TUSCAN HOAX

AN ARCHAEOLOGICAL THRILLER

DARWIN LACROIX ADVENTURE SERIES
BOOK 4

DAVE BARTELL

ISBN: 978-1-957269-90-0

To my brothers Dan and Eric, two of my closest fans and fiercest critics.

"The antiquities underworld is far more determined and far more organized than anyone has ever imagined."

Peter Watson & Cecilia Todeschini, authors of The Medici Conspiracy

"The easiest way to convince a collector to buy a forgery is to appeal to his self-conceit of being someone uniquely qualified to tell genuine from false."

Erin L. Thompson, author of Possession

PROLOGUE

Thierry Panchon exited the truck into the quiet desert morning and breathed in the cool air. He studied the thin indigo horizon that foretold the coming dawn, still an hour away. *We have time*, he thought.

A bright flash tore the night sky and then faded to an orange semi-circle. He counted *one thousand, two thousand, three thou*—whump! The pressure wave pummeled him, forcing him to step backward. "It's less than a kilometer away!" he shouted. "Open the door. Move the truck closer." They had to get the priceless artifacts out of harm's way.

A fighter jet shrieked overhead, driving them to the ground. He lifted the arm covering his face to see twin yellow streaks peel from beneath the craft. The missiles struck near the earlier explosion, blazing the sky in a deadly inferno.

He raced to the locked shed and fumbled with his keys. Finally opening the padlock, he stood back and waved the workers through. "*Allez, allez!*" Thierry, a French native, had been excavating here in Sidon, Lebanon, as director of *La Mission Archéologique*, and the storage bunker held the treasures from the Temple of Eshmun, which dated back to 360 BCE.

As he turned to go in, his voice was drowned out by a roar that would have made Thor jealous. He looked up at three UH-1 Iroquois helicopters, better known as Hueys, whose rotors whopped the air like maniacal gods. Soldiers leaned out the doors with their weapons ready as red tracer fire from the Huey's forward guns arced into the flames, now close by.

"Mon Dieu! The Israelis. Get moving!" He pulled his scarf tight against the acrid air and blinked to flush foul smoke from his eyes. The desert silence had been a ruse. *God only knows what's burning. Or whom.* He shuddered and entered the makeshift warehouse storing the artifacts pending completion of the exhibit in the national museum.

Tensions had been rising since 1975, but the Lebanese civil war, now in full stride, was bringing its destruction and death to Beirut's doorstep, a mere forty kilometers north. He needed to get the contents to a safer location, and he hoped it was not too late.

One by one, the men hauled the crates into the waiting truck. As they wrestled with a statue, he slipped past and moved to a refrigerator-sized safe. Once alone, he spun the dial, carefully ran through the combination, and then pulled open the massive door. Inside lay a pine box nearly half a meter on each side. Its lid was screwed shut, and "C-17" was stenciled on its sides.

He left the safe door ajar as he emerged with the box, figuring the incoming attackers would not blow up an empty safe. For all he knew, they might return to use it again. Then he placed the heavy crate on the truck's rear deck and climbed in after it.

The men piled into the truck, and one of them pounded on the cab. Moments later, the driver pulled away. The French archaeologist watched the site recede as smoke from the encroaching battlefield billowed in the morning light. He had dedicated thirteen years of his life to the Temple of Eshmun. *Will I ever see you again?* He shuddered at what might happen to it in the advancing war.

Just over ninety minutes later, the truck arrived at the Byblos Citadel, a twelfth-century fortress built by European Crusaders.

Now, far from the war, they unloaded the truck and placed the crates in the citadel's basement. Thierry insisted on carrying C-17 himself, despite the strain of hauling it down steep steps.

Sweat poured from his brow as he set the crate atop another. After wiping his face, he placed his hands on the wooden box until his breathing settled. His fingers grasped the wood tighter as he heard the metal groan behind him.

"Time to go. You need to pay the men," his assistant, Sabah, said while holding the iron gate.

I can't. Thierry's feet were rooted to the floor, and his stomach sagged as he stalled for time. The C-17 box contained the treasure of a lifetime, a solid-gold bull mask, exquisitely cast and flawless. He had never seen its equal, and no one else knew of it except for Sabah. On the day of its discovery, Thierry and Sabah had conspired to send everyone home.

"We'll come back later," said Sabah. "No one knows what's in it. Let's go."

A minute later, he stood, leaving sweaty handprints on the pine, and left the jail cell where they had secured the artifacts. Sabah wrapped a stout chain around the bars and fixed a large padlock to its links. Then she turned and took his hand. "Come, I'll make you breakfast," she said. When they reached the top of the steps, she released his hand to keep their relationship as secret as the box below.

Later that afternoon, as the two drank coffee in a quayside cafe, everyone around them talked of the spreading civil war. For now, Byblos remained far from the fighting near Beirut, but a palpable tension hung in the air. With Israel's border to the south and Syria everywhere else, the Mediterranean offered the safest option, as some families had already packed cars and left on ferries.

I must get it out of here. The golden bull mask had become the Frenchman's obsession since he had unearthed it seven months ago. He had lain awake at night, working out ways to keep it from going to

3

the national museum. He loved archaeology, but it was a low-paying occupation, and he enjoyed fine living. A wealthy collector had approached him last year, offering cash for exceptional pieces. He had shown the man a photo of the bull mask and been offered a sum that equaled decades' worth of salary.

This war's the perfect opportunity. He turned to Sabah. "We need to catch the ferry to Cyprus and then to Nice or Marseilles."

"I need a visa," she said.

"No time. We'll work it out in France. You're fleeing a civil war. We can get you refugee status."

"What about the mask?"

"I'll sell it to the collector."

As Sabah stared out at the harbor, her black hair gleamed in the slanting sun, and her large, dark glasses shaded her eyes.

"Why sell only one? Why not three or four?" she asked.

"What the hell are you talking about? We only have one. Where would we…" His voice trailed off when he saw her mischievous smile.

"I know a man. An expert restorer. Used to work with me at the national museum. Until they caught him working on the side. They still say five or six pieces in the museum are no longer original."

"A forger?" he asked. She nodded, and he continued. "How do you know him?"

She let the sandal slip from her foot and ran her bare toes under his trouser leg. "I have my ways."

T he next morning, Thierry left Sabah as she slept and went out to rent a car and buy ferry tickets. The more he thought about the forgery idea, the better he liked it. Over dinner the previous night, she had explained how the museum sent pieces out for restoration, adding that some had been copied and carefully aged to the right millennium. The originals went underground, sold by unscrupulous dealers to the highest bidders. Of course, the pieces could never be seen again in public, but buyers who acquired stolen antiquities were driven by possession, their desire for a private, personal collection.

After coffee, he had listened to her converse on the telephone with a man she called "the Albanian" and arrange a meeting the next day. "Where?" he had asked, but she had then led him to the bedroom, and he had become absorbed by thoughts of wealth during their lovemaking.

Now, walking back to the flat, he mentally inventoried getting access to hundreds of rare artifacts. *No one's harmed. National museums keep their treasures. The greedy get to admire their precious acquisitions in private. I'm paid handsomely to broker transactions.*

"I'm back," he said, dropping the keys on an entry table. At that moment, footsteps pounded down the outside hall behind him, and he turned to see a slender man with close-cropped hair, dressed in the uniform of a citadel guard.

"We've been robbed!"

"What?"

"*Al-Katā'ib*," said the man.

Thierry froze at hearing the name of the Phalangist Party's paramilitary force. Then he ran to get Sabah in the bedroom. Empty! He rushed back into the front room, his eyes wild, feeling gut-punched.

"They kidnapped her, sir."

Hours later, the police left the basement storage room in the citadel, and Thierry tried to piece together what had happened. The guards had described being disarmed by hooded militia and knocked unconscious. They remembered little except a blindfolded figure with hands tied and wearing a floral dress—Sabah.

When the guards awoke, they had found the chain cut and a half-dozen boxes gone. Now that the adrenaline had drained away and the pounding in his ears had subsided, a rising sense of wanting to hurt someone flooded his thoughts. *They took my bull.* His fists balled, and his fingernails bit into the skin. The pain helped him focus.

How did this happen? He considered the hired men. *No, not them. No one knew the crate's contents.* But that was not true. His lover had called a man—the Albanian—yesterday.

Putain! His blood boiled, pounding in his ears as he stared at the empty spot where C-17's crate had lain. "I will get you back. No matter how long it takes."

1

Darwin Lacroix sat on the two-thousand-meter ridgetop, his watch showing a heart rate of 191. At this elevation, the reduced oxygen, combined with hard climbing, had him belly-breathing to maximize air intake. He pressed against the rocks to shield against another sleet spray from an early spring cloudburst.

Darwin and his best friend, Zac Johnson, a former US Army Ranger, were in the notoriously difficult section of the GR20 route over the Corsican spine where teeth-like sections of granite peaks took the trail to its highest points. The last two hundred meters had required hand-over-hand hauling up a chain anchored in the near-vertical chimney between two peaks. And despite training throughout the autumn and winter, the trail had pushed him to his max.

His face stung from the lashing it had taken a few minutes ago as ice sprayed off the lower rocks. Biting one glove, he yanked out a hand and put it to his tender skin, momentarily soothing the windburn. The raw feeling reminded him of a skinned knee, and when he pulled his hand away, he half-expected to see blood.

"Let's go," said Zac as he climbed the last section of the chain. "You're wasting time."

Merde! Darwin shoved his now-icy fingers back into the glove, got to his feet, and crossed the few meters over the summit before dropping onto a narrow trail that hugged the ridge's backside. His right foot shot sideways on the scree, and he quick-stepped to regain his balance as rocks careened off the mountainside toward the river a hundred meters below—a fall from this height would be fatal. He focused on the waist-width trail as a blinding light forced him to squint.

The setting sun had burst beneath the cloud layer, raking the alpine landscape in glaring light. Unfortunately, its rays offered no warmth against the frigid wind rocketing up the canyon. A sudden gust pitched him backward. He compensated and then drove against both it and the time. What felt like a doable task this morning rapidly receded as the trail stretched to infinity—an optical illusion of altitude and the horizon.

The wall of peaks marched on several kilometers, leaving the two men exposed to the elements. What would have been a breathtaking summer hike was now a race for survival. He pushed away thoughts of spending a night on this ledge in sub-zero temperatures.

His shadow on the rock wall to his left leaned downslope as if willing him to go faster. On flat ground, it would have stretched several times his height, but on the seventy-degree face, it was just shoulder level. Darwin increased his pace, thinking of Eyrún being held in the rock hut seven kilometers ahead. *We need to get her before nightfall,* he thought, glancing at his watch again. *Shit! I'm behind.*

While Eyrún, in truth, was comfortable in their warm mountain house, Zac had created this scenario to make the exercise seem more real. Darwin had wanted an experience akin to Zac's special-forces training. While Darwin's life as an archaeologist had involved more danger than typical academic digs, he wanted to toughen his survival skills. Since arriving back in Corsica, his Lacroix family's ancestral home, he had been drawn to its independent nature. His forebears had built a shipping empire that had spanned the Mediterranean Sea, based in Ajaccio, three hundred kilometers to the south.

C'mon, you wanted this. He pushed on but slipped on his next step. He stayed upright, but more rocks spilled off the edge. *Easy.*

"Careful, bro!" yelled Zac.

"What?" Darwin hollered back as a wave of rocks cut between them.

————

D arwin turned to see Zac jump back. A boulder tumbled less than a meter away, pulling a wake of granite that plunged into the river. "Shit, that was close," Zac said, his voice barely audible over the wind.

Each now stood on opposite sides of the trail. Between them, a three-meter chunk had dropped into the canyon below. They determined that hiking up and over the gash was not an option. The loose rocks and sharp angle meant any misplaced foothold was a one-way trip into the boulder-strewn river. And even if they miraculously survived a fall, the violent, storm-gorged water heralded certain death.

"Get the ropes!" Zac yelled while surveying the best crossover points. Darwin shrugged off his pack and braced it a couple of meters down the trail. Then he removed the climbing rope from its side and unclipped a loop of anchors. Searching along the trail, he found a crack in a solid part of the cliff and wedged a spring-loaded cam in it. He snapped a quick-draw carabiner on the cam's loop, tested its hold, and passed the climbing rope through the quick-draw's other end.

"Careful movements, Darwin! Get it right. I'm solid over here," Zac shouted across the gap as he stepped into a climbing harness.

"Got it!" Darwin put his own climbing harness on, set another cam in the rock, and attached himself to it. This system created separate anchors—one for him and one to belay Zac across the now-widening chimney between them. The water from higher up splattered down the gap. It would be a wet passage for Zac.

"Zac! Let's do your pack first. We'll clothesline it across."

Darwin grasped the coiled rope in his left hand and moved it back and forth, testing his balance for the throw. He released with an outward arc, aiming for a point upslope from Zac, but it landed farther up from where he intended. The rope's midsection caught the water, and the torrent sucked it down. Zac stomped on the end as it whipped by him. He pulled it in, clipped one end to his harness, coiled the rope, and sent it back to Darwin, who completed the clothesline.

Zac then knotted a small loop in the rope and attached his pack with a carabiner, and they reeled it across the gap. Darwin unhitched the pack, placed it next to his, and then attached a belay device to the rope. He tightened the rope to his anchor point and dug his boots into the rocks to belay his best friend across the wet, now-darkening gap. The sun had dropped below the adjacent peaks.

"I'm going to drop like a rock when I come off the ledge!" yelled Zac as he fixed a handheld ascender to the line. "It'll be wet as hell. Get ready."

"Ready," said Darwin, angling himself to take on Zac's weight once he jumped off.

"On one." Darwin nodded to Zac in acknowledgment. "Three, two, one."

Zac pushed off, scrambling sideways across the wall as he dropped. Darwin's hips pulled upward as Zac's full weight snapped the line. He pressed against the wall like doing a kettlebell squat and leaned back over the canyon. A glance at the roaring water below brought out an expletive, but Zac had bottomed out, and Darwin stabilized his stance.

He looked down again at Zac as he worked the ascender with his right hand—reach up, engage, lock, haul up, and repeat.

"Damn good thing you spend time in the gym," said Zac.

Darwin laughed to himself. His friend's sense of humor never failed.

"Almost there." Zac's voice came from below Darwin's left foot. "I'm coming up close, right next to you."

Half a minute later, he reached Darwin's left shoulder, and they both pulled upright. As Zac steadied himself on the trail, water poured off his hair like he was a dog just out of a lake.

"Well, that was a walk in the park," said Zac, wiping water out of his eyes. Within two minutes, they had derigged the climbing gear. "Let's go. We're behind."

Darwin turned toward the packs just in time to see a large rock careen into his, knocking it into the ravine. It bounced three times before being kicked outward and into the rapids. Fortunately, he grabbed Zac's pack just before it tipped over.

"Shit." Darwin's shoulders slumped as he wagged his head in disbelief.

"Thankfully, there wasn't much in it," said Zac.

"Yeah. Just dinner and the tent."

2

Eyrún Stephansdottir braked hard and steered around the mudslide across the lower slope of the T20 road that ran over Corsica's mountains and into its capital city, Ajaccio. As she paddle-shifted into third gear, its turbo-powered pistons churned like a cheetah. The fat tires gripped the pavement, the racing compound rubber and track suspension concealed the Porsche Macan's soft, grocery-getter appearance.

She exploded out of a curve, smiling as the engine howled at six thousand RPM and the wide shoulder belt held her in the racing seat. The modified car had just returned three days ago on the ferry. She had sent it to a famous racing builder in Marseilles two months ago. Besides the suspension mods, the engine had been transformed from a worthy, factory-built 348HP to an astounding 730HP Ferrari killer.

Later in the year, she had plans to take it to her native Iceland and take part in rally races. For now, it served as her commute vehicle from her mountain home to work at the Agrippa Center for Archaeology, which she had founded with her husband, Darwin. They had chosen Corsica because of its centrality, surrounded by ancient cultures, and for the Lacroix family roots. She had fallen in love with the Mediterranean lifestyle; its climate was much kinder than that of her previous home in Reykjavík. As part of France, Corsica benefited from economic support while keeping its self-determination alive, not unlike her native Iceland.

Down on the valley floor, Eyrún stomped on the acceleration. The turbo whined like a shop vacuum as the G-force mashed her into the seat. A lone white sedan occupied the lane ahead, and she nudged the steering wheel to pass. The speedometer hit 271 kph before she braked for a roundabout.

Downshifting through the empty circle, she exited onto the first right and adhered to the posted fifty-kph limit as a gleaming glass building came into view. She whooped in exhilaration as the blue vehicle rolled into the car park. After shutting off the engine, she sat a moment, thinking about the day's must-get-done-list before gathering her purse.

When a white sedan pulled in several spaces over, she exited the Macan and waited for its occupant to get out. A middle-aged man with thicker hair in his gray beard than on his head slung a pack over one shoulder.

"Good morning, Barry," said Eyrún.

"Good morning, Eyrún. I figured you were the tornado back there. Any faster, and you'll need a pilot's license."

Eyrún laughed. "How's the family settling?"

"They're great. Zoe is laying down the vegetables. Says we'll have a real crop here, not the soggy, stunted varieties up north."

Barry Hodgson had arrived last month from the northeast UK, where he had been the chair of the archaeology department at the University of Newcastle. Eyrún had first met him six months ago, though she had known of him by proxy the last two years. Barry had been Darwin's professor during his master's degree in archaeology. The two had bonded, and Barry's team had helped Darwin with fundamental research on two of their previous discoveries.

Now that Barry's kids were university age, he and his wife had been looking for a warmer climate. In addition to running a well-known archaeology department, he had collected a global following of corporate research clients. Eyrún and Darwin had easily settled on

Barry as their first choice for chief archaeologist of the Agrippa Center for Archaeology.

"Lupita accepted our offer," he said, pulling the building's front door open and waiting for Eyrún to go first.

"Wonderful. When will she arrive?"

"Two weeks, as she needs to close a project in Newcastle and then wants to visit her family."

They walked to the kitchen to make tea as Barry updated her on the progress in building the M8B project—a machine-learning and artificial-intelligence effort to find crossovers between research in the hard and soft sciences as well as the arts and cultural studies.

While Barry explained, Eyrún's thoughts drifted two months back, when they had conceived the idea while sitting around a fire. At the time, Barry and Zoe had been house hunting and staying at the Lacroix mountain house.

Under a black new-moon sky, with the Milky Way shimmering like a silver fleece, and deep into a third bottle of a bewitching Châteauneuf-du-Pape, Darwin asked, "What if there was a way to link all human knowledge to come up with novel ideas?"

"No simple questions with you, eh, Darwin?" asked Barry. Up to this point, the conversation had lapsed into comfortable silence among friends as they leaned back, gazing skyward.

"I'm serious," said Darwin. "There's so much research and in ever-narrowing disciplines. Each day, we're losing whole swaths of human experience. Zoe, how many languages have gone extinct this century?"

"Hard to know exactly, but hundreds for sure," said Zoe, a professor of anthropology and linguistics who wrote books in elvish as a hobby.

"Maybe AI?" Eyrún speculated while pointing out a satellite arcing eastward.

"Yeah, the algorithms are getting better. Sift through a million unrelated papers and make connections. What if the ACA creates an AI department?"

"Who would we get to run it?" asked Eyrún.

"We don't even need a Magic Eight-Ball for that," said Zoe.

"Lupita!" Barry and Darwin answered simultaneously. The two

began recruiting her the next day and used Zoe's comment as the project's name.

So much had happened so fast as Eyrún signed large purchase orders. Fortunately, Barry took over the day-to-day setup and operation of M8B. He wrapped up the impromptu report and handed her a teacup, snapping her back to the present.

While costs for the new department were staggering, they were less than she had imagined. The principal work involved software, which was Lupita's domain. The young woman from Kenya had a gift for imagining computer models. While Eyrún had a Ph.D. in volcanology, an increasingly data-intensive field, she dealt better with the physical world of geology, energy-transfer mechanisms, and, increasingly, business acumen.

During a conversation with Lupita in Newcastle last month, Eyrún had been entranced by Lupita's intuition with data models. She rivaled Darwin at crazy, out-of-the-box thinking. At one point, Lupita had said, "Any researcher's greatest problem is their own point of view and its tendency to restrict questions and starting points for investigation."

"How do we avoid it?" Eyrún had asked, and the answer had staggered her.

"We don't. We step away from questioning entirely. We let the software look at all the data—the history, the geological records, and the archaeological evidence—and form its own questions."

"Can you think of an example?"

"That's the thing. We can't know what we don't know—we're blind to it. But let's take an example from history. For centuries, Rome was protected by the swamps that surrounded the city. Attacking enemies would die in large numbers and retreat. The Romans even had a name for it, *mal-aria*, or bad air. Today we know that mosquitoes living in fetid water spread a bacterium that causes the disease malaria."

"So you're saying, we're limited in the connections we can make because of—"

"Our culture, gender, language, religion, poverty, you name it. The opinions and hypotheses we form are obscured by our inability to be truly objective."

"Can we program software to not behave in the same way?"

"That's the million-pound question. We can't be sure, but if we program the *machine* to *learn* as it gathers data, we hope it will generate novel lines of inquiry."

Eyrún remembered thinking, *Intuition. It's how Darwin comes up with his crazy ideas. He connects things that others don't see.*

But she knew his weakness: as talented as he was, there was no way to duplicate his talent. Even he could not describe how he worked. It wasn't guessing. Darwin's brain hoovered up data from vast resources and popped out connections. People called it instinct or prescience, but the scientist in Eyrún knew the human brain was still little understood. And some brains, like Darwin's, had limited capacity to focus. She chuckled to herself, picturing the overflowing trash bin in the bathroom. *If something doesn't interest him, it languishes. What if this software could duplicate Darwin's gift—and broaden it?*

E yrún walked to her corner office, a perk of being a founder of the ACA. She and Darwin had committed a substantial sum of their wealth to found the center from the near-billion euros they had earned from discoveries in Iceland, Egypt, and central France. In addition, her royalties from flue-gas patents and stock in the Iceland company that delivered geothermal energy to Europe funded a comfortable life.

But money did not drive her. It was a benefit of being in the right place at the right time. She knew the false logic that hard work alone brought riches. If that were the case, there would be billions of billionaires. She and Darwin had co-founded ACA to give talented scientists the means to pursue knowledge and be free of limits imposed by lack of funding and political pressure.

She looked at the roster of incoming interns, a collection of archaeologists from countries that did not have funding for deeper training. Eyrún circled one name, that of a woman whose country was listed as "none." She had grown up in a refugee camp in Syria and struggled her way through schooling.

Eyrún had also created a special team to help the interns become comfortable living in Corsica. She knew from relocating, learning French, and adopting new customs that the trauma of everyday living was the largest obstacle to fitting into a new situation. Her team had arranged a group of flats in town, and some key staff members lived among the interns, helping them become part of the community. The mayor of Ajaccio had added the commune's support, as she welcomed the jobs and the international attention.

As strong sunrays fell across the worktable and loosened Eyrún's shoulders with their heat, she looked at the first item on her list. She turned to watch the light slice through the scattering cloud cover. The trees swayed in the offshore winds as the trailing storm continued south toward Sardinia. Last night, the same wind had howled like a banshee in the canyon below the mountain house. *I wonder how Darwin and Zac got on?*

3

Early light and a freezing cabin brought Darwin out of a dream in which he was struggling to climb out of a collapsing lava tube in Azerbaijan. He crawled out of the blankets and coaxed the embers in the woodstove to life, feeding the flames with split pine stacked in the hut. He stood and reached overhead to ease through the stiffness. The night before, after their debacle on the trail, he and Zac had hiked eleven miserable kilometers, reaching the cabin well after dark. His cheeks felt sunburned this morning from yesterday's freezing rain.

Navigating the treacherous cliff face where his pack had tumbled into the ravine had required an agonizingly slow pace until they had reached a gap between two peaks. Though the gap widened into a bowl that surrounded an alpine lake, they found no shelter and made for the nearest cabin, another seven kilometers. They found it still closed for the season, but, with numb fingers, he had slammed a chunk of granite against the padlock until it split from the doorframe.

"Survival has no rules except stay alive," said Zac.

Fortunately, the winterized shelter had stored supplies like wood and blankets. After firing up the woodstove, they had stripped and hugged fleece blankets until life-giving heat permeated their bodies.

Then they had eaten a makeshift meal of protein bars and collapsed into sleep near the fire.

This morning, when the heat filled the cabin again, Darwin placed a pot of water atop the stove. He contemplated how to brew the coffee he had found among the leftover supplies, which included two cartons of ultra-pasteurized milk. The noise of milk shaking in the carton brought Zac out of his slumber.

"What're you doing?"

"Making a latte. Too bad there're no filters," said Darwin.

"Whiner. So we drink it cowboy style."

"What?"

"Move aside, city boy, and I'll show you how coffee's made in the wild," said Zac, stretching and pulling a blanket around his shoulders. Once the water was boiling, he poured in the ground beans.

A calming wave eased down Darwin's shoulders and lower back as the rich aroma filled his nostrils. The very idea of the brew brought comfort. He closed his eyes and turned, letting the fire's heat continue to aid the muscular release.

A couple of minutes later, a metallic sound brought him back around as Zac added two spoons of cold water to the coffeepot. "It'll help settle the grounds. Too bad we don't have eggshells," he said.

"Huh?"

"Removes the bitterness and further settles the grounds. Get the cups ready."

Darwin poured heated milk into mugs, and Zac topped them off with the steaming brown liquid, careful to keep most of the grounds in the pot. They unstacked two chairs from the corner and sat by the fire while the caffeine and calories did their work.

Darwin brought one leg across a knee and massaged a sore spot on the ball of his foot. Setting the mug down, he worked his foot with both hands. The closing moments of the dream replayed as he stared at the flames through the stove's front glass. He was not given to literal interpretation of his dreams, but the struggle aligned with the gut feeling he had had last month in Azerbaijan.

"Where'd you go, bro?" asked Zac.

"Thinking about Azerbaijan. It doesn't feel right," Darwin said, massaging his arch.

"Why not?"

"Too much conflict."

"That's never stopped you before."

"Dunno this time... Got a bad vibe." Darwin walked to the sink, where he poured out the muddy mixture in the bottom of his mug.

Zac asked, "But it's Alexander the Great. What's not to find?"

Darwin made another cowboy latte and sat down. "That's just it. No doubt, Alexander transformed his world, but he was a pirate, looting and leaving destruction in his wake."

"He founded Alexandria."

"He founded something like twelve Alexandrias," said Darwin. He took a sip of his coffee and got a mouthful of grounds. He set it down. "I gotta pee."

They exited the cabin and stood on the edge of the deck. Steam rose from the puddles they made in the dirt. Sunlight scored a hard orange line across the distant peaks, and the pale blue sky foretold of a much drier day as Darwin resumed his explanation.

"I traveled to the town where they found the coins," he said, referring to a small cache of silver drachmas stamped with Alexander the Great, exhibited in the Azerbaijan state museum. "It's on the edge of Nagorno-Karabakh, where all the men carried guns and everyone eyed me with suspicion. Besides, we can't just dig around. We'd probably get blown up by a landmine."

Within the hour, they had packed up their belongings and set the cabin back to the condition it had been in when they had arrived, except for the door. Darwin wrote a note explaining the need to break in and left his contact data to pay for repairs. Zac extinguished the fire.

"Okay, so you give up on Azerbaijan. It's not like Alexander's stuff is going anywhere. What'll you do?" Zac asked as they hit the trail.

"I'm going to take up the directorship the pope offered."

"Cool."

In a little under twenty kilometers, the GR20 trail would arrive at a mountain village, where they could find a ride.

4

A knock on Eyrún's office doorframe drew her attention away from a construction bid. Her assistant, Hervé, apologized for interrupting and said, "A truck's at the loading dock. It's…er…" He flipped over a page on a clipboard and continued. "Vases and artifacts from La Citadelle Museum. It must be the donation they offered last month."

"Oh, right." Eyrún took the clipboard and scanned the waybill. "Let's go see what we're getting."

She and Hervé collected Barry along the way to the ground floor and pushed through an office door. An icy wind swirled in the open dock, and she crossed her arms tightly around herself.

"Thought I left this weather in Newcastle," said Barry.

Eyrún and Barry stepped into the lorry and gave the crates a once-over. Barry inspected the waybill against a numbered inventory, and once they had accounted for all the boxes, Eyrún signed the receipt. Three men from the shipping company unloaded the crates while Hervé activated the roll-up door to the storage area.

Twenty minutes later, with the door closed, Barry and a research assistant, Katrina, used crowbars to open the crates. Eyrún put a finger in each ear as the bars clanged when hammered under the lids. A moment later, Hervé returned with her coat and a hot cup of tea.

"Thanks. You're a godsend." As she sipped, she jerked at a harsh noise and scalded her lips.

"Sorry 'bout that," said Barry. He levered up the lid on the largest crate, and its nails shrieked in protest.

Eyrún and Hervé approached the crate as Barry and Katrina removed the packing material. A meter-high, bubble-wrapped object stood in the center. It was too heavy to lift out, and Barry warned them to cover their ears again as he pounded the sides apart. Then Katrina removed the bubble wrap as Barry held the piece steady.

"*C'est magnifique*," said Hervé.

They stood back as a group to admire a black and red-ochre clay vase resting on a block on the crate's bottom. The vase swept outward from its base and rounded inward, forming a heart shape with a broad mouth. Stout handles connected the widest part of the vase to its thick rim.

The vase's main body featured a scene of three figures gathered around a fountain. One, clearly a woman, was washing her braided hair. Her lithe figure was illustrated by simple black lines fired into the clay. A second figure, masculine but with breasts, reclined near the woman, and one hand grazed her arm. The third figure, a female in a flowing robe, stood watching the two with a hand raised as if blessing them. The vase looked barely scratched, except for the handles, where the black glaze had been rubbed away from hard use.

"I've never seen one so fine," said Barry.

"Says here it's a krater used to mix wine and water during banquettes. It's late fifth century BCE, found in a tomb near Falerii, north of Rome." Katrina read from a document that had come in the crate. "The scene depicts the Fountain of Salmacis. The greek goddess Aphrodite watches over her son Hermaphroditus and the water nymph Salmacis."

"It's stunning." Eyrún moved closer to the krater and knelt to study it. The artist had given three-dimensional energy to the flat surface. It exuded sensuality. Her hand moved reflexively, drawn to the figures.

As she traced the minute black lines of the nymph, her fingertips tingled, and she thought of the exact location for it in her gallery. She had never possessed a thing so exquisite.

5

I n his mountain home above Ajaccio, Darwin dozed on a leather couch in front of a log fire. He and Zac had hitched a ride to Ajaccio with a local woman in the village where they had exited the GR20 trail.

Earlier, Darwin had stood under a hot shower until the water had cooled. Then he had made a mushroom and gruyere omelet. After the second bite, his stomach had perked up, and he had wolfed down the rest almost without chewing. He had brewed a triple cappuccino and taken it, along with a rustic baguette and some berry jam, to the couch, where, after a few sips, fatigue had tugged his head deep into the cushions.

The front door opening brought him back from dreamland. "You're here," said Eyrún, smiling and setting her purse on the entry table. "What happened? I thought you'd be gone until the weekend."

He stood and stretched. The sunlight angled across the room as it reached its nadir on the far side of the canyon. "Change of plans." He walked around the couch and leaped up the shallow steps toward Eyrún. They kissed, and he pulled her into a hug.

"You're warm," she said.

He buried his face in her long, dark hair and breathed her perfume. "We got more adventure than we wanted."

"I thought about you during last night's storm."

Darwin recounted the misadventure, and Eyrún swept a hand to her mouth when he got to the part about his pack tumbling into the ravine. She tried to stifle a laugh, and he joined her when the effort failed.

"It's so Zac and Darwin. What did you do?"

"We kept going. It was a survival simulation." He told her of the cabin and their trek to the mountain town. "There wasn't much more for it. The storm sucked all the fun out of the adventure. Besides, I've decided to take on the pope's gig."

"No surprise in that. I figured you would," she said, moving to the fire where she kicked off her shoes and threw her socks in a corner. Then she stretched toward the flames and wriggled her toes in the radiating warmth.

"What's for dinner?" he asked.

"I have leftovers from last night, but there's not enough for two."

"How about the village? You liked the new chef's style."

"Okay." She squirmed closer as he slid an arm under her back. They watched the flames slowly dance across a new log.

The fire popped, and they jumped. He reached atop the couch and swept a blanket over their heads.

"We're marooned in a cabin by a raging storm, desperately clinging to each other for warmth."

"Sounds dire. What do we do?"

He began unbuttoning her blouse. "The science says skin-to-skin contact shares heat better."

"And they also say exercise generates heat," she replied, easing a hand under his shirt.

6

Zac leaned on the railing of his flat. It overlooked Ajaccio, where, three kilometers across the horseshoe-end of the harbor, a jet was lifting off from the airport. The growl of its turbofan reached him as it banked over the Mediterranean Sea before arcing out of view. A random thought popped into his head: *I should learn to fly.*

He had the time and money, and Ajaccio International Airport had low commercial traffic with plenty of wide-open space over empty ocean. *Maybe para-gliding.* Corsica had abundant hills from which to descend. *I don't know what I want to do.* It was a genuine dilemma.

Zac had left the lab an hour and a half ago and gotten dinner alone in a brasserie, where he had sat at the bar while watching a football match. He had no opinion about the two teams, but having something to focus on had made eating alone more palatable. The listless feeling was new to him, as his life up to this point had been purposeful pursuit, from sports through high school in his native Oakland, California, to West Point Military Academy and rising to captain as a US Army Ranger.

His Ph.D. in earthquake prevention at the Colorado School of Mines had taken him to a career with the US Geological Survey, and during that period, he had met Darwin. They had kindled a friendship, and a later adventure in Iceland had brought them both riches.

Zac had used the money to start a company that used microsats, football-sized satellites, to triangulate data for an early earthquake warning system. Following his grandfather's death in the 1989 Oakland earthquake, he had pursued geology, determined to find a solution. His firm developed sophisticated algorithms using machine learning and artificial intelligence to estimate earthquake probability based on the satellite images. When they forecast three minor earthquakes to within a day, investors had come calling.

But after a year, he had divested his interest in the company as the venture capitalists looked to monetize what he considered a public necessity. He had also felt the pull to be closer to his partner, Stevie Leroy, whom he had met in Iceland. He had moved in with her in her home Orange, France, to build their relationship but found himself alone as much as he had before moving to France. He loved her, but Stevie's free spirit kept her forever chasing projects. She was a gifted cave biologist, highly sought after and, it seemed to him, always underground. They were great when together, but it turned out to be much less often than Zac wanted. And family meant a lot to him. Five generations of Johnsons had thrived in Northern California.

Three months ago, Zac had begun helping his friends Darwin and Eyrún build the Agrippa Centre for Archaeology. The pure research aspect appealed to him after coming to terms with investors' expectations of creating products and revenue. While he deeply appreciated capitalism, he viewed development in human health and well-being as social enterprises.

He had agreed to take on the ACA challenge while sorting out his direction and had laughed off comments about a midlife crisis. "Not my style," he said. "I'm more like an actor between blockbusters." As always, he became absorbed in the challenge, only feeling adrift in moments like this, when he wondered, literally, where in the world Stevie was.

His eyes drifted down to the harbor club, just coming to life. The neon lights of its back deck cast a garish glow onto the water. The colors seemed to dance on the rippling water. Without thinking, his body moved to an imagined beat. On a whim, he decided to visit.

Thursday night brought a larger crowd to the club, including mainlanders on weekend mini-breaks. He grabbed a beer and took in the scene. A few dozen people danced as the club's energy picked up with the growing number of bodies. Halfway through his beer, he noticed one woman dancing alone in a spot cast by one of the fixed lights. She moved to the rapidly pulsing sounds put out by the DJ in a manner he could only describe as Middle Eastern. Her hips rocked, following a circular rhythm, while her arms, held out from her body, seemed to float on the beat. But it was her hands that mesmerized him. Rather than just follow the ends of the arms in a Western style, her hands led the movement, as if telling a story, and their motion flowed back to her core, in unison with her hips.

Zac put down the empty bottle and danced in her direction, following his own beat but gaining inspiration from her fluid movement. The DJ transitioned the music down-tempo, and she flowed with the change. The beat kicked up in another song, as did her hips in response. Zac found himself lost in the music and the grace of the woman. At one point, their eyes met, and they shared glances as their dancing spiraled them closer to one another.

His heat built from the rhythm, like stoking a fire, until the DJ dropped a driving beat. Cries went up on the now-crowded dance floor, and the woman surged with the energy, her hips rocking. He matched her in the style of street dancing from his native Oakland, where he had loved to attend street parties. He mimicked her movements, and she improvised off his, finding a playful rhythm. Anyone watching would have said they were a couple.

When the music slowed, she leaned in and said, "Buy me a drink." He nodded and cut a path toward the bar with her in his wake. As they moved toward the back wall, she grabbed his hand. "No. Let's go upstairs. I need some air."

He followed her up a wooden staircase to a level that ringed the old warehouse. She continued out its rear door onto a wide deck over-looking Ajaccio Harbor. The pounding music receded as they stepped outside. Zac ordered two drinks and turned back to her.

"I'm Jasmin," she said, holding out a hand as she leaned against the bar.

"Zac." He took her handshake.

L ater, Zac lay spent atop the bed, feeling as if he were floating just above the sheet. All of life's cares had paused, and he dared not move for fear the glorious sensation, tenuous as a silk thread, would break. The angst and frustration that had built over the last year had suddenly left him, or at least, they no longer mattered. He had surrendered.

He closed his eyes and slipped into a lucid dream, tumbling in a series of movie-like fades until gravity grasped hold of him. He resisted, but the intoxication dissolved, leaving him naked and sweaty in an Ajaccio flat.

He sighed and rolled his head left. Jasmin lay on her back, her eyes closed and her arms overhead, fingers lightly entwined. His gaze traversed the slope of her nose, down her neck, and over her chest, glistening with the perspiration pooling slightly between her breasts. A trickle spilled into her navel. He roamed down one leg, splayed to the side, knee bent. Her slender feet were quiet after a night of dancing and urgent movement.

He willed back the memory of the last hour. After making love twice since their return from the club, she had sat across his thighs and coaxed him forth a third time. At first, he had said, "I can't," but she had tapped her mobile to play Ravel's "Bolero." Her hands played with him, slowly, softly, almost without purpose as the music rolled through its quiet rhythm, seeming to go nowhere until a sultry wood-wind conjured a deep, soulful yearning.

At that point, she leaned over and, with the grace of a dancer, brushed her hair over his thighs. His belly stirred as his internal melody matched the snare drum, growing from a whisper to a recognizable beat. Her nimble, repetitive movements gathered his internal vibration into a tension that sought release. The beat grew until she mounted him and rode the unstoppable cacophony, climaxing in a cymbal crash before collapsing in utter release.

God, that was amazing. Who is this woman? The air had cooled, and he rolled off the bed to gather the mess of coverings they had flung to the floor. He gently lay the sheet and duvet over her, pausing a moment to drink in her lithe form, and then crawled in beside her. She groaned in contentment and moved against him.

Zac drifted to sleep, enveloped by her musky perfume.

7

Twilight closed over the warm spring day as Zac arrived at the restaurant. Jasmin had gotten up just after sunrise, saying she needed to be somewhere later that morning. "Have dinner with me tonight?" he had asked before she left his flat.

"I'd love to." She kissed him, and he watched her from his balcony as she got in a taxi. Late that afternoon, she messaged him, and they agreed on dinner at a quayside restaurant at eight.

He sat at the bar, and ordered a cocktail. About ten minutes later, Jasmin walked in. She wore jeans and a black silk camisole beneath a knee-length black silk top with a gold-edged hood draped across her shoulders. Her coal-black hair splayed across the hood and accentuated her amber eyes, set beneath generous eyebrows. A slender, almost petite nose played a quiet part between fan-like eyelashes and full lips, glossed in a coral rose that drew just enough attention.

"*Bonsoir.*" Her voice was brighter than the throaty, sultry tone of the previous night.

"*Bonsoir.*"

They kissed cheeks in greeting. Then she kissed him on the lips, lingering a few seconds before whispering, "I thought of you today. Last night was magnifique."

Zac's groin erupted like a match on spilled petrol. "Yes, it was. You made it hard for me to get work done today."

Her lips spread in a sultry smile, and she squeezed his hand. "I'm thirsty. What are you having?"

"A Vieux Carré," he said. When she raised her eyebrows in question, he added, "An American classic from New Orleans."

She tasted it and said, "Too strong. I'll have a Champagne."

When her glass arrived, she raised it. "*Tchin-tchin!*" The crystal rang out, and they sipped. "Tell me about your day," she said.

Zac described working on the computer system, though he carefully avoided buzzwords. When she asked him about the research, he delved another layer deeper. "It's a multi-purpose system. Since we're on Corsica and internet connections are at a premium, we have some racks of super-high-performance servers on-site. I'm helping set up these systems and connect them to other resources in the cloud."

"Sounds complicated," she said and drank more Champagne.

"Sort of, but I'm just helping Lupita get the lab set up so she can focus on the algorithms."

"Lupita?"

He noticed Jasmin's eyebrows pinch together. "She's the main scientist. It's her department. My friends who run the ACA asked me to help out. Just to get the systems up."

She smiled and lightly touched his knee. Zac realized his response was more than needed and sipped his drink to mask embarrassment.

"What's the ACA?"

"The Agrippa Center for Archaeology. My friends Darwin and Eyrún Lacroix founded it last year." He described the ACA charter.

"Wait. I remember. The announcement in Paris last year at the Sorbonne. They found the Knights Templar treasure and announced their foundation."

"That's the one. How did you hear about it? The news had died down by the time they made the announcement."

"I lived in Paris then."

32

They talked for a while longer at the bar. She asked Zac about how an American came to be living in Ajaccio, and he told her the story of meeting Darwin in Berkeley while the latter pursued his Ph.D. He described their developing friendship as they had gone on caving trips around the American West and how he had joined Darwin's expedition in Iceland.

"After that, I started a company in California," he said.

"What does it do?"

"Earthquake early-warning systems." He described the company and told her about selling his shares after being offered a crazy amount of money. He rocked the ice cube in his drink and sipped it.

"And you came to Corsica to visit your friend Darwin. That's an unusual name," she said.

Zac laughed. "That about sums him up." He went on to describe a relationship that had not worked out as his reason for being in Corsica and his adventure with Darwin on the GR20. Thankfully, the host rescued him from the downbeat story and guided them to a table near the water.

"It sounds like you two are quite the adventurers," said Jasmin as she slipped between the tables.

That's an understatement, he thought, flashing back on their excursions into deep underground places. When they had sat down and been handed the menus, he asked her, "Where in Paris did you live?"

"L'Île Saint Louis."

"Then you saw the fire," he said, referring to Notre-Dame de Paris.

"Yes. It was terrible, but I lived at the far end of the island in a flat facing downriver, opposite the cathedral. I chose not to watch."

The server arrived and took their orders, and when she left, Zac asked Jasmin how long she was on holiday in Ajaccio.

"I don't know. It's like you Americans say, complicated."

"I'm good with complicated."

"I owned two antiquities galleries, one on L'Île Saint-Louis and the other behind Musee d'Orsay."

"Owned? As in, you sold them?"

"I still own them, well, half of them." She sighed heavily, slumping her shoulders and absently fingering the stem of the Champagne flute. "I'm going through a divorce."

"I'm sad to hear. You don't have to talk about it." He reached across the table and touched her hand holding the glass. She rolled her wrist and grasped his hand.

Zac forgot his own pain for a moment as she went on. "It's okay. I need to talk about it. I miss the galleries but not my husband. He's controlling and abusive—no, no, not physically," she added when Zac stiffened in his chair.

"He questioned everything I did. Changed my decisions. Talked behind my back to the employees. I finally grew up and left. He doesn't know I'm in Corsica, which is good. I need to keep a low profile until the divorce."

Their appetizers arrived, and the conversation drifted away from their current relationships. Jasmin told him of growing up in Paris after her family fled the civil war in Beirut, Lebanon, confessing she remembered little, as she had only been six when she had arrived in France. Zac described growing up in Oakland, California, in the large Johnson family. He had traveled little before attending the US Military Academy in New York and going overseas for Army duty.

Following dinner, they walked along the quayside in the pleasant spring evening. She grasped his hand as they moved past the silent powerboats and they stopped near a three-masted sailboat moored at the end of one long pier. Lights poured from its interior windows and a small group of people sat on its stern. The night sky away from the harbor lights blazed with stars. All was quiet save for the murmur of conversation from the large boat and the soft metallic tinkling of rigging on the surrounding sailboats.

She turned to him, and they kissed. Slowly at first, then with more urgency, her tongue probed his mouth. Zac's hands grasped her ass, pulling her in. She moaned and then leaned her head back and whispered in his ear, "This boat looks nice."

They turned and climbed aboard a sailboat moored in a slip toward the bow end of the large boat. The craft rocked gently as they made their way to cushions on the stern, where they resumed their embrace. The mast's rigging soon clanged with more vigor.

8

Darwin stood and looked out his window of the library office building in Vatican City. The bright afternoon sun beat down on the pavement outside, casting hard shadows of the pedestrians scurrying on various church matters. A knot of tourists, some listening to a translation on headphones, followed a guide walking backward as he led them towards the broad gardens behind the building.

Darwin had just come from an informal lunch with the pope to kick off his role as the director of Special Archaeological Investigations. Basically, he would explore documents that had been sequestered for centuries in a secret papal archive. As mighty and dignified as the pope appeared in public, he ate most meals casually at the Vatican cafeteria. Darwin imagined the chief of staff and aides scribbling notes as soon as the trays were cleared.

A knock on the doorframe captured his attention. "Your espresso, sir," said a young man dressed in a smart black suit but no tie.

"Thank you. Come in, Paolo, and, please, call me Darwin."

"As you wish, sir, er—Darwin." Paolo set the espresso cup and small plate of biscotti on the desk. Then he smiled and retreated.

Darwin stirred the espresso, set down the tiny spoon, picked up the cup, and swallowed the hot liquid in a quick gulp. The heat burned a path to his stomach.

"Ah." He breathed out hot air and, after replacing the cup, walked around the desk and sat. He placed his hands, palms down, wide on the desk and surveyed his domain. A series of documents fanned out across the deep mahogany surface. Their crisp whiteness provided a stark contrast to the rich brown and much-used surface. His right fingertips played over the wood grain as if trying to read the grooves.

He had accepted the pope's offer on the condition that he remain a free agent. When the pontiff questioned this, Darwin said he and Eyrún had established the Agrippa Center for Archaeology to give them the independence to explore without undue influence from corporations or donors. "Besides, you don't need me here full time," he said. "My work habits disrupt well-run processes. Even Eyrún doesn't want me in the day-to-day operations of the ACA."

The pontiff chuckled and reminded him why he had been offered the role. "Without your uncompromising commitment, the Library of Alexandria and Christ's papyrus would have remained hidden."

Darwin smiled at the recollection. Then he moved the espresso cup and saucer to a side table, gathered up the documents on the desk, and laid an acid-free blotter over the wood. He went to a wall safe, swiped his badge, and placed his fingers on a special pad. An electronic chime sounded as the lock mechanism snapped open and the door popped outward a centimeter. Opening it wide, he withdrew a hermetically sealed plastic tube and removed its cap.

Donning cotton gloves, he laid the tube's contents, a scroll from the fourth century BCE, atop the desk and rolled it open. He leaned forward, closed his eyes, and slowly inhaled. An odor similar to the stacks of an old library filled his nostrils, but it also had subtle undertones of decayed straw and the pungent carbon of a cold hearth. He let his mind wander back in time to that of the scroll's creator.

Darwin opened his eyes and ran them across a map of the ancient world of Greece and Persia. "*By my hand*," began an inscription written by Alexander III of Macedon, better known as Alexander the Great.

The map had been among scrolls found in Alexander's unused tomb in an obscure oasis in the Sahara Desert, close to Libya. Darwin had found the empty tomb three years ago. *Not completely empty*, he reminded himself. Alexander had died far from the elaborate tomb he had commissioned in Siwa Oasis, and his body was never transported to the forgotten tomb. Six hundred years later, Hypatia of Alexandria, a renowned scholar in the Mediterranean coastal city founded by Alexander, rediscovered his tomb. With the once-magnificent library under threat of destruction by religious fanatics, she had organized a clandestine transfer of the ancient scrolls across the Sahara Desert seventeen hundred years ago and sealed them in Alexander's unused tomb.

Darwin smoothed the edge of the scroll, one of many that had been found in the tomb. He flashed back to an underwater knife fight in the Siwa Oasis that had nearly cost him his life. He shook it away and refocused on the map.

While all the scrolls from the library of Alexandria had been scanned and made public, Darwin had held this one back. Its papyrus had been sampled and dated to 334 BCE, and some of its ink had been scraped off and authenticated, but putting it online would have drawn treasure hunters the world over, each poking shovels into sensitive archaeological sites.

He also knew this map had been drawn early in Alexander's campaign in this region. After initial battles against the Persians, Alexander had turned toward Egypt, where he was recognized as the son of Ammon. He had journeyed to the far oasis to consult Ammon's oracle before making the long trek back to conquer Persia and spill its treasury. But at the time of this map's creation, Alexander had possessed none of that later wealth.

Over the centuries, countless books had been published on Alexander, and Darwin had studied many, including many in their original Latin and Greek. His gift for languages and knack for making obscure connections had earned him the nickname—the Great Finder. Darwin peered into gaps that others overlooked. A decade ago, he had suffered ridicule for unconventional thinking, but after a series of astounding discoveries in Iceland, Egypt, and France, he had attracted a following.

Though he was a wild risk-taker during explorations, Darwin valued family and friendships. He considered Eyrún, whom he had met in Iceland, his most valuable discovery. That she thought so as well had led them to marry and build the Agrippa Center for Archaeology together. He pictured her glacier-blue eyes and smiled.

He returned to the map, withdrew a silver drachma from his pants pocket, and rolled the tiny gray-green coin between his thumb and index finger. He alternated his gaze between the coin, stamped with Alexander's likeness, and the map. After a moment, he placed it atop modern-day Azerbaijan—a place Alexander had never gone.

"How did you get there?" he said to the lump of silver. A year and a half ago, he and Eyrún had visited Baku, Azerbaijan, and learned of a coin cache found by a farmer in one of its western towns. Unfortunately, the details were sketchy. The farmer had broken a clay pot while digging a well, and the drachmas had spilled out. The coins had ended up in the Azerbaijan national museum, but Darwin, figuring a poor farmer might have held some back, had bought one from the man. In addition, the ACA had contributed substantially to modernize the town's school.

He had no desire to explore in the Caucasus conflict zone, but he wanted another look at the scroll. He returned the tube to the safe and locked its door. *You're someone else's worry now. Well, maybe someday…*

9

Eyrún opened a second-floor door of the ACA that connected to a steel catwalk along the building's exterior. She moved a few paces onto the new platform to join Barry, who was yelling over the cacophony of construction below. "Be careful with that!" The builders were stretching a tarp over an archaeological site.

Three months ago, when tearing up the car park to expand the building, workers had found Paleolithic artifacts. Construction had stopped after Barry and Darwin had determined a substantial settlement existed on this spot over a twenty-thousand-year period. The alluvial plain on which the ACA was built had been an ideal site for early dwellers on Corsica.

However, rather than abandon the expansion, Barry came up with the idea of enclosing the space as a working project to train interns. Eyrún had thought it a brilliant idea, and Darwin had consulted with the firm that had designed the Necropolis of the Via Triumphalis, an ancient cemetery found beneath the Vatican and Castel Sant'Angelo.

The architects had designed a metal-and-glass structure with louvered roof panels to vary the sunlight and roll-up doors for broad equipment access. Visitors would criss-cross the dig on elevated walkways from which they could observe real-life archaeology just meters away. The upper walk, where Eyrún and Barry now stood, would be used by staff only to access the labs on the second floor.

"How's it going, Barry?" she asked, handing him a cup of tea.

"That's lovely. Thanks." He sipped the beverage and sighed before answering. "Well enough. The gorillas just needed a reminder to go easy. We don't want any more trouble from that French building inspector—she's a ball-buster."

"What is it with you Brits and the French? The historians named the Hundred Years War about a thousand years too short."

"You think?" He grinned.

Weeks earlier, Barry had offered to supervise the expansion project, and now he had an update for her on its progress. As Eyrún had suspected, it was on schedule; she knew how eager he was to complete construction and get back in the pit. Darwin had told her Barry was most happy when digging.

"What was it you wanted to ask?"

"It's…" He stopped as a hammer drill rattled into concrete. Once the noise abated, he continued. "About the eight-ball project. Lupita's tech guy turned us down, and she's worried about getting behind. Would Zac consider staying longer?"

"He might be. Where's she stuck?" asked Eyrún.

"She had an entire team of technicians to help set up and test the sensors at our Newcastle lab. She's by herself here, dealing with the computer hardware, and the satellite feeds need calibrating. That's more Zac's expertise."

Lupita had run Barry's artificial intelligence lab and had broken new ground in sifting through mountains of data to discern patterns and relationships. While the software did not possess anything close to human intuition, it reduced the sheer number of hours spent gathering and collating data. In addition, the AI system could work twenty-four hours a day without fatigue.

"I think it's a great idea. I'll ask him," she said. "He's been nosing around for something to do, and he even mentioned going back to the States."

"Fantastic," said Barry. "What about that collection we got this morning?"

"That one vase, the Fountain of Salmacis, is stunning. I've thought about it all morning, and I know just the place for it," she said, envisioning the spot in the ACA's lobby where she would see it every day.

They spoke about it a few minutes before Eyrún's watch chimed, letting her know she had an important phone call. She asked her voice-activated assistant to record an action to talk with Zac and, following Barry's suggestion, to have a staff member verify the provenience of the vases.

10

The next day, Darwin awoke to a glorious spring morning that bathed Vatican City in warm sunlight. The last month of rain had taken its toll as winter's vise-like grip had squeezed everyone's mood to the point of snarling at each other. He walked the two kilometers to his office, noticing that people's wardrobes shifted to more vibrant fashions and the office conversations had more energy to match the changing season. He spent the morning on administrative duties, attending a staff meeting, reviewing budget requests, and proofreading two research drafts.

At a quarter past noon, he left his office in the Vatican Apostolic Archive for a lunch meeting, walking through the tapestry and maps galleries to a ground floor exit into the gardens. Descending the short steps outside, he was greeted by the sweet fragrance from a cluster of orange trees. The blossoms triggered a memory of another spring day three years ago.

While teaching at the University of California, Berkeley, his grandfather Emelio had phoned about a discovery that had taken him to Iceland. Darwin let the mental clips play, smiling about the first time he had met Eyrún, her take-charge demeanor and skeptical attitude that had melted into wonder when they had found a massive lava tube leading under the North Sea.

I wonder how it's going. Her frustrations had been high when she had dropped him off at the Ajaccio Airport three days earlier. She threw herself into work, especially at her former company, Stjörnu Energy, but as chief scientist, not its principal. The ACA was theirs, and, as managing director, while she applied her passion for organizing a complex operation, all of its biggest problems stopped at her desk. *We need to do something fun, get away, even if just for a long weekend.*

A vibration from his mobile showed his lunch companion was waiting. Darwin picked up his pace towards Saint Peter's basilica, and, a hundred meters later, he angled toward the Governor's Palace. Once inside, he found Richard Ndembele, a robust man with a voice that rumbled foundations. They hugged as Darwin braced himself against his friend's lung-emptying crush.

"It's good to see you again. How's Eyrún?"

"Fabulous, and she says hi."

Richard turned to a man standing next to him. "Gavin, this is Darwin Lacroix." Turning to Darwin, he said, "Darwin, Gavin Kane."

"Nice to meet you," said Darwin, shaking Gavin's hand.

"Likewise. Richard's told me a lot about you," said Gavin, whose voice lilted in an Irish accent.

Richard led the way to a private dining room. "Let's get some food. I'm famished."

He was wearing a cassock, as was his style, but Gavin was dressed in less formal black trousers and shirt. His short sleeves added to his informality. But what Darwin noticed most was Gavin's emerald eyes, bright with energy and a probing intelligence.

While they waited to be taken to their table, Gavin said, "Richard tells me you've taken on a special project for His Holiness."

"Yes. Heading a task force to review objects and documents in extended storage, hidden away and forgotten," said Darwin.

"Don't let him fool you," said Richard. "He's solved two great mysteries from long-forgotten documents in His Holiness's secret archive. My friend here has unusual methods, but he manages to find things where others have failed."

"I read about the Templar's reserve bank you found beneath Cathédrale Notre-Dame-de-l'Assomption in Clermont-Ferrand. Impressive," said Gavin. "I also read that you and your wife used a substantial part of your fortune to found an archaeology center in Corsica."

"And Eyrún's the loveliest woman I've ever met. What she sees in him..." Richard burst into uproarious laughter, causing the diners at the surrounding tables to turn.

Darwin blushed. "You get used to him."

"That, you do." Gavin chuckled.

They studied the menu, and, once they had ordered, the conversation shifted to Darwin's plans for his Vatican directorate. Darwin also learned of Gavin's work at the Vatican Bank, where he had had a career in finance before his calling to the priesthood.

"He heads back tomorrow, and I thought you two might enjoy meeting," said Richard.

"Where's your parish?" Darwin asked. "I got my Ph.D. in Berkeley."

"Mountain View. Lovely city but, as you know, on the less-well-heeled side of the tracks from Palo Alto and Stanford University."

Gavin talked about his parish, the energy of Silicon Valley, and his love of hiking in the green hills. Darwin shared stories of Berkeley, and they discussed trails, agreeing on the Dipsea Trail in Marin County, north of San Francisco, as their favorite. Gavin said it reminded him of his native Northern Ireland.

They concluded their lunch, and, as they made for the door, Gavin asked, "Darwin, do you have a few minutes? There's something I want to show you."

"Sure. I've no meetings until three," said Darwin, knowing this request was coming. Richard had said earlier that Gavin had discovered something about an object in the Vatican collection that fit Darwin's new mission.

A s he and Gavin emerged from the Governor's Palace, Darwin shaded his eyes against the light concentrated in the marble courtyard. They walked in silence for a few minutes through the Vatican's contemplative gardens. A few tourists ambled about, but they had it mostly to themselves. Gavin asked, "Do you mind if we detour a moment? It's on the way."

"Not at all." Darwin followed Gavin to the Casina Pio IV, a patrician villa built in the sixteenth century. Entering its courtyard, their hard-soled shoes echoed on the travertine. When they reached its center fountain, Gavin ran a finger in the water and rubbed it against his thumb. "I've always enjoyed this spot. Amidst all the glorious buildings in Vatican City, this vision of a Roman courtyard draws me in."

Darwin studied the white marble Italian Renaissance façade, covered in a fusion of ancient Roman and Christian iconography. This style had become the benchmark of modern classical tastes and permeated design catalogs.

Gavin continued. "It's fitting that Pius the Eleventh established our Academy of Sciences here."

"How so?" asked Darwin.

"For all his controversy, he sought to align the Church with the world's technological leaps. He saw the need to promote mathematics and the sciences, but also to align their pursuit with epistemology. What do you think?"

"If you mean to fuse scientific method and religious experience with our search for meaning, then I've always thought it makes perfect sense."

"Precisely. The more we explore, the more we learn. But it creates a paradox: the more we learn, the more questions arise."

Darwin looked at two couples taking selfies and wondered where this conversation was going. Gavin continued. "Look at these buildings, this courtyard. We replicated an ancient style and associated it with elegance, knowledge, and power. We call it classical. Look at the statues. How many would you say are original, that is, from ancient Greece?"

"Probably none," said Darwin.

"And you're correct. They're copies." Gavin paused and then added, "You're also probably wondering if this conversation is going anywhere."

"Er…"

"Come on. Let me show you why I wanted to meet."

They exited the grotto and headed to the museums. Darwin answered questions about the ACA, adding, "So much ancient knowledge is under threat of plunder or commercial development. By teaching young archaeologists the value of their past and proper conservation, we can prevent the loss of our human history and development. At least, that's what Eyrún and I hope to achieve."

"It's a worthy mission," said Gavin as they crossed the Cortile della Pigna, teeming with tourists.

They entered the Chiaramonti Museum, and Darwin glanced down its long front wing toward Saint Peter's Basilica. During one of his earliest visits to the library, he had asked about the Sistine Chapel and been told, "It's just down the hall." The answer was an inside joke, as the long parallel buildings that made up the museums and libraries each stretched nearly a kilometer; their narrow construction allowed for natural lighting.

Gavin explained his Vatican Bank investigation as they spiraled up the Bramante staircase. "I gathered a ton of data. I learned in my finance days how perpetrators laundered money by using everyday transactions to hide currency flows. For example, you and I know the price of a cappuccino, but to someone who does not, a thief could add two euros. Multiply that by ten thousand cappuccinos… Well, you get the point."

As they reached the top floor and entered the Gregorian Etruscan Museum, Gavin hit on the reason for the excursion. "As a side project, I was asked to audit Vatican Museum pieces sent for restoration over the last eighty years. I found some of them have gone out more than once, which looked odd to me, but I'm not an archaeologist."

"Possibly," said Darwin. "Maybe the conservator missed something?"

"Perhaps," said Gavin, leading the way into the hemicycle above the Pine-Cone Courtyard. The window's shades protected the ancient works and gave a gauzy effect to St. Peter's dome towering above the visitors below. They strolled through rooms with terra-cotta vases fired with black painted designs. Most were whole, but many had been reassembled, their cracks and lines left on display.

Gavin stopped before one case and waited until a nearby couple moved out of earshot. "I thought like you, that the restorers missed something." He pointed to a vase about a half meter tall featured in the display. A woman, face and arms painted in white, stood over a naked dead man whose armor hung on tree branches. Reds highlighted the woman's dress and a warrior's plumed helmet. Aside from chips around its mouth and scratches on the handles, the amphora stood out because of its completeness.

"It's striking, but what brought it to your attention?"

"It's been sent out for restoration three times since nineteen-twenty-one."

Darwin glanced at the nearby cases to confirm an impression that this vase was whole. It had not been found broken and reassembled. *He's right. There's nothing to indicate it needed restoration.* He moved around the case, studying the vase's perfection. When Darwin reached full circle, Gavin said, "I think Vatican pieces have been used to create forgeries."

Darwin's eyes widened as he looked back and forth between the vase and Gavin, who added, "It's worse. I fear some pieces in here are no longer the originals."

A cold void opened within Darwin. He was no stranger to tomb looting, but this was a bold theft of priceless heritage. *I have to stop this.*

11

Eyrún rounded the traffic circle to the T20 road leading up to the mountain house and asked her digital assistant to ring Darwin. He had messaged that now was a good time to talk.

"Hi, love," he said, sounding a little out of breath.

"Hi. What're you doing?"

"Just finished a workout. The Vatican gym's great. I talked the Swiss Guards into letting me join their mixed martial arts session."

"Nice," she said and listened as Darwin filled her in on the secret library documents. He paused, and she heard him gulping water before he asked, "What was it you wanted to ask about Zac?"

"Barry came to me with an idea, and I wanted to run it by you."

"Okay."

"It seems Lupita's assistant declined the offer. Hang on—" Eyrún downshifted, and the Macan's turbo screamed as she passed a lorry. Once back in her lane, she asked, "Do you think Zac would want to stay longer? I mean, it would give him something to do. Get him out of his funk."

"I think he would jump at it. You want me to ask him?"

"No. I'll ask him when I get the full scope."

"Super. By the way, did you ever hear from Stevie?"

"No. I swear I don't know what makes her tick. I got used to her self-isolation, but I can see how Zac wouldn't put up with it."

"We talked about it on the trail. Zac knew what he was getting into. He was running from his own frustrations as much as he was falling for Stevie. He's in a lost patch right now," said Darwin. Then added, "He'll get through it."

"I hope so. I wish I had another friend to introduce him to. He's such a great guy." She paused and then asked, "See you tomorrow?"

"Five twenty-one arrival."

They said goodbyes, and Eyrún lost herself in the drive. After a few minutes, she remembered that she had forgotten to ask him to explain provenience. There were so many things to learn about archaeology. *Every day, it's something else.*

Earlier that day, Hervé had interrupted a meeting to let her know about a surprise shipment that required her personal signature. After the meeting, she went to the loading dock and found another seven crates from the Ajaccio museum. However, this shipment had come from the museum owner's personal storage locker in Basel, Switzerland.

The waybills gave few details, and a quick search showed it was a freeport customs facility on Switzerland's border with France and Germany. She had not been expecting another shipment, nor had the collector said there were more. Barry had taken the day off, and she had filed her question away to ask Darwin later.

Strange why it needed my signature. The crates contained more Greek and Etruscan vases, none as beautiful as the original collection. For now, she asked the staff to store them. *This better be it. We're not a warehouse.*

She reached Bocagnano and pulled in to pick up dinner. *I wonder if there's more trout?* She salivated at the memory of last week's fresh catch.

12

D arwin set down his iPad and rubbed his eyes. The spreadsheet, even on his large tablet, taxed both his vision and concentration. Multiple restorations were not unheard of as the technologies for cleaning and repairing got better. However, this document showed a recurrent history of objects that went outside the Vatican for repairs. And the last line of Gavin's email still gave him pause:

`Be careful who you ask about this.`

How many people are involved? He looked at the row with the Amphora of the Vatican Mourner. The perfect specimen depicted either Eos or Aurora weeping over the body of her son Memnon. Its opposite side featured Menelaus bringing Helen back after the Sack of Troy. The notes listed its painter as from an Attic ceramics studio, possibly a student of Exekias, circa 530 BCE. It had been excavated in 1836 in Vulci, a key destination for amateur collectors during their nineteenth-century grand tours.

Darwin knew certain Etruscan schools exhibited mastery sought after by collectors and that Vulci's tombs had given up objects of immense value but also left many questions of provenance. Given the sparse documentation for this amphora, he surmised it had been dug up by grave robbers and sold to a wealthy traveler.

His watch vibrated. *Time for coffee with Richard.*

They met in a cafe behind the museums and carried their cups outside to a shaded garden bench in a section closed to tourists. Richard listened attentively as Darwin explained Gavin's spreadsheet and the objects sent out multiple times. After a couple of minutes, Darwin sensed he was confusing Richard. He paused and then asked, "What can you tell me about Gavin?"

Richard gazed at him a long moment, and Darwin sensed the deep brown eyes penetrating his soul.

"Hmm, where to begin? Gavin came to us on a wider path. He's Catholic, from Northern Ireland, and a product of conflict similar to my own in Soweto. Violence would have swallowed him too were it not for his gift with maths, which gave him a way out of an impoverished life.

"He found a career in finance, where he excelled, but he lost sight of his moral roots. His brilliance took him to fantastic gains but also to the wrong side of the financial regulators. Gavin's work on the investment products sold by his firm obfuscated the risks in esoteric language and inordinately complex derivatives. The investigators offered him a choice of working with them or going to prison. He chose the former and assisted the European authorities in unraveling abstruse evidence in the two-thousand eight financial collapse."

Richard sipped his coffee before continuing. "After the investigation and fulfilling some community service duty, his faith led him to the priesthood, where he worked on the Church's banking matters. I brought him in two years ago to unravel the banking mess created by Cardinal Keenan."

Darwin blinked, surprised at hearing Keenan's name again. The former camerlengo had manipulated Vatican Bank deposits to funnel money into groups that opposed the pope. Officially, Keenan had retired to his home parish in the US for health reasons, but Darwin knew the full story.

"Yes. That's how we did it," Richard added upon seeing Darwin's reaction. "Gavin was the perfect outsider to investigate. He has uncommon forensic abilities, and none of Keenan's crowd remembered him. He sees patterns and clues. If he gets a scent, he follows it, not unlike you, Darwin, and your crazy adventures."

"Okay." Darwin started to answer, but then he paused to reframe his question. He had learned Richard always had other forces at play. "Why involve me? I'm here to query ancient documents in the library."

"True. But consider this mystery. Gavin asked me a question: why would priceless Vatican objects go to an outside restorer for months and the services cost so little money? And why, within a month of their return, did the same restorer make a generous donation to the Vatican Museums?"

"Dunno. It seems odd. But I'm an archaeologist, not a financial analyst," said Darwin.

"Precisely. Who better to sort out these antiquities restoration irregularities?"

"But—" Darwin stopped as Richard held up a finger and withdrew an envelope from a cassock pocket. He took it and furrowed his eyebrows at the cross-key papal embossing. A wavering hand had addressed it personally.

Darwin,
Before settling too deeply into your new role, I ask that you look into
the odd movements of some of the treasures in my museums. As before,
please communicate only through Richard on this task.
Yours in faith,

The note ended with the pontiff's scrawled signature. Darwin looked up at Richard, who said, "Consult with Gavin discreetly. He's convinced something unethical is going on, but he said the task requires your expertise."

13

Just after lunch the next day, Eyrún's assistant alerted her that Zac had arrived. They embraced outside her office. His burning the candle at both ends appearance reminded her she could also use an afternoon boost. "Coffee?" she asked.

"Love one," he said, adding, "This place is really transforming."

As they walked toward the kitchen Eyrún noticed the bounce in his step. His usual effervescent personality had returned since she had last seen him. He looked happier and she said so.

"I slept well."

"You look like you haven't slept at all," she said with a knowing smile.

He laughed as they turned into the break room. She got a tea, and they carried their drinks to the rooftop garden overlooking the harbor. A soft onshore breeze carried the scent of the Mediterranean, and they sat at a cafe table, where Eyrún caught him up on the ACA. "Darwin's due back tomorrow night. You should come to dinner again."

He agreed, and then she turned the conversation to Lupita's project. "I could use your help on something here," she said. "I know you were thinking of going back to California, but I think it'll only take a couple of days."

She watched him gaze over the harbor and sigh with a smile. "I might stick around a while longer."

"I know that look, Zac. You met someone?"

"Guilty as charged." He grinned.

"That's great!" She had grown to love Zac like a brother and could only imagine his frustration as he came to realize what Eyrún had settled on years ago—Stevie would not change.

"Yeah, we'll see where it goes. It's early, but we're having fun," he said.

"And sleeping well."

He raised his mug in a mock toast and asked about the AI project. Eyrún described it as best she could, a combination of onsite computer servers and mainland-based cloud servers. It seemed Corsica's internet connections were too slow to do all the computations in the cloud.

"Lupita said something about load balancing and data storage access. I'm sure I could understand it, but I've got another unexpected problem."

"Only one?" He laughed. "It's why I sold my company. Loved the research, but the day-to-day operations sucked the life out of me. I'll get with Lupita. I'm sure, between the two of us, we'll have it figured out in short order."

"Thanks. I was secretly hoping you'd say yes. And now you have another reason to stick around," she said, glancing at her watch, which had vibrated. "I have a call in fifteen minutes. Sorry to cut our visit short."

"No problem. I'll get started." He stood and went to the computer lab to meet Lupita.

As they entered the building, he asked, "What's your unexpected problem? Darwin got another hairball idea?"

"Ha! For once, it's not his doing." Eyrún explained the donation from the local museum and the crates that had arrived from the Basel freeport. "With Darwin starting up on the pope's job, I've no one on staff to sort out these vases."

"I might have an idea. Got another minute?" When Eyrún nodded, he told her about Jasmin's experience in antiquities. "Perhaps she could look?"

"That would be fantastic. Maybe we could meet over drinks or dinner?"

"Sure. That'd be fun." They paused at Lupita's lab, and he added, "I'll ask her and text you later."

"Thanks," said Eyrún. "It's great to have you here."

14

After dinner, Darwin strolled through the neighborhood to ease the rich meal through his system. The osso buco sauce was among the best in memory and paired well with the vibrant Tuscan red. He preferred the work of small vintners for their creativity in extracting unique soil and climate signatures.

The warm day had given way to evening air stretched thin by winter's dying grasp. He flipped up his jacket lapel and tucked his hands in his jeans pockets. A chill had taken hold by the time he reached the boutique hotel, and he ordered a digestif at the front desk before hiking the stairs. He took them two at a time to generate heat and, on reaching his fourth-floor room, closed its window, switched on the gas fire, and swapped his jacket for a thick cotton robe.

A knock on the door heralded room service, and, a few minutes later, he loosened the robe in the combined warmth of the fireplace and amaro. Then he grabbed his iPad from the chairside table to study Gavin's spreadsheet. After orienting himself to its layout, he sorted the pieces by the restoration date and found seventeen that had been sent out for multiple restorations.

He read the notes on each and determined seven were legitimate because of poor workmanship or an improvement in technique.

Narrowing his focus to the most recent dates, he fixed upon four pieces sent out in the last decade. Their notes were brief, and the gap between restorations averaged twenty-three years, but the data did not connect in any way he could discern.

He swirled the amaro and watched the chocolate amber liquid meander down the glass. He sipped, letting the burnt caramel flow over his taste buds. As his olfactory senses processed the herbal nuances in the drink, a question formed: *Who's conspiring with the restorers?*

He looked up the department head who had signed off on the restorations: Giuseppe Tonto. But then he found each department's curator had changed between the first and second restorations. He pictured one possible workflow. *A piece gets sent out. Years later, a new curator is hired on who has no memory of a restoration and, wait... There must be records showing the times a piece went out.*

He messaged Gavin in California.

Darwin: Hey Gavin, how's Cali? got a sec to answer a question about the xls?

Gavin: Sure. Nice spring day here. But you know that from your Berkeley days

Darwin: Don't miss the morning fog tho. What's the process for sending pieces out on restoration

The mobile rang. "Hey, Gavin."

"Hi, Darwin," said Gavin. "Faster to talk this through. Besides, I'm walking a couple through a wedding set-up."

"Sorry. I can call later."

"No problem. They're discussing flowers. Ask away."

Darwin asked about the records process.

"Good. You caught the same thing. The records prior to 2003 have not been digitized, and there's no objective auditing process. I've seen firsthand how coconspirators create a sign-off loop that only they see."

"But I looked into the current process. The curators determine whether the in-house talent can do a restoration; if not, they send it outside. There's a rigorous approval process that requires Guiseppe's sign-off."

"There's been a lot of turnover in recent years, and the newer computerized records make it harder but not impossible. Remember what I said about audit loops. I had to be discreet, but I found two of the curators started a restoration request on Guiseppe's suggestion. They didn't think the pieces needed restoring but didn't want to question their new boss."

"I can see why. Don't want to get on his bad side."

"Right. Did you find out how many pieces he recently approved?"

"Four."

"Correct. And what else did you notice about them?"

Darwin studied the spreadsheet, sensing that Gavin was leading him to a conclusion. He wiggled straighter in his chair like a student eager to get the right answer.

"Hard to distinguish them except... Wait..." He paused, swiping his finger up and down to compare some numbers. "These four have a higher appraisal value."

"Precisely. Listen, the couple looks like they've decided, and I need to get back to them. Look at my notes on the Oedipus kylix. I ran out of time to investigate it. Text me if you have other questions."

They said goodbye, and Darwin slumped back in the soft chair, scrolled to the row with the Oedipus kylix, and read Gavin's note.

```
Original in the Vatican, but a near-identical
piece turned up at auction two years after
the last restoration in 1997. See catalog
here.
```

He followed the link to a London auction house catalog from 1999 that had been scanned and added to a back catalog section of their website. The page with the kylix gave its provenance as from an anonymous Italian collection obtained in 1969, one year before the 1970 UNESCO convention on illegal transfer of cultural property. *Convenient. Clears any repercussions of a looting charge.*

But not forgery. He enlarged the photo and, setting his tablet in split-screen mode, brought up the photo from the Vatican's Etruscan collection. He could see no discernable differences between the zoomed images.

Who bought it? he wondered, but he knew in the same instant that the auction house would never disclose it. He searched the Web, using various phrases until the results narrowed, and he found a news article from 2011. It referenced an online article about a small museum in New Mexico that had received the kylix as a donation. The museum mainly featured objects from the American Southwest. The story quoted Debbie Anderson, the museum's curator:

```
While different from our main collection, we
think this vase will offer our visitors a
beautiful comparison of the ancient gods and
stories in the Old and New World cultures.
```

He zoomed in on the picture, which pixelated badly, having been scanned after printing, but he could see it was the same kylix as the one in the London catalog. He called the museum, and the man who answered introduced himself as a volunteer docent.

Darwin asked to speak with Debbie but was told she had left. Darwin explained the reason for his call and asked, "Can you tell me anything about the kylix?"

"Well, the new curator's not here, but if you're a buyer, you'd better hurry. It's at the auction house in Los Angeles."

"What? When?" Darwin's heart dropped.

"Next Tuesday."

Darwin left a message for the curator, Daniel Lopez, to call him as soon as possible, giving his title as director of Vatican antiquities, which, while not strictly accurate, hopefully, would create a sense of urgency.

15

Darwin's flight from Rome landed on time the next afternoon in glorious Ajaccio sunshine, and he walked the two kilometers to the ACA. After a long day of sitting and the cramped cabin of the small jet, the movement refreshed him. Less than half an hour later, he walked into Eyrún's office.

"Hi, love." They kissed, and he lifted her off the floor in a hug.

"Stop," she whispered in his ear, gently admonishing him for a stray hand on the back of her jeans. "We're in the office."

He put her down and looked through the office's glass walls. The staff had left for the day, except for Hervé, who was on the phone and looking the other way. She asked him about Vatican City as she tidied the desk and put her laptop in her bag.

"Richard says hi."

"Oh? How is he?"

Darwin filled her in as they walked downstairs to the loading dock to see the crates from the Basel freeport. As he opened the door, he said, "I have to go to Santa Fe, New Mexico."

"When?" She stopped in the doorframe.

"Tomorrow morning. I need to learn if this Oedipus kylix was really copied from the original in the Vatican."

"But we've got dinner with Zac and Jasmin tomorrow night."

"Sorry. I thought about not going, but His Holiness..."

She frowned. "I get that, but why is this piece suddenly important?"

"If there's really an inside conspiracy forging and stealing Vatican antiquities, this is the only chance I'll get to see the kylix before a private collector buys it."

She remained impassive, so he continued. "If word gets around that the Vatican Museums are full of forgeries, it casts doubt on all their treasures, including relics upon which the Church bases its provenance all the way back to St. Peter and the rock." He realized his voice had risen, and he took a breath. "So far, I only have a paper trail. This kylix may offer a more tangible clue."

"Then you should go, love. How long will you be away?"

"Three days, four at the most," he said as they went over to the crates. Letting go of his wheeled case, he walked around the box. He unlatched one side and peeled back the packing material to reveal the vase inside. Then he picked up the clipboard with the waybills, which offered little description of the crate's contents:

```
Etruscan vase, circa 500 BCE, found near
Vulci. From a private collection.
```

He set down the waybills and looked at the wide-mouthed vase. Its body featured two bulls, horns locked, and birds painted in a circle above the bulls. Its cracks had been left unfilled, a typical conservation practice.

"It's a krater, used for mixing wine and water at large gatherings, like a banquet. But you can see from its reassembly that it's average quality. All these crates arrived with no explanation?"

"None. Just required my personal signature. The driver knew nothing," she said.

"Hmm. Seems odd that one of the receiving guys couldn't have signed for them."

"Barry said the same thing."

He looked over the clipboard again. "And we know nothing of the krater's provenience besides this?"

"No. Is it important?" she asked, her brow furrowing. Then she added, "I've just been so busy."

"I know, love. You're doing a great job here." He ran a hand gently up and down her arm before crouching by the vase. "There's actually two things: provenance and provenience. Provenance is a record of ownership. Provenience is the object's find spot. It's the bedrock of archaeology. When tomb raiders lie about where they found an object to cover up looting, it creates a false history. For example, Urartu art claimed to be found in the Caspian area implies trade routes that did not exist. I could go on, but any unexplained gaps cast doubt on an object's authenticity."

"But these pieces are okay?" she asked.

He fingered the ridges in the cracks. "It's so hard to tell, as different countries have different laws regarding excavations. And looting has been common since, well, since people got buried with their valuables."

He stood and asked, "Where's that Fountain of Salmacis wonder vase you want to show me?"

"No time now. We have a six thirty appointment."

Darwin raised his eyebrows in question.

"There's a boat I want you to see."

16

Just before seven on Saturday night, Eyrún arrived at Raffaellu's, her favorite quayside restaurant. *"Bona sera Carulina,"* she said, taking a seat at the bar.

"Bona sera Eyrún. Cumu si?"

"Va bè è tù?"

"Busy, busy, but good, like you," said Carulina. Her dark hair swished from side to side as she arranged wine glasses. "Your Corsican's improving. You'll be a native before you know it. Are you meeting Darwin?"

"No, he's off to San Francisco."

"Oh?" asked Carulina, pausing her work.

"He's visiting a friend from university days. I'm meeting friends for drinks and dinner," said Eyrún, giving an obscure reason for Darwin's travel. She had learned that gossip spread quickly in Ajaccio.

Her task complete, Carulina came around the bar and greeted Eyrún properly. Then she checked her makeup in a small mirror and smoothed her floral dress before resuming her job as hostess. She and her husband, Petru, had taken over the restaurant when the original owner, Raffaellu, had retired.

"Champagne, s'il vous plaît," Eyrún said to the bartender when asked what she would like to drink.

The cool liquid fizzed down her throat, and she sighed as the alcohol warmed her belly. Zac and Jasmin were late, but Eyrún was glad for the moment to unwind by herself. Setting up the ACA had become running from one crisis to another. Between the construction and hiring department leads, she worried her decisions came too fast, like throwing darts. She gulped a mouthful of Champagne, a tonic against her chaotic feelings.

Her mood eased, and she remembered a deliciously hedonistic weekend spent in a deserted cove, not another human in sight. She shifted on her barstool and scrolled to the photos of their trip. Darwin had rented a boat to show her some of Corsica's remote southern coastline. She had enjoyed the experience so much that she had spent two lunch hours during the past week looking at boats, which had led to her showing him one that had attracted her eye.

A minute later, she found herself reading emails again. *Stop*, she reminded herself, putting the device face down on the bar. *You moved to Corsica to let go of the stress.* She sipped more Champagne, telling herself that this phase would pass. *And tonight's about getting help.*

She turned toward the back of the restaurant, where it opened onto the docks. The sun cast long shadows and reflected in bright flashes off the glass and metal of the pleasure craft. She was thinking about the yacht again when a soft voice came from behind.

"Eyrún?"

"Oui," she said, turning to see a tall, slender woman with dark hair.

"I'm Jasmin. Pleased to meet you."

Eyrún slid off the barstool. In her low heels, she was almost half a head shorter than Jasmin. "Nice to meet you as well," she said. "Is Zac with you?"

"He's coming. Said something about waiting for a cloud connection. I don't know. It's a computer thing," said Jasmin.

A knot in Eyrún's stomach unwound slightly as she thought, *There's one thing solved.*

"What may I get for you?" the bartender asked.

As Jasmin ordered, Eyrún studied the woman who had captured

Zac's attention. Multiple thin bracelets jingled on her wrists, and gold rings adorned her fingers. Her jet-black hair was pulled back over one ear, revealing flawless skin, and her low-cut emerald dress flowed over ample breasts and a slender body, stopping over one knee, slightly bent as she leaned on the bar. The tips of her manicured toes peeked out from high-heeled sandals straight out of Paris.

No wonder Zac likes her. Eyrún suddenly felt underdressed in jeans and a simple blouse. *She's the polar opposite of Stevie.* Jasmin turned, drink in hand, and Eyrún caught a whiff of her musky perfume. Another thought burst through: *Probably a rebound relationship.*

"*Santé,*" said Jasmin, smiling warmly. "It's so nice of you to meet with me."

"*Santé.*" They clinked glasses and took a drink.

Eyrún then said, "Zac tells me you have a lot of experience with Greek and Etruscan vases."

17

The next day, Sunday, Jasmin went with Zac to the ACA. He had to check on a computer system set-up, and Eyrún agreed it would be a great idea to let Jasmin assess how she could help.

"You two seemed to get along," said Zac as they drove from his flat.

"Yes. She's nice and quite beautiful. A little intense, though."

"Well, she's a scientist, and Nordic folks take a while to warm up. But she likes you. I could tell." Zac parked and showed her to the archaeology lab, saying he would be just down the hall.

When the lab door closed, Jasmin took in the setup. Everything smelled of new equipment, metal and plastics, blended with the off-gassing of the newly remodeled building—not unpleasant, but sterile. The lab had all the instrumentation for inspection and analysis of the chemical composition of artifacts.

She moved to a row of vases on a table under the rear windows and leaned in to sniff one vase. Dusty, but also with an older, harder-to-describe character, like a museum smell. She had once been in an Egyptian tomb and remembered its distinctive odor—a colleague had called it the breath of antiquity.

She looked out the window at the verdant mountains behind Ajaccio and thought ahead to the picnic Zac had promised later. The air had been cool when they had arrived a few minutes ago, but the cloudless sky foretold a hotter afternoon. She stepped back to survey the project, remembering Eyrún had told her an intern had arranged the vases with descriptions and duplicates of the waybills.

Her cursory inventory of the pieces took just over an hour. She compiled a list of questions, including which vases to test for material composition and carbon dating, which the intern would run during the week. Then she sorted the vases based on value—those she knew clients would pay top money for, particularly the krater with Aphrodite.

A soft knock at the lab's door drew her attention. "How's it going?" asked Zac.

"Slow. Most are average." She stood and stretched as Zac crossed to her and massaged her shoulders.

"And this one that Eyrún likes?

"It's absolutely stunning." She ran a finger lightly across its surface. Her fingertip registered the smooth clay and the ridges of fired black paint. "It's perfect." She frowned and thought, *Almost too perfect.* She had learned to trust this suspicious sixth sense. Buyers could be misled, but her reputation had been built on delivering quality.

"But it's broken," he said.

"That's not a problem, as most vases of this era are found damaged. See how the cracks are left unfilled? It leaves the artist's original work intact. Our imagination fills in the gaps."

"I get it. Sort of. I have maybe another half-hour. Then we can go on our picnic. Got a surprise for dessert."

She purred, and he retreated from the lab. She put a hand to her tight shoulder, where Zac had rubbed, and returned her attention to the Fountain of Salmacis krater. The vase's note read, "Late fifth century BCE, found in a tomb near Falerii." The period and style matched. *Let's see what else you can tell me.* She slipped on a magnifying headset. After adjusting its light, she laid the vase on its side and studied its bottom.

As expected, the unglazed base was rough and porous. Any organic material absorbed in the clay should give a definitive date. She scraped a tiny amount into a glass dish for testing and then squatted to bring her eyes level with the base. *Oh my God*. She inhaled sharply. Someone had made a clear mark inside the base's ring. Few artists in antiquity signed their work. Any who did caused the piece to shoot up in value.

The krater's maker had carved a U into its top, intersected by a shallow curve, and the resulting symbol looked like a crude bull's head. She knew it as an aleph—the ancient letter Romans had fashioned into the modern A.

Brilliant technique, right down to mimicking a signature. She took a photo and then swiped to a photo of a mark on a comparable vase she had taken five years ago. *Identical.*

As she sat on a lab stool, her heart raced. *It's him.*

18

D arwin landed early Sunday afternoon in San Francisco, where he was to meet Gavin for an early dinner. Soon after clearing US passport control, he called Eyrún, knowing it was her bedtime soon.

"How's San Francisco?" she asked.

He described a typical windy and cold afternoon with fog poised on the hilltops behind the airport.

"I met Jasmin, Zac's new flame."

"And?"

"She's nice. Very different from Stevie."

"Something in your tone says you don't like her."

"What do you mean?"

"The way you said she's different from Stevie," he said as he slid into a rideshare south to Mountain View in the heart of Silicon Valley.

"I didn't say I didn't like her. It's just that... I don't know. It's only been a month since they split up."

"I like Stevie, but Jasmin sounds more like two of Zac's former girl-friends in California," said Darwin.

"I know she runs off on her explorations, but..." Eyrún let the statement hang.

"Look. Like you said, Stevie's a free spirit. Zac moved to France to see if the relationship would work. Let them figure it out. They're both grown-ups."

Eyrún stayed silent a moment, and Darwin held back the urge to fill the dead air.

"You're right," she said, picking up the thread again. "And Zac seemed happy. That's what matters. Anyway, I think Jasmin could help us with the vases."

They talked a few more minutes before Darwin wished her a good night and hung up. He napped the remaining twenty minutes to Gavin's church.

19

On Monday afternoon, Zac found Jasmin strolling through a labyrinth near the ACA's back patio, where Darwin had created this space for contemplation. A trio of menhirs, crude stone figures carved by Corsica's Palaeolithic peoples, watched over the maze from a surrounding rock garden, and Roman column sections lay strewn on the opposite side.

He crossed the marked semicircular rings and joined her. She asked about his AI work. After explaining it for a couple of minutes, he paused and said, "You're not following this, are you?"

"I get the concepts, but I'll admit it's not my passion. I like to do things I can see and hold in my hands."

"I got just the thing for you." He grinned and embraced her.

"Is it unique?" She slipped her hands in his rear jeans pockets.

"One of a kind."

They kissed more passionately and then parted. She hummed, "Can't wait for later. But I wanted to ask your opinion about something."

"Hit me."

Jasmin described her examination of the vases and the shipping documents. "Some of the poorer-quality pieces are genuine, but five of the finer ones look forged."

"Holy… How can you tell?"

"I'll know more when the carbon dating comes back tomorrow, but two of the fakes have a mark from a modern artist." Zac's eyebrows shot up, and she added, "Forgeries are common, but these are the best I've ever seen."

He whistled. "You need to tell Eyrún."

"I'm worried how she'll take it."

"She's a straight shooter. Just tell her."

20

C lose to eleven the next night, Darwin landed in Albuquerque, New Mexico. After meeting with Gavin on Sunday evening, he had hung out with former colleagues on Monday at the University of California Berkeley. One had invited him to give a guest lecture on his discoveries.

His visit with Gavin had revealed nothing new, but Gavin had agreed with Darwin's hunch to meet with the curator in Santa Fe, saying people revealed more when face to face. Unfortunately, Darwin still had little else to go on besides getting a better grasp on the spreadsheet.

As he walked outside the terminal to the ride-share location, a blast of frigid air sliced through his jacket. The near-freezing temperature forced him closer to the waiting area's infrared heaters. While spring's warmth had penetrated southern Corsica, Albuquerque sat nearly two thousand meters higher in elevation.

Fortunately, the driver arrived less than five minutes later. The SUV's black leather interior bristled with creature comforts, not unlike the AirBus 350's business class seat from Paris. Best of all, the heat radiating from beneath the seat warmed his backside. Darwin settled in, shivering off the chill.

"Cold enough for you?" asked the driver.

Darwin laughed and leaned back for the hour-long trek to his hotel in Santa Fe. As the New Mexico high desert swept past, he thought of the yacht Eyrún had shown him on Friday night. It was nice, but he had figured she needed to learn more about watercraft before choosing one, so he had introduced her to a family friend, Marc Denis, who owned a charter boat company. "No one knows these waters like Marc. He can help you figure out what kind of boat you want," he had said.

Eyrún wasted no time meeting him, and, before her bedtime last night, she had emailed photos of a yacht that Marc had known about. Darwin now scrolled through the pictures and laughed to himself about the powerful-looking blue yacht with gleaming black windows. He dozed, thinking about Eyrún and her need for speed.

When the vehicle slowed in Santa Fe, he awoke, and, minutes later, the driver let him off at the Inn and Spa at Loretto. As he checked in, the desk agent described the fabulous features that Darwin would not have time to enjoy. He thanked her and went straight to his room, where he slipped into bed, fearing the jet lag would awake him long before sunrise.

21

S unrise finally topped the mountains behind the Inn and Spa, sending a blaze of light into Darwin's room. He had been awake since four o'clock and had coaxed several cups of brown liquid resembling coffee from the in-room setup. It tasted awful but delivered much-needed caffeine. He called Eyrún when he felt more awake.

"Hi, love."

"Hi. How's New Mexico?"

"So far, it's freezing and dark."

She laughed and launched into a litany of the activities at the ACA, including a construction delay and a surprise shipment from the Basel freeport.

"What will you do with the new vases?"

Eyrún said Jasmin was assessing them, but then she cut their call short for another interruption.

To help wake himself up, Darwin went for a run, but one step outside in Santa Fe, even higher in altitude than Albuquerque, sent him to the hotel's gym treadmill instead. After working out, he ordered a triple cappuccino and breakfast from room service. Then he read up on the history of the American Southwest to kill time before his meeting with Daniel Lopez at eight.

His watch vibrated, alerting him that it was time to walk to the restaurant, and he exited into a robin's egg blue sky that stretched between horizons. Despite wearing a sweater beneath his jacket and a scarf coiled about his neck, he picked up his pace to generate heat. While it might be warm enough at midday, the low morning sun failed to provide warmth.

He noticed that most buildings had a pueblo motif. Their mocha walls sloped inward as they rose, and all corners had been rounded. The window frames mimicked the thickness of the adobe blocks used in the ancient construction, and it took him a couple of blocks to figure out why Santa Fe had a familiar feel. He passed a shop named Oxygen Oasis. Its title reminded him of the salt-mud buildings in the Sahara Desert's Siwa Oasis, where he and Eyrún had found Alexander the Great's tomb.

New Mexico's geography offered similar challenges—small areas of habitable land surrounded by massive desert. The crucial difference was that Santa Fe looked more like a theme park version of an ancient pueblo than the hard-scrabble Egyptian oases.

A block later, he reached the Coyote Cafe, wedged between Casa de Turquoise and an art gallery, one of many he had passed on the way. Inside, a few patrons occupied tables, most with notebooks and tablets —business people meeting to start their day. A black-haired man about his height rose to meet him. His fleshy face and a substantial belly showed a man who enjoyed his meals.

"Darwin?" The man thrust out a hand when he saw a positive response.

"Yes. Daniel? Pleased to meet you," said Darwin, shaking the offered hand.

Daniel Lopez wore an open-necked white shirt with a bolo tie held fast by a large turquoise piece. The aquamarine mineral also covered his broad silver watchband. Darwin saw a black cowboy hat on an adjacent seat that, together with black boots, completed the picture of a southwest business person.

"Nice to meet you as well. Did you sleep well at the inn? It's one of our nicest," said Daniel.

"It's very nice. Thank you for the recommendation and the

upgrade." Darwin had been given a suite on check-in, and now he knew why.

"You're the first official from the Vatican Museums to visit us. This vase must be a big deal."

Their server greeted them, and Darwin ordered a blue corn tortilla breakfast burrito blanketed with a New Mexico chile sauce and topped with a fried egg. Daniel asked for the same and returned to questioning Darwin, who steered the conversation toward the vase.

"We're not sure, but we think the kylix in your collection may be related to several in the Vatican's Etruscan collection."

"Huh." Daniel tilted his head. "I've always wondered about that piece."

"How so?"

"We're entirely focused on this region. None of our collection comes from farther away than three hundred miles."

"So, how did the museum get it?" asked Darwin.

"Came before my time. I heard it showed up one day—out of nowhere. We know nothing about its provenance and think it came from a donor the old curator knew. But that's it."

Their breakfasts arrived, and Darwin breathed in the pungent aroma melded with the more familiar scents of butter and egg. A mouthful brought out the nutty taste of the blue corn beneath the stronger chile, and, despite this being a second breakfast, his appetite kicked in as he scooped up the delicious combination. At one point, he leaned forward and grabbed a napkin to stop the sauce from running down his chin. Daniel, being more aware of the peril of the messy dish, had tucked his napkin into his shirt collar.

When their eating slowed down, Darwin resumed his questioning. "What can you tell me about your predecessor? Debbie, is it?"

"Never met her. Heard she came to Santa Fe in the late nineties. A real wheeler-dealer. During her time, our collection grew substantially. Mostly through donations."

"Why did she leave?"

"Funny things went on back then. Pieces showed up as donations, were exhibited a while, and then went out to auction. Good money for the museum, so the board never asked about it. But the IRS, that's the

US tax authority, started poking around. About a year later, Debbie suddenly retired to Costa Rica."

"You think there was fraud?" asked Darwin.

"I studied the records closer yesterday while you were flying in. She appraised the kylix at two million dollars."

Darwin whistled and drank some water.

"Exactly," said Daniel. "Comparable kylixes have auctioned for under a quarter-million, which is what we expect to get for this one."

"Why the drop in value?"

"Your question should go the other way. Why did she appraise it so high?" Daniel paused while Darwin considered the question. Then he said, "The donor got a huge tax break for the donation."

"But won't you be losing money at the auction?"

"Nope. Remember, we got it as a donation. I deaccessioned it to refocus on our Southwest collecting. Whatever it brings in goes to our operating budget, minus the auction house commission, of course. Are you considering buying it?"

"Dunno," said Darwin.

They finished breakfast and walked to the museum, where Daniel gave Darwin a personal tour. Two hours later, Darwin was en route to the airport for a flight to Los Angeles, where the auction was to take place that night.

Staring at the desert again, this time in daylight, he mulled over Daniel's revelation about the kylix. Darwin was no stranger to tomb-robbing and forgeries. He knew the business first-hand from an Egyptian antiquities network. But this was his closest encounter with antiquities tax fraud.

22

J ust after six on Tuesday, Jasmin waited for Eyrún to finish a call
and then entered her office. After greetings and small talk, Jasmin
got to the point. "I'm afraid I have some bad news about two of
the vases."

Eyrún's eyes widened. "Ugh, what now? That was the contractor
telling me about another delivery delay."

"I'm sorry. I can come back another time." Jasmin moved to stand.

"No. No. It's okay. Just tell me."

Jasmin explained her suspicion that the quality of the vases was too
perfect to have been buried for two thousand years.

"And...?" asked Eyrún.

"The glaze also used manganese, a compound the Etruscans didn't
have."

"They're fake?" Eyrún slumped and raised her hands to massage
her temples. A few moments later, she stopped. "So, what does this
mean? The collector bought fakes and didn't know?"

"It happens all the time."

"But the Fountain of Salmacis? It's amazing. How could..." Eyrún
squeezed the chair's arms, remembering her first encounter with the
vase. *Its colors are so vibrant. Its surface...* Her fingers tingled at the

memory... *It felt so precious. And now...* she flushed, recalling the time a coworker had tried to steal a discovery, and suddenly stood. "I need to see it."

She followed Jasmin to the lab, brushing off her assistant along the way. "Not now, Hervé." When she reached the table, she studied the krater, grasped its middle, and turned it. "It looks real," she said to Jasmin.

"Yes. It does. I'm sorry—"

"No. It's not your fault, Jasmin. I'm sorry. I don't know what caused me to get so upset. It's just that..."

"You thought it was real, a piece of history. Not a deception." Eyrún nodded, and Jasmin continued. "To an untrained eye, this piece is everything it claims to be. The techniques, proportions, and materials are perfect for a fifth-century Etruscan vase."

She described how its artist had even copied a known workshop's style. Then she carefully laid the vase on its side and pointed to the aleph mark on its base. "Almost no artists signed their work."

"Who's the artist? And what about the cracks? Did they forge it and then break it?" asked Eyrún.

"Exactly. A fully intact vase is rare. The repair adds to its authenticity—found in a tomb crushed under a modern city. It's also easier to hide a fake. To answer your first question, I've seen this forger's mark before, a legendary artist—the Albanian Master."

Eyrún crossed her arms. Her blue eyes radiated an icy expression.

"I know. You feel taken advantage of. But here's another thing," added Jasmin. "You wanted it to be real. We all do. And so, wealthy collectors will overlook inconsistencies. Worse, their desire to possess an authentic vase shades the truth, and they believe it's real. One day, when they grow tired of it or need money, they sell it as a legitimate antiquity. Then a skilled dealer or auction house places the vase within a group of pieces with known provenance as cover and sells it as genuine."

Eyrún's mouth hung open, and she moved a hand to cover it.

"Don't feel bad. I've had to explain this to clients who brought pieces to me for appraisal."

"Did the collector know this was fake?" asked Eyrún, bending to study the aleph.

"Maybe, but I doubt he would tell us."

"Where did he get it?"

"That's a harder question to answer, but I know an Egyptian dealer who sells his pieces as real."

"Who's that?"

"Nahla Al Mahwi."

Eyrún went rigid.

"You know her?"

"We've had dealings with her."

23

What the hell's going on? Eyrún's heart raced as she printed out documents from the museum, whose collection now sat in the ACA's lab. Both Barry's and Darwin's questions about provenience rolled around in her head as she pored through the museum's records.

Her blood boiled at the mention of Nahla, who had caused them no end of trouble during their investigation of the lost library of Alexandria. She shuddered at the sudden memory of the dark tomb, a fire, and her nemesis, Tessa, in a pit. Despite her friend Stevie's reassuring words, "You did all you could, Eyrún," the horror of watching someone die resurfaced from time to time.

The awful vision passed, but it was replaced by another she had never shaken off: Nahla's thugs entering their home and taking the Alexander treasure scroll Eyrún had personally located and given to Darwin as a wedding present. Her heart pounded, and her fists shook as the violation replayed in her mind. Only when the pope had returned the scroll to Darwin had she let go of her visions of revenge.

She stood and returned to the problem of the donated forgeries. With the documents spread across her desk, she read one and then the next, writing questions in the margins, but she made no sense of it. The connections came into focus and then went out again. *Dammit, I need*

Darwin. She tapped her mobile to call him, but it went straight to voicemail. She called again. Voicemail. *Shit. He goes into his own universe sometimes.* Not knowing what kind of message to leave, she disconnected, laid down the mobile, and massaged her jaw.

Calm yourself. Relax. She breathed deep and glanced at her watch, figuring it was just past noon in the Western US. *He's on the flight to LA. Of course he can't answer.* She groaned, hating when emotions got the better of her. *Work the problem. Leave a message he can act on.*

In twenty minutes, she had figured out the basic flow. The museum's collector had accumulated the pieces over a thirty-year period from multiple sources, random at first and then narrowing down to two specific dealers. The Salmacis vase and four other fakes had been acquired from Alexandria Antiquities Ltd. She laid the purchase receipts side by side. *Interesting.* The Alexandria Antiquities purchases had well-documented provenances, down to the date and tomb in Vulci. *If I were to fake something, I'd want to make it look as real as possible.* A quote from a university professor came to mind, "If you can't dazzle them with brilliance, then baffle them with bullshit."

However, Googling on her laptop turned up no connection between Nahla Al Mahwi and Alexandria Antiques Ltd. No surprise. Eyrún knew Nahla maintained a high-profile status as a benefactor to the New Library of Alexandria, yet a tightening in her belly added to her sense of a linkage between Nahla and the donated forgeries. *What are you up to?* The association eluded her, but she knew Darwin's intuition might find a tie-in.

She composed an email documenting what she had found in case he did not call before her bedtime. Just before driving home, though, she had a premonition. When busy, Darwin tended not to look at his emails for a day or two. Scrolling through her photos, she found the best one of the aleph and messaged it to him. *That'll get his attention.*

In the car park outside her office, a breeze drifted down the mountains, infused with maquis. The sun had baked the native shrubs all day, its heat extracting the aromatic oils that permeated Corsica. She paused for a cleansing breath and relaxed her neck muscles as the angst over Nahla diffused.

24

___

"Can I get you anything else, sir?" asked a woman's voice, penetrating Darwin's lucid dream. He came to as reality set in at the poolside cabana in Beverly Hills. The palms cast long shadows, and the air had cooled in the last half-hour.

"Er... No. Thank you," he said as she collected the plates from his late-afternoon meal. But then, struggling through the fog of jet lag and needing to focus on tonight's auction, he changed his mind and asked for a pot of coffee. He checked the time: four forty-three. *Too late to call.* It was near midnight in Corsica, besides he had chatted with Eyrún earlier while waiting for the flight in Albuquerque.

After the auction, his current plan called for a trip back to Berkeley in the morning, where his colleagues had scheduled a guest lecture at the University of California's archaeology department. He would catch the afternoon flight from San Francisco tomorrow.

Earlier he had gone directly to the auction house from the Los Angeles International Airport to view the kylix. The auction house had said it was closed to set up for the evening's bidding, but Darwin's Vatican credentials had convinced them to give him a special tour. The kylix, while beautiful, had no outstanding qualities except that the vase's paint seemed too bright for an artifact buried in soil for the past twenty-five hundred years, as if the restorer had gotten too heavy-handed.

He puzzled over the kylix, comparing pictures he had taken at the auction house to photos of the original sent by a trusted assistant. Unfortunately, those had been taken in dim light, as the Vatican kylix was in the basement storage. *Why copy this one? It's unremarkable. And Daniel Lopez expects it to sell for under $250,000.*

Earlier, a woman at the auction house had asked him, "Not what you expected, Mr. Lacroix?" Darwin had realized he was frowning but made no reply. *Maybe they took my lack of interest for a poker face.*

Shadow covered the pool deck, and the breeze forced him to retreat to his room. Fatigue dragged like an anchor as his body's internal clock ticked deep into the night.

D arwin returned to the auction house at eight, entering the main gallery, which had been filled with rows of chairs separated by a central aisle. Most attendees stood around the perimeter or near the wine and hors d'oeuvres along the back.

He studied the program listing the objects on offer; the bidding would culminate with a gold necklace, said to be late Persian. He had eaten dinner, but he salivated over the desert table. While, in his opinion, no one beat Parisian patisseries, Los Angeles added its experimental flair to all things creative. He chose a small plate that simulated an archaeological dig. Chocolate columns, molded like the hexagonal basalt found in Devil's Tower, stood in a dark Oreo cookie crumble, sprinkled with crushed caramel. An amphora in white chocolate lay beside the columns, and the dessert was finished with bits of gold foil.

Ingenious. He carried a plate to a stand-up table, where he snapped a photo next to his glass of cabernet sauvignon. He swirled the wine and held it to his nose. *Impressive.* He had never heard of Frank Family Vineyards, but he knew Calistoga, California, had rocked the French wine world before.

"Superb wine, isn't it?" asked a well-dressed woman with silver hair.

"Yes. Very drinkable," he said.

They chatted for a couple of minutes as Darwin ate the dessert. Fighting an urge to lick the plate, he excused himself to get another. He offered to get one for her, but she declined and had left when he returned. Shortly before nine, he got a third and used a finger to swipe up bits of Oreo as the auction for the Oedipus kylix opened.

It's starting price of two hundred thousand dollars moved briskly up to 250. The bids then crept up to 280, alternating between the silver-haired woman and a man leaning against the wall to Darwin's left. Darwin watched the man cup a hand over an earpiece running from his mobile and figured the buyer was on the other end of the call.

What's going on?

On a whim, Darwin raised his number as the auctioneer asked for 290. The man with the earpiece offered three hundred, fifty thousand over the price that Daniel Lopez had expected. *Interesting.* Darwin's enthusiasm spiked. *Did I miss something earlier?* He took out his mobile to look at the photos he had taken in the gallery and saw the red dot on his messages app. He tapped it to see a reminder about his flight for tomorrow and a message he had missed from Eyrún.

Eyrún: Found this on Salmacis vase. Jasmin says it's fake. See email.

He swiped to her email, tapped back to the photo she had sent, and zoomed in. *What!* He tapped to the kylix pictures as the auctioneer rattled off, "Three twenty." He pinched to enlarge the base of one of the kylixes. There was a mark, blurry from the glare in the plexiglass, but it was an aleph—same as on the Salmacis vase. *Merde!*

"Three twenty going twice."

Darwin's arm shot up, waving his bidder number.

"Three thirty," said the auctioneer. "Do I hear three forty?" Almost immediately, he said, "Three forty," nodding toward the silver-haired woman. The man countered. "Three fifty."

Darwin remembered something he had read earlier while researching vases: "Most of the works come from a master's studio and are not marked. The pieces signed by the master are the most valuable."

He scanned Eyrún's email again, aghast at its revelation. *It's connected.* He looked up on hearing, "Three sixty. Going twice." *I need this piece.* He thrust up his number.

"Three seventy," said the auctioneer.

All heads turned toward Darwin. The conversations in back increased in volume, as if the bidders were at a racetrack and a preview horse race, booked to fill time until the main event, had unexpectedly become a crowd-pleaser.

"Three eighty. Three ninety. Four hundred." The number volleyed between Darwin and the man on the mobile. Darwin paused and slowed his breathing, wondering if he was nuts, his fingers tingling. Then he remembered Gavin saying, "I fear some pieces in here are no longer the originals."

Merde! To hell with the cost. It's the answer to the restorations. I know it. This isn't about money. It's the authenticity of the Vatican's museums.

"Four ten," came the call at Darwin's latest bid.

The man at the wall talked into his headset. Darwin's heart hammered against his breastbone.

The man raised his number. "Four twenty—"

Darwin's hand was up before the auctioneer finished speaking, and the crowd gasped in delight. The man shook his head no at four forty. Less than a minute later, it was over.

"Vatican." Darwin heard a woman whisper to another as he walked to the office to settle the transaction. After declining to bid higher, the man had pulled his earpiece, studied Darwin for a long moment, and then left, apparently there only for the kylix. The auction arena led to fierce competition, no physical contact, but losses still hurt.

While arranging a funds transfer for $430,000, Darwin asked about the man on the phone, knowing the art world was secretive but also liked to name drop.

"Our policy protects the privacy of bidders, but in this case, I can honestly say, Mr. Lacroix, we don't know," said the man, taking Darwin's banking details. "He presented an invitation and said he was here on behalf of his client. But I detected a touch of an Eastern European accent."

Darwin left shipping details for the ACA in Corsica before returning to the hotel, where he took a warm shower to unwind and then crawled into bed and passed out.

25

Bob Marley's "Exodus" blasted from Darwin's iPhone, tearing him from sleep. *What the hell?* He fumbled around the nightstand, grasping for the device. His brain computed something was wrong as he saw the caller ID.

"Zac?"

"Darwin. Sorry to wake you, bro, but Eyrún's been arrested."

"What! Why?" Darwin sprang out of bed, fumbling for the bedside light.

"The French antiquities police say she's trafficking illicit cultural heritage. It's the vases from La Citadelle Museum," said Zac, rattling off details.

"Putain!" Darwin got the light on, saw 3:57 on the clock, and gently rubbed his eyes to ease the raw feeling. He got that Zac was in the Ajaccio police headquarters, where they were holding Eyrún. Sleep was over, and he moved to switch on the in-room coffee machine. He understood Eyrún was waiting for their attorney before answering questions. While the brew cycle began, and now more awake, he asked Zac to start over.

"Sure, bro. You okay, it's like…four in the morning there," said Zac.

"No! My wife's been arrested, and I'm on the other side of the planet. What the hell's going on?" The machine hissed, emphasizing his own boilover.

"I agree with you. It's fucked up."

A flashback seized Darwin as he sipped the steaming brew. He and Eyrún had spent a rough night in a Paris jail after breaking into a tunnel beneath Notre-Dame Cathedral. *Hope it's better in Ajaccio. At least Zac's there.*

"Darwin?"

"Yeah, yeah, I was thinking about Paris. Go ahead."

"It's not exactly the same, but I hear you. About ten this morning, Hervé ran into the computer lab saying the French police had a warrant for Eyrún's arrest and a court order to seize everything in the lab. Barry and his team were kept out while the customs officers packed the vases. I talked to Eyrún as they walked her out—"

"Handcuffs?"

"No. They were civilized about it. The gendarmes made the arrest, but they were backed up by a guy with a warrant from the Marseilles branch of the OCBC. The ah...*Office Central de*—"

"I know who they are. Sorry, didn't mean to be so abrupt."

"I get it, bro. Listen, I'm staying with her until the lawyers get here or we get bail."

Darwin stood at the window, looking across the ocean of lights that spread to the mountains ringing the vast city. His mind raced through getting a flight from LA to Paris and then to Ajaccio. It would be night-time when he landed in Corsica.

"When does our lawyer arrive?" he asked.

"Early afternoon. I chartered a jet to bring her and her team down from Paris."

"You didn't have to—"

"Don't worry about it. But, something's not right. This is messed up."

"What do you mean?" Darwin stiffened.

"Think about it. The ACA gets a donation. Then a surprise shipment with forgeries arrives from the Basel freeport, and, within days, the OCBC shows up? C'mon, it's bullshit. This ain't a coincidence."

Darwin's brain kicked in as the caffeine boosted his time-zone-challenged neurons. *He's right. The donation, the shipment, the matching alephs. But how could this happen so fast—*

"Shit!" he said, scrolling to Eyrún's email.

"What, bro?" Zac's voice sounded tinny over the phone's speaker.

"Nahla!" yelled Darwin. "That bitch is screwing us again."

26

Two days later, Darwin sat with Eyrún, Zac, and the lawyers in an ACA conference room. He had flown to Ajaccio via London on advice from their lead attorney, Astrid, who had said the French police had a warrant for his arrest. He had hired a jet from Heathrow to Ajaccio to avoid a public scene at the main airport terminal, and the police had taken him into custody at the private terminal. Astrid's team had arranged bail, and he had been released almost immediately.

Darwin paced the conference room, fueled by restless energy from nonstop traveling the past week. He stopped and gripped a chairback as the meeting had started. Zac read through a pile of documents opposite his friends.

Astrid said, "Here's what we know. La Citadelle Museum owner's nowhere to be found. Ajaccio commune records show the museum building and collector's residence are owned by a shell corporation in Monaco that's a subsidiary of another shell corporation in Grand Cayman. The artifacts shipped to the ACA came from the Basel freeport and were owned by the same corporate organization. However, when Eyrún signed the delivery receipt, those artifacts became ACA property—"

"But, we didn't know their provenance when we signed. How does that make us guilty?" asked Darwin.

"Technically, you owned them as soon as the ink on your signature dried."

"That's bullshit!" He slammed the chair against the table and turned in a short loop before continuing. "We've been set up by Nahla Al Mahwi. Her company's been selling forgeries by this Albanian Master, whoever he is. She needs to be arrested."

"Perhaps," said Astrid, unmoved by Darwin's outburst, "but nothing in the document trail directly implicates her or Alexandria Antiquities."

"We just haven't found it yet. She's pissed off that we got back the Alexander scroll, and now she's bringing her vendetta here. She wants to ruin the ACA!"

Eyrún joined Darwin and took his hands. She looked into his eyes a moment before saying, "I agree that something's not right, love, but let's work the problem. Astrid's digging into the museum's paperwork. Anger won't help."

"The hell it won't. Shit, I should've been here helping you with this, not chasing the damn Vatican kylix. If I'd been here—"

"You'd have been thrown in jail with me."

He growled and shook his head. He had spent a fitful night brooding over his failure to protect her.

"C'mon. We went through this yesterday," she said. "Let's work the problem."

He opened his mouth to speak, but she squeezed his hands. She had been in problem-solving mode since he departed LA. After a moment, he sighed heavily. "You're right."

Astrid said, "I'm sorry for you both. I know this is difficult, but we'll get to the bottom of it."

Zac held up a document from the pile and waved it at Astrid, who added, "Yes. There's something else…" She took the paper and slid it toward Eyrún. "The French prosecutor says she has someone in a Marseille prison who confessed to excavating the vases you signed for."

Darwin pounded the table. *"Putain!"*

93

27

The afternoon sun warmed the balcony of Zac's flat, where Jasmin poured tea. A soft breeze lifted the steam as Zac removed the sachet from his cup and placed it on a saucer. He breathed in the aroma before sipping the pungent liquid. "I get the bergamot, but not the royal blue flower taste," he said, reading the label from the famous French brother's tea house in Le Marais, Paris.

"You will as your palate improves," said Jasmin. "It's like wine, where you learn the varietals and then the terroir. It takes practice."

He sipped his tea again. Zac had stretched his horizons to fit his lover's preferences. He thought tea tasted like weak coffee, but the strong oil from the Seville orange gave him something besides the tea's astringency.

Earlier, after Eyrún and Darwin had dropped him off, Zac had paced his flat, moving about randomly, straightening objects that were not out of place while trying to sort out who would have set up his friends. *Get a grip*, he chided himself, and then he ran through mental exercises given to him by an Army psychologist after a roadside IED had injured a soldier under Zac's command. He had blamed himself for not seeing it, not protecting his soldiers, and the ongoing anger had clouded his judgment. *Why would someone set such a device?* The same sensations now overwhelmed him. He hated perpetrators of cowardly action.

By the time Jasmin arrived, he was so wound up that he launched into a diatribe. She listened patiently and then held a finger to her lips and moved it to his. He stopped talking, but his short, fast breaths flared his nostrils. She wrapped her arms around him and pressed her head against his chest, quietly soothing his agitation.

His breathing slowed, and his shoulders settled as her fingertips made small circles on his back. Not long after, she led him to the bedroom, where they made love, slowly at first and then vigorously, until Zac's anguish exploded in a yell. He flopped onto his back, panting. Jasmin rolled over, lay her head on his heaving chest, and moved a knee over his thigh.

An hour later, after a brief nap, they had moved outside, with Jasmin wearing one of his T-shirts. He tried the tea again, and its heady fragrance and her presence combined to soothe him. He studied her and realized she had deftly taken his angst and redirected it, defeated it. *Like a counselor,* he thought. Then chuckled. *She uses her body in ways no counselor can.* An electric buzz radiated through him, but he checked it. *Too early. We just met. It's the sex talking.*

Her eyes engaged his. "What is it?"

"This is good. It's growing on me," he said, looking over the harbor to conceal his feelings.

"Tell me what happened this morning," she said.

Zac gathered himself and then went through the meeting with the lawyer, ending with learning about the tomb raider's prison confession. "Why would Nahla do this?"

Jasmin looked into her tea and did not answer.

"You know her, right? You mentioned her to Eyrún."

"Yes."

When she did not elaborate, Zac gently prodded. "Talk to me. She's done this kind of thing before, right? You must've seen it."

"It's..." She looked away and then closed her eyes a long moment.

"It's what I'm trying to get away from. This whole business of deception and lies. Nahla set me up once when I was younger. My husband…" Her eyes flooded, and a teardrop rolled down one cheek.

Zac moved behind her. "I'm sorry. I didn't mean to bring up the memories." He stroked her shoulders.

"I have to deal with it eventually," she said with more strength. "Maybe what I know can help Darwin and Eyrún."

"Only if you want to. They have good lawyers. I'm sure we'll figure out this was a mistake, that Eyrún did nothing wrong."

"I hope so," she said, tipping her head back and locking eyes with him, "because these people are vicious."

Zac straightened at her ominous tone.

"You've no idea, Zac. Unbelievable entitlement fuels their greed. Millions of euros are involved, and these people will stop at nothing to get what they want."

Her sudden mood shift perplexed him. *She doesn't want to talk about her husband, but something about their business triggers her?* As casually as possible, he asked, "So, how does the antiquities trade work?"

28

The next afternoon, Saturday, Zac and Jasmin were at the mountain house to spend the weekend with Darwin and Eyrún. A cool breeze wafted up the canyon as they sat around the rock-lined firepit on the back deck. The pine logs crackled, and the sweet smoke swirled away over the house.

Eyrún had laid out a tray with coppa and two cheeses: a sharp Niolu and mild, nutty Venaco, to which she added grilled figatellu. To go with the rustic Corsican fare, Darwin poured Faustine, light spicy red from Domain Abbatucci. They dabbed the rich sausage juices with crusty bread, and greasy fingerprints coated their wine glasses. Zac coaxed the last drops from the second bottle and asked, "Which grape?"

"Sciaccarellu. A native," said Darwin.

"Eyrún, this is yummy," said Jasmin. "You have to take me to this market. What's its name again?"

"I Mazzeri," said Eyrún. "It roughly translates to 'the seers.' The chef-owners, Sylvie and Anne, came from Paris and are reviving traditional Corsican dishes with touches from other parts of France."

"They make the sausage, too?" asked Zac.

As Eyrún explained where the meats came from, Darwin went to the kitchen where he seared a veal roast and, in between turning it, decanted a magnum of 2011 Châteauneuf-du-Pape from Vieux Télé-graphe. As he poured, the robust, unfiltered Mourvèdre-backed wine gave off its characteristic garrigue, an herbal bouquet that reminded him of Corsica's native Maquis. *That's gonna be good.*

He set down the empty bottle and looked across the living area to his friends at the firepit. *We needed this.* Zac had called him last night to relate Jasmin's forgery story. "Bro, you need to hear this shit firsthand. Reminds me of a drug cartel." Darwin had invited them up for the weekend, figuring a night of drinking would chase away the lingering tension.

After transferring the veal into the oven, he rejoined the others by the fire, where the wine had uncorked emotions. Within moments of him sitting down, Eyrún spat out, "I don't deserve this! What've I done to her?" She thrust a heel at the rocks ringing the pit, sending one into the flames and showering Darwin with sparks.

"Jesus, Eyrún." He jumped up, brushing himself off.

"Sorry, love. I didn't mean… You okay?"

He glowered but said he was unharmed.

"Glad that's out of your system." Zac smiled. "Anyone else?"

"No." Darwin thrust out a hand. Eyrún apologized again and asked Jasmin to start her story over.

"I'm sorry this happened," said Jasmin. "What you're doing with the ACA is wonderful. If it's Nahla's doing, I don't know what she's up to."

"If?" asked Eyrún. "I thought you said…"

"I said she's sold pieces by the Albanian Master. Let me start by saying most antiquities dealers and collectors have a genuine passion for preserving our ancient past, but like anything, the ambitions of some individuals get the better of them. Arrogance, entitlement, and greed cause them to skirt the law."

"My galleries in Paris dealt only in pieces with a rigorously docu-mented provenance. Sometimes clients would ask me to appraise pieces they had acquired elsewhere but with shoddy provenance. I refused. Sometimes it cost me a client, but I held to a higher standard as part of my brand. Owning a looted antiquity is illegal, and many of my clients had public reputations they did not want at risk."

"What do you mean by shoddy provenance?" asked Eyrún.

"One piece I saw listed at auction described itself as having been 'In the MacArthur family collection since the great-grandfather brought it back from the Crimean war—'"

"Spoils?" asked Darwin.

"Yes," said Jasmin. "As unscrupulous as the Nazis forcing cheap sales of artwork during the pre-war purges."

"What's good provenance?" Eyrún looked at Darwin.

He answered, "A bill of sale that shows provenience, its findspot, preferably from a registered archaeological dig and with permission from the country of origin to remove the artifact from its borders, and an unbroken record of all its transfers of ownership."

"Which is rarer these days," said Jasmin. "Many objects are either looted by professional tomb raiders, have altered documentation, or both. A thousand-year-old vase doesn't change, but when and where it was found can be. And its provenance is *laundered* by moving it through transactions in legitimate businesses, similar to how drug cartels legitimize their cash.

"For example, a typical flow goes like this. Tomb raiders, people who need to feed their families, dig up what the ancient rich took to their graves. Some clans specialize in looting. They get up and go to work just like you and me; only, their office is a tomb. Police are paid off to look the other way.

"They sell an artifact to a dealer, who legitimizes the piece by cleaning it and sending it to auction, where the agent plants one of their people to pose as the buyer. The repurchased piece now has the stamp of approval from a major auction house. From there, the dealer sells the piece to a collector or stores it in a freeport."

Darwin checked the temperature on the veal with his mobile app as Jasmin continued.

"At this point, multiple things can happen, the two most common being a collector buys a piece for their private collection or buys it and donates it. Less scrupulous curators compete for donations by marking up the appraised value. The museum gets a brilliant piece, and the collector writes off a large tax deduction."

Zac jumped in. "Wait, I read about this, where an American comedian got caught committing tax fraud. She bought a vase or something at auction for, like, thirty thousand and then donated it to a museum in Malibu, whose curator appraised it for a million. Would have gotten away with it except for a suspicious IRS lawyer with an art degree."

"I know that case," said Jasmin. "It exposed a vast corruption ring, where the curator had been making millions on the side of his museum salary. I remember it because the French tax authorities began scrutinizing my clients' dealings more closely—all the more reason to keep my galleries clean."

A buzzing sound from Darwin's mobile alerted them that dinner was ready, and they moved indoors.

They tucked into the veal, rubbed generously with arba barona, mountain thyme, that the Lacroixes had foraged on an earlier hike. The side dishes, a ratatouille and lemony potato mash, had come from I Mazzeri. Partway into the meal, Eyrún picked up the conversation again. "Where does forgery come in?"

"It's as old as time," said Jasmin. "Our forebears wanted a token from the pharoah or a piece of Christ's cross. In our time, it's money. Antiquities are investment grade. The wealthy buy them to diversify their portfolios, which creates a high demand for quality assets."

The conversation paused as Jasmin took a bite of the veal. Eyrún's eyes widened in recognition of the problem.

"Exactly," said Jasmin. "There are more wealthy people but a finite number of tombs. Forgers provide a steady flow of goods by copying ancient techniques and selling pieces for tens of thousands of euros, if not hundreds."

"The best even work on commission," said Zac. He swallowed a bite of veal with a mouthful of wine and added, "This is a fabulous pairing, Darwin."

Darwin tore a slice of baguette and dragged it through the plate's juices.

Jasmin said, "It's mostly money, but there are buyers who want a hand-painted copy of a famous piece. It's been going on forever. Art students copy masterworks to learn techniques. Some excel at it, and, well, it's hard making a living as an artist."

"How much forgery is there?" asked Eyrún.

"Difficult to say," said Jasmin. "The art and antiquities world is rife with fraud, but, in my experience, it's as high as thirty percent."

"That can't be right," said Eyrún.

"I'm afraid it is. These people have no regard for history. They're obsessed with money and possession. My husband became consumed by it and lost perspective. Three years ago, I found a shipment from Alexandria in our warehouse and learned he was dealing in counterfeit antiquities behind my back. It's why I left him."

Zac reached over and rubbed her shoulder.

"I'm sorry," she said as a tear ran down one cheek. "He destroyed everything I stood for."

29

The two couples spent a quiet Sunday together once they had shaken off the effects of Saturday night. Darwin, thinking he was up first, saw Jasmin and Zac outside on the patio, doing yoga. He paused, watching her direct Zac through one stretch. Her hair glistened in the morning sun. *They're good for each other*, he thought. *Still, I wonder how long it will last. She seems genuine, but...* He ground the beans as he pondered his doubt. *Dunno. She's used to wealth, and he says he wants a down-to-earth life.*

The espresso machine beeped ready, and he poured the last of three shots into the steamed milk and spooned a dollop of froth on top. He carried the cup down to the main living area and switched on the gas fire to ward off the morning's chill.

A few minutes later, Zac brewed tea for himself and Jasmin, and they joined Darwin.

"Thanks," said Jasmin, taking the tea from Zac. She got settled and picked up the conversation from the previous night. "Eyrún mentioned you've had dealings with Nahla, but she didn't say how."

"Ow. As if my hangover wasn't enough, you want to stir up that shit again this morning?" said Zac.

Darwin shrugged. "It's okay. A couple of years ago, I worked with another archaeologist pursuing the lost library of Alexandria. Turned out she was Nahla's former employee and wasn't happy about being left out of the deal."

Zac snorted. "He makes it seem casual. The woman kidnapped Eyrún, and her psycho accomplice nearly killed Darwin. In the end, Nahla got the corrupt Egyptian antiquities authorities to claim what Darwin had found."

"Sounds familiar. Nahla gets her objects by any means," said Jasmin.

"Do you really think she's behind what's happened to us?" asked Darwin.

"She's vindictive," Jasmin replied. "Have you done something to anger her?"

"Not that I know of." Then, like a light in a dark room, he knew the answer. *Merde! The scroll.*

He brought the last of the cappuccino to his lips to cover himself. The pope had intervened with the Egyptian president to return the Alexander scroll to Darwin. He had always suspected she was behind the crooked officials. *Could she be this vicious?*

But he already knew the answer. His blood boiled, and his temples throbbed. He massaged one side gently as Eyrún emerged from the master suite with her hair wrapped in a towel.

"Good morning," she said. "Looks like I'm last to the party."

———

Eyrún drove everyone into town on Monday morning, dropping Jasmin and Zac at their flats before continuing to the ACA with Darwin. "They're fun," she said after leaving Zac's place.

"Yeah, they are," said Darwin.

Yesterday they had procured a picnic from I Mazzeri and hiked a trail along Mount D'Oro before spending a lazy evening at the house.

As they entered the ACA lobby, Eyrún said, "The lawyers arrive at ten. Meet me in the upstairs conference room."

"Okay." He wiped a raindrop off one eyebrow. The sunny days of the past two weeks had given way to a gloomy drizzle that had brought a chill with it.

Once settled in his office and checking emails that had come in over the weekend, he opened Gavin's spreadsheet again, this time to look for evidence of Alexandria Antiquities or other links to Nahla Al Mahwi. It was a tangled mess. He yawned after an hour of poring through the rows and columns and went to the break room, mostly just to get some energy back in his body. His watch alerted him to the lawyer meeting in five minutes, and he collected his iPad on the way to the conference room.

"B*onjour*. How was your weekend?" Darwin asked Astrid, who had arrived early.

"*Bonjour. Magnifique.* My husband flew down—without the children—for a mini-break," she said. "It's lovely here, and the water is so blue. I miss the sea after being land-locked in dreary Paris."

Eyrún joined the conversation, and they talked about life on Corsica for another five minutes. She invited Astrid to visit them in the mountain house on their next trip. "It's a different side of the island."

Astrid thanked her as Hervé delivered coffee, and after he left, they shifted to business. "Nothing developed over the weekend. This week, my team will focus on the transfer of ownership and explaining that you had nothing to do with the museum collection and its prior transfers."

"What about that looter in prison?" asked Eyrún.

"That he confessed to looting the objects and selling them to the agent means little. I doubt he kept any records. Then there is the question of motivation. He's in prison for another offense, tomb looting, which exposes him to Italian laws and longer prison sentences.

"I suggest you get on the front foot. Spin this story in a favorable direction. Acknowledge the event. Say it is a misunderstanding, that you intended to exhibit objects of historical value to show the cultural development of the Mediterranean but a corrupt museum owner manipulated your trust. You could even insinuate that he donated the collection to avoid being caught—dumped the problem on you, so to speak.

"Anyway, assert the ACA's mission. Introduce a few of the new interns and their home countries, whose heritage you are protecting. Perhaps make a donation—not too extravagant. You want to show your good works, not throw money around to deflect a problem. What do you think?" Astrid asked, warming her hands on the mug.

Eyrún looked at Darwin, who shrugged. "That could work. I don't know what else we would do," she said, turning back to Astrid.

"Also, highlighting your work shows you are not tomb raiders but reputable archaeologists working to preserve French heritage."

"I like it," said Darwin.

Everyone agreed, and Astrid offered to connect them to a trusted marketing communications agency to take the story to social media. As they wrote ideas on the whiteboard, Hervé knocked and delivered an envelope addressed to Darwin.

"Who's it from?" asked Darwin, turning over the plain manila paper with only his name printed on its front.

"*Je ne sais pas*," said Hervé. "An intern found it on the lobby floor."

Darwin slit the envelope roughly with a pen and withdrew a single printed page. Eyrún leaned over his shoulder to read it.

"What is it?" asked Astrid.

"*Putain!*" said Darwin as he slumped in his chair.

"The bastards. It's extortion!" Eyrún shoved her notepad across the table.

Astrid jumped from her chair and stood behind Darwin as they all read the note again.

```
Darwin,
We apologize for the ACA's unfortunate inci-
dent with the authorities. We can make the
misunderstanding go away in exchange for a
favor. Send this item out for restoration:
1897.017.127b
```

When you comply, provenance documents for the
vases will be made available to the OCBC.
Details to follow.

30

Back at their mountain house gym, Eyrún yanked the handle to lift the weights on the cable machine and then let the iron stacks slam back down. Ninety minutes ago, after Astrid's departure, she had told Hervé to cancel her schedule for the day. Now she imagined Nahla's head beneath the clanging plates.

She had run for half an hour on the treadmill before moving to the weights. Sweat poured down her face, and a glance in the wall-to-ceiling mirrors showed her pale Nordic skin was flushed red. She yanked away strands of dark hair stuck to her perspiring neck and started a new set.

Everything's screwed! The ACA! My reputation!

Twenty kilograms banged down, shuddering the cable machine. Her arms thrust the handles down, sending the weight stack up.

I want that bitch exposed for what she is!

Bang—she finished the set. Her pulse pounded, and she was breathing heavily as she sat on a wooden plyo box. Darwin walked in and put a hand on her shoulder. "Don't!" She shrugged it off, and he turned to go about his own workout.

Eyrún did another two sets, but, this time, she kept the weights under control, watching herself in the mirror. The self-disciplined movement checked her emotions—a technique that had served her well since her father's death in an explosion while investigating a steam vent under a glacier. She had been seventeen, and, when her mother had fallen apart, she had had to act as head of the family.

She glanced at Darwin's reflection as he warmed up across the room. When they had first met three years ago, she had thought him weak, too scattered, and even dangerous as they had undertaken a lengthy expedition in a lava tube. She had insisted on bringing more experienced guides to compensate, but it was Darwin who had kept the team together and reached her emotionally.

She continued watching him as she worked her core with a medicine ball. Her anger at his running off to LA fueled her twisting side to side. *His stupid adventures. The way he leaps into situations. He... No.* She caught herself and set the ball down, panting. *Going to America had nothing to do with what happened.*

Her rest timer went off, and she grabbed the medicine ball again. As she finished the set, Eyrún recalled a conversation with Stevie where she had complained about Darwin's impulsiveness. Stevie's reply echoed in Eyrún's mind: *But you love the excitement.* She looked across the room at Darwin, and the corners of her mouth turned up. *Dammit. She's right.*

Eyrún attacked the ball as Stevie's other comment played in her head: *You two make a wonderful team. He's the Great Finder, and you're the Fixer.* Halfway through the set, she grunted, "We need to get them back."

"What?" asked Darwin, pulling out an earbud.

She repeated herself.

"I was thinking about that."

"And?"

"We give them what they want."

"You can't be serious," she said, rolling the heavy ball away.

Darwin sat on the edge of the padded gym bench and massaged his shoulder. "I am. There's got to be a way to do it. I'm not sure exactly what's going on, but the spreadsheet shows regular questionable restoration."

"But we're talking about a priceless Vatican treasure." She stood and leaned against the wall with her arms crossed as she tried to process her husband's latest crazy idea. "How...? No. No. Not how, why? It's a ridiculous idea."

"I excel at ridiculous." He grinned, and Eyrún responded by knitting her eyebrows. "Okay, it's total lunacy, but hear me out."

Here we go again! She huffed and crossed the room to open the sliding glass door. A cool breeze splashed her sweaty body. "Fine," she said, turning to face him. "Let's have it."

Darwin swiveled on the bench, tracking her movement. "I've been thinking about this for two weeks. Something's been going on inside the Vatican Museums. Who knows? Given what Jasmin told us, it's gotta be happening at other museums."

He described a plan to let the piece out for restoration and track its movement. This would allow them to figure out who was involved and stop the wider forgery.

"You really think that's going to work? Look at what these people have done. These are sophisticated thieves who've been at it for decades. You're just gonna show up and bust their forgery ring?"

"Well, obviously, my plan needs more work, but yes."

She sighed and tipped her head back.

"What do you propose we do? Let them destroy everything we've worked for?" he asked.

"I didn't say that!" she yelled. "Dammit, Darwin. You go at everything with half a plan. You nearly got us killed in Siwa."

"It's still just an idea. Of course we plan it out. I'm not stupid." He walked out of the room.

Eyrún winced at the door slam and listened to him thud up the steps. Then she walked outside, picked up a rock near the firepit, and hurled it into the canyon.

For the next three minutes, she watched the sun sinking on the horizon. Finally, feeling chilled from the air sweeping up the gorge, she went back inside for a glass of water.

Darwin was gone.

31

"**D**arwin?" Eyrún called out as she walked to the front entry. The door was ajar. "Darwin? Are you inside?"

She turned, listening for the shower, but heard nothing. *Shit! Where'd he go?* She looked at the entry closet where they stored the hunting rifles. *Stop it*, she told herself. *Corsica's safe*. Still, she moved cautiously.

She stepped onto the porch—and heard the crunch of gravel. She jumped behind the Macan, took a defensive stance, and then blew out relieved when she saw Darwin standing near one of the large pines that isolated their property from the mountain road. He jumped up to grab a thick rope hanging from a branch and climbed it hand over hand. Seconds later, he tapped a marker of red tape at the top and reversed course.

"You left the door open," she said when he hit the gravel after letting go from two meters up.

"Sorry, love," he panted with hands on his knees. "Thought I closed it."

She grasped the rope and pulled herself up five times before dropping to the ground. "Oomph." She massaged her upper arms. "Guess I shouldn't try that after lifting."

"Yeah, it's a killer. That was my last set." He brushed off his hands and flexed his fingers.

They stretched for a few minutes while the sun sank behind the far ridge, deepening the twilight and taking the temperature with it. "I'm chilly. Let's go back inside." Eyrún moved toward the house. The exterior lights highlighted its stone facing and stout wooden door.

Darwin followed, and their footfalls were the only sounds beneath the vast western slope of Mt. D'Oro. She paused for him to catch up and then said, "I'm sorry. I didn't mean to suggest your ideas were stupid. I'm mad at Nahla."

"I know, love." He put an arm around her shoulder, and she leaned into him as they reached the porch together. "It's risky, but we have to sort this out."

"Maybe Jasmin can help," she said, opening the door. "I mean, right now, Nahla's got the upper hand, and Jasmin's the only person we know who seems to know how this works."

"Sure. I'll explain what I'm thinking over dinner. After I shower."

"Soap my back?" She ran ahead to the master suite. He kicked the door closed and hurried after her.

An hour and a half later, Darwin popped a slice of Sartenais cheese in his mouth, enjoying its smoky taste. He tipped back the last of the Muscat from Cap Corse, the northern peninsula. Their simple salad and sauteed trout with foraged mushrooms had been the right refreshing combination after their workout and weekend of rich eating.

Sylvie's and Anne's small market and restaurant in Bocagnano had become a hit with the locals and a godsend for Darwin and Eyrún, who were still getting used to thinking ahead about meals. They loved life on the mountain, but the local shops were no longer steps from their front door like in Paris or Reykjavík.

Eyrún sighed and leaned back, propping her feet on an adjacent chair. "I feel better. More relaxed, anyway. Now, tell me what you're thinking." Earlier, while cooking, she had asked him to wait until she could give him her full attention.

"It'll be complicated and not without risk, but it will allow us to nail Nahla once and for all."

"Cheers to that." She tipped back the last of her wine.

"I looked up the piece they want. It's got plenty of gaps and spaces to hide a GPS tracker inside it."

"But is it going to Nahla or someplace else?"

Darwin paused before answering. "That's the complicated part, as I don't know what they want to do with it. The note just asked for it to be sent out for restoration."

"What if this backfires on us?"

"How do you mean?"

"They keep asking us to do more. How do we know they'll live up to their end of the bargain." She chewed a slice of cheese while mentally running through the scenarios. Like most of Darwin's plans, this one morphed in real time. "Push back. Tell them it's too risky getting the piece out of the Vatican."

"But—"

"Think about it. They pulled this stunt to show we have looted goods. So what? I've been reading. A high percentage of the vases in most museums have been looted. I say we do what Astrid suggested: give the donated pieces back to cities they came from, along with sizable contributions. We continue our mission, and, a few years out, no one will remember."

Darwin narrowed his eyes. "But what makes you believe Nahla will stop at this? I think she wants to destroy us. I say we attack."

Eyrún pursed her lips as she considered their nemesis.

"She's not going to quit, love," he said. "She lost millions not getting the Alexandria Library scroll. Hit her business hard. We won that round. But she's now launched a vendetta against the ACA."

Eyrún's eyes widened. "And the pope got back Alexander's treasure scroll. You're right. She's out to get us."

32

Darwin used the short flight to Rome and drive into Vatican City to rehearse his upcoming conversation with Richard, who was similarly unconventional. During their first encounter, Richard had all but encouraged Darwin to break into a crypt after the Church had refused them both permission to explore.

But Darwin knew that his typical method—asking for forgiveness after a questionable operation—would not play well in Vatican City. Richard had now risen to a prominent position as assistant to a cardinal considered a papal contender. Asking to send out a priceless treasure to fulfill a ransom request seemed, at moments, ludicrous even to Darwin.

As Saint Peter's dome loomed larger, he ran through the video call with Gavin last night. "It's an insane proposal," Gavin had said.

"But will you support it?" Darwin had pressed after floating the question a couple of times.

"Provisionally. The tracking device must be rock solid, and be careful to conceal your actions. Don't trust any of the curators."

Darwin's heart thrummed as they reached the security checkpoint. He showed his credentials to the Swiss Guards, and, a minute later, the driver let him off inside the Belvedere Courtyard. He walked to his office in the library, where he busied himself with email, but he could not focus.

Merde. He looked at his watch for the umpteenth time since arriving—two more hours until lunch with Richard. He hated waiting, so he walked about the office, introducing himself to colleagues he had not met. When his admin reminded him it was time for a weekly staff meeting, he excused himself from the woman working with the high-resolution scanner and went to the conference room, glad to have something to do.

The team cataloging the items in the pope's secret vault had gathered in there, and conversation had begun about summer holiday plans. Eventually they moved on to business. One by one, the team members summarized documents that no longer held historical urgency or whose damming information applied only to the long deceased.

While the team members debated the relevance of one document's centuries-old conspiracy between obsolete ruling families, Darwin paged through a printout. Its Carolingian script in old Latin with no spacing tested his skills, but he quickly reached the opinion that the document was fodder for historians. He concurred with the team, who agreed to release it into the main Vatican archives. And so it went. While much of the discussion bordered on tedium, it passed the time until his lunch with Richard.

A t twelve thirty, Darwin met Richard behind St. Peter's. They went around its south side, through a maze of buildings, and exited Vatican City into Rome. When time permitted, they preferred to lunch in a tiny cafe on Via Nicolò III, less than a five-minute walk from the bustling capital of Catholicism.

Richard queried Darwin on the arrest and proceedings at the ACA, and he agreed that the coincidental timing sounded suspect. "How is Eyrún taking it?"

Darwin sighed, and shoulders slumped, "She's angry, and it's piling onto the stress of starting up the ACA."

"I'm sorry to hear it. She doesn't deserve this treatment. But Eyrún's tough."

They walked half a block in silence before Richard continued. "Do you really think it's that Egyptian woman Nahla?"

"So far, we can't think of anyone else."

Richard asked about the lawyer's strategy.

"They plan to tie it up in court while we investigate," said Darwin.

"That'll cost you two a fortune," Richard said as they turned into the restaurant.

They took a table in front. Darwin's stomach growled at the herbed aroma wafting from the kitchen that melded with the fragrant spring air.

"*Bonjourno*, Richard," said the owner, a man with a gray mustache the size of a small broom. "And Darwin, too. Heaven only knows what Vatican conspiracy you're debating today."

"*Bonjourno*, Fabrizio," they said together, and the three of them gossiped about the goings-on in the nation-state down the street. Richard gave Darwin a look that said, "Caution."

A year ago, Fabrizio had grabbed a chair and regaled them with tales of tunnels beneath Rome. He had come across a blog about a Knight's Templar discovery in France. Darwin had shared unseen photos and let him handle one of the Aquila coins the Romans had minted. The old man, his mustache twitching, had turned the coin in his fingers. After a time, he had reluctantly handed it back and said, "You should look under Rome sometime. Lots of Roman tunnels. Maybe you can find a treasure here, no?"

They had been treated like family since that day. Now, each time they dined here, Darwin flashed back on the tunnel beneath a wine shop less than a kilometer away and wondered if Nero's gold was still there. *I really should look.*

An hour later, their lunch plates were cleared, and Richard steered the conversation to business. "Tell me about this idea that you say I won't like. I can only imagine it's something like digging up St. Peter's floor because you found another parchment with an obscure text." His booming laugh reverberated in the small restaurant.

"How did you know about that?" asked Darwin.

Richard sputtered powdered sugar as his eyes grew as wide as saucers.

Darwin grinned. *Gotcha.*

"Good one." Richard wagged a large finger and wiped his mouth. "Your sense of humor's improving."

When Darwin explained what he really wanted to do, Richard sat straighter and said, "You've got to be kidding. No. Wait. I know you are not, so slow down and take me through that again."

Darwin removed three folded sheets of paper from the inside pocket of his jacket and smoothed them out in front of Richard.

"These are the major objects restored in the last hundred years. The list doesn't count the smaller, in-house work. The highlighted pieces have all been sent outside to the same workshop. Some of them have gone out multiple times.

"Now, I've consulted with experts and found it's rare that pieces would undergo a restoration more than once, unless there is a significant improvement in technique. Notice how these three pieces were sent out a second time, *but*"—he tapped on the paper—"only after new curators took over the individual departments. The common denominator in these recent restorations is Giuseppe Tonto." He paused to let the story sink in.

Richard put on reading glasses and scanned the sheets. After a minute, he said, "But Giuseppe's dead. Problem solved."

"But he wasn't the first. We've uncovered a forgery ring whose key insider died. They probably have one or more candidates, working their way up the ladder, but it may take years, so they're looking for another method."

"Like blackmailing you and Eyrún?"

"Precisely."

Richard set down the papers, removed his glasses, and massaged the bridge of his nose. His chest swelled, and he sighed. "I'm troubled by what's going on, Darwin, but I can't see risking an irreplaceable artifact. His Holiness would never approve."

"I get it. It's risky as hell, but you've got a serious problem."

Richard's eyebrows raised in a "what now" fashion.

"My deeper audit of this list found twenty-one forgeries. It's not just curators at the top, Richard. There's corruption throughout the museum ranks. If we don't stop this, there'll be nothing real left in the Vatican Museums. And, if word gets out—"

"Stop." Richard held up a hand. "I get it." He then asked, "How would you do this? I'm not saying I agree, but how would you send the object out. And who can you trust?"

"Trust is the hardest part, as any corrupt insiders will be for watching for traps. We have to send the object out using the normal process. Do you trust the new head of security?"

"Yes. We recruited him from outside."

"Good. I'll meet with him, after you get permission from His Holiness, of course."

Richard harrumphed. "I'm so looking forward to that conversation."

"It's the only way to stop this Vatican looting, and I'll bet it's happening in other museums. Our cultural heritage is being stolen and hidden in billionaire's personal collections. We have to stop this unbridled greed."

After settling the bill, they walked back through St. Peter's Square, as Richard said he wanted to feel the energy of the visitors. When they entered the square, he said, "Whether believers or not, people come to this space for a sense of wonder and hope."

Passing the obelisk, he added, "Each person's experience is unique, but it's based on an unbroken chain of collective experience. They go to a theme park or Las Vegas for entertainment, knowing it's a copy. They come here because it's real."

Darwin stopped and swept an arm, taking in all of Vatican City. "But what if they learned this was fake? All the originals were stolen."

Richard stopped and, turning slowly to Darwin, said, "We cannot let that happen."

33

"It's that one," Eyrún said when she, Darwin, Jasmin, and Zac neared the end of a long pier. They were playing her guessing game as they walked past beautiful vessels on the fifty-meter dock. Eyrún had invited them for dinner and to spend the night on a boat she was considering purchasing.

"That's not just a boat, Eyrún," Zac said as they approached a gleaming carbon-fiber craft whose acute lines resembled a cigarette boat. Its long, sharp bow ran flat to midship and then raked over the upper deck at an angle that shouted—speed. Windows just above the water line ran the length of its black carbon-fiber hull, and a flybridge, sporting state-of-the-art radar, sparkled in the late sun.

"I know," said Eyrún, beaming and kicking off her shoes dockside. She bounced up the steps of the twenty-one-meter Azimut S7 and turned to face the others. "Welcome aboard."

Zac explored like a kid in a new play structure, while Jasmin walked more casually, admiring the galley and the table set for dinner on the main deck. They laughed as Zac flopped and rolled around on the bow cushions outside the bridge windows. He returned to the main galley, and they toured the lower deck, going first to the bow suite with a queen bed.

"Nice," said Zac. "I can see you and Darwin liking it here."

"This room's yours, Zac," said Darwin.

Zac turned and silently mouthed, *What?*

Eyrún led them to the mid-vessel master suite, directly below the galley. Six windows grouped in rectangles on each side of the room gave an expansive view from a king-sized bed that faced a massive flat-screen TV. Behind it was an en suite bath to rival a luxury hotel, complete with a separate bidet.

"It's lovely, Eyrún," said Jasmin. "Thanks for inviting us."

"My pleasure."

"I gotta see the tech," said Zac. He bounded up the spiral steps to the helm and jumped into one of the side-by-side chairs. Eyrún slid into the other, tapped the power on, and explained the data in the three flat-panel displays as Zac ran his hands over the steering wheel and trim control. He wiggled from side to side in the wraparound leather seat.

"I know," said Eyrún. "It feels like my Macan."

"What's it got under the hood?"

"Three Volvo Penta engines with eight hundred horsepower."

"Nice."

"Each," she added. "It'll do thirty-six knots."

"Holy..." Zac's voice faded as he tapped the displays, and he stopped for a moment as Eyrún explained the fuel auto-balancing that kept the vessel trim at high speed.

Darwin rolled his eyes as they geeked out, and then he invited Jasmin forward to explore the bow deck. Minutes later, Eyrún called to them, "Shall we make a toast?" They followed her to the stern and down to a teak swim deck, where Champagne beckoned. "You do the honors, love," she said to Darwin.

As Darwin untwisted the muselet, Zac asked, "it's beautiful, but how do you get to shore? You can't beach this baby?"

"Nope." Eyrún tapped a button on the hull, and a section of the stern lifted. "Voila. The garage." She waved a hand at a jet ski and Zodiac parked side by side as the Champagne cork popped, launching into the harbor. The bubbly spouted onto the wood.

Darwin filled their glasses and toasted. "To Eyrún and many more adventures."

She blushed as they repeated, "To Eyrún."

"What about a name?" asked Jasmin.

"*Hypatia*," Eyrún said without hesitation.

The early-summer sky darkened at quarter to ten as Darwin brought out a cheese plate. Eyrún shivered as a breeze wafted across the harbor; the thin fabric of her dress was not enough against the cooler evening breeze. He reached under a deck cushion storage locker and handed blankets to her and Jasmin.

"Thanks," they said as they pulled the light polar fleeces around their shoulders.

He returned to the galley to put dessert in the oven, and Zac said, "That's bull." The women laughed, but Darwin's head was behind the refrigerator door during the comment that provoked Zac's response.

He smiled at their convivial dinner and slid chocolate lava cakes into the oven. His busy brain churned freely and morphed the word "bull" into "aleph," the ancient symbol for the letter "A" that looked like a bull's head. *Wait.* He paused after closing the over door. *How did I miss that? The forger.* Eyrún had told him that Jasmin had mentioned a forger known as the Albanian Master, who signed works with an aleph. But in the chaos after Eyrún's arrest and his subsequent focus on the extortion request, he had forgotten about it.

Jasmin laughed at another of Zac's jokes as Darwin served a dessert wine. He popped a bit of pungent blue cheese in his mouth while waiting for an opening in the conversation. As the aroma of chocolate lava cake drifted from the galley, he asked Jasmin, "What do you know about the Albanian Master?"

"There's one from left field," said Zac.

Darwin realized their confusion and explained the missing context for his question.

"A little," said Jasmin. "I think most of it's myth. I first encountered him twenty years ago in graduate school when our professor asked us to identify a vase with an aleph on its base. We guessed a workshop in ancient Greece and were astonished to learn it was a forgery."

"How did he get the name?" asked Zac.

"No one knows. I heard it stemmed from the Albanian government's support of antiquities forgery to get foreign currency. When communism collapsed in the early nineties, vases with amazing quality began showing up at auction, each one with an aleph. Then, in ninety-seven, a high-profile piece turned up at the Louvre."

"The Louvre?" asked Eyrún.

Jasmin turned to her. "Many collectors and museums have been fooled. I was taken in once by one of his unsigned works."

"But why sign some pieces and not others?" asked Darwin.

"I think to throw people off. Keep them guessing." Jasmin sipped her wine. "But his work is so perfect you need detailed chemical analysis and carbon dating to detect the forgeries. And, even then, it's difficult because he uses ancient materials."

"How does that work?" asked Zac.

"Melt old metal or use ancient clay for an object's base. Most curators sample from the bottom. The material tests as ancient, and they believe its age. Once it's laundered through auction and museums, no one looks at it again."

Darwin's watch vibrated, and he went to the galley. After serving each of them a cake with vanilla gelato, he attacked his own plate. He spooned the gelato and oozing chocolate pastry into his mouth and savored its hot and cold goodness.

For the next few minutes, the only sound came from water lapping against the starboard hull. Halfway through her cake, Eyrún asked, "Does anyone know where the Albanian Master is now?"

"Not that I know of," said Jasmin. "But every couple of years, a new piece turns up at auction. They're famous on their own and fetch high prices."

"So, it's no longer a problem if people know they're buying fakes," said Zac.

"For collectors, no," said Jasmin, "but his unsigned pieces end up in museums. It devalues ancient works."

"And Nahla's his primary dealer," said Eyrún, her face flushing.

Darwin clenched the napkin on his lap, wringing it like a wet towel.

"Anyone for an after-dinner swim?" asked Zac.

They turned and stared at him like he had spoken in Swahili.

"I'm kidding. You're getting wound up. Let's get back to celebrating the new boat." He pushed away from the table and went into the galley. Seconds later, he began dancing as music erupted from invisible speakers, vibrating the deck from a hidden subwoofer. Jasmin joined him.

Eyrún and Darwin cleared and stowed the table, leaving the rear deck wide open. Between songs, Zac uncorked another bottle of Champagne, and they danced and drank as the lights of Ajaccio shimmered in the dark harbor.

Eventually they moved the party below decks, where Zac capped off the evening by saying, "If this cabin's rockin', don't bother knockin'."

Inside the master cabin, Eyrún washed her face as Darwin gazed out the port-side windows. A minute later, she slid behind him and dipped her hands into his pockets, searching. "Let's properly christen the boat."

34

On the Tuesday after their weekend boat party, Darwin caught up with Max Keller, the new head of Vatican security. Unlike his predecessor, who had risen through the Swiss Guard's ranks, Max had come from a corporation that managed executive and institutional security. After the debacle where the former head had become corrupted by an internal rogue Church faction, the pope had decided on an outside leader.

Darwin had found a refreshing air in the security offices. It seemed less about guarding an ancient order and following mysterious, time-worn protocols and more about providing appropriate levels of access to valuable assets. Employing this new business-like mindset, Darwin approached Max to support his case to send out the Etruscan oinochoe wanted by the blackmailers.

"Darwin," said Max, rising from behind his desk. While a shade taller than Darwin, he had the build of a rugby forward. His thick neck and broad upper body filled out a crisp white shirt beneath a dark blue suit. Deeply bronzed skin spoke of a man who spent much time outdoors. A white Van Dyke beard stressed his square jaw and comple-mented his equally pale hair.

They shook hands and sat at a small table. Darwin laid out the situation and his plan to send out the requested vase as a means to track the perpetrators.

Max stroked his beard for nearly a minute before asking, "And you're sure there's a broad group involved?" His voice was as gravelly as a bucket of rocks.

"Based on the audit data compiled in these spreadsheets, yes."

"Okay. We'll follow your plan, but since the normal restoration request process, as you said, takes at least a month, I'd like one of my trusted people to validate the data and see if there's anything we've overlooked."

"It needs to be discreet," said Darwin, biting his lip.

"Don't worry. I have so many audits going on that no one will notice a few more questions. This is good work."

Their business wrapped up, and Darwin moved to go. Max asked, "I heard you had a rough encounter with Miguel, the former security head."

"That's an understatement." Darwin's calf sometimes still throbbed from the injury that had slowed his escape while Miguel was trying to kill him.

Three weeks later, their lawyer, Astrid, said the court had delayed their hearing again. And Darwin found that even with the pope's consent, the Vatican bureaucracy moved at the pace of an institution whose mission concerned all eternity. Max Keller confirmed rushing the process would raise eyebrows.

One morning over breakfast, Darwin suggested to Eyrún, "Let's get out of here. Take *Hypatia* for a long cruise."

"Where should we go?" she asked, smiling and setting down her mobile.

"Dunno."

She collected a navigation chart from a nearby counter and unfolded it as Darwin moved the breakfast dishes. The map had a dozen Post-it notes fixed along the Italian Peninsula. "I've been thinking of some places," she said, smoothing the chart across the breakfast nook.

———————

They began their adventure three days later with a plan to circumnavigate Corsica, both for Eyrún to see the diverse seaside cities of her new home and to deepen her feel for *Hypatia*. In the weeks since purchasing the yacht, she had thrown herself into online training for its radar and other instruments. She had also tutored under Marc Denis, going on day trips out of Ajaccio Harbor. Darwin, who had boated around Corsica since childhood, further explained the currents and coastal waters between Corsica and Sardinia.

Six days into the journey, after looping clockwise from Ajaccio, they departed Bastia on the northeast coast and motored across the Tyrrhenian Sea toward Naples, Italy. Eyrún piloted at a modest twenty knots, this being her first venture into the wide-open ocean and shipping lanes. She knew from years of rally driving in Iceland that intimately knowing your machine made the difference between winning and not, or worse, making a fatal mistake.

The journey took twelve hours, and they pulled in, exhausted, just before eight. They moored at a marina's guest berth and had dinner in a dockside restaurant before collapsing in the master suite. After sleeping in the next morning, they visited the ruins at Herculaneum. Darwin was eager to see the newest unearthed mosaics, and Eyrún wanted to study the physics of the long-ago pyroclastic surge that had buried the city. Darwin tried to find the location where his forebear Pasquale had unearthed a box of Roman scrolls, but too much had changed in the nearly three centuries following his discovery.

After a day of wandering and eating in Naples, they boarded *Hypatia* and picked their way along Italy's southern coast, anchoring in quieter harbors. Some nights, they dined in waterside restaurants, but mostly they cooked for themselves using ingredients purchased in local markets. Four days later, they reached the Amalfi Coast, where, with the tourist season in full swing, the harbors teemed with holiday-goers. To get away from the hordes, they motored farther offshore to the island of Capri.

Ten days into their journey, they had thoroughly relaxed. Eyrún, now adept at navigating *Hypatia*, probed the islands' towering cliffs and, where they could not get close with the yacht, explored the sea caves with the Zodiac. On their last night before returning to Ajaccio, they anchored in a wide cove enclosed by vertical walls. The rock dove deep into the impossibly clear azure water, and the gentle swells slapping against the granite echoed in a high arch. Dinner had been a simple branzino over greens, served with a Gewürztraminer that Darwin could only describe as hedonistic. Its lychee and grapefruit notes dazzled their palates.

As they finished the meal, a full moon crested the cliff, its granite concentrating the light in the cove. The luminous sea bounced moonbeams into the arch's dark spaces, which appeared to Eyrún like a nighttime cathedral vault. They stood on the teak swim deck watching the shadows play. Darwin brought his gaze down to her dark hair, radiant in the silver light, and slipped his hands around her waist. She turned and kissed him. After a moment, she pulled back and sighed, and her eyes motioned toward the bow. Darwin took her hand, and they eased along the gunwale to the wide cushions, where they made love bathed in the lunar spotlight.

Early the next morning, the sea was dead calm, with not even a breeze rippling its surface. Eyrún piloted them to open water and pushed down the throttle. *Hypatia* flew near top speed over the Mediterranean, closing the 230-nautical-mile gap in just over six hours. Darwin watched the radar for vessel traffic. She slowed as they entered the channel separating Sardinia and Corsica and kept their speed low until they aligned with the Port Vecchio to Marseilles ferry route, where she went full throttle again and arced northward to Ajaccio.

35

A week later, back at his desk in Vatican City, Darwin surfed around a map of the Mediterranean, daydreaming about the trip with Eyrún. She had suggested they take an even longer journey once they got past their legal entanglement and completed the ACA construction. He was swiping to Malta and then over to Crete when his watch vibrated.

Finally! His heart thrummed as he nearly jumped out of his chair. The restoration approval had been signed a day after he had returned from holiday, and the briber had sent instructions for a warehouse drop-off in Rome.

Fortunately, the process of pulling the object off exhibit and shipping it out moved swifter than the signatories for its release. As the museum closed, he met Max and followed two curators to the top floor of the Etruscan gallery, where they opened the glass and, using protective gloves, lifted the jug onto a cart. Darwin noticed a small slip of paper fall off the base, and he picked it up and read it. *Merde.*

After looking about to see if anyone had noticed, he slipped it in his pocket as the curators wheeled the cart to the lift. He fingered the note in his pocket, itching to read it again as they walked to the lab. To occupy himself while the curators crated the vase, he scrolled through posts by archaeologists he followed. Then, when the four of them had returned to the ground floor and the curators had left for home, Max and Darwin lingered until a security specialist met them.

Back in the basement, the specialist opened one side of the crate and, using magnifying spectacles, inserted the tracking device. Once she had verified the signal and closed the crate, they returned to the ground floor, where Darwin waited until the specialist had left. Then he turned to Max. "I think you should read this," he said, handing him the paper.

T he next day, at ten a.m., a courier van arrived to transport the crate. Instructions had been clear: if the van was followed, the deal would be terminated. Darwin watched the dot move on Max's monitor. Two vehicles with Swiss Guards moved parallel to the van in case intervention became necessary.

Thirty-five minutes later, the van stopped on a street with older commercial warehouses. Max alerted the team to the location and instructed them to wait on streets a few blocks on either side.

"What do we do now?" asked Darwin after a half-hour, staring at the screen.

"It depends on how long it stays there," replied Max. "Espresso?"

"*Sí*, but we can't leave."

Darwin kept vigil in front of the monitor as Max got their coffees. Not two minutes after the security chief left, the dot moved. He swore, ran to the office door, and yelled, "It's moving."

Max hurried back. Over the next hour, they watched it travel north along the Via Flaminia Nuova, beside the River Tiber's serpentine course. Then it turned clockwise onto the A90, which rings the capital city, and a kilometer later, it made a sharp left onto E35 and up the Italian peninsula. When it passed Orvieto, Darwin asked, "Where do you suppose they're going?"

"Your guess is as good as mine," said Max.

Just past noon, they went on alert as the dot stopped. A radio chat with the pursuit cars determined it was a petrol stop and one of them rolled past to snap photos of the vehicles at the station. Max studied the pictures of two sedans and one compact SUV. The first sedan contained a group of three. The other sedan and SUV each had a single driver.

"Where's the van?" he roared.

O ver a tense next hour, Max shouted orders to find the delivery van. As the security staff made calls to the Carabinieri, he commanded one of the chase drivers following the sedans and SUV to run ahead to determine which vehicle had the GPS signal.

Minutes later, the first driver, Nico, radioed back. "I only passed the SUV." The second driver, Alain, said he had followed each sedan briefly as they exited the highway, but returned to the chase when they had determined the cars were not the GPS signal source.

Max put down the radio and yelled at his people outside the office. "Anything yet on that van?"

A young female staffer appeared at the door. "There's no activity at the warehouse. The Carabinieri went to the delivery company's depot and found the driver who said he picked up a crate at the Vatican and dropped it at the warehouse. Put it on the floor and left. That's it. Saw no one."

"Understood. Set up a detail to monitor the warehouse. Alert me on any activity. Acknowledge," said Max.

"Acknowledged." She nodded and left.

"The SUV must have picked up the crate after the courier left it," said Darwin.

"Most likely. Unless they opened it, pulled out the GPS and stuck it in the SUV as a decoy."

They debated that probability a few minutes before deciding a simple dropoff and pickup was the most plausible scenario. Then, Max radioed Nico and Alain again. "Okay, let's assume the tracker's in the SUV, but stay sharp."

A half-hour later, when nothing further happened, Max sent Darwin to grab a quick lunch at the employees' cafe where he inhaled a plate of pasta with wild boar ragu. He returned in time to watch the dot loop around Florence and veer northwest toward Bologna. The combined boredom and post-lunch drowsiness pulled on him, and, when Max left to take a scheduled meeting, he struggled to stay alert. When his head bounced off his chest, whiplashing his neck, he got up and stretched while glancing back at the dot.

Finally, close to five o'clock, the dot merged onto the A50 around the western edge of Milan and then onto a westbound highway. It exited in less than a kilometer, and Max zoomed in as it stopped at a roadside motel. He alerted the team to exit in the same location. "Park discreetly. Let's see what he does."

When no movement had occurred by ten p.m., they determined the driver had checked into the hotel. Max and Darwin prepared for an all-nighter by having a cot set up in a nearby office. Dinner had been delivered earlier, but they skipped the wine.

"You get some rest. I'm a night owl and never sleep before two," said Max.

The Swiss Guards in Milan similarly organized themselves for an all-night watch, carefully parking out of view from the hotel's windows. Darwin lay down on the cot shortly before eleven, but he tossed and turned. Sleeping in public places like ferries and planes made him uncomfortable; the myriad noises and lights kept him from settling into a deep sleep. He thought of Eyrún, but he had messaged her "goodnight" earlier, and they had agreed to restrict communication to their normal chatter. They could not be a hundred percent sure no one had access to their conversations.

His next memory was a hand rocking his shoulder. "Darwin. Darwin. Time to get up."

It took him several seconds to realize his location. "Right. Okay," he said, pushing himself to a sitting position. "Anything happen?"

"Quiet as the dead," said Max, who went back to the monitor while Darwin used the toilet and brewed coffee.

In less than five minutes, Darwin was sitting in the dim office, watching the red dot next to a building labeled "Motel 2000."

"Wake me if anything happens," said Max. "Alain's on watch. Nico's on sleep break. Don't worry about dozing. I've set an alarm if the GPS moves."

"Got it. Thanks."

Darwin finished the coffee and got a second cup at 3:13. While not feeling refreshed, he was reasonably alert and used the time to read a backlog of papers. He had to abandon reading a data-intensive paper by a forensic archaeologist and clicked to another, but soon he was struggling with that one, too. His tired eyes forced him to repeat reading most paragraphs. The monitor beeped, and he jumped as the dot moved north on A50.

"Max!" Darwin shouted and tapped the radios to alert the drivers.

"Where's it going?" asked Max, stepping into his shoes.

"A50." Darwin pointed as the radio crackled.

"The SUV's still here," said Nico.

"Get on the road behind that signal," said Max.

"Already on the A50, matching its speed," Alain said in the second car.

"Must be a vehicle switch," said Darwin.

"How come we didn't see it?" Max pounded the desk.

Darwin listened to the team's fast chatter, and then all went silent while Nico investigated the SUV. The dot now moved east onto the E64, crossing the northern edge of Milan. Max ran down the hall for a quick bio break and was hurrying back in just as Nico reported, "The SUV's empty."

36

An hour later, both cars trailed the dot. Earlier, Nico reported opening the unlocked SUV, finding the keys in the driver's side cup holder, and, determining it was abandoned, racing to catch up with Alain. Now Max considered their next moves. "How's your fuel?" he asked.

"Three hundred kilometers range," said Nico. Alain reported similarly.

The morning sun in the security office angled through a high window, which, combined with noises from the incoming staff, helped Darwin shake off lost sleep. A junior officer brought them breakfast while they debated the vehicle's destination. While Darwin ate, he retraced the route from yesterday.

The courier picked up the crate from the museum loading dock. Took it to the warehouse. Then another vehicle took the crate from the warehouse to Milan. Spent the night at the hotel and moved the crate to a new vehicle. It's now heading east. To where?

He grabbed his iPad from Max's desk and zoomed in on a map of Italy. Unless they turned north into the Alps, the vehicle would reach Venice in less than two hours and enter Slovenia in another. *Albania! They're heading towards the Albanian Master.*

He zoomed out and immediately knew that made no sense. It was over a sixteen-hour drive south through the countries opposite Italy. *No, for Albania, they would have driven south from Rome and taken the ferry across the Adriatic.* His eyes roamed the map, trying to divine the dot's destination. Then an idea surfaced. *What if they're trying to throw us off?*

As Max and his men chattered in the background, Darwin grabbed his iPad and compared the warehouse address given by the ransomer to the address on the spreadsheet. *It's different.* He went to the restorer's website and clicked a link for company history. *Merde!*

He called the number. "*Bonjourno*, DaVinci Restorations," said a young female voice.

Darwin asked her about the warehouse and was transferred to the owner. He repeated the question and learned the warehouse was their original headquarters but they had moved to their current headquarters half a century ago. "That old building's been in our family since the seventeen hundreds. It's disused now. Why?"

Darwin made up a story to explain his query and thanked the owner before disconnecting. He returned his attention to Max, who had just finished talking with the drivers about the destination. "What was that about?" asked Max.

"What if the thieves found the tracking device? Maybe…planted it on another car," said Darwin, and he filled Max in on his theory.

"It's plausible," said Max. "Nico's making a fast pass of the vehicle now. Should be—"

Nico's voice burst over the radio: "It's a family sedan."

"What?" asked Max. "Confirm." A moment later, his mobile beeped with a photo of a small blue sedan with four passengers, two of them children. As he and Darwin studied the photo, Nico said, "There's no way the crate would fit in that car with four people. Even the boot's too small."

"Dammit!" Max roared, jumping to his feet. "Nico, get back to Milan. Alain, follow the sedan. Talk to the driver when it stops." He sat down, elbows on the desk, and massaged his temples.

37

D arwin waited with Max and Richard at the papal office. Word had spread around the museum that a priceless vase had been stolen with his help, so he had avoided the office until today's late meeting.

Yesterday morning, Alain had followed the family car until it stopped, and he had found the GPS device stuck under its bumper. He then returned to the abandoned SUV in the Milan hotel parking lot, and he and Nico reviewed the hotel's security cameras. In the middle of the night, an unmarked cargo van had parked next to the SUV, and two people shifted the crate into the van. Minutes later, one emerged, bent down behind the family's blue sedan, and affixed the GPS. The entire process had taken five minutes, and Nico had admitted to not watching a hundred percent of the night.

Now, sitting in the waiting area, Darwin tugged at his jacket's sleeve a fifth time, adjusting the length of exposed shirt cuff. One of his feet was swept backward toward the door, his ankle wiggling. *Stop it.* He brought his feet together in front of the chair.

I gambled and lost. It happens. He reviewed his internal pep talk. *Work the plan.* In two hours, he would meet the owner of DaVinci Restorations at the warehouse, and he hoped a backtrack to the original transfer point would elicit some clue. He sat straight and calmed himself. *We didn't lose the original.* At least Max had already devised a story of how they would produce the object safely stored in the basement.

"His Holiness will see you now," said the pope's assistant. Darwin's stomach hardened as he realized his fretting was not over the loss of the object but the pope's trust.

Just before entering the inner office, a security officer rushed in and whispered something to Max.

Inside, the pope said, "I only have a few minutes. Let's get to it, shall we?" Once everyone was seated, the pontiff turned to Darwin. "The press is having a field day at my expense, Darwin. Tell me how you allowed a priceless Vatican treasure to be stolen."

"We didn't, Your Holiness," said Darwin. "It was a forgery."

The pope sat back, his mouth slack.

Darwin continued. "When we moved the piece two days ago, a note that fell from its base alerted us to a duplicate in the basement storage. After the curators left, Max and I found the forged duplicate and swapped it with the original."

"Why was I not told?"

Max answered this time. "My apologies. It was my doing. We wanted the situation to appear authentic, as we don't know who's involved." He explained the jug had been duplicated when it went out for restoration in 1963. Its owner had since died, and his estate had left it to the Vatican, where the curators had placed it in storage.

Richard asked, "Why leave a note under the original?"

"Who knows?" said Max. "And it doesn't matter, since it worked to our advantage."

The pope accepted this logic. Then he asked, "But we still lost the forged piece. We're no closer to the thieves. What now?"

"My office just reported the van went to the Basel freeport, where it's still parked."

"Freeport?" asked Richard.

"A customs warehouse with a duty-free designation for goods in transit," said Darwin.

"So…" Richard prodded.

"A lot of art and antiquities are warehoused to avoid taxes and police. This freeport's a known legal hiding place for illegal goods."

Max's mobile chimed. He looked at it and read the message aloud. "The crate went to a warehouse used by Alexandria Antiquities."

"Nahla," Darwin muttered under his breath.

38

Darwin arrived at the DaVinci Restorations warehouse the morning after the papal meeting, and he greeted the owner. They shook hands before the bulky man worked through a series of keys to unlock a small side door. "I've not been here in three decades," he said. "We have no use for it, but the family trust forbids selling it."

Their footfalls echoed on the concrete flooring. The space was dimly lit, as the only light came from top windows. Darwin sneezed from the kicked-up dust and pinched his nose to stop a second. He paused to assess the empty warehouse, running a light over the dusty floor and shining it back toward the door they had entered through. Crouching, he could better see the dust layer covering the floor, which had been disturbed near the large freight doors facing the street. There were tire tracks from at least two vehicles, but his and the owner's footprints were the only ones that led deep into the warehouse.

He stood and, running the light along the walls, found only two places of interest: an office in the left-rear corner and a workbench with a handful of broken wooden crates beside it. As he moved toward the workbench, he could see packing material, ranging from straw to more modern bubble wrap, strewn about the crates. He clicked a task light on the bench. Nothing.

"Electricity's been off for years. I checked," said the owner.

"Any idea who could have used this space?" asked Darwin.

"None. Like I said. I was last here when I was eleven. My grandfather brought me for some reason. I don't remember, but it was empty then."

"Well, we're the first people back here in a long while," Darwin said while examining the crates.

"I'm going to look in the office," said the owner, and he walked over to a small house-like building inside the larger structure.

Darwin examined the workbenches. He recognized brushes and other tools as those used in conservation, arranged in an orderly fashion. He scanned the dust-covered wooden surface and found two spots where tools had been moved. He swiped a fingertip about a thumb's length and then moved twenty steps opposite the crates and used a different finger to swipe the floor. When he compared them, the floor fingertip was completely black, while the bench finger was just a dirty gray.

Someone's been here within the last year or two. He wiped his fingers on his jeans. They would need a more precise survey to narrow down the time, but his gut told him this place saw sporadic use.

He moved to the crates and found one containing a carved bust. He snapped its photo in situ before moving it onto the work surface. It was classical Roman: a man, hair carved in ringlets and topped with an olive-branch crown. But the artist had carved it from basalt. *Odd.* Heads like this had always been done in more durable materials, like marble or bronze. He leaned closer. The gray rock had been finished smooth like any other sculpture, but its color struck him as strange. He had never seen such a thing.

He searched the crate but found no markings on its exterior. Then he rummaged through the packing material and found a crumpled paper. Smoothing it, he struggled to interpret its Arabic script, but he guessed it was a torn waybill, only a third remaining. He set the note next to the bust and, putting his hands on hips, surveyed the area.

Focusing on the tire tracks some twenty meters away, he mentally worked through the scene. *The delivery truck with the Vatican piece arrived three days ago.* He ran the light over the unbroken dust on the floor again. He pivoted to the bench. *But they didn't come back here...* He turned back toward the front doors and ran through the timing. *The GPS dot was here less than thirty minutes. They must have received the crate, sent the delivery driver away, and then loaded it into the SUV we followed to Milan. So, these crates can't be connected to the delivery, which means someone else used this workbench.* He puzzled over any connection, like if the driver of the SUV used this warehouse but infrequently.

The office door closed, and Darwin pocketed the waybill fragment as the owner walked over.

"You found something," he said, looking at the bust. "Weird sculpture. I've never seen anything like it."

"Me, either. Anything in the office?"

"Nothing besides old furniture."

"Can I have this bust?" asked Darwin. "We may be able to learn something from it."

"*Si.* It looks like a practice piece. Worthless unless done by Cellini." The owner laughed.

Darwin wrapped the bust in some of the packing material, and, as the owner locked up, he mused, *If nothing else, Eyrún'll get a kick out of this thing.*

On the quick hop to Ajaccio, Darwin placed the bust on a table and lay the waybill next to it. His NetJets membership allowed him to avoid a commercial flight transfer in Nice, and his Vatican credentials expedited the customs processes. The one other passenger looked up, but then she returned to her laptop.

Using the translation app on his mobile, he determined the object had shipped from Alexandria, and he held the paper to the window to read handwritten letters in the bottom corner: "YRNM." *Someone's initials?* He set the paper down and focused on the bust, rotating it, but even in better light, nothing stood out. *Strangest thing,* he thought as he carefully lay it down to look at its base.

He inhaled sharply. The woman looked up. Darwin smiled and wiggled his fingers like he had whacked one on the sculpture, and she went back to work. An aleph had been carved on its base. After comparing it to the photo from the kylix in Los Angeles, he determined the two symbols' proportions matched.

Were these carved by the same person? The aleph in the basalt had been chiseled, and the one on the kylix had been carved in soft clay. *It's plausible the Albanian Master carved it, but...*

He snapped a photo and messaged it to Eyrún, asking if Jasmin could look at it. Then, as the small jet began its descent into Ajaccio, he re-wrapped the bust and gazed out the window, contemplating the frequency with which alephs had turned up.

39

Eyrún paused halfway through reading an email from the lawyers, sat back, and massaged her temples. She considered legal documents an exercise in obfuscation. An urgent change order from the builder lay beside her laptop, and, earlier in the day, an uptight provincial official had insisted the ACA hire more local archaeologists, despite there being no qualified candidates. *Why does everything have to be so hard?*

Then she pictured the bust Darwin had brought back from Rome last night. Over dinner, he had ranted about possible connections to the vases seized by the antiquities authority. She had tuned most of it out as wild speculation. *At least Jasmin is helping.*

Her thoughts drifted to their trip to Capri. She had woken up at first light on their last morning, energized from a deeper sleep than she had had in months. The craft was utterly still. She slipped out of bed, dressed, and climbed the steps, grabbing a blanket on her way to the flybridge, where she drank in the view. The glassy surface reflected the dawn sky, and the sun's rays were just hitting a fishing boat as an orange-tinged cyclone of gulls whirled above it.

Sitting now at her desk, she scrunched her toes, recalling the cool feel of the teak decking and the freedom to motor anywhere in the world. She forced herself back to the email, but *Hypatia's* shiny carbon fiber hull kept interrupting her concentration. After rereading one paragraph a third time, she looked across her desk at a book on nautical radar. *There's so much to learn.* Her heart fluttered. *I can't think here.* She snatched up the book and pushed back from the desk.

"I need to run an errand, Hervé. I'll be back after lunch."

"*D'accord,*" he said, looking up briefly.

Eyrún parked in the owners' section at the harbor and tapped her key fob on the dock's security gate. Heatwaves radiated off the creaking, weathered boards as she walked, and her heart beat faster as the flybridge and its black radar array came into view.

While she happily shared everything with Darwin, this was her own special space. She thought of the attic in her parents' Reykjavík home, where she would get away from the stress of having to be the adult after her father died. But that sad memory faded as she boarded the craft and climbed to the flybridge in the bright sun. She gripped the steering wheel and looked across the bow. *This is mine.*

A few minutes later, she wandered through the vessel, making sure the cleaning crew had done a proper job. Then she remembered Marc had suggested an engine inspection after the yacht's first long voyage. She descended the short ladder down to the engines and ran a hand over each Volvo's manifold. The compartment smelled of fresh paint, adhesives used in construction, and lubricants. The pristine engines had less than a hundred hours on them, and she knew most of that was from her recent trip.

Eventually she got hungry and made a note to call the marine maintenance company. Then she went to the galley to prepare a plate of cheeses, charcuterie, and fruits and carried it to the outside deck table. A few bites in, her gaze drifted to the marina office, about fifty meters away, where a woman was getting into a Zodiac. *What?*

She grabbed binoculars from a drawer and confirmed her suspicion. *It's Jasmin. Where's she going?* The bright orange craft crossed to a megayacht anchored in the deeper water. *That's new.* The three-deck, all-white craft had arrived sometime since yesterday.

She zoomed to the limits of her iPhone camera and snapped photos. Looking through the binoculars again, she watched a man welcome Jasmin onboard. They kissed each other on both cheeks before going inside. *Who's that? They didn't greet like lovers. A client, maybe?* She knew Jasmin catered to the wealthy.

Eyrún went back to eating, lifting the binoculars every couple of minutes, but she saw no activity. A half-hour later, Jasmin was still aboard the megayacht, and Eyrún had to return to the ACA. Driving along the harbor road, she mentally added this newest conundrum to her issues list.

40

Late that afternoon, after attacking the problems: answering the lawyers, talking the contractor down from ridiculous fee changes, and dropping the official's complaint in the desk side bin, Eyrún was about to start a new actions list when her mobile rang.

"*Bonjour, Marc.*" She had messaged him earlier, asking if he knew anything about the megayacht.

They spoke for a few minutes about her trip. She told him about the cliffs on Capri and asked about nighttime radar navigation before turning the conversation to the megayacht.

"It's a magnificent vessel," said Marc. "Norwegian builder. In the market for a bigger one already?"

"*Hypatia* is big enough for me. Any luck finding out its owner?"

"I looked up its IMO number. That's the International Maritime Organization; your yacht also has one. It's flagged in Monaco and registered to a... Let me look... Here it is. Eshmun Holdings SARL. Does that help?"

"Not really. I was hoping for a person's name."

"Sorry. It's not much to go on. I can ask around."

"No, that's okay. I appreciate your help."

Marc described how she could look up vessels in the IMO database, and they spoke a little longer before disengaging.

After the call, Eyrún stared over the harbor from her office window, pondering what she had seen at lunch. Multiple possibilities ran through her head—none of them fit Jasmin's reasons for being in Ajaccio. Eyrún had seen her walk by Hervé's desk not long ago, and, glancing down at her list, she decided a conversation with Jasmin topped the priorities.

"How's it going?" Eyrún asked after knocking lightly on the lab's doorjamb.

Jasmin was peering into a microscope, and she sat up. "Slow. There's not much to learn from it besides the aleph on its bottom," she said, referring to the bust Darwin had brought back from the warehouse. "It's elegantly sculpted, but I've never seen a work like it."

"Did the Albanian Master carve it?"

"I can't tell. Anyone could have copied the mark. If it were marble, I could at least learn where it was quarried. I know nothing about lava."

"Maybe I can help. Some lavas have unique geology." Eyrún took a seat on a stool at the lab bench.

After Jasmin described the bust's sculpting technique and explained how she knew it was Roman, not Greek, Eyrún steered the conversation toward the megayacht. "I appreciate you volunteering to help the interns. They seem to enjoy your real-world experience."

"You're welcome. I enjoy working with them. So much energy and ambition. Almost makes me want to pick up a trowel again."

"My geology work had me spend a decade covered in dirt. Can't say I miss it," said Eyrún, pausing a moment, then continued. "I went out to my boat for lunch today. Needed to get away from the stresses here."

"I know the feeling."

"There's a yacht in the harbor that looks like a small cruise ship. I thought *Hypatia* was big." Eyrún studied Jasmin's eyes for a reaction.

Seeing none, she added, "While eating my lunch, I saw a Zodiac from the megayacht pick someone up from the marina. I got curious and grabbed my binoculars. It looked like you."

Jasmin's head dropped, and when it came up a moment later, her eyes were flooded. "It's my ex-husband's yacht. He forced me to come in person or he wouldn't sign the divorce papers." Tears spilled down her cheeks, and her voice shook. "I just want it to be over with. I hate him. I—" She broke down, sobbing. "I didn't want to tell anyone. I just thought it would be done with and he would go away."

"What a bastard. I'm sorry," said Eyrún. "Is there anything I can do to help?"

"You've done enough by letting me work here. It keeps my mind off him, and Zac makes me feel safe. But please don't tell him. He's a wonderful man, but his military background… I don't want him to do anything."

"Sure. No problem," said Eyrún, but she was distracted by the incongruity of Jasmin's emotional reaction just now and the greeting she had witnessed earlier. *It didn't look like someone she hated.*

They talked until Jasmin's mood settled. Then she thanked Eyrún, saying, "Meeting you and Darwin helps me see what a relationship should really be like."

Eyrún carried the bust back to her office while pondering Jasmin's last comment. Despite all the mounting frustrations in her professional life, her marriage was her foundation. She set the sculpture on her desk and looked at the photo on her mobile of Jasmin boarding the megayacht as she considered her story about the man. *It doesn't line up, but neither does it make her guilty of anything... But she shows up with just the right experience exactly when we needed it. We need to know more about her.*

A reminder from her laptop alerted her to a meeting in five minutes, and she set down her mobile to prepare for the call.

41

Eyrún was working on her list of actions when Darwin came in an hour later. "Ready anytime you are, love," he said, noticing the bust had been returned to her desk.

"In a minute," she said, not looking up.

Eyrún's minute sometimes took five, so he unslung his shoulder bag, dropped it onto a two-seater sofa, and sat on the other cushion. He watched her as she peered at her laptop with a furrowed brow, and as she looped a wayward lock of hair behind an ear, he smiled, happy just being with her.

The bust drew his focus again. Bands of light and shadow from the afternoon sunlight angling through the blinds sliced its gray surface. Its proportions were as fine as any he had seen, but his bewilderment returned. *Why waste time carving basalt?*

Darwin grabbed the sculpture and sat back down, turning it slowly as he contemplated its origin. He knew Eastern cultures carved the Buddha and other deities from lava. Turning it upside down, he traced the aleph with a finger. Jasmin had said that it closely matched the Albanian Master's mark, but she couldn't be certain.

In addition, she had found no organic residue embedded in the bust to use for carbon dating, and the rock's age could not be narrowed to any period within the human Holocene Epoch. Darwin's thoughts settled on the more relevant issue: *Is it related to the Vatican theft? If so, how?* His gut hummed affirmatively with the same sense that had earned him his Great Finder nickname. *The answer's here. I feel it. Someone left this in the warehouse for a reason.*

But as an answer seemed to come into focus, it blurred again, moving just out of reach. He let the sensation go, knowing it would come back. *It always does*, he assured himself. Flipping the bust upright, he stared at the face. Its exact proportions and graceful lines were so perfect it seemed cast from a living man—mid-thirties, confident, and with a full head of hair. The delicately carved eyes, while blank, as was the style, looked past the observer, evoking command. *Probably one of the caesars.*

He was reaching for his mobile to Google it when Eyrún said, "I'm ready."

He put the bust back on her desk, and they walked out to her car.

Once she had turned onto the T20 going up the mountain, she said, "Something strange happened today."

"Oh," said Darwin, looking at his mobile while swiping through photos of Roman busts.

"I had lunch on *Hypatia*." She paused while negotiating a busy traffic circle and then continued. "There was a megayacht in the harbor. Probably sixty meters, three decks above water. I saw Jasmin go out to it."

Darwin's hand with the mobile fell on his lap. "What?"

"My thought exactly. Look at the photo on my mobile."

He grabbed it from the cup holder, tapped to the photos, and manipulated one before saying, "It's pixelated. Hard to tell it's Jasmin."

"It's her. I confronted her in the lab later."

"Did she deny it?"

"No. Said it's her ex-husband's yacht and he had arrived to force her to sign the divorce papers in person."

"Sounds like a piece of work."

"Yeah. She got emotional and said that him showing up here was another of his manipulations. She seemed genuinely shaken up, so I don't think she was lying."

The road's curves hugged tightly to the lower slope of Mt. D'Oro, and Darwin swayed in the wraparound racing seat as Eyrún downshifted into a bend and powered out of it.

"Why would you think she would lie?"

"I don't know, but it's been bothering me." She described her view of Jasmin greeting the man on the megayacht. Darwin agreed with the incongruity, and Eyrún added, "I mean, what do we know about her? She's helping us and is great for Zac, but I can't help but wonder about the timing."

Darwin contemplated the events of the last three months. Jasmin had shown up in Zac's life shortly before the ACA raid, but Darwin could not link her appearance and their misfortunes to anything other than coincidence. *She certainly can't be connected to what's going on in the Vatican. But Eyrún's better at reading people.*

As they neared Bocagnano, Eyrún said, "I don't feel like cooking. Let's have dinner at I Mazzeri."

"Sure. I was thinking the same," he said.

"Maybe Zac knows more about her." She steered the Macan off the road and parked. "Think you could ask?"

"Yeah, I'll figure out a way to bring it up," he said, reading the evening's special written on a chalkboard in front of the restaurant. "That looks promising."

The next afternoon, as Darwin prepared for a workout at the gym, his phone beeped with a message from Eyrún that Marc had called to let her know the megayacht had departed shortly after four. The message ended with a line that stopped Darwin in his tracks:

He said a dark-haired woman disembarked just before it left

Why would she go out there again? He tapped to call Marc, but, at that moment, Zac walked into the gym to begin their workout.

"Hey, bro," Zac said as they bumped fists. After a series of warm-up exercises, they racked the chest press bar. Darwin went first, and he increased his weight by two kilos for a new personal best, but he was still forty kilos behind his larger friend. He wavered during his first set, struggling to get six reps.

"C'mon. You got this. Focus, man," Zac said from his spotter's position behind the bar.

When it was Zac's turn, he blew through his reps without help.

"Someone's got energy. Thought all that wild sex might take it out of you," said Darwin.

"If you only knew bro." Zac's grin spread ear to ear.

Darwin got through his second without help. "Better. I know all this legal shit's got you twisted up, but you gotta get Zen like while lifting. Focus."

Zac's second set went like his first, and, when he finished, Darwin slipped in a question. "Has Jasmin told you any more about herself?" Zac had previously mentioned Jasmin's current troubles, but he had remained guarded about her past.

"No. I'm giving her space. She's got a lot going on. I can't believe her asshole ex shows up here and forces her to meet."

"What?" asked Darwin, trying to sound surprised. As he got under the bar, Zac described Jasmin telling him about visiting the megayacht. Darwin wavered again on the set, but he got it done.

"The bastard didn't even sign the papers. Just wanted another power trip. I tried to go out there, but she begged me not to," said Zac, punching through the reps of his third set like it was his warm-up.

"They must have a lot more money than she let on. That boat's huge."

"I guess. Galleries must be a better business than we thought."

Darwin started his last set, and his gut twisted as he probed deeper. "Eyrún and I were talking about Jasmin's arrival." He paused. Zac's eyes narrowed as he looked askance. "Dunno. It's just all this trouble with the ACA seemed to coincide with Jasmin showing up."

"WTF, bro. Are you saying she's behind this?"

"No. But I called a professor I know at Al-Kafaàt University in Lebanon, and he said Jasmin Kahn had been there but didn't get a Ph.D."

"You ran a background check on her?"

"No. No. Just a call. He said she left after an arrest for antiquities looting."

Zac stared at him, mouth agape.

"I just got curious."

"Got curious? Jesus, Darwin! It's Eyrún, isn't it? I know she's cautious with people, but this is fucked up."

"It's not Eyrún," said Darwin, trying to keep her out of it.

"Bullshit! She's not saying, but I've seen her look at Jasmin. She's still pissed I left Stevie."

"C'mon, Zac. You know Eyrún's not like that."

Zac paused while moving weight onto the bar for his last set. Then he sighed. "I moved to France for her. I love her, but she kept taking off for weeks at a time. I never knew when she would be back."

"Eyrún complains about it, too. She knows how Stevie is."

Zac moved under the bar and thrust up nine reps before slamming the iron back in the rack. He sat up. "Jasmin's great. She cares for me. I don't know where it's going, but she needs healing, and so do I."

Darwin hated conflict. A maelstrom churned his insides, and his vision tunneled as he grasped for ways to defuse the conversation. "I'm not implying—"

"Yes, you are implying, Darwin. I hear you loud and clear. You and Eyrún think Jasmin's behind this. Well, fuck you. Both of you."

Zac picked up his gym bag and walked out, leaving Darwin standing by the bar and the other patrons staring.

42

Zac ran hard along the wharf, sweating out the anger from Darwin's accusations. He turned onto a trail in the eastern harbor and climbed through the maquis. Its dry, woody appearance reminded him of his native Oakland, California. The shrubs, warm in the setting sun, oozed their earthy fragrances, which mixed with a bitter undertone from the dry Mediterranean soil.

He flinched, flashing on a memory of a violent mission in similar Afghan terrain. Steadying his pace, he mentally grasped the vision and put it back on a virtual shelf. The technique Jasmin had taught him seemed to work. He had confessed to having unwanted visions after she had asked him about his occasional nightmares. While he had no problems with most of his service as a US Army Ranger, some encounters, especially with innocent civilians, had left gut-wrenching images.

"It's impossible to forget, and suppressing them will only drive the pain to resurface someplace else. Think of it like a can that falls off a shelf. You pick it up, acknowledge it, and put it back on the shelf where it belongs."

"But they keep falling," he said.

"Then keep putting them back. It's how I've learned to cope with my ex."

"But what do I do with a memory that won't go away?"

"You may want to hold it and ask why. Don't react to it. Just question. After a time, you may find it fades," Jasmin had said.

He tried this technique with Darwin's argument, but to no avail. *Why does it piss me off so much?* His heart lurched as a vision of Stevie popped up. He loved her fearlessness, whether exploring a cave, motorcycling, or, where he drew the line, base jumping in the Alps. Best of all, he loved her wicked, mischievous smile. But he had come to realize he wanted someone to return to each day. She seemed most alive when roaming. A kilometer of trail rolled under his feet as he released the bittersweet memories of his former lover.

What about Jasmin? He considered a life with her, but then he shook his head. *Too early. She's dealing with her own mess.*

He turned back toward town, increasing his pace to blur the mental noise. The endorphin rush lightened his spirit, and his attention drifted to the surrounding beauty: orange sunlight chasing shadows up the mountain through the verdant brush.

But the conversation with Darwin still banged around in his head. *His suspicion's bullshit!*

An hour later, after a shower and a post-run beer, his mood had lifted. By the time he had freshened up, Jasmin had arrived, and the tendrils of her musky perfume hooked his nostrils, reeling him into the main room.

"You smell good," he said, kissing her.

She grazed his cheek with her fingernails, and a shiver ran through his core.

"So do you," she said, adding, "I'm hungry," in response to his hand exploring her backside.

They walked to a local brasserie, where they ordered a carafe of rosé and a plate of charcuterie and olives. He shoveled in bites of coppa and slowed down after a look from Jasmin prompted him back into Corsican time. They spoke about work at the ACA, their most common activity. Jasmin mentioned an intern from Chad who hoped to preserve ancient desert dwellings.

"He comes from a family that looted tombs to earn a living. He's hoping to create eco-tourism by preserving the past. It's a lovely dream but not likely."

"Why not?"

"There's no infrastructure for safe tourism. You've seen it."

Zac nodded, having indeed seen desperate people in war-torn countries. He asked a few more questions about her work, all the while spiraling closer to what he wanted to ask. "I heard you went to the megayacht again?"

"Yes." She grimaced and drained her wineglass.

"Did your ex sign the papers?" He refilled her glass.

"No. He just wanted to talk me out of leaving again. Bastard. He's so manipulative."

"I'm sorry. How are you feeling?"

Her expression darkened as she folded her arms across her midsection. "He could have sent the papers by courier."

Zac sensed her subdued reaction was to hold in pain and keep it from exploding in public. He sat forward as if ready to pounce. "Is he still here?"

"No." Her hands went up in defense. "Zac, honey, please stay out of this. It's just his way. He'll realize it's over and go away. He's already got a lover. I smelled a perfume lingering in the galley."

Their main course arrived, and they ate in silence while surrounded by lively restaurant chatter. A cheer went up from the bar as Nice scored against Paris St. Germain. The locals supported any football squad who scored against Paris; the "team of money," they called it. Zac smiled at the universal appeal of the underdog and used the moment to slip in a question.

"Darwin said you had some trouble in Lebanon?"

"Is that what you were upset about earlier?"

"Yeah. He pisses me off sometimes. Comes from a life of plenty with an old-family arrogance. Has no idea of real-life struggles."

"What did he say?"

"He called a professor friend in Lebanon. Said you got into some trouble and didn't complete a Ph.D."

"It's a long story, not one I'm proud of."

"What happened?"

"I went to Beirut to explore my cultural roots and take up graduate studies. A year in, there was a misunderstanding at a dig site where a rival Ph.D. candidate accused me of stealing an artifact."

"Did you?"

"No. I was earning money to pay for my education. I took a side job working for a company that recovered antiquities from construction sites. The local authorities set up a sting, looking for a payout."

"That's a raw deal. I'm sorry."

"The university expelled me, and my employer did nothing to help."

"Who did you work for?"

"Alexandria Antiquities."

"Wait. Isn't that Nahla Al Mahwi's company?"

"Yes. But she said it was all legal, that her company had a contract with the government for commercial archaeology work. I spent three days in a gritty cell until my partner got me out. I hate what he's turned into now, but, back then, he was the only one who helped."

"Damn," said Zac, setting his utensils on the empty plate and took her hand across the table. "I'm sorry for bringing it up."

43

The next morning, after dropping Darwin at the airport, Eyrún carried the bust to the lab to study the basalt. The rock's chemical makeup would give them some idea of its origin. Along the way, she stopped in Barry's office to check in on the construction.

He gestured wildly as he bellowed at a voice coming from the speakerphone. "Tomorrow? Tomorrow? This isn't a musical production. I need it today." He looked at Eyrún, picked up the handset, and held up a finger, indicating one minute.

She tuned out the call as she looked for a clear spot in the mountain of papers to set down the bust. His filing system could not be more opposite hers, but, despite its chaotic appearance, any time she asked for a document, Barry's eyes would sweep the piles for mere seconds before he snatched up the needed paper.

"Thanks, mate. See, that wasn't so hard. I'll meet your driver on the loading dock at half past four—today," said Barry, his voice mellifluous. Eyrún had heard that students flocked to his lectures for the Shakespearean rants, and students across Europe competed to join his archaeological digs. He was having the same effect at the ACA, as Eyrún had received a steady flow of inquiries and more intern applications than they had spots.

As he turned to her, an infectious grin spread between his ruddy cheeks. "Eyrún! How are you today?"

She returned the smile, feeling a warmth at how Barry had also blossomed in the Corsican climate. "Always better when surrounded by your energy, Barry. I trust the construction's going well?" She nodded toward the phone.

"Don't get me started on the French bureaucracy. But, yes, we're on schedule." He moved a stack of papers. "Here you go."

Eyrún set the sculpture on the desk's bare spot and dusted her hands. As they briefly reviewed the construction, Barry tipped his head from side to side, studying the bust. "This looks familiar," he said.

"Jasmin thinks it's a Roman emperor," she said.

"Not that. I mean...now that you mention it, there's a resemblance to Suetonius, a first-century general. He, er… Never mind. You didn't come here for a lecture. I think this is in a photo that Lupita captured in her project." He picked up the bust and eyed it more closely. "Now I'm certain. This is the one Darwin found in that abandoned workshop, right?"

"Yes."

"Never seen a Roman work done in basalt. Let's go ask Lupita."

As they moved toward the door, Barry's phone rang. He looked at the caller ID and said, "It's that contractor again. I better take it. You go ahead. I'll be along."

She carried the bust a short distance down the hall to Lupita's office, where she knocked lightly on the opened door. Lupita looked up and said, "Oh, hello, Eyrún. Come in."

Her office, the antithesis of Barry's, featured neatly arranged surfaces. One large table had photos spaced as if on a grid. And, while Barry's voice boomed at a back-row audience, Lupita spoke as gently as a stream. Eyrún sat with the bust in her lap and asked how she was.

"Fine, thank you. And you?"

"Busy as ever. How is your new flat?" The Lacroix family owned a building in the old harbor, and a unit had recently become available.

"It is lovely, and I have never lived so close to the water." Lupita smiled, and her sparkling eyes conveyed gratitude.

"Tell me how your project's going. Zac says it's up and running."

"Yes. He has been a great help." Lupita blushed in the light wash cast by the two large monitors.

Eyrún smiled. *Interesting. Is she hiding feelings about Zac?*

Lupita tapped on the keyboard in answer to a beep, and, a few beats later, Eyrún said, "Can you tell me how it works?"

Lupita brightened, describing how she had coded an algorithm that used artificial intelligence to develop linkages between the Art Loss Record database and records of worldwide museums'. She surmised the algorithm could find missing pieces in vast collections that individual curators could not.

"For instance, the Pitt Rivers Museum in Oxford has thousands of pieces on display, but millions in storage. It has turned up a few possibilities, and I printed the photos there." She pointed at the table behind her.

Eyrún noticed Lupita kept glancing down at the bust as she spoke. "Did you find something about this bust? Barry mentioned it."

"No. Well, not exactly. I took photos of it and the other vases in the lab as an experiment. To see what the algorithm would find."

"And..."

"The bust is a copy of a statue in Bath." Lupita reached for a photo. "It is Gaius Suetonius Paulinus, a Roman general."

"So, this means your system works."

"Yes. It proved it worked, so I began testing another idea." Lupita lifted a copy of *Vanity Fair* from her desk. Eyrún had seen it when she walked in, thinking it uncharacteristic of Lupita, who seemed a scientist to the core. "I directed the algorithm to also scan publications, especially art and culture that the wealthy would read or at least subscribe to. In the last staff meeting, you and Jasmin talked about the super-rich and their egos."

Eyrún had never seen Lupita so animated, and she guessed the penny was about to drop.

"I figured the magazines with pictures of rich people's homes might have artworks with questionable provenance. It is still running, but..." She nodded toward Eyrún's lap, stepped over to a pile on the far table, and lifted another photo. "I found this." She handed it to Eyrún.

Balancing the bust with her left hand, Eyrún took it and swiveled her chair to catch the light from the desk. The photo showed the interior sitting area of a large yacht. The ocean was visible through a wide door to the stern. Two large paintings hung on either side of the door, and a large Etruscan vase stood on a table almost outside the frame. Lupita tapped on her keyboard as Eyrún squinted at the photo.

"Here it is," said Lupita. She pointed at a monitor and clicked the mouse to zoom in. While the photo blurred somewhat as the vase enlarged, Eyrún clearly saw the figures on the vase.

"What? That's my Fountain of Salmacis vase," she said, setting the bust on the desk and scooting her chair next to Lupita's. "At least, it looks the same. What do you think?"

"It looks identical to me."

Eyrún studied the vase's surroundings, especially the aft deck out the room's window. *Something's familiar. Wait. It can't be.* Her jaw clenched, and her pulse quickened as she leaned back in her chair to gain perspective. "Zoom out."

Lupita shrank the photo to its original size, and the ocean and horizon resolved clearly. Then she clicked to a photo of the yacht moored alongside others in what looked like Monaco Harbor.

"Shit!" Eyrún hissed.

"What is it?" asked Lupita.

Eyrún explained how she had seen the same megayacht in Ajaccio Harbor. Then, placing a hand on Lupita's forearm, she said, "I need you to keep this between us. Please. Not even Zac."

"Yes. Of course."

Eyrún's heart thudded as she carried the bust and photos back to her office. *What the hell's going on?*

44

Darwin, needing a distraction, had escaped back to Vatican City, where he gazed absently out an office window into the gardens. He no longer felt raw from the fight with Zac, but his stomach churned with each replay. They had disagreed before but never to this extent, and Zac's refusal to answer calls or texts added to his suffering.

Eyrún's consolation had helped somewhat, and she had reminded him that their concerns about Jasmin were not personal. "I like her," she had said, "but we have to question. We're under attack and don't know yet from whom."

His mobile vibrated, bringing him out of his mental tunnel.

Eyrún: Good morning. Feeling better today?
Darwin: not really

She replied with a sad-faced emoji, suggested he visit a new part of the museum to clear his head, and promised to call later in the day. He pocketed the device as his inner DVR played back the argument with Zac. *Stop! Move.* Then he walked down the long library corridor towards the Egyptian Museum.

His footfalls echoed softly on the marble floor as he passed elaborately carved cabinets with hand-hammered brass hardware. Overhead, a riot of frescoes covered the upper walls and ceiling. Centuries of creation had packed the hall, so much so that a visitor had to whisk through or miss greater masterpieces elsewhere in Vatican City.

He paused to study a scene over a doorway between corridor sections. Its artist was a lesser genius than Michelangelo but still immensely talented. As faint odors of beeswax and moldering paper tinged the air, Darwin's archaeological sense of curiosity drew him to wonder about the painter. *Who are you? What was your life like? Family, marriage, children? Was this painting your life's ambition? Or was it just a job that paid the bills? How can we ever know?*

The questions drifted in and out as he imagined the painter's life and time. Then another thought popped up: *Vatican security. They could find out about Jasmin. Of course.* He turned, and the decorations fell into the background as he beat a path to the security office.

Minutes later, he knocked on the head of security's door. "*Bonjorno*, Max."

"*Bonjorno* Darwin. Come in. How are you?"

They caught up with each other. Max recounted a busy weekend attending his children's football matches, and then they shifted to the investigation of the missing oinochoe jug.

"Nothing's happened since it arrived at the Basel freeport. We're trying to get access, but the Swiss courts are an impenetrable maze," said Max.

"Any other ideas?"

"None. But I'm sure we'll hear once they discover the jug's fake. I like your optimism that it will draw them out into the open."

"Hopefully. We'll see," said Darwin. He paused and then added, "Can I ask a favor?"

Max's eyebrows shot upward.

"No. No. Nothing like that." Darwin waved a hand, dismissing any thought of transferring another priceless object. "Can you run a background check on someone?"

"Thank goodness," Max said behind a nervous smile. "Give me the name and basic data. I'll ask one of my guys to do it."

"I'd like you to do it. I'm hoping this person isn't connected to the forgeries, but if she is, we can't risk alerting anyone."

"Sure. Sure. I understand."

Darwin wrote down Jasmin's name and the little he knew about her, including what he had learned of her failed Ph.D. pursuit in Lebanon. Max read the paper and asked a few questions, such as nationality and significant dates. Then he said, "Okay. We've worked with less. Come back tomorrow."

D arwin returned to the library offices, and, during a ninety-minute staff meeting, his thoughts kept drifting back to Max's comment about the thieves discovering the fake. *Why haven't we heard from them? They must have studied it.*

He recalled photos of the freeport's rectangular warehouse complex, enveloped by high fences and twenty-four-seven security. Last week, Max had arranged a conversation with an Italian art dealer whose company had a space in the freeport. When Darwin asked the man about looted works, the dealer's face darkened.

"We would never do such a thing," he said. Then he added, "But I have heard of dealers who traded in pieces with vague origins." When Darwin pressed him for examples of any such dealers, he had become evasive and declined to share details about the inner workings of the freeport.

As today's meeting droned on, Darwin contemplated the under-world of antiquities and art dealing. It carried the rancid odor of drug cartels: wealth and pricey lawyers at the top sanitizing the lawlessness. Those at the pinnacle deluded themselves into thinking they were a business supplying a market demand, that the problem lay with the consumer, the addict, who abused the product. Darwin saw the millionaires behind the tomb raiding and forgery as junkies whose zeal to possess justified any means of acquisition. The more he studied the subject, the more his bile rose.

Pinching his eyes closed and shaking his head, he pictured a document he had read last night. Gavin had emailed him a warrant from the Los Angeles district attorney's office that read like a whodunnit. A brazen theft of rare cuneiform tablets during the US conflict in Iraq had a list of suspects that included a corrupt museum official, the London branch of the auction house he had visited in Beverly Hills, and a husband-and-wife antiquities trading company based in Hawaii. Together with a litany of shipping companies and sketchy waybills, they had obfuscated the tablets' provenance as "Ex-Canadian private collection, obtained in the 1990s, said to be from Mesopotamia."

Obtained, my ass. Try stolen. He drank from a water bottle to wash down the sour taste in his mouth. "The bastards are destroying our past," he muttered under his breath.

"Darwin?" said his assistant.

"Huh? Sorry. I was working out a problem."

"We're wrapping up. We need a decision on the budget."

"Right." Darwin scanned the document that had been laid before him earlier. Then he looked up at the team. All eyes were on him. The tone during their debate had sounded reasoned, so he cut to the chase. "Any objections to what's been proposed?"

Heads shook. One woman said, "No."

"Okay, then. Approved." He signed it and asked his assistant to submit it to the head librarian.

45

E yrún stared absently at the bust on her desk after again scrolling through the photos of the vase on the megayacht. She messaged Darwin:

Can you talk?
Darwin: in a long meeting. an hour?
Eyrún: Look at these. Jasmin knows more than she's saying.

She included photos and a link to the publication. A minute later, her mobile chimed.

Darwin: !!!!!!!
Eyrún: I know. Maybe Vatican security can do a background check.
Darwin: thought the same thing earlier and asked Max to run one.
Eyrún: when will you know?
Darwin: tomorrow
Eyrún: ok, I'll ask her about it in the meantime.

She cleared her email inbox before Hervé introduced an interview candidate, and then she attended a series of meetings before lunch. In a break before an afternoon interview, she went to see Jasmin, who was peering into a microscope.

Eyrún tapped on the doorframe, and, as Jasmin turned, she said, "Sorry to bother you again, but I stumbled upon something with Lupita."

"No bother. I'm always happy to help," Jasmin said, scooting her chair backward.

Eyrún moved to the lab bench and leaned on it, facing Jasmin. Then she asked if Jasmin was familiar with Lupita's project.

"She described it in our last staff meeting, but I'm not technical and tuned most of it out. Why?"

"We found these." Eyrún took three photos from her jeans back pocket and handed them to Jasmin, who flipped through them. When Jasmin did not respond, Eyrún pressed, though she kept her tone light. "Why would the Fountain of Salmacis be on your yacht?"

Jasmin looked up at Eyrún. "I've no idea."

"You didn't recognize it in the lab before they seized it?"

"It was the first time I'd seen it." Jasmin shuffled through the photos again. "Where did you get these?"

"Lupita's algorithm found them in an issue of *Vanity Fair* from 2007."

"That story's over a decade old, just before my ex bought the yacht from a client in financial trouble. I was so angry when I learned what he spent, but he always did that with our money."

She's got a smooth answer for everything. Eyrún pondered this latest reply before asking, "So, you never saw it?"

"No. There was no art aboard when I first saw the yacht, and we sent it for a makeover right after the purchase." After a pause, Jasmin added, "He let me decorate it as consolation. It's how he placated me."

Eyrún shifted her inquiry. "Could your ex have a role in what's going on with us?"

Jasmin snorted. "I don't know how."

"It's okay. Let's leave it to the lawyers. Sorry for the questions. This whole thing is wearing me out, too."

"Believe me, I understand."

Eyrún thanked Jasmin and headed back to the main offices, having learned little. But a twisting in her belly left her unconvinced, and she replayed all her interactions with Jasmin as she walked. *There're too many coincidences. I can't wait to see the background check.*

46

The next afternoon, Darwin canceled a meeting and cut a swift path to the security office after Max called to say he had received the report on Jasmin.

"*Bonjourno*," said Darwin, taking the chair opposite Max.

"*Bonjourno*."

"What did you find? I talked with my wife last night. She's convinced there's more going on than Jasmin's telling us."

"She's got good intuition, and there's a lot to unravel here," said Max. He began reading from a summary page. "Jasmin had a rough start—born 1980 in Beirut. Her mom died in 1986, a casualty of the civil war. Luckily, a French family adopted her when she was six, and she grew up in Paris."

"Looks like a normal childhood after her tumultuous early years. She attended good schools and earned a baccalauréat in 1997. Her family must have had money because, despite being a middling performer, she went to the University of Paris."

"Anything about grad school or her Ph.D. attempt in Beirut?" asked Darwin.

Max picked up the full report and flipped the pages to confirm. "There's nothing on post-graduate work."

Darwin's eyes darted back and forth as he considered the alternate picture of Jasmin developing before him. "What about her business? The antiquities galleries?"

"It's legitimate. Jasmin and Thierry Panchon—"

"Panchon? She said her name is Kahn."

"That's her original family name. She and Thierry own two galleries in Paris that, according to tax records we could get, gross over seventy-nine million euros annually."

"Anything else stand out?"

"She was arrested in Lebanon twenty-three years ago for looting a tomb. No record of conviction. But there's something odd. Best if you read it yourself." Max handed the report to Darwin, who scanned the page.

"*Merde,*" he breathed out, sinking into the chair.

D arwin took the report back to his office and closed the door. He opened the folder and, skimming over the details Max had summarized, flipped to the section that caused his earlier reaction.

The document listed a lawsuit in France leveled by Nahla's company, Alexandria Antiquities, Ltd., against Jasmin's firm alleging the sale of state treasures stolen from the National Museum of Beirut during the Lebanese Civil War. The suit settled out of court, but the report contained a translated section from a French newspaper:

> Ms. Jasmin Panchon, Managing Director of Eshmun Holdings, SARL, said, "The court showed that our practices live up to the highest standards. We stand vindicated of wrongdoing and shall take action against anyone who seeks to malign our legitimate business."

Managing director? She's not as naive as she claims. I wonder what Nahla's version of this is.

He scanned the report with his mobile, uploaded it to a secure server, and texted Eyrún the link.

She called within minutes. "I knew it. That sneaky bitch. She runs the company that owns the megayacht."

"Yep. I noticed that. And, no surprise, there's bad blood between her and Nahla."

They debated how Jasmin might be waging a war against Nahla through the ACA, but they stumbled when they got to the Albanian Master. "She's got some fixation on him. Her interest in our collection definitely picked up when she found the aleph," said Eyrún.

"What do you think is Nahla's view of this lawsuit?"

"Meaning her evidence on Jasmin's company stealing from the National Museum of Beirut?"

"Exactly." An idea began to coalesce, but Darwin could not get a bead on it.

"But wouldn't the Lebanese museum sue Eshmun Holdings? They owned the stolen objects, not Nahla's company."

"Dunno," he said. Then, deciding to go with his gut, he blurted out, "What if we ask Nahla?"

A n hour later, after convincing Eyrún it was worth risking, Darwin got Nahla's contact information from a dossier gathered when the pope had secured the Alexander scroll from Egypt. After typing and deleting several messages, he decided simple and vague would best:

This is Darwin Lacroix. I need some information and have something to trade.

She texted back minutes later, and they exchanged a series of texts, ending with Darwin agreeing to meet her in Alexandria. At first, he hesitated on the location, but he agreed after pondering her message:

I bear you no ill will Darwin. We are competitors. Sometimes I win. Sometimes you win. But Jasmin is not who she says she is.

47

Eyrún warmed her hands on a teacup as she looked far beyond the horizon, imagining Darwin's flight nearing Alexandria. The hot liquid soothed the butterflies in her stomach.

Yesterday afternoon, her warning radar had gone up when Darwin proposed visiting Nahla. Initially she had argued against going, saying it bordered on dangerous, but her opinion shifted as they discussed it. The security report showed Jasmin Panchon, a savvy executive communicator, expert at selling antiquities to the super-wealthy, not the victimized Jasmin Kahn, who deflected blame onto her husband and manipulated their suspicions about Nahla.

As Eyrún had lain in bed last night, she had replayed her encounters with Jasmin. *She knows so much of our history with Nahla... But we can't trust Nahla, either...* Thinking about Darwin made her heart race, but she willed herself to relax, knowing that Max had promised two security operatives to shadow him. She had finally fallen asleep after convincing herself he would be safe.

Now, in the bright light of a new day, the prior evening's doubts returned. *What if meeting Darwin is just a distraction and Nahla and Jasmin are in this together?* She shuddered, spilling tea on one hand. The idea made sense on one level—how else could Jasmin know so much about them? But on the whole, something was missing.

She dried her wet hand on her jeans as she continued to ponder the questions that had kept her awake. *Did Jasmin seduce Zac to get into our life? And what's the Albanian Master connection?*

On top of everything, she could not connect the ACA's framing to the ransom request to send the Vatican oinochoe jug out for restoration. The more she thought about it, the more she convinced herself they had to pursue alternate strategies. Darwin's keen intuition took them in seemingly illogical directions, like meeting Nahla, but Eyrún knew solutions came from assembling multiple options.

I need to draw Jasmin out. Turn the table. Get her to react.

She recalled the idea Astrid had proposed two months ago when their legal battle had just started: conduct a public relations campaign showing the positive work the ACA was doing. At the time, she had disliked the idea, saying, "We're not guilty," but her pragmatic side had begun to consider it a decent strategy.

While Eyrún had done nothing other than talk with the marketing firm Astrid had recommended, seeing Jasmin in the kitchen across the open office prompted her to test the idea. She grabbed her mobile and tapped Darwin's number, knowing it would go to voice mail. Upon reaching the kitchen, she stopped close enough to be overheard but just out of Jasmin's sight.

"But it makes perfect sense, Darwin. The lawyer said antiquities theft is rampant and the OCBC has no solid evidence that we looted the vases. Besides, under French law, the transfer documents from the museum protect us."

Eyrún paused as if Darwin were replying. When the kitchen noises stopped, she continued. "I say we send the vases back to their countries of origin, make large donations to their museums, and begin a media campaign to apologize."

She watched Jasmin's reflection in an inner office window. When Jasmin moved closer, Eyrún cast the bait. "Forget about Nahla. The whole thing blows over, and, in a few years, it's forgotten."

Jasmin froze. Eyrún waited for a few more beats before ending her fake call. "Okay, I gotta run, too. I need another tea before my call with

Astrid. See you tonight. *Bisous*." She pocketed the mobile and then entered the kitchen. "Good morning, Jasmin. How are you today?"

"Lovely. You?"

Eyrún answered, and as she stepped toward the kettle, Jasmin asked, "When will Darwin be back? I need his help on the provenience of a cinerarium. They look so similar, and modern borders cut across the ancient kingdoms."

"Later tonight," said Eyrún, switching on the kettle. Then, thinking Jasmin might be probing based on what she overheard, she added, "He's in Alexandria today."

Jasmin's eyes blinked rapidly. "Oh. It can wait till tomorrow." She looked away.

Eyrún grinned and walked out.

48

D arwin exited customs and saw a sign for Mr. Lacroix. The slim, black-suited man holding it reminded him of the corrupt Egyptian antiquities officials who had seized his Alexander scroll. He flushed at the memory, grinding his teeth at the personal violation. For two years, the vision had plagued and humiliated him. Some nights, he had fallen asleep plotting how to destroy Nahla. *And now I'm walking into her lair. Stop it*, he chided himself. *Focus on the meeting.*

Darwin followed the man to a white Mercedes-Benz 600S sedan idling curbside at passenger arrivals. The driver palmed baksheesh to a policeman standing watch over the vehicle, got behind the wheel, and soon pulled into the hornet's nest of Alexandrian traffic.

Darwin reclined the rear seat and sighed out the tension from the morning's airport hurdles and constant barrage of noise. Sometime later, an abrupt stop jerked him from a lucid dream, and he saw they had reached the coastal road.

As the car rolled past the New Library of Alexandria, its silver dome glistening in the southern Mediterranean sun, he imagined the scrolls he and Eyrún had found. *We should visit the library and go to Siwa again.* They supported the schools in the oasis, and Eyrún had kept in touch with Illi, a local girl who had helped them, promising her an internship at the ACA.

They soon reached Nahla's apartment building, less than two kilometers from the library, and the driver strode around to open the rear door. Darwin thanked him and informed the doorman he was a guest of Ms. Al Mahwi.

The lift's mirrored inside doors reflected his tight expression; he was squinting so hard his green eyes were hardly visible. *Relax. Let it go.* He took a breath, swept back his hair, and unclenched his jaw. The doors opened into the penthouse foyer, where a young woman greeted him.

"*Bonjour*, Mr. Lacroix. I trust you had a pleasant journey?" she said in flawless English. She wore a smart royal-blue suit and white blouse and, in sandals, equaled Darwin's height.

"*Bonjour.* It was uneventful. Thank you for the airport pickup," he said. Unsure of what to say next, his face telegraphed his confusion. He had heard Nahla was in her mid-sixties.

"I'm Ms. Al Mahwi's assistant, Nadia." She opened the penthouse door and, stepping out of her sandals, said, "Please leave your shoes here."

Darwin followed her into a wide-open space whose floor-to-ceiling windows made the room feel like it floated over the vast blue Mediterranean Sea.

"Mr. Darwin Lacroix, famous archaeologist, friend of the pope and presidents, we meet at last." Nahla Al Mahwi stood before the Mediterranean panorama, having turned when he entered the room.

His vision of her shattered. He had carried a mental picture of an older woman wearing an abaya. Nahla, barely a meter and a half tall, wore an azure pantsuit that flowed over her generous curves, topped with a matching hijab woven through her lush, dark hair.

"Ms. Al Mahwi. It's a pleasure to finally meet." Darwin walked across the handwoven silk rugs, whose soft pile massaged his feet with each step. Nahla's amber eyes pulled him in like an insect about to be trapped. He shook her offered hand and, up close, noticed faint lines at the corners of her eyes and upper lip, the only giveaways of her age.

The copious gold adorning her fingers and earlobes did match his image, especially the fine gold chain holding an exquisite scarab that rested in the crevasse of her chest. He willed his eyes to her round, well-proportioned face; its mocha skin was unblemished except for a tiny mole over the left side of her upper lip.

Nahla asked Nadia to bring them tea and led him to a corner sitting area that seemed to extend over the shoreline below. Darwin glanced around for signs of any other security, half-expecting to find large men standing discreetly against the walls. *Chill. It's just a meeting.* He pushed down emotions that fought for his attention, but he had a sudden craving for the tea to soothe his dry mouth.

"Thanks for seeing me," he said.

"Certainly."

At that moment, Nadia arrived and set down a tray between them. Darwin had learned to enjoy the social aspect of tea breaks during his time in the Siwa Oasis, the simple sharing of life's everyday rhythm. He found the strong mint cleared his head, although he preferred it with less sugar.

When Nadia retreated, Darwin's eyes followed her from the room and then scanned the walls again.

"Relax, Darwin. If I had meant you any harm, you'd be drugged in the Sahara," Nahla said as she leaned back on the cream-colored leather sofa.

His chest tightened, and a lightheadedness made him grasp the teacup with both hands. The memory of waking up deep in the Sahara Desert, left to die, though two years distant, was still fresh enough to give him panic attacks. His journey into the Corsican mountains with Zac had been partially designed to help confront his fears.

"Yes. I heard about it, and I'm deeply sorry. I did not know Tessa and Fathi would go so far."

"You could have stopped it," he said with more venom than he intended. *Control yourself. Don't let her provoke you.*

"I sent Abbas."

"A lot of good that did." Darwin shook his head. Abbas Kamal, director of the Egyptian Ministry of State for Antiquities, had blundered into a standoff at the entrance to Alexander's tomb. His incompetence in aligning with the corrupt local police had led to a shootout and caused a cave-in. He later stole the Alexander treasure scroll from Darwin and Eyrún's house in Siwa.

He tried to ease the angst caused by the memory. *Breathe. Breathe.* But then, unable to stop himself, he spat out, "How did you feel when the pope convinced the Egyptian president to hand over the Alexander scroll?"

"I never saw it. Abbas betrayed me as well and hid it in the Egyptian National Museum."

"But didn't you work together?" he asked, sliding back in his chair.

"Alliances come and go, Darwin. It's a business—heartless as Wall Street and only a little more forgiving than the Marseilles cartels." She brought her cup to her lips, and her bracelets softly tinkled.

He suppressed the urge to speak. *Let her talk.* He blew across the elegantly scrolled glass cup before testing the steaming liquid. The tea burned his tongue, but the pain gave him something to focus on instead of his roiling emotions.

"I think you and Eyrún are doing great work with the Agrippa Center for Archaeology," she said. "It's a shame you're caught up in baseless charges."

Does she mean it? Or is she covering herself? He offered a tentative return. "We're at a loss to understand it, and certainly, Eyrún doesn't deserve the accusation."

"You have enemies, Darwin," she said, lowering her glass. "Don't look surprised. We all do."

Heat rose behind his eyes. "I didn't take the Alexander scroll from you. You and Tessa wanted to sell it and all the scrolls. This history belongs to all of us." He stopped himself before he went any further.

Nahla laughed and slapped her knee lightly with one hand. "Is that what you believe? Ah, Darwin, you have a gift for finding antiquities, but you have much to learn about people's motivations. Yes, I wanted the Alexander scroll. Do you know the deeper reason why?"

"To sell it or find the loot he hid," said Darwin, crossing his arms.

"I'm Egyptian, Alexandrian by birth, going back countless generations. Like you, I'm an archaeologist. And I sit on the board of directors
of the Bibliotheca Alexandrina, hardly a role for a thief. I endeavor to
preserve our Egyptian heritage, but it costs money to dig. My
company, Alexandria Antiquities, specializes in commercial archaeology. It funds more speculative explorations.

"As for the Alexander scroll, it sounds like you and Eyrún got
caught up in your own ethical dilemma. Instead of turning it over to
the Egyptian state, you kept it for yourself. Abbas, while clumsy, was
just doing his job when he confiscated it, no?"

Darwin's felt his neck and face flush, and he looked away,
attempting to hide it. Eyrún had found the scroll, but keeping it for
themselves went against the ACA's mission and his personal beliefs.
He did not want to admit this to Nahla, though, so he simply peered at
the tiny flakes swirling in his cup while regaining his composure.

She continued. "I think you're savvier than you come across,
Darwin. But let's get back to the reason for your visit, as I'm sure you
didn't come here to argue ethics. You suspect Jasmin is deceiving you
and want my opinion on the matter."

He looked up, but she had shifted her gaze out to sea as if allowing
him space to come clean about his true purpose.

"You're right. I think we've all been misled."

She turned, and her lips spread into a thin smile. "Tell me why you
came."

Darwin paused, like a kid on a dock fighting against his fear of the
black water. Finally, he scrunched his toes against the imaginary
planks and jumped. *What the hell? It's why I'm here.* He told her everything, the donation of the museum pieces to the ACA, the seizure and
accusations by the French OCBC in Marseilles, the ransom demand,
Jasmin helping, and the piece being moved from the Vatican's Etruscan
collection. He left out that the Vatican piece was a forgery.

He felt naked as she remained quiet after his monologue. Finally,
she asked, "What do you know about Jasmin Kahn?"

He described what Jasmin had said about herself and what he had
learned from the Vatican security report.

"That sounds like her. She's a clever seductress, much better than

Tessa ever was. And she's a survivor. Jasmin worked for me in her twenties, much like Tessa did. But she had formed her own company by the time the Lebanese arrested her. The Vatican's report got that correct. She tried to turn the blame on me." She paused for more tea and then asked, "Why do you suppose she's looking for the Albanian Master?"

Darwin's eyebrows furrowed. Deciding to roll with it, he said, "I've been wrestling with the same question. Many of the pieces point to him."

"How?"

He was about to answer when Nahla added, "You were going to tell me it's because of his signature, the aleph. But you know nothing about him other than what Jasmin described...do you?"

He stiffened, realizing Nahla was right. Everything they knew about the Albanian Master had come from Jasmin. She could have made him up as a diversion, and the aleph meant something else entirely. *Oh, my God. How could we have been so thoroughly taken in?* He felt like Nahla could push him over with a feather.

"You and Eyrún aren't the first. Jasmin and Thierry are the most gifted antiquities dealers I've ever encountered. I've bent the rules, but those two think the world is their personal playground. But let's get back to the Albanian Master."

She set the cup on a side table, waved off Nadia, who had moved to collect it, and locked onto Darwin's eyes. "Jasmin didn't lie about the aleph. It *is* his signature. He's a genius and has done jobs for me for decades. I can elaborate, but knowledge is precious in my business."

Darwin had been wondering why Nahla was sharing so much so freely, but then he realized how shrewdly she was bargaining. She had hooked him. Fortunately, he had come prepared to reach a détente. He lifted his shoulder bag from the floor and rested it on a knee.

"It pains me to see Eyrún suffer," he said. "Our reputation means more to us than our money." He opened the bag and laid a small, scroll-sized tube on the table between them. "In the past year, I've realized I'm not interested in treasure that lies in conflict zones, and I think your contacts could more easily navigate between the hostiles."

She smiled. "You're improving, Darwin. I mean you no ill will—

and never have. Jasmin seeks to destroy me. She's using you against me because the Albanian Master has something she and her partner, not husband, desperately want."

Darwin's eyebrows shot upward.

"Oh, no. They're not divorcing," she said at his look of surprise. "They were never married."

Darwin's face screwed up, and his heart palpitated as Nahla smiled again, clearly enjoying her cat-and-mouse game.

"Thierry Panchon is Jasmin Kahn's father."

Darwin fell back as if avoiding Nahla's claws.

49

As the pain from her fingernails digging into her palms increased, Jasmin realized she had been staring at the same carbon-dating document for a quarter of an hour. Her head swirled from the conversation with Eyrún. *What's Darwin doing in Alexandria?*

She set aside the paper. Nothing at the ACA interested her, and she was tired of keeping up appearances. Her mobile chirped:

Thierry: Darwin met Nahla

Putain! She jumped off the stool, her face flushed hot. She looked around and, seeing no one, called his sat phone.

"*Bonjour*, darling," he said.

"*Bonjour*, Papa. Where are you?"

"Anchored near Bonifacio, about fifty kilometers southeast."

"Tell me quickly. I don't know how long I'll be alone."

He recounted a conversation he had had with a Vatican curator under his influence. The previous afternoon, she had hung around the office after filing a false report about an attempted break-in and had overheard Darwin mention Alexandria. She also had seen a folder with Jasmin's name on it.

Hours later, a private detective in Thierry's employ followed Darwin outside Vatican City and confirmed that he had boarded a flight for Alexandria, where a member of an Egyptian antiquities looting gang had followed him to Nahla's penthouse.

"Why didn't you tell me sooner?" asked Jasmin.

"I just learned of it. I left the sat phone in the galley last night and went diving this morning."

"Then he'll know about us."

"*Peut-être*. But don't be so sure. Find out what you can."

She disconnected and considered her options. *Find out what I can? Easy for him to say in his floating paradise!* Her heart raced. *Compose yourself.* She slowly brought her breathing under control and reviewed her father's conversation. *I need to know more*, she decided and made a pass by Eyrún's office.

50

Darwin meandered along the seaside path in Alexandria after leaving Nahla's penthouse. The hot onshore wind tugged at his clothing, and the salty air had coated his sunglasses. Upon reaching the wide plaza of the new Library of Alexandria, he sat on a bench shaded by twin palms. The incessant honking dulled the rustling of their fronds overhead.

He stared across the road at kite surfers enjoying the strong wind and replayed his conversation with Nahla. *What the hell's Jasmin playing at?* No answer came, but he knew he had to tell Eyrún before his return flight in two hours. He stood and hailed a taxi. Once inside, he was popping in his earbuds to call Eyrún when a text from Max Keller chimed:

Call me asap

He tapped to call.
"That was fast," said Max.
"I'm in a taxi on the way to the airport in Alexandria."
"I've got more for you, but first tell me what you learned."

Darwin did, including the bomb about Thierry being Jasmin's father.

"That explains the oddities we saw in Jasmin's adoption records. But let me update you. Turn's out Thierry's a nasty piece of work." Max summarized Thierry Panchon's career, from his role as director of the *Mission Archéologique* in Beirut to opening galleries in France with Jasmin.

"At some point, Thierry added stolen art to their selling of looted antiquities. I called a colleague in the French OCBC, who said Thierry's on their antiquities watch list as a fence for a Marseille gang specializing in high-end art theft."

Darwin pondered these revelations and then asked, "I'm struggling with the motives, Max. Do you have any guesses as to what Thierry and Jasmin want from us?"

"Money. Well, indirectly. My colleague has a man in custody who says Thierry owes the gang millions from a sale gone wrong. Thierry claims he can pay it off when he finds a gold mask that was stolen from him."

"Let me guess, by someone called the Albanian Master."

"How did you know?"

51

O n her way to Eyrún's office, Jasmin stopped to chat with an intern. *Best to keep up appearances*, she thought while answering the young woman's question about the glaze used on an urn. Not five minutes later, Jasmin heard Eyrún's voice rise almost to a yell. She could not make out the words, but she knew Eyrún well enough to detect anger.

She quickly wrapped up with the intern and moved to the wall outside Eyrún's door, where she overheard, "What else did he say?"

He? Jasmin had expected Eyrún to be talking about Nahla. She strained to hear, but the voice coming from the mobile was just a tinny noise.

Then Eyrún said, "We were right... No. No. Don't tell Zac anything yet, especially not over the phone." She paused to listen and then said, "Got it. Five forty-three. See you then."

Jasmin leaned against the wall and looked across the office to see if anyone had seen her. But at half past noon, most employees had gone to lunch.

"Shit!" Eyrún yelled, and her chair rattled as it rolled across the plank flooring.

Jasmin jerked at the outburst and ran back to the lab. Once there, she closed the lab's door and leaned against it while catching her breath. She dabbed her forehead and considered her next moves. She wanted the lab to appear like she had left for the day, but, since she had no intention of coming back, she could leave nothing incriminating.

Her internal debate from the morning rekindled as she gathered her things. *But what do they know? It's Nahla's word against mine. Why should they trust her over me? Stop it.* She willed herself to focus and studied the lab again. *Looks good. Now, get the Albanian Master's location from Lupita. Then…*

Too many variables clouded the scenarios, and she ended the mental deliberation. *Just see how it goes.* Zac was still refusing to speak with Darwin and Eyrún, but she figured, with his special-forces street sense, it would take him only a day or two to sniff out deception.

She stiffened. *Darwin's impulsive. He'll approach Zac no matter what Eyrún says. I need to get Zac away from here, at least until we figure out the next step.* Taking out her mobile, she messaged Zac:

> I need a break. Let's go to Bonifacio for a few days. Come to my
> flat. We'll leave in the morning

She pocketed the device, closed the lab door, and went to Lupita's office. *Stay calm.* She rallied. *No one knows what's going on.* She smiled at a group of interns passing in the hall, turned into the computer lab, and knocked on its open door.

"Lupita?" Her eyes adjusted to the dim light and soon registered the empty room. *Dammit.* She had no time to wait. She scanned the table, but nothing looked like a printout or notes about a location for the photo.

Eyrún's voice came from outside. "Have you seen Jasmin?"

Jasmin's vision tunneled as her heart erupted. *Shit!* She swiftly backed away from the workstation and stood against the wall by the door.

"I thought she went into Lupita's office," said a youthful male voice.

Sweat blossomed on Jasmin's forehead as her trembling hands eased the door away from the wall and she slid behind it.

"Jasmin?" Eyrún asked from the doorway, just visible through the gap between the hinges.

Jasmin tensed. Eyrún moved a couple of steps into the room. Jasmin considered what to do, as Eyrún completely blocked any exit. *Keep going, keep going,* she willed.

"Lupita? Jasmin?" Eyrún stood a moment longer. Jasmin was getting ready to slam the door into her and make a run for it when Eyrún said, "Huh," and left.

Jasmin waited a long minute and then blew out through puffed cheeks as one hand grasped the door for balance. She moved around it and carefully peered out just in time to see Eyrún turn a corner to the archaeology lab.

Go. Jasmin went in the opposite direction and, after a dozen steps, willed herself to slow down. *Look normal,* she breathed and continued down to the lobby and outside. Once inside her car, she messaged her father:

They know

She backed her car from its spot and drove to the road leading to the main harbor. A half-kilometer later, she rolled her shoulders, unloading the tension. *No problem. Now find Zac.*

Her mobile rang, and she jerked the wheel, rocking the car. The caller ID showed Eyrún, so she let it go to voicemail, but it rang again half a minute later, from Thierry this time.

"What now? I'm driving," she said.

"Did you find out anything else?"

"No. Darwin called her from Alexandria. They know."

"Slow down, darling. Think. Know what, exactly?"

"I don't know *exactly*, but she asked Darwin about what a *man* said and told him not to tell Zac yet. She was referring to someone besides Nahla, so I wasn't going to stick around."

"I've thought about what you said earlier about Eyrún making donations and ignoring our demand." Thierry paused and then continued when she made no reply. "I don't think they'll risk it. We have the Vatican piece."

"But it's fake," she said, repeating what their expert at the freeport had determined.

"I doubt the Vatican knows it, and César won't figure it out. I've never seen a copy so good. Better than the Albanian Master's work. I would love to hire him, but he must be long dead."

Jasmin listened to her father's almost dreamy voice. He talked about deceiving the Marseilles gang leader, César Olmeta, as if it were a game. She had been trying to distance herself from her father, as his greed had driven him to engage in increasingly unscrupulous relationships. "What if he finds out? You should never have gotten involved with them."

"Maybe. But it is what it is now."

She pounded the horn, holding back a desire to scream. Three years ago, her father's obsession with finding the Albanian Master had led him to a partner with a Marseille art-theft gang. César had promised to help find the Albanian Master if Thierry managed the sale of objects stolen from an heiress's estate.

But when the sale went wrong and César's brother was arrested, the gang kidnapped Thierry. In exchange for letting him live, César had asked Thierry to procure a piece from the Vatican Museums fancied by César's mother.

"Jasmin? Are you okay?"

"Fine. We need to accelerate this. I'm changing the plan."

"What do you have in mind?" When she told him, he added, "I thought you didn't like the Marseilles gang?"

52

E yrún shut off the engine after stopping curbside to pick up
Darwin. He had messaged her that the plane had landed two
minutes ago. A breeze carried the spa-like maquis fragrance through
the open windows. *God, I'm overdue for a massage.* She slid her mobile in
the cup holder and breathed in nature's aromatherapy. Resting her
head against the firm racing seat, she unwound while Darwin made
his way off the plane.

Even though she had moved to Corsica to live a slower life, more
often than not, she found herself in go mode—a never-ending list of
projects and decisions at the ACA. Fortunately, key people like Barry
had taken some things off her plate. *I should let go of more.*

But a breath later, she reminded herself, *This is what I want.* She and
Darwin had created the ACA to combat the fragility of human
heritage, train archaeologists from countries with at-risk histories, and
provide resources to save the priceless connections to the past. *But
Jasmin and her partner—father! Dammit. Why?* She moved her fingertips
in soft circles on her temples.

"Hi, love," said Darwin as he opened the rear passenger door and
tossed his case inside. He got in the front and leaned across to kiss her.
"Missed you."

"Me, too," she said, grateful for the interruption. She pushed the starter, and the engine roared to life. As she navigated the airport traffic, Darwin asked about her day, and they chit-chatted about the ACA and his journey from Alexandria. When she had rounded the traffic circle onto the T20 toward their house, she shifted to the question that had been burning since this morning.

"Tell me about Nahla. Were you worried? What's she like?"

"Very businesslike. I had the odd feeling that you two might get along."

"Seriously?"

"I think so. You're both pragmatic and sensible. She knows the nuances and frustrations of antiquities dealings like you know the realities of dealing with the energy bureaucracies. There's the law, and then there's getting things done."

Her brows wrinkled as she downshifted for a curve. "I doubt we'll be doing dinner soon."

Darwin continued to describe Nahla, saying, "She looks younger than her age." He recounted the details of their discussion.

During a pause, she asked, "How did she know about Jasmin's father?"

"Through the Albanian Master."

"How?"

"He's done work for her, so I guess he told her, but she didn't elaborate."

"Interesting."

"I thought so. She did say the Albanian Master and Thierry Panchon had a falling out over looted antiquities in the early days of the Lebanese Civil War."

Eyrún grumbled at running up behind a slow-moving lorry, and, with no place to pass, she drifted back. Besides, they had less than five kilometers to home, and she wanted to focus on the conversation. "What's the connection between those two?"

"Thierry was a national archaeologist in Lebanon and, through his assistant, got introduced to the Albanian Master. Nahla's not clear how they fell out, but she made it sound like a love triangle gone wrong."

They drove in silence the rest of the way up to the house. Once there, Darwin dropped his case in their bedroom and showered off the Egyptian dust and travel fatigue. Eyrún opened a bottle of wine from Calvi and carried it to the back deck to watch the sunset across the far ridge. She had barely managed to drink half a glass when Darwin sat beside her.

"*Santé,*" he said, clinking her glass. They watched the horizon turn a deep orange as the photons refracted through thin clouds. Soon the cool air sloughing off Mt. d'Oro's shoulder would warrant a fire.

"What does Nahla think Thierry wants?" asked Eyrún.

"He was working on the Temple of Eshmun—"

"Wait! That's the name of their company. Is this about something he found there?"

"Maybe. Let me go on." When she nodded, he continued. "War broke out in the eighties, and Nahla heard many objects had to be moved into safe hiding. But she also heard the records recovered from that dig have gaps, meaning missing artifacts. For example, object B13 jumps to B18. That's not the actual record, but it's how it might appear."

"Does that mean objects twelve through seventeen were stolen?"

"Not necessarily, but in this case, yes. Nahla said Thierry had a reputation for fastidiousness and had flamed people for their mistakes."

"So, what's missing?"

"I'll have to research, but Nahla thinks it's a series of large gold objects, including a bull mask."

Eyrún poured them each a second glass and switched on the firepit gas. Bright orange flames danced, equaling the sky show but providing more heat.

"Where's the Albanian Master now?"

"She said he went underground three years ago, perhaps because of Thierry."

"And somehow Thierry and his puppet daughter, Jasmin, think we can find him."

"Yep. Thierry's desperate. He's in deep debt with a Marseilles gang who wanted him to fence high-end artwork."

"Interesting. By the way, I tried a little misdirection today."

Darwin's eyebrows vaulted as Eyrún described her fake call near the break room and how Jasmin seemed to listen.

"How did she react?"

"Walked casually back to the lab but immediately called someone."

"Thierry, I'll bet."

"Uh-huh," Eyrún concurred and then tipped back her glass.

53

The next morning, after working out, Darwin sat, showered, and dressed in the breakfast nook. The sun had climbed over the eastern slope and now slanted through the window, lighting up the steam rising from his cappuccino. During his last set of pull-ups, a thought had struck him to organize what they knew about this debacle.

He had filled half a sheet of paper by the time Eyrún walked in. The sun caught her dark hair, highlighting a few auburn strands. "What's that?" she asked, switching on the kettle and rummaging in the tea drawer.

"I listed what's happened so far and what we know about Jasmin and Thierry."

"I had the same idea when I woke up this morning. The whole damn thing seems so convoluted." She readied her cup and sliced an avocado while the bread toasted. A couple of minutes later, she joined him at the round table, holding her mug while leaning over the paper.

He touched a pen to the top line. "It all started the first week of April, when we got the donation from the Ajaccio museum. The surprise shipment came in a week later."

"The Fountain of Salmacis," she said with a sigh.

"It is a lovely vase," he agreed. "But the thing bugging me is the timing of Zac meeting Jasmin. It now seems too coincidental that he met an art and antiquities expert with spare time to volunteer."

Eyrún picked up the story. "And who, right away, starts filling our heads with suspicions about Nahla, someone we hate, and tossing in this mysterious Albanian Master." She studied the timeline and then added, "You also got Gavin's spreadsheet of questionable restorations around the same time."

"True..." Darwin gazed across the main room. "I wonder if that auction piece in LA is connected? I didn't care about it until I saw the aleph."

"I think it's a question of how, not if. Remember, I got raided while you were in LA. By the way, what did Max have to say about the raid?"

"Shit, I forgot to ask. I was so swept up in Nahla's revelations. We can call him now."

Eyrún nodded, and he tapped to the contacts on his mobile while she bit into her toast. Max answered, and, after pleasantries, Darwin switched to speaker mode. "I'm with my wife, Eyrún, and we wondered if you could answer some questions for us."

"No problem. Nice to meet you, Eyrún."

"Likewise, Max. We have a question about the raid on our organization by the OCBC. What can you tell us about them?"

"I know some. Go ahead."

Darwin picked up the inquiry. "Our attorney said it was a joint operation with the Carabiniere. But something about the timing seems odd, especially with what you told me yesterday about Thierry. Could this be some kind of inside operation?"

Max asked them a few questions about the shipment's timing and Jasmin's arrival. Once they had answered, he was silent for a few moments. Then he said, "The timing *is* suspicious. Warrants take time to get approved, especially for an international operation." He paused again before asking, "Did the warrants come from Paris?"

"Dunno," said Darwin, glancing at Eyrún, who shrugged and began tapping on her mobile. "Why would that matter?"

Before Max could respond, Eyrún jumped in. "No. It's signed by a judge in Marseilles, err...José Antigua."

"Him!" Max snorted. "I've heard, if you toss enough euros in his direction, he'll sign anything. My guess is, you've been set up."

"Fuck!" Eyrún yelled at the ceiling. "No wonder our lawyers are saying the court won't respond."

"They will, but likely not for a year or more. Listen, the freeports are clandestine vaults, untouchable by authorities. And it sounds like the gang's got its hooks deep into Thierry."

"I hate this. What're we supposed to do?" Eyrún asked.

"I recommend you call my colleague in the OCBC Paris branch, Detective Paul Nisard," said Max.

"He's OCBC. How can he help?" Eyrún huffed, throwing her hands up and shaking her head.

"I hear your frustration, Eyrún, and I can understand you not wanting to trust anyone in the ODBC, but Paul runs a covert operation inside the department. His team recovered paintings belonging to the French president's grandmother that were pilfered during the war. Trust me, he's been given carte blanche at the highest level."

Darwin and Eyrún looked at each other. She shrugged her approval, and he said, "Thanks, Max. We appreciate it."

"No problem. I'll message Paul that you'll be calling. See you on Tuesday."

Shortly after they disconnected, Darwin's mobile chimed with the contact data.

"What do you think?" Eyrún asked.

"Jasmin and Thierry must've been planning this for months."

"No. I mean, do you trust Max?"

"Richard and Gavin say his reputation is solid, and everything he's done so far's been on the level. I'll call this guy."

They spent a few minutes discussing what to reveal in the conversation, and Darwin also agreed to use his back channels to verify that Paul Nisard was legitimate. When he had their story straight, he tapped the number. As it connected, Eyrún's mobile rang.

She answered, "Hey, Barry," and moved across the room as Darwin's call went to voicemail. He was about to leave a message when she shouted, "What? Hang on, Barry, I'm putting you on speaker…" She turned back to Darwin. "Something's wrong. Barry's at Lupita's flat. She's not there."

She put her mobile on the table and said, "Okay, Barry, go ahead."

"Like I said, I stopped to pick up Lupita this morning as we arranged, but she didn't answer my texts or call, so I went up to her flat. The door was slightly open. I knocked and called out, but no answer, so I went in.

"She's not here. I'm no expert, but it looks like a struggle took place. Chair's overturned. Her backpack and mobile are on the floor. Either she ran out in a hurry, or—God, I hope not—someone kidnapped her."

54

E yrún set a personal record racing down the mountain while Darwin white-knuckled the passenger handhold. He trusted Eyrún's ability but reflexively held his breath on most corners as the fat rally tires squealed. Twelve minutes later, his heart rate settled as the harbor traffic slowed their approach near Lupita's building.

They arrived shortly after the gendarmes and were stopped by an officer at the door. They could see the other flic inside, questioning Barry.

"Stay out here until forensics arrives," said the gendarme. "Your colleague has already contaminated the scene. We will take his prints to distinguish him from any others left in the room."

"What happened?" Eyrún asked.

"*Je ne sais pas.* How do you know the victim?" said the flic, turning the questioning on them.

Darwin answered, as Eyrún's fluency still had gaps and their lawyer had advised against engaging in legal discussions in French. Fifteen minutes later, the forensics team arrived, donned their bunny suits, and went inside. They dismissed Barry, who joined them on the outside balcony.

"This is just terrible," he said. "I'm no expert, but it looks like a scene you'd see in a cop show."

"Her mobile and backpack are inside?" Eyrún asked.

"Yes. The mobile is on the area rug, like someone tossed it there."

"Jasmin! It's got to be," Eyrún hissed.

"If so, she must've had help. Lupita's no pushover. She told me about growing up in a tough neighborhood in Kenya,"

Darwin called Zac. When he got voicemail, he messaged:

need to talk to you about Jasmin

Barry and Eyrún talked in the background as Darwin called two more times. He swiped to the find friends app. "*Putain!*" he muttered.

"What?" Eyrún asked.

"Zac's on the southern road near Casalabriva."

"He kidnapped Lupita?" asked Barry.

The three looked back and forth at each other with mouths agape as if their brains could not fathom Barry's question. "No," Darwin and Eyrún said simultaneously.

"You two know Zac better than I," said Barry, "but the other day, Lupita told me Jasmin had him wrapped around her little finger."

"Where could he be going?" Eyrún asked. Her tone had shifted to action mode.

"There's a harbor in Propriano." Darwin held his mobile so they could all see it and reopened the app. *Merde. Where'd he go?* He zoomed in and out on the map. His eyes met Eyrún's. "He turned off his mobile."

55

"Bonjour," Jasmin said as she answered her mobile a little after nine a.m. A moment later, she added, "*D'accord*," and ended the call. She turned to Zac. "Ready when you are."

He carried their bags down to her car, threw them in the rear hatch of the Mini Cooper, and got in the driver's seat. She had told him earlier. "I don't feel like driving,"

Twenty-five minutes later, they were rolling through the hills of southwestern Corsica and passing small villages. Jasmin pulled back the sunroof, cranked up the music, and thrust her arms up into the wind. The swaying beneath her halter top drew Zac's eyes from the road.

He reached a hand across, but his mobile interrupted—Darwin's ringtone. "Shit. What now? Don't answer it," he said, caressing her through the thin fabric. The device buzzed twice more with incoming messages and then rang again, thoroughly destroying the moment.

"Maybe something bad happened. Can you read the message for me?" he said, placing his hand back on the wheel.

Jasmin grabbed his iPhone and held it in front of his face to unlock it. Then she read the first message.

Darwin: need to talk to you about Jasmin

"Surprise. He wants to talk about me," she said.
"Same bullshit. What's the other one? It beeped twice."
Jasmin angled the mobile away from Zac and read it.

Darwin: she's using us. the guy on the megayacht's her father not her ex.

"Just where are you?"
"Screw him. Turn it off. I've had enough of their accusations."
She coolly erased the text before powering off the device. "There," she said as she put it in the glove box, "we're off the grid." Then she leaned over and nibbled on his ear. "Let's be naughty."
Zac did his best to keep the car in their lane while Jasmin's hand roamed up his thigh.

56

Darwin's mobile rang. "It's the OCBC guy from Paris," he said and turned away to take the call.

"Barry, can you handle this?" Eyrún asked, referring to the police.

"Yeah, no problem. You two get after Zac."

Darwin followed Eyrún as she rapidly descended the stairs. One hand was on the railing as the other pressed his mobile tight to his ear. "Sorry, Paul, we're in a stairwell. Say that again."

Once outside, he slipped into the passenger seat, and then Eyrún steered them onto Cours Napoléon around the harbor. He recounted to Paul what had happened in the last few months. Then, tapping speaker mode, turned to Eyrún. "Hey, love, what are the officers' names from the Marseilles OCBC?"

"Koranyi and Gandlarz," she said.

Paul Nisard's voice came back. "I thought so. They're taking bribes from César Olmeta, but we can't prove it. What did your lawyers say about the case?"

Eyrún ran through a general status, avoiding anything he could not find out from the court documents.

"That would take care of the law, but Thierry's a dangerous man. He'll come at you another way," said Paul.

"He did. He's kidnapped one of our staff," said Eyrún.

"I'm sorry to hear. You need the local police."

"We know," said Darwin. "Is there anything *you* can do to help us?"

"We need hard evidence tying Thierry and César to forgeries and cultural trafficking," said Paul. "I know this sounds risky, but if you do exactly what Thierry wants, my resources can put him away."

Darwin muted the call and looked at Eyrún. "What do you think?"

They drove in silence as the idea gathered weight.

"Did I lose you?" asked Paul.

Darwin unmuted. "No. I think we agree. Tell us how this would work."

Paul suggested a plan, and Darwin replied, "Got it. I'll text you at this number when they make contact again."

57

Zac eased the car over the lumpy single dirt track and back onto the main road. He adjusted his shorts and then rubbed a shoulder, itchy from pine needles. He had pulled off into a copse of trees when Jasmin's teasing had threatened to run them into a ditch. Looking at the ground, she had said, "I'm not lying on that," so he had volunteered. Urgent need had won over discomfort. Now the tortured pleasure of her riding him with abandon as needles dug into his ass seemed less sensible.

He reached into his waistband, pulled out a stray needle, holding it up as evidence of his sacrifice. She thrust out a lower lip in sympathy and then lifted her halter, rocking her shoulders as a visual salve for his wounds.

"Oh, no," he said. "Next time, it'll be on a soft mattress in Bonifacio." She laughed, settled her top back in place, and then looked in the side mirror while flouncing her hair.

Zac glanced at her and smiled. Her hair streamed in the wind, and her skin was mildly flushed from their tryst. His own afterglow had soothed his earlier vexation with Darwin's incessant calling. But as he drove, the sentiment crept back into his thoughts. *What the hell's with them? Can't they see she's the victim of her husband's bullying? He's a thief, dragging her down.*

Yesterday he had found Jasmin in tears. "What have I done?" she had asked him. "I've been nothing but honest. Yes, I had to go to the yacht, but I refused to answer his questions about the ACA. And now they're running a background check."

But now, as he drove, one question perplexed him. *Her ex wants something the Albanian Master stole from him. But she's getting divorced, so why does she care?* He asked, "Just curious, but why do you care about the Albanian Master?"

She tensed and, turning to face him with a fevered stare, said, "the son of a bitch killed my mother."

58

On the road, an hour behind Zac, Darwin called Marc Denis while Eyrún passed slow traffic at every opportunity.

"*Bonjour*, Marc. Has anyone seen the megayacht since it left?"

"*Desolé*. I meant to call first thing today, but I got a boat with a leaky bilge."

"No worries."

"Jacques Tambeau said he saw it last night, anchored about a half-kilometer from Bonifacio. He arrived in port this morning after two days of diving for clams off the south coast. Can we talk later? It's madness here with the tourists."

"Sure, this is good enough," said Darwin.

They disconnected after Marc offered to ask his cousin in Bonifacio to alert them if the megayacht moored in the harbor. Darwin said thanks and fiddled with the map, scrolling to the southern tip of Corsica and zooming in. He found a road to a village that would give them a view of the surrounding coastline where the megayacht had been sighted, and he entered it into the Macan's nav system. Just under twenty minutes later, Eyrún slowed as they neared the turnoff. The maquis hugged the shoulder so tightly they could hardly see any openings.

"There!" Darwin pointed. Eyrún braked hard and eased the car onto a rough road just wide enough for vehicles to pass each other. Darwin felt like someone was throwing punches from beneath his seat as the racing suspension picked up every lump and crack in the pavement. Six minutes later, they reached the village, a collection of homes that had seen better days.

They parked and traversed a wooden path to an observation point. Scanning the horizon, they could see many pleasure craft but nothing large. "What about closer to shore, where we can't see?" Eyrún asked, pointing to inlets in the undulating landscape.

"Too shallow. I've explored most of them. Great secluded beaches but too risky to take a deep draft vessel."

"Bonifacio?"

"Maybe. But—"

Eyrún's mobile rang. "Hi, Barry." A long moment went by, and Darwin leaned in close. In response, she tapped speaker mode, and he caught the words "...open it?"

"Yes. Read it to us," she said, turning to Darwin. "An envelope arrived by courier a few minutes ago."

"Here goes," said Barry. "We have Lupita. Get us the location for the Albanian Master. You have twenty-four hours. That's it. Jesus Christ! Who are these fucking people?"

"Our sentiments exactly. Is there anything else?" Eyrún asked.

"No. Just those three sentences on a plain piece of A-four. The envelope just has your name and the ACA's address. What should I do? Where are you?"

Darwin jumped in to update him on their journey, and Barry agreed it was worth looking for the megayacht in Bonifacio. "Get the police to raid the goddamned boat. Lupita's got to be on it."

Eyrún had the car started as Darwin climbed in, and then they moved up the rough road at what seemed a snail's pace. Once on the highway, she gunned it. "How far?"

"About thirteen kilometers," said Darwin.

Nine minutes later, the road sloped downward, and the number of homes, small hotels, and restaurants increased as they approached Bonifacio Harbor. When they swept around a turn, the hills fell away, opening into a wide plaza teeming with summer tourists. Eyrún slowed. "How are we going to find them?"

They stopped in a pull-out midway across the plaza to get their bearings. A large car park lay across the road on their right, and the long, narrow harbor to their left cut between steep hills on its way to the sea. The pedestrian area, dotted with palms, spread between the harbor's sides, each lined with terra-cotta-topped buildings. Pleasure boats of all sizes crammed the closely arrayed docks.

"Anything look like the megayacht?" asked Eyrún.

"No," said Darwin as he closed the car door. He had run to an information booth to get a local map, saying it had been over a decade since he had been here. "But it could be anchored farther down where it bends near the citadel. It's almost two kilometers to the mouth."

He spread the map between them. "You can see the harbor serpentine its way toward the strait, but most of the tourist places are toward this end. They will probably be on this side." He pointed to a long, thin peninsula on the map and then out the window at the busier side of the harbor. "They'll be staying in one of the hotels along the water or one inside the old city up there."

"Why not the megayacht?" Eyrún looked out the windscreen at an enormous stone-block rampart whose side facing the harbor looked like a ship's prow. At this distance, the smooth white structure built atop the ridge appeared small until she compared it to the buildings at water level.

"Not likely. Remember, Jasmin still wants Zac thinking Thierry's her manipulative ex-husband."

"Then why bring Zac?"

"Dunno. Maybe protection until she gets away?"

A gendarme tapped on their window, gesturing for them to move along. As Eyrún pulled out, Darwin said, "Drive up to the citadel. The road tunnels under the wall." She looped around the plaza and ascended the road along the backside of the hotels. Homes abutted the right side of the lane, leaving bare limestone on its left, where home-owners had cut garages into the cliff.

They paused where the road topped the cliff at the citadel's base and craned their necks to look at its ramparts. A horn from behind got Eyrún moving. As they rounded the prow, the road split left into a tunnel and right down to the harbor. "Go right," said Darwin. At the harbor's edge, they stopped in the parking area designated for ferry traffic and peered down the crowded quayside.

"We need to do this on foot. They could be anywhere in the restaurants lining the harbor. Let's go back to the car park and walk back. If they're not there, they'll be in the old city. There's a pedestrian gate near where we stopped back there."

Eyrún agreed, and a few minutes later, they entered the car park. As they rolled toward its rear section, Darwin said, "There! That's Jasmin's car. A red Mini Cooper, right?"

"Yes."

They found a spot two rows over and, after peering inside the locked Mini, moved toward the restaurants. The scorching July sun turned the harbor into a reflector oven, and sweat rolled down Darwin's temples by the time they entered the shade along Quai Jérôme Comparetti.

The narrow lane ran between the building's ground-floor restaurants and quayside tables. Darwin searched their insides while Eyrún scanned the outdoors. A half-hour later, the restaurants petered out near the ferry landing, and they worked their way up Montee Rastello, looking in the shops on the steep path to the citadel. Finding nothing, they crossed the road and mounted the steps leading to a heavily fortified gate under the towering eastern wall.

E yrún walked along a tight street deep in shadows, relieved to be out of the heat. The buildings were a hodgepodge of reconstructions, some with smoothed walls, others bare stone, but most in an in-between condition. Modern communications wiring affixed to medieval construction was the only giveaway that this was the twenty-first century.

To her, this felt like looking for a needle in a haystack. What had seemed clear during the drive was now obscured by the reality of an ancient town full of hidey-holes. The next block had a long, unbroken wall on her left, which she figured must be the church. A glance at the map confirmed it and showed the plaza with cafes at the next intersection. She messaged Darwin:

Almost at plaza. Find anything?
Darwin: no. three cafes. no Zac. moving toward you
Eyrún: Okay. I'll wait for you in the plaza.

Darwin moved toward Eyrún as he scanned another cafe, cautious to avoid being seen first and spooking them. He knew, if they went deep indoors, they would never find them in this maze. Her earlier questions came to mind. *Why bring Zac along? If they have Lupita, why does Jasmin need him?*

A heaviness settled as he wondered how his friend could have been so thoroughly deceived, but then he realized his own misguided pursuit with Tessa Santarossa, how he had naively accompanied her to the Siwa Oasis with no rational plan or backup. It was Zac who had saved him then. *I guess it's my turn now, buddy. Think. If I were Zac, where would I go? I'd want a room overlooking the water.*

The seaward edge of the old city sat on a cliff, the rampart protecting the town from attackers. Small hotels offered rooms that opened directly onto the sea. He was turning toward the dot on his mobile that marked Eyrún's location when her ringtone sounded. He answered.

"I found them at a cafe in the plaza," she said.

"Okay, wait for me."

"Too late. He saw me. I'm going over."

"Wait!" But she had disconnected. *Merde!* He pocketed the device and sprinted to the plaza.

59

"Shit!" Zac jumped up from their café table.

"What is it?" asked Jasmin.

"I can't fucking believe she followed us here." He strode across the square to intercept Eyrún.

"Zac—"

"I don't want to hear it, Eyrún. You're out of control."

"She's not—"

"No," he said, waving his hands like he was warding off a curse. "No. I'm done."

Jasmin screamed, "Zac! Help!"

He pivoted to see two large men wrestling her away from their table. He recrossed the distance in seconds. Eyrún followed, yelling, "Thierry's her father!" but at that moment, Zac was shouldering one man off Jasmin. The guy hit the ground hard, and Zac spun behind Jasmin's back, grabbed the other man, and took him down.

Eyrún arrived, and Jasmin jumped behind her as Zac rolled to his feet. He grabbed a steak knife from a nearby table. The first thug, shaking off his fall, stumbled toward the women. The guy facing Zac reached behind his back.

"Gun!" yelled Eyrún, and she hurled a café chair at the man's gun arm. The weapon clattered across the cobblestones as patrons scattered.

"Jasmin, run!" shouted Zac. He dove for the firearm and reached it just as the man did. The gun discharged, exploding a shop window. Eyrún grasped a wine bottle off a table and moved to help Zac as a body dove into the scrum, driving the thug off Zac. The gun tumbled away again, and Darwin got to his knees.

"Get Jasmin!" he yelled, and Eyrún spun to see her exiting the square with the first thug in pursuit. She sprinted after both, tossing the bottle in a planter box.

Zac got the gun and pointed it at the remaining thug, who thrust his palms out and shouted, "Don't shoot!"

Shouts came from across the square. "*Arrête!* Police! Drop the gun!" The second thug spun away and ran in the opposite direction, drawing one cop with him.

Seeing the gendarme's weapon, Zac palmed the gun, barrel up in surrender, and tossed it wide. The cop's attention followed the gun, and Zac ran into the crowd of patrons. Darwin followed, but Zac knew speed was not among his friend's talents.

"Dammit!" Eyrún hurdled a postcard stand flung in her path by Jasmin. The thug had cut down a side alley, where she caught a brief flash of sky. She refocused and closed the gap, channeling her university days as the anchor on a champion eight-hundred-meter relay team.

Jasmin slowed and jumped left into a side street. Its gap was just wide enough for two people. Eyrún checked her stride and made the turn but collided with two bins. *Shit!* She spun and pumped hard, her eyes fixed on Jasmin just meters away, and yelled, "Where's Lupita?"

A blur from the left hit her, slamming her into the wall. She bounced off and tumbled, and her head banged the pavement. *The man!* Stars spun as she scrambled to her feet and unsteadily bounced off the opposite wall, ignoring the pain in one knee. She looked ahead and stopped cold.

Gone! Where the hell are they? The alley ended at a waist-high wall. She lunged toward it and looked over. Jasmin and the thug were in the water, twenty meters below.

60

Z ac followed the overturned objects Jasmin and Eyrún had left in their wakes. When the trail got confused, he yelled, "Gendarme! Which way did they go?" He knew from street combat that people never questioned, just pointed. *Unless they're on the bad guy's side,* his training reminded him.

"Zac!" yelled Darwin, now thirty meters back.

He ignored his friend and turned to where an older couple was pointing. He vaulted two bins, wincing at the rotting fish splashed on the path. Eyrún lay sprawled ahead of him, and she struggled to her feet as Jasmin topped a wall at the alley's end and dropped from sight.

"No!" he yelled as the thug followed her over. *Shit!* He had thought about the plunge earlier while peering over their hotel balcony —*Doable if you avoided the rocks.* He aimed for a spot to Eyrún's right. Just as she looked back, he sprang off his stronger left foot and pushed off the wall top with his right. Then he was flying over the sea, arms waving and legs, spinning for balance while he targeted a landing spot.

Fuck! Panic surged as the crystal clear water appeared far shallower. He aimed as best he could for a deeper spot, pressed his legs together to avoid a hammer blow to his crotch, and, arms in tight, clamped his hands together over his nose.

He hit the water with the force of a car wreck and thrust his arms out to create drag. His knees crumpled on impacting the sea bottom, and he rolled until his back thudded into a rock. He winced, but the liquid absorbed enough force to soften the collision.

Holy shit! He shoved back a vision of landing in a shallower spot and sprang up, pulling with his arms. His lungs screamed as the mirror surface seemed to stretch away. Finally, he broke the surface and sucked in air. Three huge breaths. Then he spun, found the cliff, and twisted back to find Jasmin. As he treaded hard to move higher in the water, he saw two heads at ten o'clock, maybe four meters distant.

"Jasmin!" he yelled and swam over to her, but his high-tops dragged like anchors. In his days as a Ranger, Zac had trained to the point of collapse. Survival meant needing to know one's range. Too hard, and you pass out. Not hard enough, and—*Not today. C'mon, Zac, dig.*

Darwin's and Eyrún's voices rang out from the clifftop, but they were unintelligible in the thrashing water. *Something about a boat,* Zac thought. He adjusted his stroke and lifted his head forward. *Shit!* They were pulling Jasmin into a bright orange Zodiac. *Have to get there!* He surged forward, and his vision tunneled as his body channeled oxygen into his burning muscles.

An arm slammed into rubber. He popped up and grabbed the Zodiac's side rope while sweeping salt water from his eyes with his other hand. The dark hole of a large handgun pointed between his eyes. The thug he had hit first in the square said, "Get in the front of the boat, Zac. Try anything, and the first bullet goes in Jasmin."

"Zac! Zac! The Zodiac!" Darwin and Eyrún yelled as they frantically pointed at the craft powering toward him. Darwin moved to the top of the wall, but Eyrún tugged him back. "That's stupid. We can't help him."

He flashed hot, but then he realized it was a dumb move. "Oh, crap. There's the megayacht." He pointed at the vessel cruising through the Zodiac's wake. It had motored into view from behind Bonifacio's peninsula.

"Zac!" they yelled again.

"He saw us," said Eyrún when Zac turned briefly, but he kept going.

They watched as the Zodiac cut its engine and the man on board hauled in Jasmin and then the thug. The man waited a few seconds for Zac to catch up and then used a gun to subdue him.

"Oh, Zac," Eyrún cried out mournfully while turning to Darwin. "Get down." She pulled him into a crouch beside a wheelie bin. "There's a flic at the intersection, turning this way."

Darwin pressed his head against the wall and watched the cop from a gap behind the bin. "He's on his radio and coming down the alley."

Just then, an older woman called to them from an open third-floor window. "Hey, you, behind the bins." When they looked up, she pointed at a door three meters to their left. "Go in there and wait," she said.

Eyrún started first and pulled Darwin inside. "Ew," he said as he slipped into a dark space a little over a square meter that smelled of cleaning chemicals.

"It's this or them," she said.

Through a small window, papered over except for scratches, Darwin saw two gendarmes pass. He put an ear to the door and heard the woman tell them about some crazy people who had jumped into the sea. A long moment passed, with the only sounds coming from Eyrún's breathing and his own heartbeat whooshing against his eardrums. Then a loud radio burst announced the people had been picked up by a tender and taken to the yacht, now powering away.

"What do we do?" asked one gendarme.

"Unless you can fly down to that yacht, they're gone. Did you get a good look at the guy with the gun in the square?"

"No."

"Then go interview the people who saw him."

Darwin watched them pass again, and Eyrún asked, "How long should we wait?"

A minute later, a rap at the door brought him back to the window, where the woman waved them outside. They followed her to the same alley where the thug had crashed into Eyrún, and she said, "You need to leave quickly. I don't like the police. Bunch of boys never got out of puberty. Follow this street and go left at Rue du Clocher. Then take a quick right onto Rue du Corps de Garde. It ends at the Mémorial du Passé Bonifacien. From there, you can find your own way under the bastion."

"I know it. Thanks," said Darwin.

Eyrún handed her a hundred-euro note. The woman refused, but Eyrún insisted, and the woman took it with a smile.

As they walked away, Eyrún asked Darwin, "You follow all that?"

"Yes." And, at the first intersection they passed, he looked at the sign mounted on the building. "This is Rue Doria. An old friend's grandparents lived down the block."

They walked at a normal pace, and Darwin took her hand so they would appear to be a normal couple out for a stroll. The deep shadows tempered the hot air, but its stillness increased the claustrophobic feeling of the tight street.

"I need water," said Eyrún, putting into words the tacky sensation in Darwin's mouth. They passed a section permeated by the aroma of cooking sausages, which reminded him that he had never properly finished breakfast and would likely not be having lunch anytime soon.

A minute later, they reached the street's end and entered a wider space at the memorial's entrance where a handful of people sat at cafe tables. They crossed under the bastion through the same tunnel they had entered and ran down Montee Rastello. The number of tourists had increased in the last hour. *Good for cover*, he thought. But shortly after turning onto Quai Jérôme Comporetti along the harbor, he pulled Eyrún into a shop.

"What're you doing?"

He put a finger to his lips as he led her behind a clothes rack and pointed. A gendarme outside the shop's window moved toward the door and stayed there. Darwin and Eyrún stepped into a dressing room and peered around its drape.

"We've lost them," the gendarme said into his radio.

"Stay in place for another half-hour. They'll have to cross that location," a voice crackled from the radio.

"Merde!" Darwin rolled against the changing room wall, considering their location relative to the car.

Eyrún peeked at the flic again. Then, shutting the drape, she asked, "How're we getting out of here? Our only options are the quayside path and the upper road."

Darwin closed his eyes and visualized getting around the harbor. "I got it. The train."

"Train?" Eyrún's face went blank.

"Yes. Drives on the street. You know, like you've seen in zoos. Anyway, it runs from the car park into the old city and back. We can catch it on the street at the top of Montee Rastello."

"That works, but what about him?" She pointed toward the gendarme camped by the door.

"Easy. If he looks in here, shout." Darwin walked around the counter and asked to borrow the phone. He called the local police dispatch and said he was a waiter at La Caravelle restaurant and had just seen the man the police were looking for.

Not a minute later, the cop's radio crackled, and he took off in the direction opposite Montee Rastello. They beat a path up the steep street, and, when Darwin caught up with Eyrún, she asked, "How long before the train?"

61

Z ac fell beside Jasmin in the Zodiac's bow as the pilot shoved the throttle and swung hard toward the cliffs. He swiveled around to see a man descending a stairway cut into the limestone. "That would've been easier—"

"Shut up. No talking!" yelled the pilot.

The man on the stairs plunged into the rough water and swam toward them, and, when the first thug hauled him aboard, Zac recognized him as the other thug who had attacked Jasmin in the square. As the small boat pulled away, its engine echoing off the cliff, he focused on the men in the Zodiac. The two he had bested in the square had middling skills, but the Zodiac's pilot was untested. He appeared cut from similar cloth, but the gun more than tipped the odds in his favor.

Zac turned to study the approaching megayacht, estimating its size as about equal to that of a small navy frigate. Its three wraparound decks above water each had ample windows. As they closed within thirty meters, he scanned for security staff but only saw a man and a woman emerge from the interior and descend to the swim deck. *Crew,* he assessed from their casual dress, white shorts and collared shirts with gold epaulets. The man shouted to them in a Russian dialect, "Who is he?"

"The boyfriend. He followed us," said one thug.

Zac had learned basic Russian from working a joint Ukrainian operation early in his Afghan days. Unfortunately, his ability to visually judge his captors ended with a blindfold as soon as he set foot on the swim deck. He widened his stance against the loss of a visual horizon and let awareness flow into his other senses.

The surrounding conversations focused on stowing the Zodiac and another thug telling a crew member to get Thierry. Moments later, Jasmin yelled, "Leave me alone!" He smiled, as, from the slapping sounds, she seemed to be fighting like an alley cat. Then Thierry must have arrived, because she let loose a tirade worthy of a drunken sailor, screaming, "Leave me alone! I signed the goddamned papers!"

More struggling led to Thierry saying, "Stop it now, or he goes over the side." Zac felt hands on each arm, and they partially lifted him. The command had an immediate effect, as Jasmin went quiet. "Good," Thierry continued. "The same goes for you, Zac. Cooperate, and I won't hurt her."

"What do you want?" asked Zac.

"Take her away," said Thierry.

"Zac, I'm sorry," said Jasmin. Her voice sounded small, like that of a child speaking to a bully.

All went quiet. Zac could feel the sun's heat move across his body, and he guessed the yacht was turning. A voice from his left said, "Move." Then it instructed him to step up a short stairway to the main deck. They walked a short distance, and the hands turned him. "Sit."

Zac's calves sensed an object, and he lowered himself onto a cushioned seat. The sound of wood on wood scraping was followed by Thierry's voice. "What do I want? I thought I have been clear, Zac, but maybe your friends are not as smart as they think."

When Zac did not respond, Thierry moved closer. "What I want is for your friends Darwin and Eyrún to complete my request—find the Albanian Master. I asked nicely...well, with some unpleasant legal leverage, but they seem to think throwing their money around can get them out of the ACA's embarrassing situation."

"Why can't you find him yourself?" asked Zac. *Keep it neutral. Let him talk.* The first rule of captivity—survival—meant understanding your captors, letting them know you will comply and help them get what they want.

"Believe me, I've tried, but the Mediterranean's vast, with thousands of islands. I had almost resigned myself to letting him go, but he has something of mine that I need as collateral."

"How can Darwin help you?" Zac tried to imagine what the man looked like. His voice flowed like a hypnotist's. His English was perfect but with a heavy French accent.

"Zac...both you and I know he has an uncommon ability to find the unfindable. And he's acquired powerful resources. But they think this is a game. I even sent Jasmin to help them get started, but she failed, so I engaged an alternate strategy. And now look. You've volunteered yourself as another hostage. I'm sure Darwin and Eyrún will do their utmost to find me the Albanian Master."

62

Darwin scanned the road toward the citadel as a taxi coming from the lower harbor stopped at Montee Rastello to let out passengers. As the last person exited, Eyrún got in. "Let's go," she said, pulling Darwin's arm. He slid in beside her and closed the door.

"Car park, please. We're in a hurry," Eyrún said to the driver and held two twenty-euro notes over the seat. The man took the cash and shot down the hill. Two minutes later, she and Darwin bolted from the car, and he paused at a street vendor. "I'm getting water. Bring the car around."

She did, and she barely stopped as Darwin hopped in, dumped four water bottles on the front carpet, and secured the seatbelt. Then she cut into the stream of cars and headed back toward Ajaccio as fast as traffic allowed.

Darwin opened a bottle, handed it to her, and snagged another for himself. After slaking his thirst, he said, "Let's not make a habit of running and jumping in the car."

"Be glad it's not a horse."

"Tell me that's not another of your secret talents."

"Horses? No. They smell." Her phone chimed, and she asked the in-car system to read the message.

"You have two new messages. Shall I read them?"

She grunted. "Yes."

"Message from an unknown number: 'We have them both. Your twenty-four hours to give us the Albanian Master's location is down to twenty.'"

"Shit! How the hell are we going to find him in twenty hours?" she asked.

When the digital voice asked if she wanted to reply, she shouted, "No!" and stomped on the accelerator, taking them to 180 kph before downshifting into a series of curves.

"Didn't the assistant say there were two messages?" asked Darwin.

"Siri, read the second message," Eyrún said.

"Message from Barry Hodgson: 'Lupita left this photo and a note in my office. Sorry I didn't see it yesterday. She put in under a pile. Call me when you get this and I'll read you the note.'"

Eyrún ignored the question about replying. "Darwin, look at the photo."

Darwin picked up her mobile and tapped the image in Barry's text, enlarging it to full screen. A woman and a girl stood before a dark cliff about three times their height. Bright sunlight bore down from a clear, pale sky and, combined with fading from age, washed out the color. He pinched the image.

"Merde! Look at this. No, pull over. You need to see it close."

She stopped in a turnout and manipulated the photo. "The woman looks like Jasmin. Wait, so does the girl. Jasmin and her mother? What's this about?" She looked at Darwin, who shrugged. Then she said to the in-car system, "Call Barry Hodgson."

He answered on the first ring. "Eyrún, where are you? Have you found her?"

"No. Well, not exactly." She filled him in on their chase, Zac's kidnapping, and the message that they had both Lupita and Zac now. "We're assuming they're both on the megayacht."

"Dammit," said Barry.

"I got the photo. What's the note say."

They heard rustling over the phone's speaker as Barry said, "Let me get my glasses. Okay. Here we go:

```
Barry,
I wanted to run something by you that's
making me suspicious.
Jasmin came by with a photo, asking if the
algorithm could find its location. I agreed,
thinking it would be a good test of the
system and our searches for looted sites.
The photo is of a woman and a young girl
taken in the 80s (see attached). Jasmin said
it was her mother and sister. When I asked
why she could not ask them the location, she
said they are dead and she wants to find
their burial place.
Then she asked me to keep the search between
us, but she was emphatic about telling no
one. Why would it be such a secret?
Lupita
```

"That's it," said Barry.

"I understand Lupita's suspicion. If Jasmin's looking for her mother's and sister's graves, why keep it between them?" asked Eyrún.

"Wait," said Darwin. "Zac said Jasmin doesn't have a sister. She's an only child."

"That woman's smarmy. No wonder Lupita doesn't trust her," said Barry.

"Jasmin's got to be looking for something else at this location. Maybe her mother's grave, but why would she lie about a sister?" asked Eyrún.

"No idea," said Barry. "I've already turned Lupita's office upside down. There's nothing else related to this. What else can I do to help?" said Barry.

"Dunno yet, Barry," said Darwin. "We're on our way back and should be there in an hour."

They disconnected. Eyrún continued studying the photo as the car idled like a slumbering dragon. "Something about this." She looked up at Darwin. "Jasmin's from Lebanon, right?"

"Yeah."

"Well, this photo's not taken there. Look." She zoomed in tight on the dark rock formations. "This looks like basalt, but it's much younger than anything in Lebanon. I'd say it's from an eruption during the Holocene and maybe more recent."

Darwin understood geology in vague terms. As an archaeologist, he knew the Holocene as the age when modern humans started cultivation and built cities, but little beyond that.

"She's lied to us about everything: her business, her father. She's not looking for a sister. This is her and her mother," Eyrún said as she continued to scroll around the photo. Then she repeated what Barry had read, "Jasmin's looking for the place this was taken."

"Maybe that's why she's been so curious about the bust?"

"What?" She jerked up in her seat.

"The bust. It's basalt, right? She asked me once about the style, trying to narrow if it was Greek or Roman. Said that would help determine where it came from. I didn't—whoa!" He gripped the passenger handhold as Eyrún shifted in gear and the Macan fishtailed in the gravel until grabbing the pavement.

"Dammit. I should have done it before. I kept thinking it wasn't important," she said as they flew over the hills towards the ACA.

"What?"

"Examined the basalt. All rocks have a signature. Its composition can help us narrow down its origin, at least its geographic region."

"You think—"

"Yes. She remembers this place. There's something there."

"Or someone," said Darwin, bracing for a corner.

63

In just under an hour, they reached the ACA and ran upstairs to Eyrún's office to get the bust. Darwin followed her as she carried it to the lab and set it on a worktable. After a preliminary study, she said, "I have to break off pieces to sample it."

"Sure. I don't care if you grind it up if it helps find them," he said.

She chipped pieces from its base and a curl of carved hair and then studied each under a microscope. Darwin sat on a stool a few steps away, turning the sculpture in his hands, admiring its lifelike lines and striking proportions.

He looked up at a tinkling sound. Eyrún was stirring a solution in a beaker, and he refocused on the sculpture, rolling it upside down. He traced the aleph with a finger, seemingly in a trance. *Who made you? The Albanian Master, or did someone copy your signature?*

But he sensed there was more to the mystery. *This isn't just a practice piece.* A lengthy amount of time had gone into its creation. He set it upright on the bench and stared into its eyes. *Why carve you in basalt? Surely, marble would have brought a higher commission?*

And why bother shipping it to Rome? His only clue was the partial waybill he had found in the warehouse, which listed Alexandria and the letters YRNM. Weeks ago, he had gone through guessing names for initials and then anagrams, but he had arrived at nothing convincing. Now he reconsidered. *A cipher? If I were someone creating an ancient code name, I would...* His brain rolled through all the cipher techniques and codes he knew from antiquity.

Interrupting his flow, Eyrún said, "I need the spectrograph to do this right."

"What?" He looked up.

"I need to run a slice of this through infrared and other wavelengths to get its chemical signature. All rock has a taxonomy, the same as organic life. I can see it's a fine-grained igneous rock, but it's also a vitrophyre because of its porphyritic texture."

"Huh?" His brow scrunched as her words flowed past him like they were in a foreign tongue.

She added, "It's full of phenocrysts, large crystals in layman's terms. It looks peralkaline. A spectrographic analysis will tell me which kind."

Wait! A language! He returned to the bust and started writing on a blotter atop the bench, a mental exercise he used to jog ideas.

YRNM which language?

Then he wrote:

Greek
Assyrian
Egyptian
Roman
Hebrew

"Canaanite!"

"I've never heard of Canaanite," said Eyrún.

"Sorry, it's a language, not a rock. Why didn't I see it before?" He tapped rapidly on his iPhone.

Eyrún's eyes went wide in a "Tell me" expression.

"YRNM is the ancient Canaanite word for Kossyra." He opened a map on his mobile to a wide blue swath of the Mediterranean Sea between Sicily and Tunisia. Then he zoomed to a tiny island not far from the African coast. "Here. It's modern Pantelleria."

Eyrún grabbed her mobile and typed furiously. Then she went back to the microscope. She looked back and forth between the eyepieces and mobile before announcing, "It's a peralkaline rhyolite, but from Pantelleria, so it's a pantelleric rhyolite, or pantellerite for short. Brilliant!"

She turned to the satellite view of the island on Darwin's mobile. "I remember pantellerite from university. It's not rare, but not common, either. You can find it in Canada, Antarctica, Ethiopia, but it's named for Pantelleria in the Strait of Sicily."

She brought up the photo of Jasmin and her mother again and zoomed in on its rock. Then she compared it to the highest zoom on Darwin's mobile of a formation on Pantelleria.

"Can't tell anything from this. Hand me the bust."

Darwin reached for it but misjudged the distance and knocked it over. The bust rolled off the bench and hit the floor with a thud. "Shit!" He jumped from the stool.

They squatted to examine the carving, which had split into two main pieces and scattered fragments about. Each half had a cylindrical borehole that had been sealed expertly at the bottom. Eyrún reached for a small paper scroll lying in one half. "What's this?"

They stood together, and she laid the scroll on the benchtop. Darwin pressed a finger on one edge of the tight scroll as Eyrún unrolled it. The paper contained a series of boxes with names and lines that connected in a hierarchy. "It looks like a family tree, but the names make little sense," said Eyrún.

"It's an organogram."

"A what?"

"An organization chart." Darwin pointed to a name they both immediately recognized.

64

J asmin sat on the rear sundeck of the megayacht, watching its
wake trail into the distance. The churning azure water settled to a
smooth surface before the wind tugged at it, erasing their path. As
the yacht made a slow turn to port, the sun angled in from behind her
sunglasses, obscuring the view of a broad-shouldered young man
setting a drink on a table beside her. "Your cocktail, Mademoiselle
Panchon."

"Thank you," said Jasmin, uncrossing her feet and swinging her
legs off the chaise lounge.

"Monsieur Panchon asked me to tell you that dinner will be at half
past eight in the Manet salon." He bowed slightly and then turned to
leave.

She watched him pad across the teak decking, his deep brown skin
contrasting with his white shorts and shirt. As he mounted the steps to
the upper deck, his glutes flexed beneath the shorts. *Must be him*, she
thought. Earlier, her father had said she would like the new man.

"Didier?" she called out to him.

He stopped on the third step and looked back. "*Oui*, Ms. Panchon."

"I'd like to have my drink on the flybridge. And, please, call me
Jasmin."

As he walked back, she stood. Her white cotton coverup fluttered in the breeze, and her skin tingled as she left the heat of the cushion. Didier put the drink back on the small silver tray, and she caught him studying her breasts. He smiled, covering his glance, but she wondered, *Maybe not.*

She returned the smile, locking briefly on gray eyes that, combined with his thin nose and angular face, told of his Bedouin ancestry. Then she led the way up the stairs, knowing the thin green material of her bikini left little to the man's imagination.

By the time she reached the flybridge, she felt the need for the iced cocktail, partly because of the sultry Mediterranean air, but also from imagining his eyes on her thonged bottom. She stretched out on the padded bench across from the captain's chair. Didier pulled out a small table and set the drink down. "Will you need anything else, Jasmin?"

"Not at the moment, thank you."

"As you wish." He turned and left the flybridge.

But maybe later, she thought as she watched him descend.

The sun hung over the northwest horizon, and the warm breeze whipped her hair back. She shifted stray strands behind one ear as she sipped the delightfully cold cocktail, a French 75, its savory gin kicking in behind the lemon-tinged Champagne.

She sucked an ice cube as the alcohol kindled a fire in her belly and she wriggled into the cushion. Another sip, and, moments later, a soothing wave radiated through her, lightening the day's tension. She savored more of the drink and reached for a sore neck muscle, digging her fingers into it while recalling the jump and swim in Bonifacio.

Dammit! Zac was not part of the plan. *Well, he is now.* Two hostages gave them more leverage. She removed a faded photo from a pocket in her coverup and flipped her sunglasses atop her head to study it. She recalled the man taking the picture but could not recall his name. No one had called him the Albanian Master then. It had been made up later.

She thought back to the day it had been taken. Heat radiated like an oven as she stood with her mother near a cliff. Or at least, it seemed that way to a six-year-old. A few days later, she was back in Lebanon, in the care of friends, when the police came. Her mother had been killed. Someone showed her a picture of the man who had taken the photo by the cliff, and they wanted to know where he was.

A series of images cascaded, and she slipped into its stream, dragged along surging rapids: a woman saying, "She's dead"; a building full of kids, knowing no one; a man they called her father taking her away; a crowded city.

A hollow quivering in her gut replaced the alcohol's warmth. Rapid memories assailed her of growing up in Paris but traveling months at a time, never able to sustain friendships. All the while, she longed for affection, but her father remained distant, cold, always searching for something. In her later teens, she learned his true obsession—a golden mask—stolen by a man who had also killed her mother.

For months afterward, she lived in a haze, experimenting with alcohol and drugs. She had sex for the first time and craved the closeness it made her feel, but the relationship failed, and she tried a series of others. When an accidental overdose landed her in the hospital, she vowed to turn over a new leaf. She focused on school and soon discovered that she could win her father's attention by aiding him in his search.

The more she helped Thierry, the more he seemed to love her, praise her, give her the warmth she hungered for. In her university years, he introduced her to wealthy clients, and her ability to coax them into making ever-larger purchases from their galleries won even more of her father's devotion. In time, her father's vengeance became hers. And now, closer than ever to finding the Albanian Master, her chest tightened, and her breaths came faster as she imagined her mother's voice: "Avenge me, darling."

"I will, Mama," she said, and one white-knuckled hand squeezed the railing as she visualized coming face to face with the man who had deprived her.

65

Zac heard a door close behind him, and he pulled off the blindfold. He assessed the small room, functionally appointed but likely crew's quarters, as it lacked luxury. He tried the door. Locked. But he estimated it could not withstand a hefty kick.

He pulled off his wet shoes and stripped, wringing out his clothes in the tiny water closet. After hanging everything to dry, he went to the fixed window above the mattress. The sea rushed past roughly a meter below and stretched to a horizon that contained nothing but water. He lay down and planned his attack. *There's got to be a weapons locker aboard. Probably a panic room as well.* His training had briefly touched on yachts, but with limited detail.

One part of his conversation with Thierry perplexed him. *What did he mean, another hostage? Jasmin? But who's he holding her hostage from? She's divorcing him. Maybe he's forcing her to spy as a condition for signing the divorce papers?*

His muscles tensed as he envisioned getting Thierry one on one on the bow and dropping him into the surging water to be sucked into the screws. He grinned. A moment later, he thought of Jasmin. *She's probably in an upper-deck cabin.*

The engine's thrum and post-adrenaline rush drew him into the soft bedding. He replayed meeting Jasmin and dancing at the club. While their relationship had started purely sexually, it had developed. *Hadn't it?*

But then he paused on something Darwin had said: *You have to admit, the coincidences are piling up: her arriving right before the raid and knowing all about this Albanian Master character.*

He had blown it off. Coincidences did not mean connections. But now, as a captive, the special-forces-trained part of his brain began assessing the situation, exploring all plausibilities. *Could I have gotten this wrong?*

66

Darwin and Eyrún stared at the flattened organogram under a piece of Lexan.

"Gavin assembled one of these to connect who was involved in the banking scandal," said Darwin. "It shows the players involved, but also the transaction flows."

"It doesn't appear overly incriminating," said Eyrún. "No evidence that links anyone to a crime."

"No. You're right. It's disappointing. Why go through all the trouble of concealing this inside a carving."

"Maybe there's some kind of code in it?"

"Dunno." Darwin leaned in and examined the paper.

Eyrún read a text block in the lower right corner. "What's this? Banco di Trapani 173."

"A bank address?"

"But there's no street name."

"A safe deposit box—where's the key?"

They looked at each other and then at the two halves of the bust. Then they turned to the lab floor, where tiny pieces of basalt still lay scattered about. Darwin switched on the overhead lights and joined

Eyrún on hands and knees. He lowered his face to floor level and scanned with the beam on his iPhone.

"Here it is." Eyrún flattened herself and reached under a cabinet along the wall. She stood and returned to the workbench, where she laid the key next to the scroll. "I wonder what's in that box?"

"That depends on how big it is."

They split up again. Eyrún scanned Pantelleria for locations for Jasmin's photo, but even the island's small size, ten by six kilometers, left far too many possibilities. The entire island was basalt, having been created from an undersea rift in the Strait of Sicily 100,000 years ago.

Darwin had an easy time locating the Banco di Trapani in the Sicilian city of the same name. Zooming in on a street map showed a small building whose façade mimicked the structures of ancient Rome, including four Doric columns.

They stopped work with a call to dinner, which Barry had volunteered to bring them when he learned they had hardly eaten all day.

67

As they finished the meal in the second-floor break room, Darwin rubbed the outside of his left knee. With a full belly, his brain alerted him to a nagging pain he guessed had occurred during his fight with Zac and the thug.

Eyrún dabbed her mouth and said, "That was delicious, Barry. Tell Zoe she's an amazing cook. And she grew all the vegetables?" Their meal had begun with heirloom tomatoes, drizzled in a vinaigrette and sprinkled with basil, before moving to a veal and figatellu sausage pie with a side of ratatouille.

"Yes, and she's quite proud of the bumper crop. There's never enough sun to coax this harvest out of the Newcastle soil. She's gone to town with Corsican cookbooks, too." Barry patted his middle.

Darwin stood to gather the takeaway containers, but Barry told him to leave them. "We need to answer them tonight."

The three walked to the computer lab. All four of Lupita's screens scrolled through photos from Kenya. Eyrún tapped the main keyboard, waking up the system, and entered the master password that Lupita had given her for emergency access.

"Do we know what we're looking for?" she asked.

"Start with Jasmin," said Barry.

She typed "JASMIN" in a search block, which returned three results: the photo of Jasmin and her mother, the document Lupita had written for Barry, and a file none of them recognized. She clicked on the unknown file, and a window opened with a dashboard for an application: a dial labeled "Percentage Matches" showed zero point three. A clock listed hours running at ninety-eight, and its seconds ticked in real-time. Other blocks on the dashboard showed rapidly scrolling text.

"Makes no sense to me," said Barry.

Darwin pointed at the text. "It's a visual of her algorithm. This text shows files it's searching, but I'm sure she didn't know about Pantelleria when she entered the search parameters. Maybe we could give the algorithm a hint."

"I don't know how to do that. Barry?" asked Eyrún.

"Don't look at me." Barry waved her off. "Lupita's the genius. Zac maybe could do it, but they're on the yacht together."

"Wait. That's it," said Darwin. Eyrún's and Barry's expressions implied, "What's it?"

"We tell them Lupita and Zac are the only ones who know how this algorithm works." He pointed at Eyrún. "We say you've looked at the bust and can only tell it's some kind of, I dunno, general basalt that could come from any island from Greece to Sicily. Keep them thinking about the Eastern Mediterranean."

"Okay," Eyrún said tentatively.

"It's worth a try," said Barry.

They determined what to say, and Eyrún messaged the number from earlier that she had saved as Thierry:

We need more time. Only Lupita & Zac know the algorithm. The bust is a normal crystalline igneous rock. Could be anywhere in eastern Mediterranean.

Six minutes went by. Darwin checked the time again, eighteen twenty-three, and stood to go to the toilet. Eyrún's mobile chimed as soon as he stepped into the hallway. He ran back.

Thierry: You need to do better than that Eyrún. Aren't you a famous volcanologist? You still have 16 hours and I hope you have a better answer in the morning.

"Shit!" Eyrún stamped her foot.

After another two hours of trying to figure out Lupita's program, Barry suggested a break. "It's been a helluva long day. Let's rest and give our story a think. Hopefully, the algorithm magically spits out a location overnight."

They agreed, and Eyrún and Darwin headed to Maison Lacroix, where Emelio kept a room for them. If anything happened overnight, they wanted to be closer to the ACA.

"Eyrún, how are you?" said Emelio, hugging her as they entered the foyer. She sighed heavily into the old man's embrace, which had always brought comfort. Three years ago in Scotland, when people had crowded Darwin about their discovery, she had been left standing apart. As she had shivered from the cold and trauma, Emelio had taken her in his warm arms and said, "You're safe now, Eyrún. It's okay. You're safe."

A similar wave now melted the tension in her neck and shoulders. His arms squeezed as if drawing darkness from her body, somehow accessing an emotional layer that words could not penetrate. She inhaled in his loosening grip, feeling light and energy flow in. As they pulled apart, his hands slid around to her shoulders and paused, and his bright green eyes twinkled above a knowing smile. The moment passed in less than a minute, but Eyrún felt as restored as she would have after a week's holiday.

"How about a nightcap?" asked Emilio. "Help you relax."

"I'll get it," said Darwin. "I have something in mind."

Emelio raised his eyebrows and, as Darwin disappeared into the cellar, nodded toward the sitting room.

"Thanks," Eyrún said. He squeezed her hand.

She fell into her favorite chair, whose angle seemed to create an anti-gravity field with just the right combination of softness and support.

"That was my wife's favorite chair," Emelio said.

She knew. He had told her at least half a dozen times. *He won't be with us forever.* A brief shroud of sadness dampened her mood.

"Tell me what's going on," he said. "Darwin told me about the kidnappings before you drove over."

As Eyrún was bringing Emilio up to speed on the last few days, Darwin returned from the cellar with a half bottle and three small glasses. He pulled its cork while Eyrún described finding the organogram and key in the broken bust.

"What's this?" Emelio asked, taking a glass from Darwin.

"Something I remember seeing in the cellar. It's a Passito di Pantelleria. This one's from the Donnafugata winery. I had forgotten about it until Emelio mentioned nightcaps. It's the Zibibbo grape from the Muscat family and originally from Alexandria. They grow it across the Mediterranean, but mainly in the Sicilian islands. *Santé.*" He clinked glasses, moving between Eyrún and Emelio before taking a seat.

Six hours ago, Eyrún had a vague knowledge of Pantelleria, and now she was staring into a glass of amber liquid that had come from the volcanic speck off the Tunisian coast. She sampled the nectar. Intense, aromatic fruits, as if candied and drizzled over citrus, flooded her palate. But it was smooth, fresh, not overly sweet. She drank again, letting the wine slide down her tongue and catch every taste bud until a reflexive swallow carried it down her throat, where the alcohol warmed her insides. Between the hug, the chair, and the wine, she wanted to suspend time.

But reality pulled back hard as Emelio said, "I've been to Pantelleria. My search for lava tubes took me there before you were born, Darwin."

She sat up. "Would you recognize a place on the island?"

"I don't know. It's been so long."

Darwin dug the photo from his tablet's case and handed it to him as Eyrún explained what they knew about it.

"It doesn't look familiar, but, if I remember correctly, there's a ridge that runs along the island's northeast from a massive ancient caldera.

This cliff face," Emelio said, tapping the photo, "could be that part of the island."

Eyrún finished her glass. "I need to wash my face. Get ready for bed." She stood, said goodnight, and then headed for the stairs.

"I'll be up in a minute," said Darwin. She paused on the first step when she heard him say to Emelio, "Thanks, Grand-père. She loves you."

"You know, she's the best discovery you've ever made."

"I know."

She floated up the steps, knowing she was exactly where she wanted to be.

68

Once dinner was cleared away, Jasmin followed her father to the aft deck, where he had a cigar. As the smoke drifted in the moonlit wake, she asked, "What did you want to talk about?" The yacht cruised into the swells on just enough power to counter the sea's motion.

"Eyrún messaged me a little while ago. Said they don't know how to work on the woman's computer system. I told her she needed to do better than that." He paused to draw on the cigar, and then he huffed out a smoke ring that lived briefly before being swept away. He smiled as if pleased with the effort. "What's your opinion?"

Jasmin knew there was more. The man loved toying with people; she had been an object of it herself before becoming a student of his manipulations. "I saw you laughing while you texted. What else did you tell her?"

"That she, being a famous volcanologist, should be able to do much better and to text us back in the morning with an answer."

"Did she say anything else?" Jasmin knew Eyrún to be serious and, while a savvy negotiator, not likely to bluff when people's lives were in the balance.

"Something about igneous rock in the eastern Med and an algorithm. Maybe she doesn't know more, but I want to push her. Let's find out what she has to say when the twenty-four hours are up."

Jasmin looked over the side at the black water flowing along the white hull and she turned from the railing. "I watched Lupita set up the algorithm to search using the photo. She typed a lot in some unintelligible code. It's plausible that only she knows how to do it."

"They must have someone else."

"Yes, and he's in the cabin below, next to Lupita."

"That's a problem. What if we let one of them go? Tell them they have to find the location or the other one goes for a swim."

"Which one?"

"Let's decide tomorrow."

E yrún awoke as the sky lightened, and she lay quietly in bed, watching the last of the stars twinkle out. Darwin breathed softly beside her. The wide double-casement windows had been opened all night, and the morning air carried the fragrance from the neighbor's rose garden. Emelio's friend Mateo, a regular champion in the annual Ajaccio competition, grew several dozen varieties in the wide space between their homes. She rolled her feet to the floor, grabbed a throw blanket from off a chair, and wrapped it around her shoulders as she walked to the window.

The light pouring in over the mountains had chased the darkness to ground level. Science ruled her world, but she could see the appeal of believing in sun gods and underworlds. It lent a magical mystery to life that data-driven explanations left dry and mechanical. In the growing dawn, the paler roses emerged first, tinged with purple and yellow. She inhaled the perfumed air, teasing her senses, and stretched the moment as long as she could to hold away the day's impending decisions.

Upon waking, it had been clear to her that honesty was the best course of action. *This isn't a game. Our friends' lives are at stake.* She would tell Thierry about Pantelleria, but she could not narrow it further. Emelio's comment about the ridge helped, but if she told them,

Thierry might do something rash, like cut off communication and search the ridge himself.

She decided to get Lupita and Zac involved. She was not sure how, but her navigational studies of her yacht, *Hypatia*, had taught her that modern vessels teemed with sensors that left a trail like digital bread crumbs. *And so does Thierry's sat phone.* She smiled wryly. Behind her, the sheets rustled.

"Good morning, love. Did you sleep well?" she asked.

"Surprisingly, yes. What about you?"

"Not bad at first, but I woke a while around three. Hope I didn't disturb you."

He stood and joined her at the window. Sliding his arms around her, he rested his chin on her shoulder as they looked at the roses. "I don't know how Mateo does it, producing such magical blooms year after year."

"They're beautiful."

"So are you." He kissed her neck. She closed her eyes and tipped her head back, thinking of his and Emelio's comments last night as she had paused on the stairs. His hands lowered to her hips.

"Not now," she said, gently covering his hands with hers. Their fingers intertwined, and they stood for a few moments longer in the calm. The darker roses morphed into red as the sunlight crested the mountain and fanned out across Ajaccio.

They showered after a quick run along the harbor to the citadel and back. As Darwin got dressed, his stomach growled loudly at the rich aromas drifting through the house. He headed downstairs and found Emelio in the kitchen, chopping herbs.

"*Bonghjornu,*" he said.

"*Bonghjornu!* It's another beautiful day," said Emelio. "I know you two need to find your friends, but you'll need energy." He waved the knife at chestnut polenta as he sliced sausage into a pan.

Fresh croissants wrapped in thin paper lay on another cutting board next to a jar of Mateo's rose jam. Darwin's palate leaped, teased by a riot of yeast, figatellu, and hot butter. He tore a piece from one croissant, spooned on a bit of jam, and popped it into his mouth.

Eyrún walked in with a towel across her shoulders to protect her top from her damp hair. *"Bonghjornu,* Emelio. You're a godsend. I'm starved."

He said good morning, adding that she was a feast for the eyes as he cracked the eggs into the pan. Minutes later, they were sitting in the breakfast nook, Darwin eating like a wolfhound, when Emelio asked, "What have you decided?"

"We tell them *we think* it's Pantelleria based on the lava's signature, but it could be another island" said Eyrún. "We don't disclose what Darwin deduced about Kossyra. And we say that Lupita's algorithm will narrow it down but we do not know how to operate it."

"That's good," said Emelio.

"We ask them to release either Lupita or Zac to come back and modify the program."

"Which one?" Emelio looked back and forth between Darwin and Eyrún.

"Ideally, Lupita, as it's her code," said Darwin. "They'll have to come into a port. If we can get them to Corsica, the OCBC guy, Paul, can seize the vessel."

"Do you think it will work?"

"Thierry wants the Albanian Master. I think Jasmin's smart enough to figure out hurting Lupita or Zac buys them nothing."

They worked the idea over the remains of breakfast then headed to the ACA. Eyrún messaged Barry that they would arrive about seven thirty, giving them three hours before the twenty-four-hour deadline.

As Eyrún, Darwin, and Barry sat at the small table in her office, she stared at her mobile, willing it to respond. "Why doesn't he answer?" She had messaged Thierry just after eight o'clock. "I hate waiting,"

"Don't we all," said Barry.

Moments later, her mobile chimed.

Thierry: A better answer. But maybe Pantelleria? Why "maybe"?

"Good. He's grabbed the bait," Darwin said as Eyrún tapped a reply:

The bust is made from a pantelleritic rhyolite found in the Sicilian island chain. Can't be certain which island, but Pantelleria is far enough off the grid and still accessible.

When Thierry did not respond after a reasonable wait, she added:

Lupita's program can narrow down which island, but only she knows how to run it. Let her come back here. When she finds the Albanian Master, release Zac.

"Let's see how that flies," she said. Seconds later, her iPhone rang. She punched the green button. "Thierry?"

"Eyrún, it's Lupita." Her voice was shaking.

"Lupita. Oh, my God. I'm so sorry this happened to you. Are you okay?" Eyrún asked.

"Yes. They are not mistreating me, but I am standing on the back of the boat. They said they would push me in the water if you did not help—"

Lupita screamed.

"Lupita?" Eyrún yelled. "Lupita?"

Jasmin's voice came from the speaker. "She's still here, but I've moved away from her. The less she knows, the better, and we want you to know who's in control."

"Where's Zac?" asked Darwin.

"Darwin? Good, you're there. Zac's fine."

"He cares about you, Jasmin."

"That's sweet."

Eyrún wrote on a sheet of paper between them:

ask about Lupita

Darwin read it and said, "We can help you find the location in the photo, but we're not lying. We really can't do it." He paused a few beats and then added, "Only Lupita knows the algorithm. Let her come back here to tweak it. Keep Zac as a hostage."

"That's so nice of you to offer your friend's life, but we need to discuss it. Right now, Zac thinks Thierry has kidnapped the both of us."

Eyrún leaned in and was about to say something when Jasmin's voice came back at them.

"Zac will figure out his situation soon enough, and his military training will make him a difficult hostage. However, we might be willing to trade Lupita for someone."

Darwin tapped the mute button as he looked at his wife.

Eyrún's stomach churned at the memory of her captivity in Egypt. A tingle surged down her neck and arms as she remembered awakening in alien surroundings, ignorant of her captor's language. She shuddered but refocused on Lupita. *This is my doing. I convinced Lupita to move to Ajaccio. I hired Jasmin and signed for the vases. I need to fix this.*

She inhaled, steeling herself to volunteer, but then Barry suddenly said, "I'll go. Lupita's like a daughter. Zoe and I sponsored her into the EU."

"Barry, you can't. It should be Darwin or me—"

But he unmuted the call. "Jasmin, it's Barry. I'll trade with Lupita."

69

J asmin stopped Thierry on the swim deck steps after the call. "Wait," she said. "You made your point with her. Let me talk with her over breakfast. Alone. We need her skills."

"What about my breakfast?"

"Have it anywhere you want. I'll keep her here a while, and you can talk to Zac. Get a sense of what he knows about Lupita's program."

"Good idea, darling. We'll compare notes later," he said and turned to a crew member to request that a light breakfast be brought to his study.

Jasmin continued to the breakfast table on the aft sun deck, where Lupita was eating in silence. While filling her teacup, she tried to gauge the other woman's mood. *Is she in shock? No. She's eating. But she's scared and doesn't know what's going on.* Jasmin knew well the feelings of having one's sense of familiarity and stability torn away and not knowing what would happen. She decided to talk to Lupita as one victim to another. "I'm truly sorry this happened to you. I had no idea my ex would do this."

Lupita stared at her plate, so Jasmin added, "If you help us, I'll get you out of here unharmed."

"What do you want?"

"I need to find the place in the photo. Eyrún has narrowed down the search to an island off the Sicilian coast, but they can't update the algorithm and need your help."

"Well, I cannot do that from here, can I?"

Jasmin smiled. "No, of course not. I suggested to Darwin that you tell him what to do, but he pointed out that only you could do it, or maybe Zac."

"Zac doesn't know the algorithm."

"Could you explain it to him?"

"No, I coded it in Python. He does not know it."

"I thought it was something like that." Jasmin reached for a croissant, adding, "I told Thierry it was stupid to kidnap you."

As Lupita huffed and looked out to sea, Jasmin chewed and refilled her cup from a small silver pot. After a mouthful to clear her palate, she said, "They need you back in Ajaccio. Barry offered himself as a hostage in trade."

Lupita's eyes snapped back to Jasmin's, who continued. "Now comes the tricky part. We need to swap you two without the authorities getting involved. I don't trust Darwin and Eyrún not to try something, so we need you to convince them to cooperate."

"How do I do that?" asked Lupita.

"Simple, really. We have Zac as a hostage."

Lupita froze.

"He followed me to the yacht in Bonifacio. I told him not to, but he insisted, and Thierry locked him in a cabin below."

When Lupita said nothing, Jasmin went on. "I need you to convince Eyrún and Darwin to leave the police out of this when we exchange you with Barry. You go back to your system in Ajaccio and find the location in the photo. Then we let Zac and Barry go—unharmed. If not…"

"There is no need to threaten my friends. I was helping you before."

"I know, Lupita. I know. I told Thierry that, but he…" Jasmin paused, looked around, and then leaned in. "Please help me, and I'll get you all out of this. I promise."

As Lupita was led back to her cabin, Jasmin began plotting her trade with Barry. She chewed the inside of her cheek as she considered her most immediate problems. *Zac will figure me out soon enough and try to break out.* She had seen the yacht's thin walls during remodeling. *We'll need to double the guards on his section.*

Her other problem was Thierry. *He's becoming irrational. His ego's getting more and more in the way.* She groaned at his ludicrous partnership with the Marseille art gang.

70

Zac stood at the second knock on his cabin door. Earlier, they had brought breakfast, one thug with a gun forced him to sit on the bed as the other left a food tray on the desk.

"Housekeeping this time?" asked Zac.

The same thug waved him back to the bed and moved against the wall as Thierry entered, followed by another thug, who blocked the door.

"Good odds. Three against one. But you'll have guessed my first move is to take out the gun."

"Sit down, Zac," said Thierry. "Jasmin told me about your constant joking, but if you want to get yourself killed, go ahead. One less complication. We only need Lupita."

"What?" Zac tried to project calm, but his mind raced. *Lupita's here? Why?* One leg reflexively stepped backward and hit the mattress.

"Yes." Thierry smirked. "She's in the next cabin. We kidnapped her the morning you and Jasmin left Ajaccio. You see, Eyrún and Darwin stopped cooperating, and we needed more leverage, but we seem to have made a minor miscalculation in thinking Jasmin could get away from you."

Zac sat on the mattress like a deflated balloon, his heart racing at the image of Lupita being seized against her will. He had seen the panic in too many hostage situations. *She doesn't deserve to be caught up in this.* He shifted topics. "What have you done with Jasmin?"

"She's in her room. I'd let you see her, but you've proven to be a distraction from what I sent her to do."

"I want to talk to her."

"You're in no position to make demands," said Thierry. "But perhaps an information exchange will change my mind."

Bingo! He needs something. "What would you like to know?" Zac asked in a neutral tone. Sound disinterested, one special forces instructor had said.

"Lupita's computer thingy is searching for a location in a photo. How does it work?"

"Which photo?"

"That's not important. Will you help me, or do we force it out of Lupita?" Thierry nodded to the thug by the door, who moved into the hall.

"No. Wait," said Zac. "I was just curious. Let me explain."

Thierry called the man back, and Zac continued. "It's a simple concept. The software scans a photo into millions of digital pixels and then compares those pixels against other photos and ranks them from best to worst. Ideally, the best photo has what you seek: an object, person, or location. Humans still do it better, but just imagine holding a photo in one hand and comparing it to millions of photos—it would take you months."

"So, can Lupita's program do this faster?"

What's he driving at? If the algorithm's running, why kidnap her? There's more going on here. "Yes and no."

"Stop fucking with me, Zac." Thierry stepped towards Zac, stopping a body length away, and stared down at his face. "I told Eyrún that Lupita goes overboard unless I get a result."

"I'm not messing with you, Thierry." Zac put his hands up in surrender and then leaned away as he studied the man's reactions. *He's desperate. And desperate people do crazy shit. Bring this back down.*

Calming his voice, he continued. *"Yes,* because the machine's much faster than humans, but also *no,* since a huge dataset requires a lot of time to analyze. And it's also not a straightforward process. The algorithm learns as it goes, gets smarter, so to speak, by reworking its evaluations. It only takes milliseconds per photo, but if there are a billion photos, that's a bunch of time. I can explain it in more detail, but that's the gist."

Thierry dragged over the desk chair and sat facing Zac. "Where do these billion photos come from?"

"Anywhere, really. People post hundreds of millions a day in various clouds, Instagram, TikTok, you name it."

"How could you make the computer go faster?"

"You narrow its search criteria based on what you're looking for, say an object or a person. Are you looking for the Albanian Master?" Zac watched Thierry's face closely for a reaction to his question.

"A place," said Thierry.

Cool as a cucumber, this guy. Zac held his answer a moment and then said, "Same technique regardless. For a place, you feed the algorithm a photo or group of photos from the region, along with search boundaries, like GPS."

When Thierry's eyebrows scrunched together, Zac jumped ahead of the anticipated question. "All digital photos have location data embedded. You'd tweak the algorithm to first sort by location, which eliminates millions, and then do a pixel compare of the remaining photos."

"Perfect," said Thierry. "I knew you would cooperate. Lupita may not need to go swimming after all. But she will need to tell Darwin what to do. Thank you for being so instructive, Zac."

As Thierry rose to leave, Zac's mind raced through the conversation, teasing out its essence. *Jasmin asked Lupita to find a photo's location, but she didn't know where it was taken. And—*

"You discovered the photo's region, didn't you?" he asked.

Thierry turned and smiled, but he said nothing more before leaving. The last thug closed and locked the door.

Shit! Darwin's no programmer. He has no idea how to update the algorithm. How the hell... Wait... He said Lupita's in the next cabin.

He looked at the walls. *Which one?* He knocked on each. Nothing. He removed a shoe and pounded its heel against the aft wall. Nothing. He did the same on the bow-facing wall. A knock came back.

"Lupita!" he yelled.

"Zac?" came a faint voice through the wall.

71

Zac found an air vent beneath the desk, and while its angled grate was secured by starred screws, preventing him from removing it, a faint light inside the duct suggested an opening into the opposite cabin. He squeezed sideways under the bolted-down desk and called Lupita.

"Zac! Oh, my God. I am so glad to hear your voice."

"Agreed, but I'm sorry that it has to be this way. How are you?"

"I am fine. Not so scared now. Jasmin just told me you were here."

"When? Tell me what happened?"

Lupita explained how she had had breakfast with Jasmin and how two men had pushed their way into her apartment as she had opened the door to meet Barry. "They had a gun and told me not to struggle. Then they blindfolded me and drove a long distance, maybe an hour. The last part was bumpy. Then they put me in a rubber boat and brought me here."

"Did you see anyone besides the men who took you?"

"No."

"When you were just up on deck, did you see any land?"

"Maybe to the west, but small on the horizon. I am not good with distances."

They speculated a couple of minutes on their time at sea. Zac noted the engines had been on low power and the light in his window had changed multiple times, like the yacht was cruising in a wide circle.

Lupita said she had talked to no one until she had been taken to the upper deck this morning. "Jasmin called Darwin and Eyrún. Barry's with them, too." She described what she remembered and then added details from her breakfast conversation. "That is when I learned they had you. They want to trade me for Barry. This is all wrong. Are they going to hurt us?" Her voice sounded about to break.

Zac put a hand to the grate, sensing her fright. "Lupita." He paused for her to acknowledge and then said, "It's all going to be okay. Trust me. I've been in much worse situations." He gave her a brief picture of his military duty in the Middle East, especially routing insurgents in Kandahar, Afghanistan.

"What do we do?"

"I need to know more about the yacht. Did you get a good look around?"

"I think so, but only the back part."

"Good enough. I'm going to ask you some questions. Close your eyes and place yourself on the rear deck with Jasmin. Can you do it?"

She said yes, and Zac asked her simple questions about the decking, furniture, and colors of the sky and sea before moving to more specific queries about the model of the sat phone and the radar array on the flybridge.

"Lupita, you have phenomenal recall. I would have loved to have you on my recon team in Afghanistan."

"I am on your team now," she said.

"Yes, you are." His energy soared as a plan coalesced. "Can you access the algorithm from outside the firewall?"

"Yes, but I need someone to open a port."

"Darwin can do it. He's played with some code as part of an ML project with the British Museum. Is a sat phone connection fast enough?" he asked, adding, "It's typically twenty-four hundred bits, but I might be able to get us ninety-six hundred."

"That would work," she said. "The algorithm is text based, and we could buffer the entries."

"Perfect. We could connect it to the laptop from here and keep Barry safe at home, but, Lupita, I need you to be brutally honest with me." He paused.

"Okay?"

"I'm very good at this kind of work and have never lost a Ranger, but they have guns, and this could get dangerous. I need you to tell me now if you feel you can't do it."

"I am scared."

"Scared is good. Keeps you alert. I'm scared, too. Can you work through being scared?"

"Yes. I would never forgive myself if I left and something happened to Barry."

"Good. Then let's beat these bastards. Here's what I think we should do. Give me your feedback, and let's work it."

She agreed, and they went back and forth on a plan that involved them convincing Thierry to allow them to connect a laptop with the sat phone.

Five minutes later, Zac stood and stretched, thinking through an alternate strategy. As much as he trusted Lupita's algorithm, he wanted a backup plan. While connected via the sat phone, he would contact colleagues in the OSINT, a global citizen collective that exposed what governments wanted to hide. The open-source intelligence community laid bare anything from illegal mining to political education camps to military downing of civilian aircraft.

Zac figured it would be child's play for them to track a yacht with hostages. He grinned while going into battle mode. *We're gonna need your eyes and ears, people.*

72

D arwin hung up with Paul at the OCBC. "We're set. The French navy is positioning two ships, one off Sardinia and the other north of Pantelleria, near the main shipping lanes. They'll wait for our signal and deploy their special-operations forces onto the megayacht."

"Will Zac and Lupita be safe?" Eyrún asked, and then she quickly added, "You, too, Barry."

Darwin nodded. "It would be lunacy for them to fight the French navy."

They worked through the plan again. Eyrún would pilot *Hypatia* to an agreed location where each yacht would deploy its Zodiacs, which would meet and exchange Barry for Lupita.

"As soon as the exchange is made, the navy will intercept you," said Darwin.

"Are you okay, Barry?" asked Eyrún. "You don't have to do this, you know. Darwin or I will do it."

"No. Lupita's my responsibility. I'm going."

"Then there's nothing for it but to wait," said Darwin.

As the three sat in Eyrún's office, Barry fidgeted with a small case with his things and some clothes for Lupita that his wife had grabbed from her flat. A half-hour later, Eyrún's mobile rang and she put it on speaker.

Jasmin said, "We changed the plan. Zac and Lupita came up with an idea that negates the need for a hostage swap."

The three looked back and forth at each other with blank expressions.

"Go on," said Eyrún.

"They'll use a sat phone hookup to a laptop to access the system remotely. Darwin?"

"*Oui.*"

"Zac says he needs you to open a port, whatever that means." When Darwin objected, she added, "Don't worry. Zac said he can talk you through it."

Before disconnecting, Jasmin told them to get ready for a call back within the hour.

"But I thought..." Barry started to say, but Darwin and Eyrún were already out her office door and running to the computer lab.

"Let's go, Barry. We still need you!" Eyrún yelled from the hallway.

73

*Z*ac and Lupita sat in an upper-deck guest cabin with a view of the sea, not that it mattered as they stared at a laptop with the room's shades drawn. One thug sat deskside as Thierry had instructed. Earlier Zac had been emphatic about getting the tech parts they needed after the yacht's engineer said, "Just use the Wi-Fi."

"Too many packets get dropped. We need hardwire for speed," said Zac. They ended up pilfering a micro USB cable from a crew member after the captain called all hands on deck.

Thierry had also requested a step-by-step talk-through of the operation, and Zac answered honestly, figuring he could hide any trickery in plain sight. "Some things have to happen fast, so I won't be able to explain each step in real time. I'm going to authenticate into my Iridium account—that's the satellite network—and then open a secure window to let Lupita access her system."

"The one at the ACA?" Thierry asked.

"Yes," said Lupita, glancing at Zac. They knew the servers doing the computations were scattered among various cloud data centers, but they had agreed earlier to keep it simple for Thierry and the thug.

Zac continued. "Lupita then calls Darwin on speaker mode to instruct him on how to open a port." Thierry raised his eyebrows.

"It's like one of the watertight doors below decks. When closed, it's sealed; nothing gets in or out. Same principle, but it's a software door."

Thierry stood behind him, watching as Zac opened a small black window with a blinking cursor. He typed:

```
AT+CBST=71,0,1
```

"What's that? Thierry asked.

"A scripting shell. I'm asking the satellite modem to make a faster connection. To leverage the cable I asked y'all to find." He patted the small black wire running between the sat phone and laptop.

"Good. It's done." Zac opened a web browser and keyed in an IP address, saying, "It's the same as a URL but faster from here. No need to use the internet lookup tables." Less than half a minute later, he added, "Okay, we're in. Lupita, you drive."

Zac vacated the chair, and Lupita slid into it and tapped Darwin's mobile number into the sat phone. "This call will slow us down temporarily, but once Darwin opens the port and we drop the voice connection, we will speed back up," she said.

Perfect, thought Zac. He stood a couple of paces to the side of Thierry and the thug so he could gauge their reactions. He and Lupita had planned a fast-paced execution: get into the algorithm as fast as possible and not let them linger too long on any step.

Thierry read off the GPS coordinates of the search area as Lupita's fingers flew across the keys, entering numbers. The thug double-checked the numbers she typed against Thierry's paper.

Zac thought it a brilliant move by Lupita, getting them involved. She now talked them through the dashboard display, mesmerizing the two as data scrolled at lightning speed in two boxes and an odometer-style counter ratcheted up the number of images scanned. A second counter moved more slowly.

Lupita pointed at it. "This one is the number of photos requiring a deeper scan. I set the parameters to thirty percent. Roughly, anything with a dark, cliff-like structure is sorted for deeper scanning, where it will look for a cliff *and* people. I programmed it to keep refining from there but always to use Jasmin's photo as the gold standard. That way, the algorithm learns."

"How long will it take?" Thierry asked.

"It depends on how many photos are geo-tagged in Pantelleria and if any match Jasmin's photo. But we should have a good idea of how this pass is working in about twelve hours."

As the thug led them back to their crew cabins, Zac secretly hoped it took at least twenty-four hours. While he had explained the need for his secure server, he did not say that it lived in the darknet among non-state bad actors and clandestine military, where his colleagues in the OSINT would find the ping he had dropped in the sat connection.

74

"What do we do now?" asked Barry after Darwin had completed the instructions to open the port.

A moment later, a window opened on the main monitor. "There's your answer," said Darwin as Lupita's dashboard mirrored itself in the computer lab. The data boxes scrolled text opposite the counters.

"Do you know what they mean?" asked Eyrún. "You did that ML project with Zac."

"This unreadable text is the search strings. It mainly lets us know the algorithm's working. This counter is probably the number of images scanned." He pointed to a rapidly spinning dial where the digits beyond the thousands columns were the only ones moving at a readable pace. He pointed at the other counter. "This is the one that matters. It's the images that fit the criteria."

"You mean it's the place?" asked Barry.

"Could be, but most likely, Lupita set a wide filter to capture images that broadly match Jasmin's photos. Then she'll refine the criteria, and, hopefully, we get a match."

"But we know it's Pantelleria," said Barry.

"True, but we don't know where on the island, and, given the whole thing is volcanically young, it could take weeks of driving around to find it," said Eyrún.

"Well, I, for one, am hungry," said Barry, and he offered to get food for them.

Eyrún went to her office to deal with a construction issue while Darwin leaned back in the chair and propped his feet on the desk. He scrolled through blogs while occasionally glancing at the dashboard. The French navy remained in play, with their plan calling for intercepting the megayacht in open water beyond Sardinia's international limit.

Three-quarters of an hour later, Barry returned with three niçoise salads. Darwin tucked in. Stress had never affected his appetite. As he used his knife to press the remaining bits onto his fork, his mobile chimed.

Paul Nisard: Problem. The yacht disabled its radar signal. We're blind.

"Shit!" Darwin tapped the browser on his iPad and looked at the vessel-tracking site. Dozens of colored arrows appeared atop the pale blue background, most near Corsica and Sardinia.

He called Paul and, after a greeting, asked, "Can the navy get a satellite picture?"

"They're trying, but they said their command won't redirect for a low priority target."

Darwin argued the point, but he ended the call after realizing Paul was doing all he could. He called Max for help.

"We have no influence over the Italian navy," said Max.

"What about the Swiss Guard? They chased the Vatican's oinochoe jug all the way to Switzerland."

"We were acting in an official capacity then. We have no clear connection to your friends' kidnapping. I'd be acting way outside my authority."

Darwin thanked him and ended the call. His heart pounded, bringing a headache with it, while he, Eyrún, and Barry studied the vessel locator. The most orderly arranged arrows indicated commercial vessels like ferries and container ships in designated shipping lanes. Between the Tunisia-Corsica gap where Pantelleria lay, these yellow and orange arrows flowed in tight eastbound and westbound rows. Other arrows in purple, green, and blue pointed every which way, mostly hugging the coastlines.

"Those are the pleasure craft and fishing boats," said Darwin. "The megayacht's last known location was here." He touched a spot on Sardinia's northeast coast.

"Well, they're eventually going to Pantelleria," said Eyrún. We'll catch them there. Darwin, check on flights." She scribbled calculations on a piece of paper. Then, after fiddling with the calculator on her mobile, she looked up. "Figuring megayacht's top speed is between eighteen and twenty-one knots, which they likely won't use, as it will burn a ton of fuel, they would arrive between ten and twelve hours at the earliest. But, given they turned off their satellite beacon, they'll run slow, especially at night."

They looked at Darwin, who said, "There are no good flights. The fastest option is seven hours with a layover in Rome, but it only goes once a day, and the next flight is tomorrow at three."

"So, our earliest arrival is ten tomorrow night?" asked Barry.

"Correct, but—" Zac's ringtone from Darwin's mobile cut him off. He grabbed it. "Zac!"

"Darwin la-croy?" an American-accented voice asked over the speaker.

"Who is this?"

"Maria Guttierez. I'm with Zac's former company."

"But it's Zac's number. How did you…"

"We spoofed the system to show Zac's caller ID. We picked up a signal in our sat network with Zac's fingerprint. It's a ping coming from a sat phone in the Mediterranean Sea. Does this make sense to you?"

Darwin let out a whoop. "Yes. Yes, it does."

M aria described to them how Zac had set up the sat phone to activate a program on a server in the darknet that would both track the phone's location and broadcast a signal—a ping. "Think of it like a flash from an ocean navigation buoy. It's a warning to anyone looking for it."

"Who's looking?" asked Darwin.

"Could be any number of people. I received an anonymous message this morning tipping me off to Zac's ping. What's going on?"

Darwin filled her in. "Oh, dear," she said. "How can I help?"

Over the next half-hour, Maria helped them connect to the sat phone ping coming from the megayacht, and they determined it had swung wide from Sardinia, east toward Italy. Darwin saw the algorithm had gathered several thousand possible photos and figured Lupita would soon adjust the search criteria.

He got an idea and ran it by Eyrún and Barry, who agreed it was worth a try. They called Maria back.

"Can you send a file to a place where Zac could get it and ping him to look there?"

"I think so. Let me check."

In the minutes Maria was away, Darwin wrote a short note as a cover to the file for Zac:

```
Background check from Vatican Security on
Jasmin. Darwin
```

Maria came back and said it could be done. Then she asked Darwin to forward his note and a link for the file. A minute later, she said, "It's done. If he's online, he'll get the ping instantly."

75

Jasmin used a second sat phone to study satellite images of Pantelleria, but between the slow speed and her vague idea of what she sought, the time proved fruitless, and she soon disconnected.

Nearly six hours had passed since Lupita kicked off the search and Thierry had brought her and Zac back to the upper cabin to assess progress. Thierry told Jasmin to stay away. "It'll just complicate things. Zac thinks you still care for him."

She had no problem complying because, unlike most of the assholes she had seduced for their business, she had grown to like Zac's company. *He's a nice man, more than just an object. Maybe in some other universe...* Her mind drifted into a fantasy where her mother was alive and both her parents had raised her. *If I'd met Zac then?* But after a few more seconds, she shook it off and focused on reality.

What's going on up there? she wondered. Then she thought, *Wait!* She realized she could eavesdrop on the conversation if she went into Thierry's office just off his master suite. Opening a panel next to the desk, she woke up a flat-screen display and, manipulating a mouse, brought up the video feed from the upper cabin where Zac and Lupita worked.

Four pictures filled the screen, one from each pinhole camera in the cabin's corners. The two sat before the laptop on the desk, with the thug adjacent to them in a lounge chair. No Thierry. She turned up the audio.

"—two to three hours, and we can narrow the criteria," said Lupita.

She and Zac were exchanging comments about the algorithm's functioning. Most of it meant nothing to Jasmin, but suddenly their conversation lowered. "Look at this," Lupita whispered. They glanced at the thug, and then Zac turned the laptop slightly toward himself, clicked with the mouse, and leaned in.

What's he doing? Jasmin turned up the audio as loud as it would go.

"It looks like a background check on Jasmin Kahn," said Lupita.

Jasmin flew out of the chair to find Thierry.

Z ac's eyes widened as he reread the document. His heart rate had settled after first becoming angered by another of Darwin's attempts to thwart his relationship with Jasmin, but the data in the report fit with everything he had experienced in the last forty-eight hours. The damning line was

```
Thierry Panchon is Jasmin Kahn's father.
```

His forearms tensed as he tried to control himself. *She used us, used me. Fuck! How did I not see this?* As a picture of manipulation formed, he said under his breath, "How could I be such a fool?"

"It could have happened to anyone, Zac," said Lupita.

He flashed on a memory of dismissing a fellow Ranger who had been seduced by an Afghani woman. He had thought him weak, but now, in a guilt-driven backlash of his own, he realized the dangers of the human heart.

The cabin door burst open.

"I told you to watch them!" Thierry strode to the laptop and pulled it away from them. He read the report. A minute later, he asked, "How did you get this?"

"The algorithm found it," said Lupita.

"Bullshit."

"You manipulating son of a bitch. How much does Jasmin know?" asked Zac.

Two other thugs joined them in the cabin as Thierry instructed them to bring Lupita and Zac down to the swim deck.

"I knew you'd be a problem, but I'm solving that now," Thierry said to Zac, who stood between two thugs, each grasping his arms. Thierry held a pistol loosely at his side. "I'll ask one more time. How did you get the file?"

"We—"

"Lupita, no!" Zac shouted.

Thierry swung the gun at her and pulled the trigger. She screamed. The bullet went wide, but she fainted and dropped to the deck. Thierry turned and made a sweeping nod at the sea. The thugs hurled Zac off the stern.

76

Darwin compared the vessel-finder website to the GPS coordinates from Thierry's sat phone. It had not moved in over an hour. Nothing else was close, and they speculated on the reasons, from lying low with the radar disabled to waiting on the algorithm to start a refined pass to narrow the location on Pantelleria.

"The screen just went dark," said Barry, who swirled the mouse in circles to wake up the monitor. "The power's on, but it looks like the program stopped."

Eyrún's mobile chimed. "It's from a different sat phone," she said, and Darwin and Barry pressed next to her to read it.

It's Thierry. Nice try. But Zac paid the price for it.

The device vibrated a second time with a video. She tapped it. "Oh, God." Eyrún cupped a hand to her mouth as they watched Thierry swivel and fire a shot and thugs heave Zac over the stern. He tumbled into the churning wake, one foot popping up briefly, and then the video cut off.

"Where's Lupita? He can't have shot her!" Barry yelled, adding with a growl, "I'll kill the son of a bitch."

Eyrún played the clip a third time, but they could not work out where the shot had gone. "Barry, that was Lupita screaming, wasn't it?" she asked.

"It's her."

"Was it before or after the shot?" asked Darwin.

Eyrún played it again. "After. Would you scream before or after getting shot?"

"Dunno," said Darwin. "I'd guess before, but...?" He looked at Barry as if he might have a better answer.

Eyrún called the number. No answer. She kept calling. "Answer it, you bastard."

"Barry," said Darwin. "Open Google Maps on Lupita's workstation and put in these coordinates. I'm calling Zac's friend Maria in California to get live satellites on this."

Barry zoomed out on the map, as the location was open sea. *Merde*, thought Darwin as Maria's line rang. A wave of dread ran through him as the maps showed that the Italian coastline was over a hundred kilometers from Zac's location.

The call went to voicemail. After leaving a message, he texted her to call immediately, telling her that Zac's life was in danger. Then he stared at the screen. *Why isn't the GPS moving?* "Barry, is the GPS right?"

"Yes, I double-checked."

Eyrún gave up calling. "Maybe they're bluffing. A fake shot, and then they threw Zac overboard and pulled him back in as a decoy. He sent the video to screw with us."

Darwin got Maria's voicemail again. "Merd—" His throat closed against the word, and his brain screamed, *No, no, no!*

77

As Zac went into the water, Jasmin ran to the starboard side, unfastened a life raft canister, and checked that its line was solidly cleated to the megayacht's hull. Just before rolling it overboard, she ran through the second-level galley to the sitting room with the laptop and grabbed the sat phone. Returning through the galley, she dropped down the short steps to water level and rummaged in a small locker for a dry bag. She checked that the sat phone was powered on before sealing it in the bag.

Once back at the canister, she stopped. *Shit! How do I get the phone inside?* Seconds later, her memory of the emergency-training exercise kicked in. *It'll open when it hits the water.* She opened a gate in the railing designed for the purpose and rolled the canister over the side. It hit the water and bobbed briefly before the line yanked, triggering inflation. After a small explosion, the raft unfolded, hissing loudly as it took shape.

In less than twenty seconds, the filled raft trailed alongside the megayacht's hull. Jasmin moved along the railing until just above the raft's protective tent. Its end flap was rolled against its roof. In an actual emergency, she knew passengers would jump in to stay as dry as possible. She leaned over the railing, holding the bag with the sat phone. *Don't miss.* She shoved down the thought and, with heart in mouth, tossed the bag.

It hit the raft's floor and skidded into its rear. Then she released the taut line from the cleat, and it zipped over the side as the raft disappeared into the yacht's wake. She let out a huge breath and sagged against the railing as she tried to gauge the time since they had thrown Zac into the water. *Maybe two minutes.*

A moment later, she hurried to the stern, passing two thugs carrying Lupita. Thierry laughed with another thug; neither seemed to notice the raft. She searched the water for Zac, but it was too dark to see more than a few dozen meters. *What if he doesn't find it?*

Gripping the rail above the swim deck, she watched the raft undulate in the spreading wake as the megayacht arced to starboard. They had been on low power, just a few knots per hour, due to the radar being turned off. She guessed Zac would be no more than two hundred meters back, and the calm air meant the raft would not drift. *He'll find it. He's got to.*

"Ah, Jasmin. There you are. We—"

"You bastard. I heard the gunshot." She jumped down the swim deck steps and got in his face. "What've you done?"

"Not here," said Thierry.

Jasmin gritted her teeth at her father's vain refusal to show any emotion in public. "Fine. After you," she said, stepping back and following him to his study.

Thierry paused at the study's door, and, when Jasmin walked in, he closed it behind her. She stopped in the room's center and pivoted, attacking him as he turned.

"When is enough for you? Now you've killed someone."

"He's not—"

"Cut the shit, Papa. You're deluding yourself if you think he'll swim to shore or be picked up by a fishing boat. You damn near killed Lupita, and we need her!"

"Darling—"

"Don't darling me. I'm not your little girl, and I haven't been for years. I built this company. Yes, you started it, but, while you were running around screwing our clients' wives, I turned the galleries into a formidable business. Now, in addition to risking it all for your golden bull obsession, you've committed murder."

"I—"

"I, I, I. That's you in a nutshell. It's always about you. Did you ever care for me?" She stopped, realizing the senselessness of the fight, and waited for a reaction, but she knew that Thierry's fetish had insulated him from reality. Three times in the last year, she had proposed solutions to his money trouble with César Olmeta and the Marseilles art gang. Deep down, she knew, even if he found the bull, he would never part with it.

Thierry, seemingly both impervious to and bored with Jasmin's accusations, moved to the desk with the laptop. Its screen saver cascaded colors like the northern lights, and he fingered the touchpad, bringing up a frozen view of Lupita's dashboard. Then he followed the cable from the laptop to its naked end. "Where's my sat phone?"

"In the raft that I released for Zac. Hopefully, he finds it."

Thierry jerked up, his teeth bared, but seconds later, his grimace transformed into a wide smile. "Darling, you're brilliant. Now those people will be looking for a raft, thinking it's us. See, I haven't killed anyone. I need to tell the captain to increase our speed." He left the study.

Jasmin crossed her arms over her stomach and stared out the starboard window. *How did we get to this?*

78

Zac tumbled in the churning wake, trying to find which way was up. He broke the surface and sucked in a breath. Then he spun around to catch the receding megayacht, now fifty meters distant and shrinking. His clothes and shoes made the water feel thick. Panic seized him as he pulled on all his training to gain control of the situation. He knew how to stay afloat and that hypothermia would be his major problem. *But that's hours away. Focus on the now.*

He scanned the horizon for other vessels. Nothing. Sardinia's dark outline filled the western sky, but not knowing its height meant he could not fathom its distance. Corsica's peaks pushed into alpine territory, making them visible from forty kilometers. *Shit. If Sardinia's only half as high, it's a long swim.* And he doubted the currents were kind to making landfall.

He looked at the receding megayacht. *Wait. What?* Something bobbed in its wake. He pushed up as high in the water he could muster. A bright orange shape dipped below a swell. Hope surged. He relaxed a moment and then thrust upward again. *A raft! Son of a bitch.*

He swam toward it, thinking someone had had a change of heart. *More likely, they wanted an excuse. I can hear Thierry saying I attacked them and went overboard in the fight. They couldn't find me but left a raft.*

After every dozen strokes, he looked up to adjust course, and, ten minutes later, he grasped the raft's trailing rope ladder. He climbed it awkwardly until he got waist level with the pontoon. Then he pulled himself aboard and flopped onto its rubber bottom. The water beneath him heaved as he caught his breath.

Minutes later, he sat up and surveyed its contents, finding a velcro-sealed compartment with five water bottles and a flare gun. Additionally, he found a drybag against the forward pontoon. He opened it—Thierry's satellite phone. *WTF*, he thought. Examining it, he found its home screen locked.

What're they up to? They could have killed me outright. Then it dawned on him. *Darwin's tracking the GPS. Dammit! Now he can't follow the megayacht.*

Zac pressed the side button combinations to bring up the emergency call screen and triggered the call, knowing one of the European services would answer. *Hopefully, English or French.* He slumped against the sidewall as the phone connected.

"Pronto? Qual è la tua emergenza?"

Ugh! He dug into his Ranger language training to stutter out, *"Ciao. Lei parla inglese?"*

D arwin called Maria once more. At the first ring, his phone beeped from an incoming call. "Italian number," he said aloud, accepting the call. *"Pronto!"* he answered, tapping speaker mode.

"Signor Darwin Lacroix?"

"Sì."

"This is officer Lorenzo Carli of the Carabinieri in Milan. We have an emergency call over a satellite phone from a man named Zac Johnson requesting you at this number. Shall we connect you?"

"Sì, yes, of course."

"Hold the line, please."

All went quiet for a long moment as Darwin, Eyrún, and Barry looked back and forth at each other. Then a voice came over the speaker. "Signor Johnson, you are connected. We will stay on the line."

"*Grazie mille. Grazie.* Darwin?"

"Zac, where are you? What's going on? How's Lupita?" The three pummeled him with questions.

Zac answered everything, including that he had called 112, the pan-European emergency number, and had no idea how the police in Milan had gotten the call.

"I'm fine. Lupita's fine, at least she was two hours ago, but they need her more than me for the algorithm," said Zac, going through the event like a mission debrief. "I got the file on Jasmin, and somehow they found out. That's when everything went to shit. How did you know to send it to me?"

Darwin described Maria finding Zac's ping and sending him Jasmin's background check.

"Enough of this," said Eyrún. "Zac, are you okay? What's your situation?"

"I've got water and a flare in the raft. I'm good here for at least forty-eight hours. You need to get after Lupita. Thierry's a fucking madman."

"Zac, can your cube-sat people find the megayacht?" asked Darwin.

"Hell, yeah!" Zac said, and then he told them who to contact.

"We're coming to get you," said Eyrún. "It's a straight shot from here to you and then to Pantelleria."

When he objected, saying to focus on Lupita, she overrode him. "Shut up, Zac. We're coming."

They flew into action as Eyrún issued commands. It had taken her seconds to realize their fastest practical way to Pantelleria would be on *Hypatia*. Taking their yacht would also give them the opportunity to figure out where the megayacht would anchor in Pantelleria.

While Darwin and Barry argued options, she opened a navigation app and roughly calculated the route from Ajaccio to Pantelleria. The most direct path went through the Strait of Bonifacio into the Tyrrhenian Sea and along Sardinia's eastern coast.

She connected with the harbor office. "I need my yacht fueled for an emergency departure."

"We're backed up right now," said the young man dockside.

"I'll pay you whatever's needed to make it your top priority," she said, "cash." She smiled at his understandable rearrangement of the fueling order, putting *Hypatia* first, and asked him to call back with an ETA. Then she turned to Darwin and Barry.

"Darwin, get to the store. We're going to need food for at least three days, and Zac will be hungry. Barry, we need you here to monitor the workstation and relay anything to us if it comes back on. Can Zoe bring food for you? I texted Hervé to join you for relief."

Both men nodded and moved for the lab door. "Wait," she said. They turned to her. "It's a ten-hour run at top speed to Pantelleria's main harbor. Hopefully, stopping for Zac will not take long. I'll draw up the route and leave it for you, Barry. Darwin, see you on *Hypatia* in an hour. Got it?"

They nodded again, and she went to her office to plot the full route and pull cash from the safe.

———

Darwin found *Hypatia* at the petrol dock, and he stashed the cold foods in the refrigerator, leaving everything else atop the galley counter.

"*Pardon*," he called to the fuel attendant, and he soon learned it was at least another forty minutes to top off the tanks. He paused and mentally ran through what they might need—clothes, they had on board. *Zac! He'll need clothes.* His friend was larger by twenty kilos. Glancing at his watch, he saw he had twenty minutes until Eyrún's arrival. *There's time.*

He went to Zac's flat, located the spare key kept under a flowerpot, and made a quick grab of shorts, underwear, and two shirts. He looked around, wondering what else Zac would need—shoes popped into his head. *He's been in the ocean.*

Darwin grabbed a pair of sneakers and flip-flops and looked at a box in the back of the closet. *We might need that.* He scooped up Zac's military pistol and headed back to the harbor, arriving just after Eyrún.

He dropped the clothing bundle on the banquet seat around the galley table. "What's that?" she asked.

"Zac's gun."

"Good thinking. I hope we don't need it, but…" She let the thought trail off.

As Darwin stowed the food, Eyrún slid into the captain's chair and entered the route coordinates into *Hypatia's* navigation system. The marine radar system would autopilot using a combination of GPS and known navigation charts while also using onboard radar sweeps to pilot around anything in its path.

The fueling completed, and they circled the hull, securing anything that might fly about. Once out of the harbor, they planned on cruising at top speed. At thirty-six knots, anything not tied down would fly off or cause drag that they did not want.

Eyrún used the joystick to maneuver them away from dockside, and, when in the deeper harbor, Darwin joined her in the side-by-side captain's chairs. The setting sun blazed into the slanted windscreen, and he adjusted a visor as Eyrún bumped up the throttle.

"Sunset's at nine thirty-five, and we'll have the sun at our stern once we clear the harbor," said Eyrún. "It'll be easy to see what's in front of us until we hit nautical twilight, basically dark, but we should be around the northern tip of Sardinia by then."

Darwin looked out at two sailboats ahead to port. Their white sails were tinged orange in the fading daylight. He looked down, confirming their shapes on the radar sweep, and gauged their distance at five kilometers. Eyrún explained how to tune its resolution.

"The higher the resolution, the more it picks up," she said, adjusting a graphic slidebar as the screen went nearly white. "At this level, it's catching the wake from that fishing boat." She pointed to the craft to starboard.

"Got it," he said.

They cleared the outer harbor, and Eyrún throttled up. Once they were running trim, she pushed them up to top speed. The sea rippled from a cross-breeze in a consistent one-meter swell. Darwin jumped up to secure a ballcap that had slid from the galley top, and then he put on coffee for the long night.

"Text the sat phone. Let Zac know we're on the way," she said.

"Guesses on time?"

As he measured coffee, she calculated. "Four and a half, five hours."

"Got it." He sent the message and turned back to Eyrún in the captain's chair. Her right hand shielded her eyes from the sun just above the starboard horizon. He smiled. It would be a long night, and there was no one else he wanted to spend it with.

79

Zac watched the Milky Way brighten and checked his watch. Still over four hours until Eyrún and Darwin reached his GPS location. If all went well, he would be in Pantelleria with them tomorrow. *If that bastard harms one hair on Lupita's head...*

Something splashed. He looked over the side. Nothing. He slumped back, and his eyelids, sticky from salt water, would not stay open. He drifted into a fitful sleep.

A heavy vibration awoke him, as a sound like strong surf came from his left. *What the hell?* Sitting up, he looked through the raft's side window at a massive black shape bearing down on him, pushing a churning white wave three meters high.

A ship!

In the time it took for his brain to resolve the shape, his body had already taken him overboard. He swam like hell as the bow wave surged him forward. Then, it sucked him back as the displaced water came together at the stern. *Pull! Pull! Pull!*

He shoved away pictures of him being drawn under and turned into hamburger by the giant screws—a bright pink puff and then shark bait. The water thrummed like a kraken. Just as he thought the beast had him, he flipped end over end in savage rapids as the ship passed.

Air hissed around him as bubbles surfaced and the water reached equilibrium.

"Hey! Hey!" he yelled at the retreating stern on the chance that a sailor against the aft railing might hear him.

It was over in a minute, and he bobbed in the black water—no sign of the raft. He tapped his watch; its backlit face showed less than an hour until his friends arrived. *Gotta find the raft.* He scanned the horizon as before, but the sea was pitch black. The stars and quarter moon offered just enough visibility to find Sardinia, so he knew which direction *Hypatia* would be coming from. *Not that they can see me.*

He turned slowly, using the rising swells to push up and look. After two full turns, he was about to stop to conserve energy when a blue flash strobed the surface about fifty meters east. He rolled and side-stroked toward the flash, not recalling if the raft had a survival beacon.

It took half an hour to reach it. One side had been punctured, leaving a banana-shaped pontoon trailing the deflated half. He could drape across it to rest and get his body out of the water. He surveyed what was left of the raft and sighed heavily at finding the side containing water and flare pouch, now ripped open and empty. The dry bag with the sat phone had also been lost. *Why can't this be easy?*

As Zac fought the fatigue brought on by lowering body temperature, he played memory games to stay awake. *Just a short nap,* some part of him begged. *The brain consumes the most energy. Shutting it down will keep the other organs functioning better. Stop it.* Zac kept returning to his training. Discomfort and pain could be overridden.

A look at the time: four hours until nautical twilight, when the upper sky lightened, but longer to better visibility at water level. *Darwin's connected with all the right people. They're working the problem. Your job's to stay afloat.*

They'll come from the north. He paddled his banana-shaped boat around, keeping Sardinia on his left. He listened with eyes closed, trying to intercept any incoming sound, but he heard nothing above the water sloshing against the raft.

They should've been here by now, another look at his watch told him. *Shit! What if they can't find me?* A voice from his training sounded out: *You will not die alone, soldier.* He stared at his reflection in the dark water, a shape outlined by moonlight. Suddenly everything went white.

D arwin forced himself to stay alert. At this speed, the Volvo powerplants vibrated the floor, creating a loud hum that, combined with the wind tearing over the superstructure, made it hard to concentrate. Eyrún had the wheel, which kept her awake. He scanned the radar console and his iPad again. "Shit! Zac's signal's gone!"

"What do you mean, it's gone?" asked Eyrún, twisting toward Darwin in the seat next to her.

"The GPS signal's gone. Disappeared. No longer there."

"Restart the app."

"I did, and the sat signal's still connected."

Darwin called Maria in California. "We lost the GPS here."

"Same here," said Maria. "Two minutes ago. I see you at twenty-three nautical miles from its last known location."

"What about satellite?"

Maria said she would roll back the satellite feed, and Darwin waited a tense minute for her to finish.

Eyrún glanced at him every few seconds. "Stay on the radar, Darwin."

He rapidly scanned *Hypatia's* radar console, knowing, at their current speed in darkness, they would have mere seconds before visual contact with any object. *Including Zac!*

"Oh, Jesus!" said Maria.

"What?"

"A large ship went over Zac less than five minutes ago."

"Is he okay!" Darwin yelled. Eyrún's hands jerked at the shock, and *Hypatia* rocked until the autopilot stabilizers took over.

"I'm looking. It's a mess of readings down there. I'm adjusting the... I've got a heat signature. Human-sized!"

"Is he—" Darwin stopped.

"I can't tell from this altitude. If it was daylight, we could get a visual, but infrared is the best we can do at night."

Maria stayed on with them as they closed the gap, and Eyrún throttled back a half-hour later.

"Oh, crap. We just lost the IR sat below the horizon," said Maria.

"You can't see him?" asked Darwin.

"Hang on. Hang on. Okay, I just tapped a feed from one of Bluefield's sats." She explained how the organization tracked illegal emissions. "I've got a heavy oil trace. Yep. Same path as the ship. Move to your left."

"On it, Maria. We're heading up to the flybridge now."

Darwin followed Eyrún up the aft stairs, and he scanned the horizon as she activated the flybridge's controls. Three minutes later, Maria announced they were directly over the slick, and she guided them as Eyrún moved along its route.

"If he's there, you'll see him any minute."

Darwin stood on the bench, sweeping his eyes across the dark surface.

"Y ou're on top of his last known spot. Allowing for the current drift, he's anywhere within a few hundred meters," said Maria.

"Zac!" Eyrún yelled to starboard. She had *Hypatia* throttled down to a crawl.

"Screw it," said Darwin. "Sound the horn. We need him to know we're here." He held up a flare gun and fired.

As Eyrún leaned on *Hypatia's* horn, the flare arced forward and burst into a white-hot ball, forcing them to look away. The sea's black surface broke into a kaleidoscope of stars. Darwin launched another flare aft.

"Holy shit, you guys. My screen went bonkers. What happened?" Maria said into Darwin's earbuds. He explained, and she disconnected, saying she would stand by.

"There!" Eyrún pointed. "There! I see arms."

Darwin followed her finger to a pair of arms waving about two hundred meters off the portside bow. They slipped back into the water and moved to grasp half of an orange raft.

Eyrún throttled up in Zac's direction. Minutes later, she eased off and swung *Hypatia's* stern toward him. Darwin heaved a rope and, a minute later, pulled Zac onto the swim deck.

"We thought we lost you," Darwin said as he bear-hugged his best friend.

"Me, too, bro."

Eyrún threw her arms around Zac. After a minute, he pushed away. "We gotta get Lupita."

80

Eyrún stood and stretched as *Hypatia's* autopilot guided them towards Pantelleria. The windless night made for a smoother passage across widely spaced, shallow swells. Deep in the hull, the engines hummed, and, in the forward passenger cabin, Zac slept. He had run a hot shower and shoveled in some sausage and cheese before crawling under blankets.

Darwin had thrown Zac's wet, salty clothes through the washer and dryer, and now slept on the galley bench converted into a bed. She was due to wake him in a half-hour.

After some deep squats to increase circulation, she returned to monitor the radar and three vessels about ten nautical miles ahead of them. Only one appeared to cross their path, and she scanned the horizon, getting a visual of its starboard lights as it moved from her port-side. *Container ship—a big boy at that*, she thought, knowing it threw a wake large enough to surf.

Thirty minutes later, *Hypatia* undulated in the ship's wake, and Darwin rolled into a sitting position. "How long was I out?" he asked and yawned.

"A little under three hours," she said.

"Zac?"

"Not a word."

She caught him up on their position in the wide-open Tyrrhenian Sea below Sardinia, coming level with Sicily. "We're about three hours out."

"Thanks, love. Get some rest." Darwin took over the helm as she snuggled into the still-warm banquette.

T wo hours later, the steel gray swells reflected the pink dawn from cumulus clouds high over the Sicilian coast. The radar now showed dozens of blips as they neared the major shipping corridor between Sicily and Tunisia. Their destination, Pantelleria, was traffic furniture in the middle of a major waterway.

For a moment, Darwin imagined the time of his forebears and their shipping empire. While they had never had a craft of this speed, their ships had plied this same route thousands of times from the early Renaissance until the early 1900s. He thought of his three-times great-grandfather Pasquale, whose portrait hung in the mansion on Rue des Orangers and imagined him at the helm of a Lacroix vessel.

Pasquale's escapades had been passed down through the generations, and Emelio had regaled Darwin with fantastic tales about him. Pasquale had been among the earliest explorers of the rediscovered cities of Pompeii and Herculaneum and had found a now-famous box of Roman scrolls. But Darwin's favorite tales were about Pasquale the privateer. Legend had it that he operated for the Genoese, the French, and, for a short period, even as a corsair out of Tunis.

And here I am, captaining a modern Lacroix vessel. Hypatia's power surged into his hands as he piloted her across open sea. Gooseflesh bristled across his tired body, and he breathed deeply, swelling his chest at the sense of belonging with his seafaring ancestor. He reached up with one hand, raked back the hair that had drooped across his left eye, and smiled broadly. *I'm one of you.*

He basked in the fantasy as a line of cargo ships in tight formation resolved on the horizon. He had been watching them on radar. In actuality, their lanes were separated by a quarter of a nautical mile, but they appeared bow to stern from *Hypatia's* position. Darwin figured passing between their wakes would be rough, so he switched off the autopilot and eased the throttle to come around behind them.

Eyrún stirred. "What's up?"

"Sorry, love. I didn't mean to wake you." He explained their situation as she stood and gathered the blanket against the cool morning air. Ahead, the sun hit the vessel's hulls, highlighting their red water lines against the dark horizon. The containers on the largest ship looked like a pile of Lego blocks towering over the water. *How does that not tip over?*

"I've always loved mornings out here," he said, as much to himself as to Eyrún.

They discussed their position, fifty-six nautical miles from Pantelleria's main harbor on its western side. "Not likely they went there," she said. "We're going to need Zac's satellites."

As if on cue, he popped up the spiral staircase below the bridge. "Good morning! Did y'all have a good night's sleep?"

Darwin mumbled something unintelligible at Zac's unwavering early-morning cheer and added, "I'm making coffee."

"Never thought you'd ask, bright eyes," said Zac. "Where are we, Eyrún?"

Zac found that Maria had passed monitoring to others in the OSINT network and, by the time of his second cup, they had found the megayacht. A watcher somewhere in the Russian steppe, going by the name *tigereye37*, had located it anchored in a Pantellerian bay between Punta Rubascchi and Faraglione di Tracino.

He brought up a live image on Darwin's iPad that showed the megayacht to be the only sizable craft in the tiny harbor on Pantelleria's northeast coast, facing Sicily. Unfortunately, the resolution was not high enough to show any human movement.

Eyrún navigated them toward the looming island, now fully lit by the morning sun. Greenery blanketed its volcanic peaks, whose height squeezed moisture from the humid air, irrigating the lower slopes.

Ground-hugging vegetation covered the volcanic soil, and signs of cultivation appeared where the verdure had been arrayed in orderly rows, touches that had revealed lost settlements to archaeologists years later. The natural world was random. Humans arranged it.

Darwin folded sausages into an omelet in the galley kitchen. The butter and curing spices melded with the aroma of crusty bread wafting from the oven. He grabbed the loaf between fingertips and half-tossed it onto a cutting board.

"Damn. If the Navy served up luxury like this, I might never have left," said Zac.

"I thought you said the Rangers were Army," said Eyrún.

"They are. But we hitched rides from all the other services. Now that we have a Space Force, I might re-enlist." Eyrún's face screwed up, and he smiled. "I'm kidding."

Darwin buttered a thick slice of bread and slathered it with a generous dollop of apricot preserves for Eyrún. He devoured his portion of the omelet and exchanged positions with her so she could eat.

Halfway through his plate, Zac said, "I'm sorry, Eyrún. I fucked up."

"Don't worry about it," she said.

"No. Seriously, you guys. You tried to warn me. I've never been taken in like that, and after all my training."

"You're not in combat, Zac," said Darwin.

"But that's the point. I was taken in, not thinking about any danger. I…"

Eyrún put a hand on his arm. "It happened, Zac. We forgive you. Now, let's turn it around. What did you learn that will help us get Lupita back?"

81

By midnight, Lupita's algorithm had narrowed the photo of Jasmin and her mother to an area downslope from Monte Gibele, the second-largest volcano on Pantelleria. It most closely matched photos taken around a nearby historical site with four Byzantine tombs. Jasmin and Thierry had zoomed in and out of Google Maps and found only a handful of dwellings in the area. The most promising of them was up a dirt road on the dormant volcano's steep south-eastern slope, but there was no street-level view. Before going to sleep, Thierry had instructed the captain to make for Tracino, a village with a harbor close to their target, where they dropped anchor before sunrise.

As the early-morning sun climbed the cloudless sky, Jasmin and Thierry ate their breakfast and, through binoculars, studied the activity on the shore. A dive boat departed, and a few fishing vessels returned, but the tiny harbor was mostly tranquil. A light offshore breeze carried a faint smell of the maquis—similar to Corsica but with a dusty, volcanic undertone. Her light cotton top hung limply in the humidity, somewhat elevated from a light overnight rain.

She finished the last bite of her breakfast just as the tender returned. The thug who had jumped the wall with her in Bonifacio reported what they had found. "The village is small, just a few shops. People are curious about the yacht, but we made it clear you wanted privacy. We hired a car. It's ready anytime." He pointed at a sedan parked dockside.

Thierry leaped from the table, dropped his napkin on his plate, and ran to his office. Jasmin was glad for the time alone, as, over the last two days, he had increasingly acted like a child overexcited about a birthday party. He had talked incessantly about finding his mask.

Her gaze drifted from the shoreline toward the distant mountain, and her heart palpitated. For over three decades, she had thought of this confrontation. At times, she had imagined crushing her mother's killer with a car or stabbing him with a kitchen knife. Just yesterday, while watching one thug clean his pistol, she had envisioned shooting the Albanian Master. Her chest tightened as she pictured coming face to face with him. *God, I just want to get this over with.* Revenge seemed much simpler in concept than reality.

"Are you ready?" asked Thierry when he returned from inside the yacht.

"Give me a few minutes." She stood and moved towards her cabin.

"You're sure you can recognize the place?" he called after her, but she ignored him.

Forty-five minutes later, the thug at the wheel steered them onto a dirt track that cut between knee-high basalt rock walls. The main road, Contrada Dietro Isola, had sloped upward from the harbor and through rolling hills terraced with basalt walls. Ground-hugging grapevines grew in a manner little changed since Roman times. The car rocked over the rough ground, causing Jasmin, Lupita, and the other thug in the rear seat to sway against each other like Newton's cradle.

"That's it," said Jasmin, and she pointed as a steep slope angled to the right. All heads turned toward a white structure tucked behind lava rock walls. More than a dozen cacti, each twice the size of the largest thug, filled its front garden. Their pale-green ping-pong paddle blades angled every which way. Low shrubs surrounded the house, further isolating it from the road and the gravel track looked little traveled.

Except for electrical wires stretching between poles that ran up and over a hill, the property's construction said nothing of its age. Two buildings sat in proximity. The larger featured a cover extending from its front. Both had water-collecting domed roofs, a practice introduced by Arabs in the late Middle Ages.

They stopped short of the shade structure. Its wooden slats protected a table and chairs that appeared recently used. Thierry burst from the car and ran into the house. Jasmin exited more slowly, and, as she ran a hand across the table's clean surface, she said, "I know this place." Her static post-card memories played: a dinner at the table, running through the garden, and getting pricked by a cactus. She reflexively rubbed her right index finger.

"Where is it?" Thierry's voice carried from inside.

She walked to the place where the photo of her and her mother had been taken: the rock wall of a cistern built into the larger building's side. It had seemed much taller to a six-year-old girl. She looked at the cliff across the road, rising thirty meters before sloping away toward Monte Gibele's peak. As she moved into the house, Thierry passed her, coming out. "It's not here. It must be in the outbuilding."

Jasmin crossed the threshold, and the smells carried her back in time. She brought a hand to her chest, fingers tracing her breastbone to soothe a sudden heaviness in her heart. *We were here.* The kitchen where her mother had cooked, glass of wine in one hand, stirring a pot with the other. Jasmin's fingers tingled as the memories eased her sorrow. She stepped lightly into the back of the house, stopping at the sound of footsteps. *Mother?*

Jasmin turned to the front room, but it was only Lupita and the back-seat thug walking in. *Stop,* she scolded herself. *She's not here. He killed her.* Darkness cloaked the happy recollections, and she refocused on finding the Albanian Master. *Where are you? Thierry can have his mask, but you're mine.* She glanced at the thug, picturing the gun tucked in his back waistband. Her earlier anxiety about her face-off with the Albanian Master vanished as she pictured shooting him.

"Jasmin!" the other thug yelled from the other building, his voice carrying through open windows. She tore out the front door and raced to the outbuilding to find Thierry frantically pawing through the shelves along one wall. They contained various works ranging from rough to nearly finished. A large table dominated the room's center. The interior was completely different from the rustic exterior. Inside, modern lighting, a forge, and ventilated hood formed a combination of art studio and chemistry lab.

"It's here. It must be," said Thierry, panting and sweeping his hands over every object. He rapidly shifted things about until, pulling open a drawer, there was a flash of gold. He cried out and pulled away a cloth to reveal sections of a gold-leafed picture frame. His head dropped, and then he launched into a blistering invective as he swept the workbench's contents onto the wooden floor.

Jasmin rushed over. Thierry screamed and pounded on the bench so hard that blood splattered over its surface. "Stop it. Stop it," she said, grabbing his arm.

"It's not here!" he yelled.

"Of course not. It's his workshop. He put the mask and anything valuable someplace more secure." She motioned the nearest thug over, and he locked his beefy arms around Thierry, restraining him from behind while Jasmin examined his bloody hand. She saw a small razor tool on the floor and guessed it was the source of the injury. After wiping away the blood with a towel, she tied it around his palm.

"It's not deep," she said, placing the wrapped hand in his other. "Squeeze. It'll stop the bleeding."

"He must keep it in another part of the house," said Thierry.

"There's nothing in the house. Calm down." She looked out the only window. "It has to be someplace else entirely. Someone's been in the house recently, probably even today from the water in the kitchen sink." She scanned the room and then said to the thug near Lupita, "You, check anything that might conceal a cellar door."

They returned to the house. Thierry and Lupita sat at the kitchen table while the remaining thug stood by the door. Jasmin put on a kettle to make tea as she considered the possibility that the Albanian Master may have left the house for the day. *Which means he has no idea we're here and could return at any moment.* She turned to the thug. "Move the car up the road and park it out of sight."

When he had left, she asked Lupita if she would like some tea, and she set out two cups upon hearing an affirmative answer.

"I'll have coffee," said Thierry.

"He doesn't drink coffee," said Jasmin, stiffening. *How do I know that?* She opened the cupboards to confirm her assertion. She put out another cup and poured hot water over the tea bags.

"He's got to have ano—"

"Quiet! I need to think." Jasmin carried her cup into the middle of the main room, letting her mind drift back again. She sipped the hot brew while moving to the bedrooms, and she paused at the smaller one. Slowly she entered and sat on a futon, compressing its tired cushion. From low down, she remembered playing with a dollhouse and then standing up and hiding behind the doorframe as she watched a man remove something from behind a painting.

The key! She had followed him once—gotten in trouble with her mother for running off without telling her—but she had seen the man cross the road to the cliff and enter a dark space. She had been afraid to go in after him, but she had later seen him replace a key. Moving to the doorway, she eyed the painting, still hanging in the front room.

"I know where it is," she said, crossing the room and setting her teacup on the table as she passed. She pulled the painting away from the wall with one hand while feeling around its back with the other. A key hung on a small hook set in the wooden frame behind the canvas.

She turned, key in hand. "He keeps everything in a cave in the cliff."

As soon as the thug returned from moving the car, they called for the other thug. Then Jasmin led them all across the road.

82

Darwin cleared breakfast as Eyrún throttled up. She would take them northeast of Tracino and cruise along the coast past Punta Rubasacchi, where Zac and Darwin would study the bay with binoculars. He had messaged Barry earlier and learned nothing had come back onto the workstation. Despite a long boring night at the ACA, they were still eager to do anything they could. Darwin asked them to update Max Keller in Vatican City on their position and alert the Carabiniere for help once they figured out the situation.

As Eyrún swung them parallel to the shoreline, she said, "The village is close to the foot of the two main volcanoes, but the slope there is too shallow for cliffs. The photo could have been taken anywhere along the steeper southeast slopes."

"Once we make port, we're going to need better intelligence and a bit of luck," said Zac. "The locals will probably be curious about the megayacht and might know where its passengers went."

"Won't Jasmin recognize *Hypatia*?" Darwin asked.

"It's possible, but she was only aboard once and approached it from dockside," said Eyrún.

"It's a chance we'll have to take," said Zac, "unless we want to make a frontal assault. Not a good idea with a hostage."

Ten minutes later, they passed the bay at twenty knots. Eyrún glanced at the vessel, whose bow pointed into the shallow swells. The placid water contained a few fishing vessels and a beach. A clutch of buildings hugged one side of the cove. She turned her full attention back to navigating past Faraglione di Tracino, a tiny island barely detached from the main body.

She turned wide, throttled back, and let *Hypatia* drift as Darwin and Zac returned to the galley. "Damn, it's going to be hot. I can feel it already. Africa's less than twenty kilometers beyond the island," said Zac, adding, "I saw a single crew member on the stern, smoking, but no other activity."

"There are people on the dock and some guys in a fishing boat, but no one who looks like Jasmin or Lupita," said Darwin.

"What about Thierry?" Eyrún asked.

"No middle-aged men fitting the description."

"Okay. It's time to play tourist. Eyrún, take us into the cove," said Zac.

In less than five minutes, they had anchored *Hypatia*, and Eyrún took their tender to the Cala Levante beach to reconnoiter the town. She tightened her hair in a ponytail and put on a ball cap and dark glasses.

Darwin and Zac readied the jet ski to await her signal.

E yrún tied the Zodiac beside a long cement boat-launching ramp as two curious boys with their mother watched. A long concrete patio extended from the ramp, ending at a pebbled beach that, at this hour, had only a few dedicated sunbathers occupying the lounges.

She walked past boats in various stages of decay and followed the ramp's lane around to a hotel and dive shop. While most of the village slept or was quietly emerging, the shop had a handful of people going in and out with gear. She paused outside, looking around for signs of Jasmin, Thierry, or Lupita, then went in.

"*Bonjourno,*" she said to a woman behind the counter after a couple left with their tanks.

"*Bonjourno.*"

After exchanging pleasantries, Eyrún determined the woman spoke English, and she asked about any fishermen with fresh catches, saying she was buying for a yacht that had just docked.

The woman directed her to the larger harbor a short walk down the road. Eyrún reached it in two minutes, saw men unloading their catches, and let out a sigh of relief, knowing they could still stick to their primary plan.

"*Bonjourno.*" She chatted with the men, asking about their catch before steering the conversation to her purpose: "Would you like to earn some extra money this morning?"

"Who do you want us to kill?" one man asked with a laugh.

She explained the task. "Go to that megayacht and offer to sell fresh fish, and don't take no for an answer." She further explained that it was a practical joke. When they balked, she asked, "Would a thousand euros change your mind?"

Eyrún heard one of them mutter, "Crazy rich people," as he pocketed the cash and pushed a boat into the bay with three large fish. Then she turned back to the village to avoid being seen by anyone on the megayacht and messaged Darwin:

Go now

83

I t took Thierry's group half an hour to locate the cave in the cliff after one thug climbed atop the house to see a hole in the greenery. The shadow cast by the steep rock created a microclimate that gathered rainwater and allowed vegetation to avoid the harsh sun. A path had been concealed behind overlapping branches that formed a crude gateway at the road's edge.

Thierry pushed through, and Jasmin followed, but she stopped as Lupita cried out. She turned back to find Lupita on the ground, rubbing her knee as a thug helped her up. "I am fine. I only tripped," said Lupita. She shrugged him off and pressed through the brush.

Jasmin looked down the road. Any car coming to the house would leave a dust trail. On impulse, she scoured the ground to see what had tripped Lupita. The dirt road was relatively smooth, mostly gravel in this part, but—*a rock pile!* Lupita has stacked three stones near the opening.

Nice try. Jasmin kicked the rocks and then checked for footprints. The gravel extended back to the house and, as best she could tell, had not been disturbed. She turned to the sound of Thierry yelling, "It's locked!" Shaking her head at his stupidity, she grasped the key in her pocket as she made her way to the cave.

A narrow gap in the rock broadened into a modest portico-like entrance that ended at a stout wooden door. Basalt blocks had been mortared together to form a doorframe beneath a substantial lintel. She guessed the door swung on inward-facing hinges, as the rusted metal plate with the keyhole was the only exterior feature.

"Open it. Open it." Thierry nearly danced with anticipation.

"Hold him," Jasmin said to the thugs as she keyed the lock. She had expected difficulty, but the deadbolt slid with ease from the steel mortise on the doorjamb. The door opened with a groan, but other-wise, it felt regularly used. She fingered on the light on her mobile and peered into the darkness.

84

Eyrún took her tea and Sicilian brioche to a small table outside the cafe across the road from the dive shop to settle into her next role as the lookout. She, Zac, and Darwin were assuming Jasmin and Thierry were already on land, looking for the Albanian Master's house, but if Lupita had been left aboard, they needed a well-executed distraction.

She angled her chair for an optimum view of traffic coming into the village. After a sip of tea, she pulled the tuppo from the brioche and popped it into her mouth. Its delicate crunch gave way to a soft, yeasty texture, mildly sweet. *Nice.* She tore a piece of the bun and chewed it while watching peoples' morning rhythm: divers leaving the shop, tourists deciding on breakfast locations, and a woman arranging vegetables in a pop-up market stall. Her neck and shoulder muscles relaxed a little from the tense all-nighter she had spent gripping *Hypatia's* wheel.

"*Bonjourno,*" said a white-haired man at the next table when she made eye contact.

"*Bonjourno,*" she replied.

"How does a beautiful young woman find herself alone?" he asked in English.

"My husband went on a dive. It's not my thing," she said, taking a bite of the pastry and hoping her "husband" comment would dissuade further conversation.

He went back to reading a newspaper, and Eyrún licked her fingers after another bite of brioche. A few moments later, it occurred to her that the man might have seen people from the megayacht. She asked, "Do you live here? It's a lovely village."

He laid down his paper and said, "Up the hill. And, yes, it's charming. A little overrun in the season but quite peaceful. Are you staying in one of the hotels?"

"No. We've just arrived. Our boat's anchored in the bay."

"The big one?" he asked, raising his eyebrows.

"Ours is in the smaller bay. We saw that one and decided to stay away. They had a rather menacing security man aboard."

"Ah, yes. We get some of those. Besides diving, what brings you to this part of our island?"

"We're art collectors and heard of a fantastic artist here. We were hoping to meet him."

"Most artists here are of middling talent."

Eyrún gambled that he knew more and shifted tactics. "Actually, my husband and I are more than collectors. We founded an institute on Corsica to preserve cultural heritage, the Agrippa Center for Archaeology. We seek a restorer of exceptional skill recommended to us by a dealer in Alexandria."

The man folded the paper and smiled while adjusting his rolled-up white cotton shirt sleeves. His blue eyes sparkled, bringing a more youthful appearance to his lined face. "I read about it. Impressive mission." He sipped from his cup and replaced it on a saucer with a teabag.

"Thanks. I'm Eyrún Stephansdottir, by the way."

"Valon," he said, offering a hand. "A pleasure to meet you, Eyrún."

She shook it and noticed a tattoo on his forearm. Its dark lines were hard to make out against his deeply bronzed skin. He added, "I think I know the artist you mean. He sometimes comes here."

Eyrún nearly came off her chair. "Could you introduce us?"

"He doesn't like collectors. Calls them a greedy lot."

"If you've read about our center, you know our mission is to safe-guard and conserve. We have pieces that our experts say have been restored by this man. I would like to talk with him about them."

"He must be very popular today," he said. Eyrún knitted her brows, and he added, "You are not the only person asking about him. The coffee shop owner said a large, bald man inquired about him earlier."

She blurted out, "He's in danger."

"From whom?"

"The people on the yacht. They mean to hurt him. Please tell me where—"

A gunshot came from the harbor.

85

Darwin's legs dangled from the swim deck into the crystal clear water. He watched fish schooling in the rocks seven meters below. When Zac started the jet ski to warm up its engine, the fish shot off, but they returned and settled down a few moments later.

"You're sure this'll work?" Darwin asked.

"Almost guaranteed."

Earlier Zac had explained their plan for Eyrún to organize a diversion. "We did this kind of thing all the time, pay the locals to create a disturbance."

"What if they refuse?" Eyrún had asked, to which Zac had replied, "Only the most hard-core zealots would turn down a month's wages in cash."

Eyrún's text arrived. "Let's go," said Darwin.

Zac checked the gun in the back of his waistband and jumped on the jet ski. Once Darwin slid in behind him, they powered away from *Hypatia* and around Faraglione di Tracino.

Not two minutes later, they drew even with the megayacht, and Darwin confirmed the fishermen were at its stern. He could see one of them holding up a fish in each hand while someone on the rear deck tried waving them off. "Go for it," he said to Zac.

The jet ski banked sharply, closing the gap in seconds. Zac slowed the craft, and they drifted alongside the vessel's port side, with Zac looking ahead and Darwin watching for anyone on the above deck. The hull lowered as the went aft, and Zac whispered, "Get ready."

Another few meters, and Zac stood on the seat, grabbed the railing, and hoisted himself over the side. Darwin pushed off toward the stern and surprised two crew members trying to chase off the fishermen.

"Hey!" yelled the larger crew member. "This is a private vessel."

"Move away. Now!" Zac shouted, pistol in hand, from behind them.

Darwin disarmed the remaining thug, the one who had piloted the Zodiac in Bonifacio, and tossed his pistol overboard. He then thanked the fisherman in their boat behind the megayacht, who withdrew as Darwin joined Zac.

"We mean you no harm," Zac said to the crew, "but we need to know where Thierry went and how long ago."

"We will not help you," said the captain.

"Perhaps we can change your mind," said Darwin, and he crossed to where the crew sat. He pointed back at Zac. "If you haven't figured out, this man holding the gun is an American special forces agent with extraordinary talents. You tossed him overboard yesterday, yet here he is again. Now, let's consider your situation. Your employer kidnapped a British intelligence officer, the tall woman, and attempted to kill this man, who, by the way, is still furious."

Zac glowered at them from behind crossed arms, one finger on the gun's trigger.

"Who are you?" asked the captain.

"Your worst nightmare if you don't drop the attitude. You and your crew have two options." Darwin paused a few beats while he made eye contact with each of the seven crew members and the thug. "Option one: you voluntarily tell us where Thierry went. Option two: I look away and let this angry American coax the answers out of you."

The captain looked left and right at his crew as if to silence them. "Option two, then," said Darwin. He moved back to Zac, who handed him the pistol and unsheathed a diver's knife from his lower leg.

"They went to a house...at the base of that mountain," said a young crew member, pointing above the village. "I heard Thierry ask Jasmin about it. That's all I know. I swear."

Zac asked him a few more questions, but the young man had nothing more. He recrossed the deck to Darwin and said, "I need to see the location they discovered on the laptop. You good here for a minute?"

"Yes." Darwin focused on the crew. A minute later, as the morning sun beat down on his neck, he shifted into the shade. His watch vibrated, and he glanced at it.

Emelio: Got the documents

The captain used the momentary distraction to pull a gun from a seat-back compartment.

86

Zac burst from the upper galley at the shot, knife in hand, and flattened himself near the deck railing. *Dammit!* He had trained Darwin with handguns and knew he hunted, but practice and combat were different.

Fearing the worst, he moved beside a bench and peered over the edge. The crew had gathered around the captain. Blood covered the shoulder of his white uniform. A woman cried out, "Get the medical kit!"

"Darwin!" yelled Zac.

His friend moved into view. "I'm fine. The captain reached for a gun."

Zac picked up the laptop he had dropped on a table and rushed downstairs. Darwin's arm shook as Zac took the pistol from him. "I got it, buddy. You okay?"

"Yeah. I'm fine. Asshole had to be a hero."

Zac crossed the deck to the captain, who sat against the railing. "Move away, people." He knelt, pressing the gun barrel into the man's gut, and checked the wound. The bullet had torn the shoulder's skin but not deeply. "You're lucky. A bit to the right, and you might not be using this arm again."

Darwin's mobile rang. As he answered it, Zac stood and instructed the crew to compress the wound to stop the bleeding. Then he had them join the captain. He looked at Darwin, who, he figured, was speaking with Eyrún.

"No. No. We're unhurt. The captain grabbed a hidden gun. We dealt with him," said Darwin. He paused, listening, and then added, "Flesh wound. The crew's subdued now."

"Did she find anything?" asked Zac. Darwin nodded.

"Good. We're secure here. See you in thirty minutes or less." Darwin ended the call and turned to Zac. "Our agent on shore found the location." Then he said to the crew, "Do not alert any of your party on the island. Doing so would assist criminals wanted by Europol and the American FBI. You will be blacklisted from future travel in the EU and America."

Zac smiled and moved toward the jet ski tied to the swim deck. Once underway, he shouted over his shoulder, "Our agent on shore? Nice touch."

In less than five minutes, Darwin and Zac were stepping onto *Hypatia* to change clothes. Emelio's ringtone sounded on Darwin's mobile as he pulled on short boots.

"Hey, Emelio."

"Hello, Darwin. I'm at my bank. There's a branch in Sicily. I've removed everything from the safe deposit box in Banco di Trapani like you suggested."

"Perfect, *Grand-père*. Anything interesting?"

"Loads of documents. Fortunately, I packed a large duffel. Most are transaction records, and some look like lists of people. The most interesting is a cross-reference to the Panama Papers, you know that Wiki-Leak in twenty-sixteen. Looks like jail time for many people."

Darwin went topside to join Zac on the jet ski, and he interrupted his grandfather as Zac hit the starter button. "Emelio, sorry to cut you off, but we're catching up with Eyrún on Pantelleria."

"Go get her. I'll text you pictures of anything important."

They disconnected, and Zac gunned it the short distance to the boat launch. He slowed, and they stepped off carefully to keep their feet dry. After tying it up, they joined Eyrún at a car park, beside a beat-up car.

"I guess the Teslas were sold out?" asked Zac, looking at the two-tone rust and white sedan.

"Careful of the chicken shit on the seats," said Eyrún, smiling when Zac's eyes went wide.

Darwin elbowed him and laughed. "How did you find the house?"

Eyrún told them about the man at the cafe as they got into the car and headed out. "He's gone," she added as they passed the empty table on the circuitous route out of the village.

"It smells in here," said Zac. "Where did you get this?"

"I wasn't kidding. The guy I paid to borrow it took out a chicken cage." She watched in the rearview mirror as Zac pressed himself up from the seat and looked around.

The temperature picked up as they moved away from the harbor's breeze. Darwin brought up a map and roughly figured out their position from the cafe man's hand-drawn map. They passed a larger cross-road, and their route straightened as it climbed a wide slope covered with low vegetation grasping at life. The volcanic soil, while rich in minerals, drained away the little water that fell.

"Contrada Dietro Isola should be close," said Darwin. "There. Go left. Okay, it elbows left in two kilometers."

"He said to look for signs to the Byzantine tomb when the road bends," said Eyrún.

A quarter of an hour later, they rolled past the tomb and looked for the second road on the right. They found it, and Eyrún rolled slowly up a steep track. What little precipitation fell had rutted it deeply, bottoming out the car's ancient suspension.

"That's what he described." Eyrún pointed at a house coming up on their right.

"Darwin, duck down," said Zac as he went flat on the rear seat. "Tell us what you see as you pass."

Eyrún described a white plastered structure with a carport-like covering but no vehicle. "There's a large rock-walled structure beside the house, but I don't see anyone." As the car went into the cliff's shadow, she added, "There's another house way up the hill, but I'm sure the one behind us is it."

"Park anywhere," said Zac.

She did, and they got out. Zac scanned the surroundings. Then he cut into an opening in the shrubs and popped back out. "A car's hidden in there. Not your typical parking spot for a resident. I'm going overland to the back of the house. You two stay here. I'll text if it's clear."

"I'll go with you," said Darwin.

"Nope. This ain't a training run." Without a sound, Zac moved between the bushes.

Z ac reached the outbuilding and listened, but he heard nothing but cicadas. He considered his approach to the main building, as the cicadas would go silent on hearing his movement—a dead give-away that something was on the perimeter.

He cautiously traveled parallel to the knee-high rock wall and then slipped over it into the covered front area. Once he cleared the house and workshop, he texted Darwin and Eyrún to join him. A minute later, Darwin came crashing through the rear brush. Zac shook his head, remembering their interrupted training on the GR20 trail.

He moved more slowly through the house now, looking for details that might give away their quarry's purpose or where they had gone. "Be careful," he said to Eyrún and Darwin as they entered the main room. He studied the teacups: one was nearly empty, but the other was untouched, most likely Lupita's. He knew captives were rarely in the mood for anything but escape.

Picking up the empty cup, he smelled Jasmin's strong perfume on the porcelain. A longing gripped him, followed almost immediately by repulsion at the reality of the situation. Resisting the urge to smash it against the wall, he set it back down.

"That painting's been moved," Darwin said as he studied the surrounding walls.

"How do you know?" asked Eyrún.

"The man's an artist. Look at this place. Everything has an orderly aesthetic. He wouldn't leave a picture at this angle." He turned over the painting of a house, tinged orange in the setting sun. "There's a key missing from this hook. Judging from its offset angle, I'd say it's a big key." He squatted to study the area below the picture. "And," pointing to rectangular clear spot in the dust, added, "someone recently took an object from this shelf."

Zac walked over. "Nice eye. You're shit in the field, but your archaeology's still first rate." He waved Eyrún closer. "They may be in the outbuilding. Stay sharp. There are two thugs, and we know Thierry's a loose cannon."

He withdrew the sidearm as they stepped outside. In a few strides, they reached the workshop. Zac scanned its interior and turned back to them. "It's empty. Go inside. I'll search the surroundings."

After a sweep around the building, Zac reentered. Eyrún said, "Someone had a tantrum in here." He joined them to find tools on the floor and blood on the bench.

"What do you suppose happened?" asked Darwin.

"Thierry went crazy looking for his mask," said Eyrún. "There's nothing in the house, and this place is a workshop. Where are they?"

"Oh, they're here. And they knew we were coming; otherwise, they wouldn't hide the car. I didn't think the captain would stay quiet." Zac opened the cabinets near the vent hood and fingered the containers. "Damn. Helluva chemistry lab. This guy's serious about his work." He turned back to Eyrún and Darwin. "You two go back to the house and sit tight. I'm going to scour the property."

Three minutes later, he had come up empty-handed. Zac had seen every kind of hideaway in Afghanistan, and nothing on the property looked even remotely suspicious. He reentered the house to find Darwin studying the painting's back.

"I'm guessing the key's about this size," Darwin said, holding up a hand with thumb and forefinger spread. "I tested the frame's offset weight with my pocket knife, and it's about a hundred grams, so this key must have a substantial shaft. The kind used on an old vault."

"Why an old vault here?" asked Eyrún.

"The same reason my ancestors on Corsica built the mountain house. This island's on the Barbary Coast."

"Okay, let's say I buy your pirate story. We haven't seen anything like a vault on the property," said Zac.

Eyrún and Darwin made eye contact and simultaneously smiled.

"What?" asked Zac.

"It must be in a cave," said Eyrún. "We're on a volcanic island with plenty of hollow spots. That's why he's against this cliff."

"Why is everything underground with you two?"

87

Thierry ran past Jasmin to the shelves along the cave's left side. His mobile lit the way into the darkness. The others followed Jasmin, and each turned on a light. Lupita moved toward the door, but one of the thugs grasped her arm. "No, you don't. Besides, where will you go out there?"

Jasmin shined her light into the cave, but the bright white halo failed to penetrate beyond twenty meters. "It smells like wine," she said to herself, trying to make sense of the structure. The human-made cavern arched three meters high at its apex and was twice as wide as it tunneled straight through the basalt. Large shelves lined the left-side wall, stacked with vases in various stages of construction. Those farthest in from the door held painted vases in finished condition.

She walked to a workbench on the right wall, where a single askos vase rested next to a modern lighter. Liquid sloshed as she lifted the askos. *Of course. Lamp oil.* She moved her light across the walls beside the workbench, revealing lamps mounted about two meters up. Then she handed the lighter to the thug and said, "Light those." Orange light sprang from the walls as he did, and he moved to other lamps now visible.

Jasmin stepped back and, in the better light, looked beneath the workbench. She inhaled sharply. A rectangular cigar box with colorful writing and glitter, as if decorated by a child, lay on a shelf. Her heart seemed to freeze. Then, all at once, it pounded. *What's that doing here?*

She reached for it, afraid to open it but knowing that she had to. Lifting it like a holy relic, she placed it atop the bench. Then she brought her fingers to her parted lips and contemplated its reason for being in the cave.

After a long moment, she ran her fingers along its edges. Finally, she pushed up its lid with her thumbs. A half-dozen photos lay in the box. She moved to the nearest oil lamp and lifted them. "Oh, my God. Mama," she gasped, flipping through them. The clothing in the pictures matched the photo she had carried all these years. *These must be from the same roll.*

She slumped against the wall, set the cigar box on her outstretched legs, and studied each photo. Some were the source of her most vivid memories, such as her mother with a wineglass, but she only vaguely remembered others, like one of her riding atop a man's shoulders, her small hands intertwined in his. But the next photo in the stack froze time.

It was of her in the arms of the same man, both with broad smiles. His arms were wrapped around her midsection. A dark, two-headed eagle was tattooed on one of the man's forearms, and mirrored aviator sunglasses reflected her mother taking the picture.

Jasmin's vision blurred as she swallowed the hard lump in her throat. The box bounced when her hands fell in her lap, jostling a small cream-colored envelope addressed simply:

Jasmin

88

Zac instructed Darwin and Eyrún to wait at the table in the covered entry, and then he moved onto the road. After surveying the cliff from the house, they had determined any cave would be within fifty meters up or down the hill from the house. Any farther up would be too close to the next dwelling, and downhill, the road curved away from the cliff.

He walked carefully to avoid kicking the gravel near tufts of ground-hugging plants poking from beneath thick maquis. Their woody stems were greener because of the moisture concentrated against the cliff. Each footfall made a soft crunch, loud to him, but he knew it would not carry over the vegetation. He paused every other step and listened. Birds flitted through the undergrowth, but he detected no sound of human movement. He looked for footprints, but the gravel gave nothing away.

Ten meters past the driveway, the maquis fragrance seemed stronger. He paused, closed his eyes, and sniffed. The pungent smell triggered memories of the chaparral above his home in California. Its aromatic oils conserved water, and the odor was normally subtle unless crushed or broken.

He studied the maquis branches slowly moving up. *Bingo!* Just overhead, a handful of stems had been twisted. *That's a purposeful move. Nice work, Lupita.* Anyone passing through would duck or crouch down. There was no reason to reach over two meters in height. More signs of human activity became apparent as he looked. He dropped to his knees and moved under the heaviest growth into a space that looked as if someone had trimmed it.

Smoke! He froze as a pair of legs moved into view. A cigarette hit the ground, and a foot ground it out. Then the legs disappeared to the right. Zac waited a moment and then continued forward. The cliff angled sharply into a gap about five meters away, where a shoe stuck out. Figuring it was the cave, he backed out of the maquis and dashed back to the house.

"One of them's outside the entrance," said Zac. "We take him out. That leaves just one inside with Lupita. We need to move fast. While they're distracted exploring the inside, that gives us an element of surprise."

"But how?" asked Eyrún. "He'll hear us and alert the others."

"We make him choose." Zac arranged a knife that had been left on the table. "This is the cliff. We come at him from two sides, one from this end and the other here." He pointed at opposite ends of the knife.

"And what if he shoots at us?" Eyrún crossed her arms.

"It's not likely he could hit you in the brush at over twenty meters," said Zac. She frowned, and he added, "But we won't take that risk."

"Too bad we don't have any smoke bombs like you used in the tunnel under Notre-Dame," said Darwin.

Zac slapped his friend's shoulder. "Darwin, sometimes you don't realize the genius you are."

Ten minutes later, Darwin's mobile buzzed as he and Eyrún walked toward the gap in the maquis. He answered in a whisper, "Hey, Emelio."

"You won't believe this, but the safe deposit box had an envelope with the Albanian Master's personal documents. It turns out he's actually Albanian."

Eyrún made a cutting motion across her throat to end the call.

"That's great, Emelio, but we're about to take out one of the bad guys. Text me the documents."

"Be careful. And good luck."

Darwin pocketed the phone and felt it vibrate against his thigh as three messages arrived. A few steps later, they found the line in the gravel that Zac had made earlier. Eyrún messaged Zac:

Ready
Zac: Count to 50 then go. Make lots of noise.

89

J asmin ignored Thierry's yelling about wine bottles from farther
down the cave. She lifted the letter, pausing as if judging its
emotional weight, and then opened it. Blue ink scrolled across the
paper:

My dearest Jasmin,

*It grieves me that this may be the closest we come to meeting. Life has not
turned out the way either of us has wanted. That which we loved most — your
mother — was taken from us.*

*Thierry's greed has grown to an idée fixe so puissant it clouds all reason.
But, having been raised in his nightmarish obsession, you know this. I am
sorry that I could not keep you from it.*

*But your mother also created complications that led to her tragic demise.
For years, she would not choose between us, but after living with me for all of
1979, she became pregnant. These pictures are from your sixth birthday, the
last time I saw you. She had belatedly agreed to marry, and we soon traveled to
Beirut to clean up her parents' affairs.*

*Somehow Thierry found us in Beirut. I never understood his obsession
with the bull mask, and your mother refused to let me give it to him. I wish I
had ignored her.*

He pulled out a gun when I would not tell him its location, and your mother jumped between us. Thierry evaded prosecution because of his connections with the Lebanese government, and I became the murderer. I tried to find you, but he had already taken you away.

Your mother's death was a tragedy and could have been avoided.

Love,

Your father

Jasmin read the letter twice more, trying to make sense of it. She was about to reread it again when Thierry stormed from the cave's rear. "We need tools. There's another door, but it's locked, and there's no key. We have to break it down," he said, his voice shaking.

She stared at him from her position on the floor. Sweat covered his face, and his fingers moved nonstop. His gaze darted over the workbench and oil lamps before resting on her. Then his face screwed up, and he leaned toward her. "What did you find?"

She folded the letter, snapped the box lid closed, and moved away from him.

"What is it? He left a map. I know it. Give it to me."

"No!" She swept the box behind her back with one hand and poked a finger in his chest with her other. He flinched but stood straight, leaning his head back as she attacked. "It's a letter. Addressed to me..."

He blinked rapidly.

"From my father."

"That's ridiculous, Jasmin. I'm your father."

"No. It says you killed her. You killed my mother."

Thierry's eyes went wide. Then his face settled into a grin. "Is that what it says?" His face rolled up as he erupted in maniacal laughter.

"You—"

A deafening flash burst from the door.

90

The dense brush scratched Zac's arms and legs as he shoved through the maquis some fifty meters up the road from the cave. Once against the cliff, he pushed along the rock, raking away the growth. Seconds later, he heard Darwin and Eyrún arguing.

"You need to wait for Zac!" she shouted.

"He's taking too long. We need to get them now."

A bit too dramatic, thought Zac, but it worked. The thug had moved into a space between the maquis and the cliff. Darwin and Eyrún were still in the brush, some distance away, but his full attention was on the quarreling couple, and he held a pistol in front of his body with both hands.

Zac closed in and, as he reached the cave, sprinted across the open ground. His gun butt hammered the thug's head, dropping him like a rock. A moment later, Eyrún and Darwin stepped from the gap.

"He'll be out a while," said Zac. He slipped his pistol behind his back and handed the thug's to Darwin. "Be careful with this." He then tied the thug's wrists with a piece of rubber tubing he had taken from the workshop. "That will hold him." Standing again, he drew a plastic bag with a cardboard tube from his pocket. "Stay here. I don't know how well this will work."

His friends' eyes went wide.

"Fireworks," he said. "Your comment about the smoke bomb in Paris triggered my inventory of the lab. Potassium perchlorate and aluminum powder. It's crude. Won't kill anyone, but it'll be bright as hell." He moved toward the gap in the cliff. *This better work,* he thought, checking that matches were still in his other pocket.

Earlier, with limited time and no visible scale to weigh the powders, he had eyeballed the amounts, roughly two-thirds to one-third, and then mixed them by hand. Grabbing a paper towel roll, he had yanked out its cardboard center, torn it in three sections, crammed them together into a single tube, crimped one end, and dumped in the powder.

For the fuse, he had crushed match heads with a mortar and pestle, poured a line of powder along a piece of paper towel, and twisted it. Finally, he had tested a section under the vent hood to estimate its burn rate and then stuck the remaining fuse in the tube's other end and closed it. He had done this before, but with much more time and a better selection of materials.

Now, reaching the cave, he opened the zip-locked bag and gingerly removed the makeshift flash bomb. He pressed against the wall and side-stepped to the vault door, opened about two body widths. He squatted, set the tube just inside the doorframe, and gently strung out the fuse. Then, he struck a match.

Inside, Thierry ranted. Jasmin said something about her father, and Thierry laughed. As flames hissed to life and sputtered into the darkness, Zac scampered away.

"What's that?" yelled the thug in the cave.

Zac waited. *C'mon. C'mon.*

Nothing happened. He thought of Lupita inside. *She's in danger.* Grabbing the gun in his waistband, he took a step. The flash bomb went off.

91

Zac's ears rang as he moved into the thick smoke. Sounds of coughing came from two directions. He searched for Lupita in the hazy light cast by the oil lamps. She called out, and he spun to see the remaining thug pull her backward with a pistol jammed in her midsection. Thierry and Jasmin cowered by a table against the opposite wall.

He darted over and shoved Thierry against the wall, ramming the pistol into the soft spot under his jaw. Thierry waved his arms frantically. His mouth opened. Zac banged his head on the wall. "Speak, and your brains become a splatter painting."

Then, leaning so close he could feel Thierry's rapid, hot breaths, he added, "You thought it funny when you tossed me overboard?" He tipped his head toward Lupita and continued. "If your thug harms her, I will kill him. And then I will kill you. Do you understand me?"

Thierry whimpered and nodded.

At that moment, Darwin and Eyrún ran in. "Stop!" commanded Zac. They froze near Jasmin. Zac glanced again at Lupita and, surmising the thug would wait before doing anything, hooked Thierry's arm in his and dragged him to the middle of the cave. "There," he said, leaving Thierry and backing against the cabinets. "Now I can keep an eye on everyone. Jasmin, it's nice to see you, but I cannot say the same for your *father*."

"He's not my father." She spat the words like poison.

"I am," said Thierry. Zac shot forward and kicked Thierry's legs out from under him. The older man landed on his back with a crunch.

"I said quiet." And, to the thug, he added, "Harm her, and he dies."

Jasmin spoke again as if nothing had happened. "You're not my father. You adopted me."

"I had to," said Thierry.

Zac took a step, but Lupita screamed. The thug had moved the gun to her neck. *Shit!* He would not gamble with a friend's life, so he stood down as Thierry limped to the thug, where he said with more confidence, "The Lebanese authorities had no birth records. You are my daughter."

"Then why was this written?" said Jasmin, reaching into the box for the letter.

"It's a lie. Made up to turn you against me."

"It's signed '*your father*.' Now, why would he do that?"

"The Albanian? Because he's a deceiver. His whole life's about faking. He lives in secret. Has to."

Zac studied Jasmin, curious about the letter, but he kept his position. Darwin, standing between him and Jasmin, took out his mobile. "What are you doing?" Eyrún whispered.

But all eyes were on Jasmin, who waved the cigar box at Thierry, rattling the photos inside. "I made this box when I was six. What I want to know is why none of the pictures are of you? Who is this man with me and my mother?"

"It's the Albanian Master. They had an affair, and he tried to convince her you were his child." Jasmin remained impassive as she waited for him to come clean. "Your mother was a confused woman. We were both her lovers, but she never told me she was pregnant."

"How did she die?"

"She had come back to Beirut when her father died. We had an argument years earlier, and I didn't know where she had been living.

She wanted to clear her conscience about stealing the bull mask, but the Albanian discovered our meeting and shot her."

"That's not what it says here," said Darwin, holding up his mobile.

J asmin turned toward Darwin, who said, "It's an investigator's report that the Beirut police were paid to falsify records of a shooting—changed the gunman's name."

"Give me that." Jasmin thrust out a hand, and Darwin handed her the device. She took it and leaned against the bench. Her heart pounded through tunnel vision as she studied the police detective's confession. The woman had jumped in front of the intended target as the gun went off. The detective said nothing else in the report needed changing, just the shooter's identity.

"There's also your birth certificate and a marriage license," said Darwin.

"Where did you get this?" she asked in a breathy voice.

"From a safe deposit box in a Sicilian bank. Its key was inside the lava bust."

She scrolled to a yellowed paper signed by the attending physician that listed Jasmin Kahn born July third 1980 to Sabah Kahn, mother, and Valon Zela, father. The next scan showed a marriage license for Sabah and Valon in 1985, also in Sicily. The last document, she read through blurred vision. Sabah's death certificate, caused by a bullet in her chest.

So much of Thierry's indifference suddenly fell into place. *He never cared. I'm not his child.* She pictured the man with the tattoo holding her. She moved a hand to her waist over the imagined arm. *He loved me. The photos don't lie.*

The ache in her heart intensified, spreading to her throat. For a moment, she drifted back to that summer day with her mother and father, together, alive. She tried to hold on to the joy, the sense of unconditional love, but it faded like the colors in the photographs. The man across the cave had destroyed her life.

Jasmin looked up from the mobile, her upper lip curling back in the stark light. She ground her teeth and tensed until she shook uncontrollably. Finally, she shrieked, "You killed her!"

She hurled the mobile at Thierry. It spun past his head as she charged, screaming, "You son of a bitch!"

92

Darwin winced as his mobile clattered deep in the cave. The rest seemed to happen in slow motion, leaving him a spectator in a violent dance.

"You killed her!" Jasmin pounded Thierry's chest, sending the man back a step. The thug, still grasping Lupita's arm, tried to intervene. Jasmin thrust a knee in his groin, yanking the gun away as he doubled over.

Thierry stumbled backward, waving his hands frantically as Jasmin swung the barrel at him. "No. I loved her! You're my—"

The gun roared in the tight space—bullet ripping through Thierry's right side. He went down. Jasmin moved over him. This time aiming carefully.

"Don't—" Thierry fell back hard on the second shot. On the third, Zac sprinted at her.

As Darwin witnessed the horror, the other thug entered the melee from outside and grabbed Eyrún.

Zac pulled Jasmin away from Thierry, taking the pistol, but the thug she had kicked was up. He wrenched it from Zac's grasp.

Eyrún stomped on her attacker's foot, elbowed his ribs, and, locking her hands on his neck, flipped him.

Darwin drew the gun taken from the outside thug as Eyrún jumped on the man, pinning his arms with her knees.

Jasmin wailed hysterically as Zac restrained her. The thug with Lupita squeezed off a shot, but Jasmin tripped over Thierry's body, taking Zac with her.

Darwin swiveled toward the gunshot to see Lupita smashing a vase over the thug's head.

Eyrún yelled as her thug bucked. Darwin brought the weapon to the man's face, who thrust hands out in surrender.

"Darwin? You and Eyrún okay?" said Zac.

"Yeah," Darwin said, taking a glance to see Zac standing with Lupita over their thug.

Eyrún asked, "Where's Jasmin?"

M inutes later, Zac, Lupita, and Darwin sat the thugs together as Eyrún returned to the cave, panting. "She took the car. I couldn't stop her."

"Dammit! Get our car. We'll meet you on the road," said Zac.

She spun and was outside again when Lupita asked, "What about them?"

"We lock them in. Jasmin left the key in the door," said Zac.

In less than two minutes, they had piled into the sedan and were racing over the gravel track. The vehicle bottomed out multiple times before hitting the main road. When they reached the straight section, Eyrún asked, "Who's her father on the birth certificate?"

"Valon Zela."

"What?" The car rocked as she twisted toward Darwin. "He's the man I had tea with."

"You don't know it was him," said Darwin.

"How many Valons could be on this island?" She mashed the accelerator despite it being on the floor. The car rattled as if coming apart.

Lupita screamed as Eyrún braked late for a corner and then navigated through a series of streets, honking to get people out of the way. At the harbor shops, she slammed the brakes and flung open her door.

"Get to the harbor!" she yelled, but Zac was already out his door as Eyrún burst into the cafe. "Where is he? Have you seen him?" she pleaded with the man behind the counter.

"Who?"

"Valon!"

"He's gone. He said goodbye, that he was leaving for a while."

"Shit!" She leaned on the rolled steel counter, her head hanging, before pushing up and sprinting back outside. She caught Lupita and slowed, sighing heavily at missing Valon. Then, realizing Lupita had not said a word since the cave, she turned and asked her, "Are you okay?"

"I am okay for now," she said.

But Eyrún was not sure. Lupita walked with her head down, gazing through half-lidded eyes. Eyrún knew from her own abduction in Egypt that Lupita had to be processing a lot, especially with the rawness of captivity so immediate. She was about to ask another question, but they rounded the quay-side hotel to see two Guardia Costiera vessels blocking the megayacht. Armed officers surrounded the crew on its large rear deck. A tall, dark-haired woman stood among them.

"Got her," said Lupita. "I hope they lock that bitch up for a long time."

Eyrún smiled at Lupita and sensed she was going to be fine.

93

M y *God. I shook his hand!* Eyrún kept reflecting on the mysterious man whose invisible hand had orchestrated the tragedy that had played out over the last four months. While Darwin, Lupita, and Zac gave their statements to the police and Italian coast guard, she returned to *Hypatia* in the Zodiac, towing the jet ski. She had agreed to swing around to the harbor to get everyone when the police had finished their questioning.

Once she had stowed the small crafts in *Hypatia's* garage, she went to the galley, where she washed her hands and rinsed her face. After replacing the towel, she turned to the helm and froze. A cream-colored envelope, addressed to her, lay on the captain's chair. She seized it.

It was a pleasure having tea with you this morning, and I trust this note finds you and your companions safe.

My bank in Sicily alerted me that someone had emptied the safe deposit box. Your husband is a clever man to have picked up on the clues I left.

I also left a letter for Jasmin. She was a bright and ever-curious child. I counted on her remembering the cave, and, judging from the chaos in the opposite harbor, she must have found it.

I hope the documents aid the prosecution of theft and cultural looting.

326

Sadly, I am party to this deception, for I confess my vanity got the better of me. But this rapacious hunger to possess has swelled far beyond my impact and must end.

Your work at the Agrippa Center for Archaeology sounds wonderful, and I apologize for the trouble my work has caused. As a gesture of goodwill, the key in this envelope opens another box in the same Sicilian bank. In it, you will find the location of the golden bull mask. Find it and use the ACA to repatriate the treasure to its home in Lebanon.

Regards,

Valon

That night, they docked in Trapani, where they met Emelio, who later hosted them at a small restaurant that he said was the best in Sicily. Before dinner, Eyrún took Lupita shopping to replace her three-day-old clothes and help discard physical reminders of her kidnapping. During the journey, Darwin had reconnected with the digital universe by turning on a spare iPhone he kept in *Hypatia's* master suite.

In the morning, Eyrún retrieved an envelope from the bank containing the electronic codes to a vault in the Basel freeport. She shook her head at the absurdity of the antiquities trade, and, shortly afterward, they departed Sicily and crossed the Tyrrhenian Sea to follow the Sardinian coastline toward Corsica.

Darwin sat beside Eyrún as she navigated through the islands on Sardinia's northern coast, passing far from view of the Bonifacio cliffs where the ordeal had started two days ago. Zac and Lupita relaxed on the bow lounge while Emelio catnapped on the galley bench with a book on his lap.

"What do you think?" asked Darwin, nodding at their friends.

"I think they both need time to heal."

"Agreed. What about you, love?"

"I've been thinking about an exhibit. What if we create something that brings attention to this obsession that leads to plunder and forgery?"

"Great idea. Maybe we partner with the Vatican's Etruscan Museum," he added.

"Yes!"

By the time they swung toward Ajaccio harbor, they were well into planning the exhibit.

Over the next two months, the French, Italian, Spanish, and UK police arrested 113 people, all linked through the Albanian Master's organogram. Combined with the evidence in his safe deposit box, it led to indictments against over two dozen high-end antiquities dealers.

Paul Nisard, in Paris, cracked down on corruption within the OCBC, ousting the unscrupulous officers in the Marseilles branch. Their plea bargains helped take down César Olmeta's gang and seize €700M in paintings used as collateral in the drug trade. The forged Vatican vase Darwin had arranged to send out for restoration was among other objects recovered from the gang. The OCBC also seized Thierry's and Jasmin's company holdings and returned looted items to their countries of origin.

Separately, the French minister of culture hosted a press conference in which she publicly absolved the Agrippa Center for Archaeology of any wrongdoing and reiterated the ministry's support for the ACA mission. Eyrún had joined her in Paris to describe the ACA's role in stymieing a vast cabal that had been looting cultural heritage. That afternoon, she met with the Lebanese ambassador to France to personally return the golden bull mask found in the Temple of Eshmun.

Five months later, Richard Ndembele traveled to Ajaccio as the pope's emissary to open the joint Vatican Etruscan Museum and ACA exhibit where visitors could learn about the cultural harm caused by looting and fraud. Eyrún displayed her Fountain of Salmacis vase in ACA's lobby, as she had intended, but labeled as a forgery and with the story of its illicit creation.

Darwin had the last laugh when the LA auction house claimed no wrongdoing because the kylix he had bought had a provenance.

Richard arranged a letter from the head of the Vatican Museums to the LA auction house saying it would feature the kylix as a central example of illegal art washing. The auction house offered a seven-figure donation to the ACA and to announce publicly that it would take steps to reduce money laundering if the Vatican left its name off the display.

After the Vatican-ACA hoopla had settled, Darwin got a message from Nahla Al-Mahwi:

Congratulations. You and Eyrún continue to make waves.
Darwin: thanks. curious, did you warn Valon?
Nahla: Of course. He's too valuable to my business.

He showed the text to Eyrún, who asked, "Do you think we've done enough to stop it?"

"I think we've done all we can," he said ruefully.

As spring brought new growth to the eastern Mediterranean, Valon stood on the veranda of his home in Qeparo, overlooking the Albanian Riviera. He could see the Greek island of Corfu thirty kilometers south. Years ago, he had modernized this sixteenth-century villa in case he needed to leave Pantelleria.

He sipped from a teacup, drawing in its warmth against the cool morning breeze beneath Mount Gjivlash, and sighed at a memory of seeing Jasmin in the harbor months ago. She had grown into a beautiful woman, much like her mother, his wife. But his vision of the inquisitive little girl had been tainted by the vicious adult verbally attacking her crew.

He blew over the cup, curling the steam toward the ocean far below. A long moment later, he went to his workshop and studied sketches for a new piece. Its commission had come from a long-time customer. A flash of inspiration seized him. He grasped a charcoal pencil and worked it across the paper.

EPILOGUE

A storm much like the one that had caught Darwin and Zac on the GR20 trail a year ago had left a mess overnight at the Lacroix mountain house. While Darwin cut up fallen branches outside, Eyrún cleared the clutter that had collected indoors since they had returned from Pantelleria and launched the exhibit.

She piled books that needed moving back to the downstairs library on the fireplace coffee table and reached for another two on its lower level. The larger book covered a smaller, leather-bound volume with no title. Curious, she opened it and, on seeing the handwriting, remembered it was the diary written by Darwin's third great-grand-mère, Pasquale Lacroix's wife. The lettering flowed across the unlined pages; its blue ink thicker where the vintage pen nib had doubled back in the cursive script.

While lovely on the page, she could not read the Corsican calligra-phy. Still, she sat on the floor, her back against the sofa, and turned to the cover page. Using her mobile, she translated:

Tuscan Hoax

A Lacroix family history and,
Resolution of the great vendetta
Letizia Lacroix nee Paoli
1921

The great vendetta? Darwin never mentioned this. She had known he
was translating it, but she had not seen him work on it for at least a
year. She turned the page, and a small note fell out, landing on her lap.
Flipping it over, she saw a computer file name. Darwin kept family
research in a cloud-based folder that he shared with her and Emelio.

She retrieved her tablet, navigated to the file's location, and began
reading. Most of the early pages listed family members' births and
deaths and who was related to whom. She skimmed ahead until
reaching pages on Pasquale Lacroix's life. Some, she knew from Emelio
and Darwin, like Pasquale finding the Box in Herculaneum in 1867, but
here were stories of his adventures until his death in 1917 while
captaining a French naval supply ship.

*Pasquale loved to boast. He was a superb storyteller, but we all knew his
tendency to exaggerate. Much of his gasconading, he appropriated from his
grand-père Henrí Lacroix, who, with the backing of the French crown,
suppressed the last vestiges of Barbary pirates. Some of this history is docu-
mented. The rest I have gathered orally and recorded here.*

Eyrún remembered the volumes of Lacroix Shipping Company
records in the library. Not eager to get back to cleaning, she went
downstairs and located the black leather-bound volumes. Beginning in
1617, the books lined two rows of shelves. She pulled out one covering
1850 to 1875, Pasquale's younger years, but they were unreadable
except for the numbers, which she figured related to cargo. She imagined her own relatives in Iceland during this same period, eking out a
living in a harsh climate. Her family had kept spotty records, and she
had never understood Darwin's cavalier attitude toward his family
history. *Why doesn't he want to read this?*

Following the shelf along the interior wall, she stopped at the point
that concealed the latch to the secret room beneath the house. Darwin

had explained how the mountain house had been constructed in the eighteenth century as a redoubt against pirate attacks. She had learned of the room two years ago when they had hid the Box from intruders, but she had not been inside it since.

On a whim, she ran her fingers over the spot where Darwin had and, just as she was about to give up, found a latch. Its opposite took less time to locate, and she swung the shelf into the room. Cool air poured from the opening, carrying a musty odor. Eyrún flicked on her mobile's light and stepped inside the five-meter-wide space that went about fifteen meters deep. Pine furniture, layered in dust, made up a crude living area, with four beds lining one wall and a table and food-preparation area on the opposite. A door concealed a pit toilet. She wrinkled her nose despite it emitting no odor.

A massive armoire dominated the rear wall. She moved to it and tugged one door open. Plates, cups, and bowls were stacked with linens, unused since the Second World War. As she lifted a blue and white porcelain bowl, the shelf support gave way. The heavy ceramic tipped the board and took down the lower shelves. The armoire's top broke away as its contents cascaded down.

She dove backwards as the ancient pine collapsed before her eyes—dust cloud billowing. A coughing fit drove her out of the room. *Oh, no!* She sighed heavily at the destruction wrought by her curiosity. Then she got a larger light from the library and went back inside to survey the damage.

As she stepped over the carnage strewn about the floor, she could see the entire upper part of the cabinet had fallen away, and its backing boards angled precariously. They could reassemble the armoire, but the dishes were a total loss. She grasped one backing board and pulled it away.

What? She removed another board. *Something's behind this.* Two minutes later, she had pulled ten boards free, exposing a wooden door set into the wall. Her heart raced. Over the next half-hour, she cleared the broken mess enough to access the hidden door. After pulling its iron ring several times, she put a foot against the wall and, grasping it with both hands, yanked multiple times until a body-width space opened.

She paused to catch her breath, and, as even colder air spilled from the blackness, the hair on her arms stood up. *God, I hope this isn't some forgotten Lacroix crypt.*

Steeling her resolve, she entered.

"Eyrún? Eyrún?" Darwin had come inside from the back patio to ask about her garden. He looked about, pausing on the opened diary.

"Eyrún? Where are you?"

He scooped up the books and carried them downstairs, figuring she must be in a lower bedroom. *Or the library.* Its light was on, and cold air flooded the hallway. *Odd. No open doors.*

His stomach clenched as Eyrún screamed.

AUTHOR'S NOTE

Thank you for reading Tuscan Hoax. I hope you enjoyed it and would love to hear from you at dave@davebartell.com, and please write a review on Amazon.

The Albanian Master character came to mind after I watched a YouTube from the DW Documentary channel titled: "Fakes in the art world - The mystery conman" https://youtu.be/1lNSXB4i4fE The more I looked, the more I found evidence of forgery and looting. It is an age-old problem, and one that has its roots in possession.

Think of an object handed down to you from one of your forebears: a grandmother's ring, a grandfather's watch or, perhaps, a family holy book. Across from me as I write, is a shelf with treasures I have collected: books, an old brass lighter from an unknown relative, a watercolor painting by my cousin, an agate I pulled from the Loire river near Amboise and old post-cards from France. Each has personal meaning, offering me a chance to go back in time or to a place with cherished memories. Collecting is a normal way to transcend our life-times, but when possession goes too far, most would agree it becomes unhealthy.

Obsession and greed are the themes of Tuscan Hoax. I will not delve into judgement here, and leave right and wrong for discussion over a glass of wine. But, I want to cast light on who owns our collective human past and how it should be made available for study. More importantly, the accuracy and honesty of that heritage shapes who we are. We see the damaging aspects of inaccuracy and dishonesty it in the proliferation of "fake news".

Antiquities give us a visceral knowledge of our past. We experience the joy, the sorrow, the everydayness of objects used in the course of a life. Exhibitions are places to display these accoutrements with their stories. But ownership is tenuous—who owns a vase from a long extinct culture? Frequently, there are no clear answers.

To learn more, please consult the resources below. I have pulled quotes from a few of the sources that stand out:

"The only way to curb looting is to reduce the demand for artifacts by making the collection of antiquities socially unacceptable." Ricardo Elia, in a review of "The Cycladic Spirit" published in Archaeology, the journal of Archaeological Institute of America, January/February 1993.

"Museums have long been our civic temples, places to worship beauty and the diversity of the world's cultures. Now they are also recognized as multimillion-dollar showcases for stolen property." Jason Felch & Ralph Frammolino, authors of Chasing Aphrodite, page 2.

"As long as people or institutions feel they have a right to buy and therefore own antiquities, sites will continue to be plundered and illegal commerce will thrive. Only when we move beyond the concept of ownership for objects of cultural heritage and accept that they cannot be bought, will the black market lose interest." Jason Felch & Ralph Frammolino, authors of Chasing Aphrodite.

"… roughly speaking, 80-90 percent of the antiquities of the open market are loot." Peter Watson & Cecilia Todeschini, authors of The Medici Conspiracy, page 348.

"... the evidence shows that without exception, modern collections of antiquities—those formed since World War II—are made up almost entirely of loot." Peter Watson & Cecilia Todeschini, authors of The Medici Conspiracy, page 349.

"Antiquities that have passed through Switzerland, especially its Freeports, and have no other scientific provenance, should be looked upon as loot and treated accordingly." Peter Watson & Cecilia Todeschini, authors of The Medici Conspiracy, page 350.

"The antiquities underworld is far more determined and far more organized than anyone has ever imagined." Peter Watson & Cecilia Todeschini, authors of The Medici Conspiracy.

"We continue to see the past through eighteenth-century eyes." Erin L. Thompson, author of Possession.

"The easiest way to convince a collector to buy a forgery is to appeal to his self-conceit of being someone uniquely qualified to tell genuine from false." Erin L. Thompson, author of Possession.

"In recent years, the number of small antiquities, such as coins, sold on eBay and other online retailers has exploded. Nearly all of these antiquities are unprovenanced. And a number of investigations have revealed that in the rare cases where provenance information is given for an antiquity, it is often faked in an attempt to show that the work came from a country where export is legal, such as Switzerland, rather than its true country of origin." Erin L. Thompson, author of Possession, page 157.

Resources used and recommended for further study:

YouTube

- The Black Box of the Art Business https://youtu.be/5TSE2TcMduc
- Fakes in the Art World - The Mystery Conman https://youtu.be/1lNSXB4i4fE

Internet

- **Wikipedia**: My go-to source to discover topics and direction to deeper research
- **Panama Papers** https://en.wikipedia.org/wiki/Panama_Papers
- **Trafficking Culture** is a research consortium that produces evidence-based research into the contemporary global trade in looted cultural objects. (https://traffickingculture.org)
- **Global Investigative Journalism Network**: The need for a sophisticated, multinational corps of investigative reporters has never been greater. We live in a globalized era in which our commerce—and our crimes–are multinational. For example, https://gijn.org/2021/09/20/investigating-antiquities-trafficking/ and https://gijn.org/2021/06/15/a-reporters-guide-how-to-investigate-organized-crimes-finances/
- Greece claims provenance over a statue but is counter sued to provide proof https://news.artnet.com/art-world/barnet-case-sothebys-1883349
- **The Art Loss Register**, (https://www.artloss.com) A database of stolen art and antiquities, but, here is the catch, objects must be reported in order to be searchable.
- Switzerland's Tough New Stance on Freeports Will Shake the Art World https://news.artnet.com/market/switzerland-freeport-regulations-367361

- The Role of Freeports in the Global Art Market https://www.artsy.net/article/artsy-editorial-freeports-operate-margins-global-art-market
- Warrant to search the Metropolitan Museum of Art to look for a Lebanese antique bull's head, Matthew Bogdanos District Attorney https://culturalpropertynews.org/wp-content/uploads/2018/02/seized-from-the-Metropolitan-Museum.pdf
- The Tomb Raiders of the Upper East Side, Inside the Manhattan DA's Antiquities Trafficking Unit, The Atlantic, December 2021 https://www.theatlantic.com/magazine/archive/2021/12/bogdanos-antiquities-new-york/620525/

Books

Priceless: How I Went Undercover to Rescue the Worlds' Stolen Treasures, Robert K. Wittman

Hitler's Horses, Arthur Brand

Chasing Aphrodite: The Hunt for Looted Antiquities at the World's Richest Museum, Jason Felch & Ralph Frammolino

The Medici Conspiracy: The Illicit Journey of Looted Antiquities from Italy's Tomb Raiders to the World's Greatest Museums, Peter Watson & Cecilia Todeschini

Thieves of Baghdad, Matthew Bogdanos

Possession: The Curious History of Private Collectors from Antiquity to the Present, Erin L. Thompson

The Vatican: Secrets and Treasures of the Holy City, Father Michael Collins

The Vatican: All the Paintings, Anja Grebe

The Vatican Secret Archives, Cardinal Raffaele Farina

Vatican Museums: 100 Works Not to Be Missed, Paulist Press

ACKNOWLEDGMENTS

As this is the fourth full-length Darwin Lacroix adventure (Corsican Gold is a Novella), character development becomes a more critical piece of the series. We all naturally age and grow wiser, and our relationships mature. The same holds true for characters. Thanks to Annie Tucker, my development editor, who helps deepen my characters emotional interplay.

Special thanks to my ARC (Advance Reader Copy) team members who went the extra distance to help ferret out those niggling errors that get through the professional editors. You went above and beyond: Nancy Aiken, Wayne Bilow, Alan Cobb, Walter Curran, Linda Dershowitz, Jeff Harris, Pam Samson, and Denyse Taylor.

Every book deserves a great cover and, thanks to Patrick Knowles Design, Tuscan Hoax has one. This is our fourth collaboration as he also did the covers on Hypatia's Diary, Templar's Bank, and Corsican Gold.

And, thank you to Diane Bartell, my wife, best fan, and most important person in my life. She will soon be asking, "Got anything new for me to read."

Please write a review as we authors thrive on recommendations. If you found anything amiss in the book, please email me directly, and I'll fix it. While I worked with a translator, developmental editor, a copy editor, and a proofreader, to err is human.

Again, THANKS, and I invite you to learn about the next Darwin Lacroix Adventure by joining my mailing list at davebartell.com.

Onward to book five!

ABOUT THE AUTHOR

Imagine the wonder at being the first person to open King Tut's tomb? Dave Bartell loves reviving lost history and his novels breathe "thriller" into archaeology.

As a kid, he was frequently found tinkering in his parent's garage. His insatiable curiosity to understand how things work led him to study biochemistry and, later, fueled a career in high-technology. His what-if mindset and life experiences combine to make his fiction plausible and feel realistic.

Dave lives in Los Gatos California, a small town tucked into the edge of Silicon Valley. He enjoys hiking in the hills behind his home, where beauty is still analog.

He hopes you enjoy his stories and invites you to share your thoughts at dave@davebartell.com. And, visit davebartell.com to get a sneak peek of upcoming projects.

BB bookbub.com/authors/dave-bartell

f facebook.com/DaveBartellWriter

g goodreads.com/davebartell

instagram.com/davebartell

twitter.com/davebartell